Simon Parsons

WHEN THE FLAG DROPS

Published in 2008 by YouWriteOn.com

Copyright © Text Simon Parsons

First Edition

The author asserts the moral right under the Copyright, Designs and Patents Act 1988 to be identified as the author of this work.

All Rights reserved. No part of this publication may be reproduced, stored in a retrieval system, or transmitted, in any form or by any means without the prior written consent of the author, nor be otherwise circulated in any form of binding or cover other than that in which it is published and without a similar condition being imposed on the subsequent purchaser.

Published by YouWriteOn.com

Author's Foreword

Formula One is a fast moving, dynamic sport. Every year, there are changes to cars, circuits, teams and rules. Since starting this book the Belgian Grand Prix has been removed from the F1 calendar and also re-instated! Teams and rules have changed just as rapidly. Any novel written about F1 can therefore only be a snapshot in time. "When the flag drops" is a work of fiction set in the past. Some team names are factual, others are not – but it just wouldn't be F1 if Ferrari wasn't in there somewhere! However, the characters and situations in this book are entirely imaginary and bear no relation to any real person or actual happenings.

Finally, I'd like to thank Sue for all her support and encouragement.

Simon Parsons
October 2008

CHAPTER 1

Sunday 19th August, Spa-Francorchamps - Belgium

Ryan Clarke wrestled his car round the tight hairpin at La Source and then floored the throttle. The Formula One car responded immediately, the powerful V10 engine screaming up through the revs as the car hurtled down the slope towards the challenging Eau Rouge switchback. The one hundred and sixty mile-an-hour left-right-left flick through the bends and up the hill to Radillon was one of the greatest tests for any racing driver. Ryan attempted to relax as the car raced towards the first of the corners.

He was almost into the turn when he spotted the waved yellow warning flags. Ryan eased back on the Vantec's throttle. Rounding the sweeping Radillon corner, he recognised the green and white livery of the shattered car tucked up against the Armco barrier on the right hand side of the track. Pieces of wing and nose cone were obvious among the shards of carbon-fibre that littered the tarmac. A gaggle of marshals surrounded the smashed-up vehicle and were struggling with the release harness on the driver's seat belt. Ryan slowed his car even more and carefully picked his way round the small group. Passing the stricken car, he could see that Alberto Panetta's head was slumped forward. Ryan offered up a silent prayer for his team-mate then refocused on the race.

They were on lap thirty-seven out of forty-four in the Belgian Grand Prix at Spa-Francorchamps. Unusually for Spa the weather was good, but the circuit demanded care in all conditions. The young Italian had only raced at Spa once before, and that was in a Formula 3000 race. As there was no sign of another car being involved, Ryan presumed that the novice driver had made a terrible mistake.

With no more flags in sight Ryan put his foot down, building speed up to one hundred and seventy five miles-per-hour as the car climbed the long, tree lined hill to Les Combes. He had barely completed the next series of right-left-right turns when he became aware of yet more yellow warning flags. This time the brightly clad track marshals, safe in their outposts alongside the track, were also holding out safety-car boards. With the safety-car out on the circuit no overtaking was allowed. A hundred yards ahead, he could see Karl Wittman's scarlet Ferrari already beginning to slow.

Behind the flashing yellow roof lights of the safety-car, the racing cars gradually formed up into a multicoloured queue. The safety-car was being driven by Spencer Collins, the designated safety car driver, and a Formula 3000 driver in his own right. Collins had to work hard to keep the powerful silver Mercedes saloon at a steady 70 miles-an-hour, a pace that was pedestrian to the sleek Formula One thoroughbreds that now strained at the leash. The slow-moving convoy of primary coloured vehicles, smothered in sponsors' adverts, acted as a mobile billboard for all manner of items, from gearboxes and cigarettes to jewellery and financial services.

The twelve-car snake seemed to Ryan to take an age to get back round to Eau Rouge. As they once more climbed the hill, Ryan hoped to see an empty car, but was dismayed to see that Alberto was still on board. Over three minutes had now passed since the accident. Ryan was too young to have witnessed the dreadful tragedies that plagued Spa in the 1950s, but now images of Ayrton Senna's horrific accident at Imola in 1994 went through his mind. That no drivers had been killed in Formula One since then was largely due to the vastly improved safety features in the cars, yet high speed motor racing was still a potentially lethal sport. Ryan prayed that Eau Rouge had not claimed another victim.

The cars continued behind the safety-car, and rounding Eau Rouge on the next lap, Ryan expelled a sigh of relief as they passed an empty racing car. The track had been swept clean, and the remains of the smashed car had been lifted onto a flatbed recovery lorry. Not sure that he wanted to know the answer, Ryan anxiously pressed the radio button on his steering wheel and spoke to his pit crew, 'Is Panetta all right?' he asked. There was a pause before Chris Somerset the team's owner replied.

'We've had no firm information, but we don't think he's in any danger. How's your car?'

'It feels fine, why?' The question puzzled Ryan, for they could easily monitor the car using the sophisticated telemetry equipment on the pit wall.

'No reason. We think the safety-car will come in at the end of the next lap. Carry on as normal.'

The conversation was over. Radio chats were kept to a minimum; not only was it difficult to talk over the buzzing engine but the drivers needed to concentrate on their driving.

Approaching the Bus Stop chicane, at the end of the fortieth lap, the safety-car turned its roof lights off, which meant that the race would resume at the end of the lap. At last the Mercedes peeled off into the pit lane just before the chicane. The racing cars picked their way through the Bus Stop, then accelerated in a crescendo of noise. The spectators in the covered stands along the pit straight covered their ears. Once across the start/finish line the drivers were free to overtake again. The race was back on.

The safety car had done Ryan a big favour in allowing him to catch up with Wittman. Ryan studied the Ferrari over the next few laps of the long undulating circuit, and realised that although the Ferrari pulled away on the straights, the brakes were clearly going off, and Wittman was braking earlier and earlier into the corners.

As his Formula One car hurtled at over 180 miles an hour towards the Bus Stop for the last time, Ryan was ready; barely a car's length ahead was Wittman's red Ferrari. This was the final set of turns, and the best overtaking point on the circuit; if Ryan was to make a move it had to be now.

On the pit wall, Chris Somerset, the Vantec team's charismatic owner, studied the TV monitor, and nervously brushed a lock of dark brown hair away from his sweaty forehead. He knew what Ryan was planning, and if he looked impassive he certainly didn't feel it. On the previous lap, Ryan had radioed in saying he thought he could take Wittman at the Bus Stop, and could he give it a go. Somerset had agreed, but in the light of Panetta's accident he now pondered the wisdom of that decision. Although he badly wanted the championship point that overtaking Wittman could bring, he could do without another wrecked car, and he certainly couldn't afford to lose another driver. This was the 12th Grand Prix of the season and costs were mounting. Besides, Wittman was the championship leader and the consequences of taking him off in an accident didn't bear thinking about. Still, he had once been a racer, and he could not bring himself to deny the request. Oh well, he thought, nothing ventured nothing gained.

As the cars raced up the road, Ryan waited for Wittman to act. He was not disappointed. Wittman did as expected and edged to the right before braking for the left-hand corner. Whilst Wittman moved out and began to brake, Ryan kept his foot firmly on the throttle and dived down the inside. As the Vantec rushed towards the apex of the bend Ryan stood on his brakes, his harness pressing sharply into his body under the tremendous G force. The brake discs glowed bright orange as the Vantec slid alongside the Ferrari, the tyres at their limits of traction. Once the car had slowed enough to take the bend Ryan wrenched the steering wheel hard to the left.

Inside the Vantec pit garage, a group of a dozen people huddled round a small overhead monitor. The mechanics were concerned that if Ryan got this one wrong then all the hard work over the past two weeks would have been for nothing. While the mechanics fretted over the car, Victoria, Ryan's tall, dark-haired girlfriend, bit her lips and worried about the driver. Heads-up and open-mouthed they watched as the Vantec began to turn inside the Ferrari. For a brief moment it seemed that the cars would clash, their wheels interlocking, before the Ferrari moved aside and Ryan was through. A cacophony of whooping and cheering echoed round the concrete garage.

Ryan led Wittman through the next two corners of the chicane, then cut across the final left-hander, the wheels sending a ripple of tiny shocks through his body as they rattled over the red and white striped rumble-strip. Ryan balanced the Vantec on the throttle until he was sure the car was settled and then pushed his foot flat to the floor.

As his car straightened, Ryan anxiously looked for Wittman in the small rear view mirror. In the vibrating glass he could just glimpse the Ferrari on his outside. Ahead of him Ryan could see the finishing line, all he could do was keep the pedal to the metal and pray. He focused on the line ahead and held on tight as the engine screamed up to full power. As fast as the Vantec closed on the line the Ferrari closed even faster. Inch by inch Wittman gained on Ryan, until, just yards from the finishing line, the cars were running side by side. In a sport where times are measured in thousandths of a second, the closeness of the finish would be talked about for years. The watching spectators could only guess at the result, but as they passed the chequered flag Ryan knew he had won the battle.

Standing in front of the bank of monitors that made up the team's timing station, Chris Somerset wasn't sure how to react. Although pleased with sixth place, his joy was tempered with concern for Panetta. Word had come though that the 24-year-old had broken both legs. Despite the shade offered by the green canopy overhead, Chris was very hot ,and his team polo shirt clung damply to his body. Strain marked his face. He looked around, the packed grandstand opposite was a riot of colour, flags and banners waved in triumph. Even over the noise of the still finishing backmarkers he could hear the braying sound of hooters and horns. Further down the pit lane he could see the McLaren team celebrating, their mechanics were exchanging hugs and slaps, big grins on their faces. He surveyed his own garage. Like himself, the crews were unsure how to react. Ryan's own crew was visibly pleased, yet their celebrations were muted in sympathy for Panetta's crew, who were understandably upset by the serious injuries sustained by their driver.

    Once across the finish line, Ryan slowed to a cruise for the short drive into Parc Ferme, which was located on the inside of the tight La Source hairpin. Ryan blinked as a trickle of salty sweat ran into his eyes. Freed from the need to concentrate on his driving; he was becoming ever more aware of his own condition. The hot July sun had conspired with the 3.5 litre engine to raise the temperature in the cockpit to over 40 degrees centigrade. Clothed in fireproofed underwear and overalls, gloves, Balaclava and helmet, Ryan was literally baking. He would have swapped almost anything at that moment for a drink of cold water. Putting his discomforts to one side; he mentally replayed the race. He didn't think he had made any real mistakes. Maybe he could have made his pit stop a bit later and avoided some traffic, but crystal balls were as hard to come by on race tracks as elsewhere. All considered he was satisfied with his performance, but oh for a decent engine! Sixth place was one of his better results of the season. After good fifth and sixth places in San Marino and Spain, he had failed to finish in three races, and at best had only managed two tenths and a twelfth place in the others. It wasn't good enough. The team needed to improve on last year and as the senior driver he was expected to lead that improvement. He was all too aware of the ease with which teams could change drivers and his contract was due to expire at the end of the season. There were only another five races left in which to make his a mark. 'Roll on Monza,' he muttered, as he casually eased the car through the marshalled entrance and into the secure compound.

Ryan parked the car and killed the engine. With great relief he unbuckled his safety harness. The elaborate belt certainly did its job in locking the driver to the seat, but did nothing for driver comfort; sometimes even breathing could be an effort. Wearily he grabbed the sides of the cockpit and lifted his legs out from the cramped pedal bay. He stood up in the car, and paused for a moment, before lifting his right foot over the side of the cockpit and placing it on the ground. He then stepped out of the car, hopping for a moment whilst he found his balance. He pulled his gloves off, tucking them in his left armpit, whilst he sought to undo his helmet. After forty-four laps the helmet felt less like a lightweight racing helmet and more like something that a medieval armoured knight would have worn.

Fiddling with his helmet fastening, Ryan failed to spot Wittman approach, and was taken by surprise as the Austrian grabbed him by the shoulder and spun him round. 'What the hell do you think you were doing?' shouted Wittman aggressively, poking Ryan in the chest.

Ryan could only just hear him through his helmet and earplugs. 'Racing,' he replied. 'What do you think I was doing!'

'Being stupid! That was too dangerous,' said Wittman.

'Look, you might have the better car but there's no way you're a better driver,' retorted Ryan, who was irritated. 'You were in no danger; unless you're not as good a driver as you keep telling everyone!' Ryan pushed Wittman away with both hands, his gloves falling from his armpit and dropping to the ground.

Their raised voices caused heads to turn their way, and beyond the fencing, the massed ranks of photographers anxiously snapped away, desperate not to miss any of the action. An official in white shirt and dark trousers carrying a walkie-talkie had also spotted the commotion, and rushed over to the scene. Just as it looked as if punches would be thrown he thrust himself between the two drivers. By now both men had realised that there was nothing to be gained by continuing the confrontation, and after glaring at Ryan, Wittman let himself be led off. As he was ushered away Wittman turned once more to face Ryan; 'I won't forget today'.

Ryan couldn't be bothered to reply. He shrugged his shoulders and resumed the task of removing his helmet. He pushed the personalised helmet up and off his head before swiftly pulling off his damp white Balaclava; he didn't like the way it made him look like a nun. He removed his earplugs then ran a hand through his blond, sweat-bedraggled hair. It was good to feel fresh air on his head again. Bending down he picked up the gloves he had dropped and stuffed them inside his helmet along with the Balaclava. Next he ripped open the Velcro that fastened the neck of his green overalls and tugged down the zip, then, removing his arms from the sleeves, he turned the top of the garment down so that it hung round his waist.

'Would you like some water?'

Gratefully he took the chilled bottle of water from the young girl, taking the opportunity to look her up and down. She was wearing a short red skirt with a matching polo top. The logo on the shirt corresponded to that on the plastic water bottle. Dark brown locks tumbled out from under the baseball hat that completed her uniform. Ryan gently grabbed her by her narrow waist and kissed her on the cheek. 'Thank you,' he said. 'I needed that.' The teenage girl blushed and smiled shyly, not sure whether he meant the drink or the kiss. Embarrassed, she moved on to look for another driver.

Ryan took a long cool draught from the bottle then replaced the screw top and headed for the weighing station. Parc Ferme was a haven compared to the pit lane. A vast noisy crowd was swarming towards the main straight to watch the victory ceremony. The jostling, excited throng was a strange mixture of humanity; mechanics and team personnel alongside corporate guests and invited celebrities.

After the weigh-in, Ryan headed back towards the garages on the pit straight. In the distance he could hear the German national anthem blaring out over the public address system in honour of Weiss the race winner. Ryan paused briefly, 'Another bloody German,' he muttered to himself. With little interest in the victory ceremony, Ryan continued his walk back to the Vantec garage, occasionally having to force an apologetic way through the scrum of people. As he passed, strangers proffered mumbled congratulations and once or twice he felt a friendly pat on the back. At last he emerged from the swarm. He heaved a sigh and continued down the pit lane, his feet feeling the heat of the tarmac through the thin soles of his driving boots.

As Ryan neared the garage a strong arm wrapped round his shoulder, and a fist playfully punched him in the stomach. Derek Archer, Ryan's mechanic, had jumped down from the pit wall on which he had been sitting and rushed up the road to greet him. 'Nice one mate,' said Archer, pleased that at least the car got back in one piece. Despite his fears, he enjoyed watching Ryan throw the car around the road.

'Yeah, thanks,' replied Ryan lamely. He was more worried about Panetta. 'How's Alberto?'

'Broken legs and a bit of concussion, he won't be racing again this year.'

The pair of them ambled back towards the garage, Ryan deep in thought. He was relieved that Alberto was not more badly injured and also sorry for the Italian who had made such a good start to his career in Formula One. He would miss his cheeky jokes, even in broken English. The young driver was always smiling and cheered up what could often be a very tense sport. God knows what the replacement driver might be like - if they could even get one

Victoria was waiting for him, with arms folded, just outside the entrance to the garage. Ryan knew she would be upset about Panetta so gave her a big hug, and a peck on the cheek, before turning his attention to the others. Victoria snaked an arm around Ryan's waist as he dealt with the usual round of congratulations. Chris Somerset waited until the others had greeted Ryan, then he pushed his way though the tiny huddle.

'Well done, you gave me kittens at the end there though. Couldn't you have gone just a bit quicker, that was bad for my nerves!' teased Somerset.

Ryan smiled ruefully. 'Only if you give me a faster engine!'

'Give me a shed load of money and I'll give you a better engine!' Somerset laughed.

Despite the light-hearted nature of the exchange both men knew that the team needed a better engine if they were ever to celebrate on the podium rather than in the garage.

'Now what was that all about with Wittman?' asked Somerset; the altercation in Parc Ferme had been picked up by the television coverage.

'A minor difference of opinion,' Ryan played the incident down.

'Well, can you sort it with Karl because we don't need that kind of trouble right now!'

'Okay, I'll speak to him later'. Much later thought Ryan. He didn't really care what Wittman thought about things. Ryan changed the subject, 'What do we know about Panetta's accident?'

'It's a bit of a puzzle at the moment. The telemetry all looked fine and no other cars were involved. We won't know more until we can get a look at the car, and we can't do that because they won't let us. I also want to speak to Alberto, but he's a bit concussed at the moment, and I believe they're going to operate on his leg soon. So, you had heard?'

'Yes, Derek told me.'

'Fine, I don't know what he told you, but the latest I've heard is that he's only broken one leg, but it's broken in two places. They've flown him to a hospital in Liege and I'm going over there shortly. I don't think we should go mob-handed though. I'll be back for the party later. You are still coming tonight?' asked Somerset anxiously. The team was going to celebrate a young mechanic's 21st birthday and Somerset had always been keen on fostering team spirit.

'Yeah, sure.' Ryan liked the lad in question. The mechanic was part of the crew that worked on his car. 'Many going?' he asked.

'Some of the other teams are staying over tonight, so we're expecting a good few people.'

'Any women?' At this Victoria gave Ryan a sharp dig in the ribs. 'Only joking,' he said, smiling back at her.

'Really?' she said archly, giving him a very sideways look.

'Look, we've got to talk tonight, it can't wait because I've got a meeting tomorrow, can you meet me in the hotel bar about 9:00,' said Somerset. They were staying in the Bedford, a 17th century 4 star hotel in Liege.

Ryan nodded his agreement. Somerset touched him briefly on the arm, then turned and left the garage. Wonder what that's all about, thought Ryan.

CHAPTER 2

Sunday 19th August. Hotel Bedford, Liege - Belgium

The ice cubes made a satisfying clink as Ryan shook the tall glass of orange juice and lemonade. Pleased with his efforts, he held the cold tumbler up to his cheek and luxuriated in the refreshing chill. Putting the glass to his lips, he tipped it back and emptied half the contents in one swallow. The ice cubes rattled again as he lowered the glass, and placed it on the small bedside cabinet. He lay back on the double-bed and clasped his hands behind his head. It was a pleasure to be in an air-conditioned environment after the sweltering heat of the Vantec's cramped cockpit. It was also good to be back at the Hotel Bedford. The hotel, situated in the centre of Liege, was a solid stone building dating back to the 17th century. Accordingly few of the rooms were the same; as a result the hotel had far more character than the featureless modern hotels that they normally stayed in. Somerset had found the hotel some years ago when the team was racing in F3; now it was a team favourite - despite being some 20 miles from the circuit at Spa. The majority of the F1 teams were based in hotels just a short distance from the track, but they were glad to have some separation from the rest. F1 was pressured enough without living on top of each other.

Ryan's lips twisted in a satisfied smile as he recalled his audacious passing move at the Bus stop. It had been the highlight of his season so far; and he knew that the move would have been broadcast all round the world. There were few enough chances to show his talent in the Vantec; it was a sad fact of life that the TV coverage focused on the first few cars. It was doubly pleasurable to have put one over the arrogant Wittman; he might be world champion but he was bitterly disliked around the paddock. After the years of domination by Michael Schumacher, it was good to have a new, more challengeable target, but he wished that Ferrari had chosen a more likeable driver. Wittman certainly had an excellent car under him, but his talent could not be compared to that of Schumacher, who had the ability to make even a bad car look good. It was a shame that the day had ended with the confrontation in Parc Ferme – Ryan shook his head and grimaced at the thought of the repercussions; without doubt the incident would be blown up in the motoring press, and it was certain that Wittman wouldn't let it drop.

His reverie was brought to an end by the sound of gurgling water from the bathroom, as a basin plug was raised. Seconds later, there was a clunk as the bathroom door opened, and Victoria, Ryan's girlfriend, emerged. He watched appreciatively as the tall brunette drifted across the large suite clad only in a tiny black thong, her ample breasts swaying provocatively. Boy – could that girl move! His eyes followed her as she settled down at the dressing table to fix her hair. The sight of an attractive girl in her knickers always got him going, but right now he was too tired to do anything about it; and besides, he was due downstairs for his meeting with Somerset.

Ryan's mobile phone began to trill. Victoria looked at Ryan and he nodded. She quickly picked up the tiny chrome-plated Motorola cell-phone to halt the tinny rendition of Colonel Bogey. For the umpteenth time, Victoria wished that Ryan would change the ring tone; but he seemed to enjoy the irritation it caused.

'Ryan Clarke's phone.'

Victoria listened patiently as the caller, a local Belgian newspaper reporter, introduced himself in faltering English, and asked if Ryan was available for an interview.

'I'm afraid he's not available tonight, and tomorrow we are returning to England,' she apologised. 'But if you'd like to give me your number perhaps he could give you a phone interview?' As they spoke, Victoria made her way over to the coffee table, on which sat a tiny notebook.

The reporter seemed happy with the compromise, and after taking down his details, Victoria politely ended the call.

'Anything important?' asked Ryan.

'I expect it was important for the caller,' replied Victoria tetchily, irritated by Ryan's evident lack of genuine interest. Although Ryan was keenly aware of the importance of good public relations, and had improved his attitude, it was still not an area of his work that he enjoyed.

Victoria tore off the page from the notebook and handed it to Ryan.

'Can you enter these details into your PDA, and make a diary entry to call this guy back tomorrow.'

Ryan got off the bed and went in search of his Palm Pilot; he knew that he'd get no peace if he didn't do what Victoria said. He quickly entered the details into the tiny computer and then returned to lie down on the bed.

Victoria worked as the public relations officer for Advanced Motor Parts, a medium sized engineering company - one of several companies owned by her wealthy industrialist father. Ryan and Victoria had first met at a Vantec promotional event. A.M.P made a number of suspension parts that were used by the car. Although Ryan was very fond of her, she could sometimes be a bit too straight for him. However her abilities as a personal assistant were very useful; besides, she was rather beautiful! Furthermore, having been brought up around cars and racing, she seemed to know just when to leave him alone. All in all, he was more than happy to have her around in a semi-permanent capacity.

'Isn't it time you got shaved?' Victoria asked as she once again began to brush her long dark hair.

Ryan gave a grunt, then picked up the glass and quickly finished his drink. Stiffly, he swung his body off the bed and headed for the shower. He stayed under the powerful shower for nearly fifteen minutes. The hot water worked its usual magic and restored some semblance of life to his aching muscles. Shaving wasn't quite such a pleasure, as he had to keep wiping a clear patch in the misted up mirror in order to see himself. The demister and extractor fan had both miserably failed to keep up with the steamy shower. However, it was a much rejuvenated Ryan that paddled out of the bathroom dressed in a large dark-blue kimono-style dressing gown.

Victoria was already stylishly attired in a black dress, a string of pearls round her neck. She shook her head in despair as Ryan threw on a blue denim shirt over a white T-shirt and a pair of beige chinos; the only concession to style being the leather Gucci belt and shoes. He switched on the large TV in the corner of the room, and sought out the race reports whilst he waited for Victoria to put the finishing touches to her makeup. As expected his 6th place didn't even get a mention. Unless you are on the podium you are nowhere in the world of Formula One. He turned the set off.

Ryan and Victoria went down together in the small, glass-walled lift. Ryan couldn't imagine how the lift could possibly hold the seven people detailed on the safety notice. The elevator jerkily descended from the top floor to reception at ground level, and then carried on down another floor. The bar was located in the cellars of the cosy old hotel. The white-washed stone walls of the cellar were lined with alcoves. In each bay, a comfortable white leather sofa half surrounded a small brass topped table. The furniture in the middle of the cellar was rather more prosaic, consisting of wooden benches and bench seats. Once his eyes had adjusted to the dim lighting, Ryan spotted Chris Somerset sitting in one of the alcoves. As usual, Somerset was dressed in what Ryan liked to call his country squire outfit: twill slacks, fine checked jacket with waistcoat, checked shirt and tie. The mild affectation never failed to amuse Ryan, who knew that

Somerset had been brought up on a council estate in Reading. An unexpected, but familiar, figure sat beside Somerset.

As Ryan and Victoria approached the alcove, the two occupants stood up.

'Ryan, Victoria,' said Somerset, gesturing towards the elderly man beside him, 'I think you know Pierre Demaison.'

In contrast to Somerset's rather idiosyncratic clothing, Pierre was smartly dressed in a well-tailored blue suit. His shirt was just the right matching shade of blue, and was set-off by a deep-blue tie with subtle motif. Gold cufflinks sparkled in the light. Money and class effortlessly radiated from him.

Ryan nodded his acknowledgement as Pierre Demaison took Victoria's hand and raised it to his lips. After Ryan had in turn shaken hands the four of them sat down.

'That was a nice move this afternoon,' said Demaison, 'almost worthy of me but...' he didn't finish the sentence, but instead, punched Ryan playfully on the arm. Ryan liked the 68-year-old man and smiled at the jest. It was still hard to believe that the balding, paunchy, man had once been a double World Champion. Although Team Demaison had seen better days, it was still regarded as one of the classic teams in Formula One. Pierre Demaison was still highly active, and a popular character around the paddock. His stories from the "Golden Age" were beginning to wear a bit thin, but were always humorous.

A bow-tied waiter had respectfully waited, until all the greetings had been completed, before he approached the table and took an order for their drinks. Whilst Victoria ordered a glass of red wine, Ryan asked for a large orange juice and lemonade; he was still feeling very dehydrated and it was likely to be a long evening.

'We would have had champagne in my day,' observed Demaison, 'But we were much tougher then!'

'Now we have to use our brains as well!' retorted Ryan. He turned to face Somerset.

'Any news on Panetta?'

'I've just got back from the hospital, and it's mixed news I'm afraid. His injuries aren't too serious, but he does have a broken leg; they reckon it could keep him out of action for eight weeks. That's the bad news!' Somerset sounded rueful.

For some twenty minutes, the group chatted happily over the rest of the days events. Eventually Somerset glanced at his watch and turned to face Demaison.

'Pierre, I really need to talk to Ryan, would you mind taking Victoria upstairs to the party?'

'I'd be delighted, I expect she would prefer my more mature company anyway!'

Victoria had been around long enough to know that business came first, and after throwing a wry smile at Ryan, stood up.

'I'll see you upstairs then, don't be too long because I might just choose to stay with Pierre!'

Ryan could sense she was slightly miffed; her curiosity aroused by the need for Ryan and Somerset to talk alone.

Ryan and Somerset both watched as the charming Frenchman led Victoria away from the table; a fat hand resting on her back - guiding her towards the exit.

'I hope you don't mind me sending them off like that,' apologised Somerset.

'Fine by me. What did Demaison want anyway?'

'He was offering us Jason Kramer, his test driver, until Panetta returns,' Somerset explained.

'Why would he do that? Surely he'd want Kramer for himself?' Ryan was puzzled by Demaison's generosity.

'He says his two current drivers are tied in by contracts for this season that would be too expensive to break, and besides, he'd like us to break Kramer in this season so that he's up to speed for next year.'

'I guess that makes sense, but I was hoping you might give the drive to Warren.'

'No, I know he's been our test driver for some months now, but he doesn't really have enough race experience at this level. Kramer on the other hand was third in the American Champ Car series last year, and who knows, he could be another Villeneuve.'

'Agreed but they haven't all worked out, just look at what happened to Zanardi!' said Ryan taking a large swig of orange juice. 'What I don't understand is why he's only a test driver for Demaison? I would have thought he'd have been in great demand, either in the States or with one of the F1 teams.'

'It appears that he started this season racing for Team Radtke, the same team he came third with last year. After two or three races he went down with glandular fever - which knocked him out for several months. It seems that his team weren't prepared to wait and dumped him. There's not a lot you can do if you're dumped mid season so I guess a test role with Demaison was a reasonable option. I'd be pretty pissed off with Champ Car racing if I was dumped, so an F1 drive must seem quite appealing.'

'Anyhow, the way things are going, I need someone with good race skills in the car; which is why I wanted to talk to you.'

'It sounded quite serious at the track.' Ryan wasn't too concerned, for he knew that Somerset liked to be a bit melodramatic.

'That all depends on how you look at it,' said Somerset, 'but yes it could be. I am very aware that we haven't yet sorted out your contract for next season. You know I don't like pissing you about - but things aren't very easy at the moment, and Panetta's accident really hasn't helped!'

Somerset paused for a moment to look around before continuing.

'We both know that our engine is the weak link in the whole shebang. We'll only move forward as a team if we can get a better engine; without it I'm not sure how I can justify continuing. Getting sponsors is becoming harder each year, and the costs are going through the roof; I'm not a young man and the wife's getting a bit edgy. I've given it a good shot, but unless I can see more success, I could pack it in at the end of the season. I have been approached by a group prepared to buy the team, and if the team goes backwards next year - maybe they won't come back.'

Ryan listened in stunned silence. This was the last thing he had expected. Somerset had always been around. It was Somerset who had spotted Ryan in Formula 3, and then later given him his break in Formula One. He couldn't believe he would just sling in the towel.

'You can't just quit like that ….'

Somerset held up a hand to stop him, 'I'm not quitting - not if we get our act together; so let's look at what we have to do.'

Ryan leant closer to Somerset and gave him his full attention. His eyes shone brightly. This sounded like fighting talk.

'We are equal 6th with Sauber at the moment on just 5 points. We can assume that Ferrari, McLaren, Williams and Renault are going to be out of range by the end of the season.' He looked at Ryan who nodded in agreement.

Somerset talked quickly and confidently on the subject he knew intimately.

'That leaves just Kodama ahead of us on 10 points - well in range. Any of the teams below us could catch up at this stage but certainly Demaison are our main threat.'

The French 'Equipe Demaison' team, owned by Pierre Demaison, were just behind Vantec in the constructors championship on 4 points.

'With five more races to go. Italy, America, Nurburgring, Malaysia and Japan,' Somerset counted the races off on his fingers. 'That means we could finish anywhere between 5th and 8th place. This is all hush-hush, but I have been talking to one of the other engine suppliers. I'm afraid I can't say who; but their engine is a definite step up from the one we are currently using, and from what they are saying, it will be even better next year. Apparently, they are growing unhappy with the team they currently supply, but will not work with us, unless we can demonstrate that we are moving forward. Informally they have told me that if we finish in the top six then they will agree to supply us. That is where you come in!' he poked Ryan in the chest.

'In what way?' asked Ryan.

'By setting a good example. You are the team's number one driver, and now with Panetta out, you must act as the team leader - it's not just a pretty title you know! You are going to have to help your number two, and make the engineers believe in the team. You can race hard, but no stupid stunts. I was as pleased as anyone with the move you made today - but you are going to have to race with your head, rather than your heart, for the rest of the season. Points finishes are the order of the day. And I don't want to see any more post-race punch-ups. The last thing we need is to start getting a bad press. You could have thrown away all the good you had achieved by that spat with Wittman. Mind you – I can't blame you, Wittman's such an arse!' Somerset paused to let his words sink in. 'Under the circumstances I won't tie you down with a new contract - just yet, and I would understand if you wanted to look elsewhere, but if we can grab a top six place, then we can all look forward to better times! Are you in or out?' Somerset asked; his speech over, he sunk back into the sofa.

Ryan didn't need to think about that one. 'Of course I'm in.'

The relief broke out on Somerset's face; he reached across and slapped a hand on Ryan's shoulder.

'Then it's time we had a drink to celebrate!' Somerset raised an arm to attract the waiter.

Two beers later, Ryan decided he had better go and find Victoria. Knowing the mechanics, he imagined that things could already be getting out of hand. Somerset accompanied him as they took the lift back up to the ground floor. Once back in the reception area, they trod a well-worn red patterned carpet down a long corridor to the rear of the building. The pair were spotted almost as soon as they stepped inside the private function room that lay at the end. A raucous cheer went up.

'It's Chris's round!' yelled a voice, from near the bar that occupied the far end of the large room. Somerset reached into his jacket, pulled out his wallet and waved it high over his head.

'You can have all the Belgian Francs I've got.'

'Yeah, and what about the moths?' cried another.

'They can buy their own drinks,' said Somerset.

The crowd parted to let Chris and Ryan make their way to the well stocked bar. Already the room was beginning to fill-up. An open invitation had been extended to the other teams; and being well aware of the Vantec team's usual hospitality, many of the British based teams had decided to stay. Unlike the majority of races they would easily be able to get back to Britain in the morning. Now that the room was beginning to fill, the DJ smoothly increased the volume. Chart music pumped out from the large black speakers, mounted on stands, either side of the even larger DJ and his twin record-decks.

Ryan ordered a beer; then went in search of Victoria. He found her with Craig McDonald, his Australian personal trainer. They were standing close to a table laden with tempting snacks. McDonald could see Ryan's eyes wandering over the fat filled delicacies and shook his head. 'It'll cost you a really hard workout if I catch you,' said McDonald.

'Just looking,' replied Ryan regretfully. He knew his trainer meant well, but surely he was allowed some fun. Still, the night was young. He gave Victoria a squeeze and kissed her on the cheek.

'Did you miss me then?' he asked.

'No, Pierre was really charming, and then Craig showed up. We were just wondering what you and Chris were up to?' There was an inquiring note in her voice.

'Oh just contract stuff,' answered Ryan, hoping to leave it there. 'Anyone interesting here?'

'I saw Stuart Underwood come in but I haven't spoken to him,' said McDonald. Underwood was a driver with Kodama - the only Japanese team in the championship. Ryan knew Stuart well from his days in the Japanese Formula 3000 series, and from last year when they were team-mates at Vantec.

Ryan looked around. As he looked for familiar faces, his eyes took in the dance floor. As expected there were only a few girls dancing. Much drinking and talking needed to be done before any of the mechanics would sally forth. The teams all employed a number of women: there were catering and hospitality staff, public relations officers, secretaries and a few physiotherapists. Some of the girls, bored with all the car talk, were self consciously dancing. Ryan was amused at the contrast between the girls, all dressed up in their party finest, and the mechanics - some had made an effort, but a number were severely fashion challenged.

'It's still warming up then,' said Ryan, looking at his watch. It was just coming up to ten o'clock. He didn't think there would be much happening for another hour yet. 'Where's the birthday boy?'

Victoria pointed in the direction of a huddle of mechanics standing by the bar.

'I'd better go say hello.'

'Wait,' said Victoria, 'Don't forget the present.' She reached into her handbag and brought out a neatly wrapped parcel. 'In case you've forgotten, it's a pair of "Ray-Ban" sunglasses.'

'You're a treasure,' said Ryan as he took the gift from her.

'I wish you meant that,' she said.

Ryan smiled and blew her a kiss as he headed over towards Andy Pedley.

The tiny group welcomed Ryan into their midst, and before he could protest, someone thrust a glass of Stella into his hand. He would have preferred a Leffe, or one of the other special Belgian beers, but he gratefully accepted the cold drink. The drinks he'd already had were beginning to make their mark - and he had a feeling it was going to be a long night.

'Happy birthday Andy,' he said handing over the present, 'I think you might need these tomorrow.'

The mechanic ripped open the parcel, as the rest of the group craned their necks to see what he'd got.

'Thanks, Ryan,' said Pedley, immediately putting the glasses on 'They're brilliant!'

Ryan stayed with the group as they traded jokes. Once they started talking about women, their second most popular topic of conversation after cars, he decided he had better return to the others. He took his leave and headed back across the now crowded room. It looked as if someone must have done a good job rounding up the locals, as there were many more young ladies on the dance floor than earlier - he didn't think they could all be from the teams.

'You took your time,' accused Victoria, although she didn't really mind.

'I couldn't just give it to him and run, now, could I?' he replied.

'Well, you can amuse yourself now as I'm going to have a dance with Craig!' With that, she grabbed an unprotesting McDonald by the arm, and hauled him towards the dance floor. As they squeezed through the crowds, Ryan grabbed a couple of sausage rolls from the buffet.

'What the eye can't see, the heart can't grieve over,' he said to himself. As he happily munched on the savouries, he felt a hand first caress and then firmly grab his bottom.

'Hiya Roxy,' he said, turning to face her. Typically, the short red-head was dressed to kill. Her tiny black dress emphasised her black nylon clad legs, and the low scooped front exposed a magnificent cleavage. Subtlety was not one of her qualities.

'How did you know it was me?' she squealed.

'Probably because I can see you in that big mirror,' he replied, pointing at the mirror behind the table on which the food was stacked. He was amused at her failure to sneak up on him.

'Oh, doesn't matter' she said, 'I still think you've got one of the cutest bums in motor racing! Are you still shacked up with Miss Iron Knickers?'

'If you mean Victoria, the answer is yes - and she's not that bad.'

'If you say so, but I bet she's not as good as me in bed, is she!' asserted Roxanne Prendergast. 'I rather think I'm even better now than when you last had me. It's amazing what I've learnt over the last year!'

Ryan wouldn't be at all surprised if she had improved her bedtime skills. Some people collected postage stamps; twenty-four year old Roxanne collected racing drivers. Spoilt rotten by her father, and not having to work, she had little to do - other than spend her time with the people in the paddock. Despite that, she was good company, and Ryan enjoyed meeting her - even if he no longer felt inclined to bed her. Ryan needed a woman with rather more in her head than Roxy. Their relationship had only lasted a few weeks and that was now several years ago.

At that moment Victoria and Craig returned from the dance floor. Victoria shot both Ryan and Roxy a withering look. Before Victoria had a chance to say anything, Roxy pecked Ryan on the cheek and slid off into the crowd.

'What did she want?' asked Victoria tartly.

'Just being friendly,' replied Ryan as McDonald winked at him.

'I know exactly what her sort of friendly means,' said Victoria, 'Just watch it!'

Ryan wasn't too bothered - the two girls had never hit it off, due to Roxy pinching one of Victoria's previous boyfriends.

'It's okay, I'll be good,' he reassured her.

McDonald spotted a few pastry crumbs on Ryan's chin.

'Looks like you've already been bad! I thought I told you to keep away from food like that.'

'But I haven't eaten for hours,' protested Ryan.

'Maybe not, but pasta, chicken or fruit – yes, sausage rolls and pork pie – no! You know the rules. No pain no gain! I'll see to you in the morning. Early!' McDonald placed heavy emphasis on the word early.

Ryan inwardly groaned; he knew McDonald wasn't joking and he could look forward to a harder than usual workout the next day.

As the evening wore on, voices grew louder and louder until people were shouting at, rather than talking to each other. The wooden parquet floor was becoming increasingly sticky in places as drinks were carelessly slopped. Every now and then an item of food, or a damp napkin, would skim over their heads. In other words it was developing into a typical mechanics' bash. Gradually the more decorous or timid guests slid away - leaving a hard core of hardened partygoers. Soon the games would start.

Immediately after the race, and for some hours later, Ryan had felt drained; but as the stresses and tensions of the day ebbed away he began to come alive. For sure his muscles were protesting but you didn't reach Formula One unless you were very fit - and the very fit recover very quickly indeed. He was enjoying himself, and looked forward to the Wheelbarrow Grand Prix that was de rigeur at the Vantec parties.

Just before midnight there was a flurry of activity, as a group of mechanics herded the few remaining dancers off the floor and towards the edges of the room. Next, chairs were placed at strategic places round the room to create a rough and ready circuit. When he was satisfied that all was ready, Derek Archer, Vantec's Chief Mechanic, grabbed the microphone from the bemused DJ.

'Ladies, Gentlemen, Mechanics and Drivers.' Archer was very particular about the sequence of worthiness. 'Welcome to the Vantec Grand Prix, the fourth running of this prestigious event. As usual there will be two teams from Vantec; and this year we have issued a challenge to Kodama, who have accepted and agreed to field a team that includes Stuart Underwood.'

Previous races had only ever featured Vantec personnel. Stuart Underwood had been Vantec's most successful driver until his move to Kodama, and was still very welcome at Vantec.

Archer allowed the applause and catcalls to die down before continuing. ' There is still space on the grid for one more team, are there any takers?'

Ryan grabbed Craig McDonald's arm and thrust it into the air.

'We have a volunteer – well done my son! Can all teams please assemble at the start…,' he pointed at a chalk line on the floor, 'for pre race briefing.'

The race would consist of four laps of the circuit. Teams were made up of two people, a driver - the one who stood up and steered, and an engine. The driver held the engine's legs whilst the engine supported himself on his hands. At the end of each lap the team had to pit. At the pit stop, both team members would have to drink a glass of lager, before swapping roles and continuing. As an added complication they would make a Le Mans style start. In this context that meant the team members would each have to down a drink in turn before they could begin. The race was becoming an institution within the team; and Somerset had donated a magnificent silver trophy that was inscribed with the names of the previous winning combinations.

Ryan and Craig had taken part before; and last year just missed winning by inches. Although as a combination they might be fitter, the mechanics could generally drink quicker. Furthermore, the Grand Prix proper normally took a fair bit out of Ryan. Still, they were both keen to do well. At the start, Craig was going to be the driver. Ryan studied the other teams as he waited for the race to begin. He knew that Stuart Underwood and partner would give them a hard time, as the Kodama driver was very competitive and had a point to prove. Stuart had raced for Vantec up until the current season, but had been moved out to make way for Panetta - who brought considerable sponsorship money into the team. Fortunately things had worked out well for Stuart and he was having a good season with the improving Kodama team. Furthermore his name was already on the trophy. Ryan recognised Andy and Wayne, two of the mechanics who made up one of the Vantec teams. The two mechanics worked on the number two car. The final team comprised the tall muscular Dave Morrison - one of Ryan's mechanics, and a young man that Ryan didn't recognise. He guessed it must be another mechanic, but he couldn't recall having seen the tall sandy-haired man before. He made a mental note to find out more about him later. Ryan liked to know everyone he worked with.

The DJ had got into the spirit of things and had put on the 'Chain' by Fleetwood Mac. The song, that was forever associated with motor racing, thundered out as the four teams stood ready beside a table on which were placed eight glasses of beer. Derek Archer held a green flag above his head and counted down. 'Three, two one …' On the count of one, he dropped the flag and the race began. Craig McDonald was going to drink first for the team. The Belgian lager was no challenge for the thirty-two year old Australian, and he was easily the first to finish - holding the glass upside down over his head. Ryan struggled with the gassy beer, and by the time he had finished, the pair had fallen back to third place. Ahead of them, two teams had already assumed position and set off across the line on the first lap.

By the end of the first lap McDonald had managed to bring them up to the feet of the second placed team. In the pit stop they again fell back a little but the mechanics were starting to breathe more heavily. The Kodama team had obviously been pacing themselves - as by the end of the drinking they had made up a few valuable seconds.

The arms were normally a weak link in wheelbarrow racing, and both Grand Prix drivers - with their well-developed arm muscles, had an advantage over the mechanics. By the end of the second lap both Ryan and Underwood had passed Andy and Wayne - the slower of the Vantec mechanic based teams, even with having to overtake on the outside!

The next pit stop saw Ryan and Craig nearly catch the leading team, whilst behind them Underwood and his partner drew closer still. At the second corner Ryan saw a gap and went for it; McDonald barged past the burly Dave Morrison knocking him to the ground, an incident that was later declared to be a racing accident and therefore perfectly acceptable. Whilst the mechanics recovered, the Kodama team also got past.

Ryan and Underwood started the last lap side by side. However, as on all circuits, the inside line gave the driver who got there first a major advantage. In this case it was Ryan. Despite feeling sick, and with his arms screaming in pain, he and Craig were able to hang on and win their first race in the series. Stuart Underwood offered a tired hand in congratulations; whilst the Vantec mechanics in third place shot them a black look and went off to protest about the overtaking manoeuvre on the penultimate lap.

Ryan hoisted the trophy high in the air, and in a loud voice said, 'May this be the first of many victory ceremonies'. The proclamation was met with a barrage of good-natured jeers and whistles. True to motor racing fashion, the trophy was followed by the presentation of an even larger bottle of champagne. As Ryan made to shake the bottle and spray the crowd, he spotted a number of smartly dressed ladies beating a hasty retreat and changed his mind. Instead he raised the giant bottle to his lips and took a good long glug - much to the disgust of his trainer. Before he could take a second swig, the bottle was wrestled away from him by McDonald, who took an even longer draught, before passing the bottle on to the runners-up.

'I think you've had all you need,' said McDonald.

'I think you're probably right,' said Ryan, who had already reached that conclusion as he fought to keep the drink down.

Victoria had emerged from the crowd and was now standing next to Ryan and Craig. She could see Ryan was worse for wear.

'Bedtime?' she asked.

'Bedtime,' Ryan agreed.

They said their goodnights and headed towards the exit. As Ryan followed Victoria towards the door he had a flashback of her getting dressed earlier, he slid his hand over her bottom and whispered in her right ear, 'I'm not feeling very sleepy.'

'Ryan!' she hissed. 'Surely you must be too tired.'
'You can always steer,' he whispered back.
They headed for the lift hand in hand.

CHAPTER 3

Monday 20th August, Liege - Belgium

The racing car ahead braked unexpectedly - and before Ryan could react, his front nearside wheel ran up over its rear left wheel. Instantly, Ryan's car was launched into the air - as his car shot skywards it flipped over, flew fifteen metres, then crashed heavily back to the track. Ryan scrabbled unsuccessfully at the seatbelt fastening as the leaking fuel ignited in a horrific fireball. He screamed.

He was still screaming as Victoria, stunned into sudden wakefulness, reached over and shook him awake. He was covered in sweat. As he woke, Victoria cradled him in her arms and whispered in his ear.

'It was only a dream, baby,' she said. 'Everything's okay.'

Ryan took a few deep breaths to stabilise his pounding heart; and then held Victoria tightly.

'Do you want to talk about it?' she asked, gently.

He looked towards the window, and then at the clock beside the bed. It was five-thirty in the morning so there was not much point in going back to sleep. The nightmare was a frequent visitor - usually after races, as his body and mind tried to unwind. Victoria had not experienced it before, so he felt he owed her some kind of explanation. He stroked her forearm absent-mindedly as he sought the right words.

'I had a really bad crash when I was in Formula 3.' He paused as images of the real crash rushed through his mind. 'My car was flipped over and I was trapped inside for what seemed an age. I could smell fuel all around me - anything could have set it off. Fortunately, the marshals got me out before anything happened - this is the only physical reminder….,' he pointed at an old white scar round his waist. '…that was caused by the marshals cutting me free - the seat belts wouldn't unfasten. The crash in the nightmare is very similar - except that the fuel does ignite.'

'How often do you have the nightmare?'

'Generally before and after most races. But not very often out of season.'

'My god,' she said. 'And yet you still carry on driving! Why on earth do you do it?'

He shrugged his shoulders in resignation; he was quite used to answering that particular question. 'Because I like it, and because I'm good at it.'

'Surely there's more to it than that?' She didn't often get to have serious talks with Ryan, so she was going to make the most of the opportunity.

'Yeah, I guess there is, do you really want me to talk about it?'

'Of course I do.' She briefly stared into his eyes, then contentedly rested her head on his chest, and waited for him to continue.

Ryan gazed at the ceiling as he got his thoughts together.

'I don't think it's the speed - so much as the act of being in control. The challenge is to control something - to make it bend to your will. A car at slow speed doesn't provide that challenge, but almost any vehicle at speed can. Obviously, the more powerful the car - the bigger the challenge. Then you have the fact that most racing drivers are very competitive animals. There is a desire to be better than other people - at everything, all of the time. I bet most drivers always had to win at Monopoly or table tennis when young. The competition is with oneself as well; I get frustrated if I can't do something as well as I would like. There's a lovely story of Ayrton Senna, who - having been beaten in a wet kart race, by people he normally thrashed -

realised he didn't know how to drive in the rain; so he would go out in his kart every time it rained until he mastered driving in wet conditions. I think we all have a bit of that in us.' He paused briefly to marshal his thoughts. 'Then there is the adrenaline-rush; a motor race is a bit like a long fairground-ride. You are always just moments away from the next thrill. Each lap can be different; the weather conditions may change - the car certainly will; and you are forever seeking to find the limits of the car. Unfortunately, the only way to know where the limits are, is to exceed them! The ability to go over the limit and recover safely is the mark of the great driver. Most of us are very, very good, but not in the same class as the true greats: Fangio, Moss, Clark, Stewart, Lauda, Prost, Senna, Schumacher.' Ryan wistfully reeled off the litany of great drivers then stopped talking.

'Could you give it up if you wanted to?'

'I don't know about wanted to,' he said. 'The way things are going I might have to!'

'How come?'

'Chris is getting a bit edgy. He doesn't seem sure about carrying on next season - unless we get better results. He won't give me a new contract yet, and if he goes, anything could happen.'

'Couldn't you just get a place in another team?'

'It's not quite that simple. There are always new drivers wanting to come in; and they might just prefer a new, up-and-coming, driver over an experienced one who hasn't had good results. So far I haven't exactly set the racing world alight!'

'But surely you've never been in a really good car?'

'Exactly, but I won't get a seat in a top car unless I look the business in an average car. Sadly it can be a bit of a chicken and egg scenario. I really need a drive next season. It's taken me a while to get used to Formula One; but I think I showed yesterday what I can do. It would be terrible to lose out now after all my parents have done for me - it nearly broke their hearts when I turned down a University place in order to go racing.' Ryan went quiet as he thought about the sacrifices his parents had made for him. Despite their reservations, they had foregone holidays and the chance to move to a better house in order to support him.

Victoria realised she wasn't going to get anymore out of Ryan. She squeezed him, 'Thank you. You're the first driver who has actually explained it to me.'

'So how many other drivers have you slept with then?' he asked playfully.

'None, stupid, and if you all have nightmares, I'll stick with just the one, thank you very much!'

Ryan rolled her over and kissed her. Her lips were relaxed and loving - taking that as a good sign, he slid his hand down to her left breast. His fingers gently teased the nipple to a peak and then moved further down her body.

'What I need is a bit of tender loving care,' he asserted.

Victoria parted her legs in response to his gentle caresses.

'Fine,' she said. 'But you can steer this time, I'm feeling too lazy!'

McDonald tried the door handle and, finding the room unlocked, quietly let himself in. The bedroom curtains were still drawn, but there was sufficient light for him to see that Ryan and Victoria were still asleep. Ryan was lying face down; his head buried deep in the pillow –his right arm was draped across Victoria, who lay on her back, her mouth open. The duvet was a crumpled mess, half way down the bed, exposing Victoria's breasts to Craig's appreciative gaze.

'Some guys have all the luck,' he muttered, before remembering why he was there.

'Come on folks, training time!'

Ryan and Victoria awoke with a start. Victoria hastily pulled the duvet up to cover her nakedness.

'Don't you ever knock!' she hissed.

'Sorry Victoria, but it's not always easy to get Ryan out of his pit from the other side of the door!'

'Well, think about me next time, will you!' She was still angry.

'Okay. Okay. Well, can you get him up on time then please.'

'Did you just say "training time"?' asked Ryan sleepily.

'You know I did. Come on, it's seven-thirty - five easy miles to wake you up a bit!'

Ryan groaned and slid his legs out from under the duvet.

'Your idea of "easy" isn't exactly the same as mine,' muttered Ryan, as he got to his feet and headed for the bathroom. His bladder urgently reminded him of his excessive drinking the evening before. A pounding head and dry mouth confirmed the abuse meted out to his body. Ryan didn't normally drink very much during the racing season, but the annual Vantec bash was an occasion. With two weeks until the next race there was plenty of time to get his body back to a peak of fitness – especially under Craig's watchful eye.

'I'll just wait outside then,' said McDonald, backing out of the room as Victoria continued to glare at him

'Women!' he muttered. 'Why can't they be more like men!'

Five minutes later, Ryan stood in front of McDonald in T-shirt, shorts and well-thrashed Nike trainers. The pair walked down the corridor. Ryan watched with regret as McDonald continued past the elevator and towards the stairs.

Outside the stone arched front of the Hotel, the early morning air was fresh; but already it promised to be another fine day. Directly ahead of them, heavily laden barges slid slowly up and down the Meuse. On days like this, even Ryan could enjoy a morning run – if only he didn't have to get out of bed first! Whilst Ryan was still thinking about it, Craig McDonald had turned right on the Quai St Leonard and headed off down the waterfront street at a brisk jog. Ryan groaned and set off in pursuit.

Liege was a fairly tricky town in which to run; the medieval city contained few parks within easy reach, and both of them would both have preferred a country run, to a jog through crowded streets - suffocated by petrol fumes. Fortunately, it wasn't a Sunday, otherwise the ancient street-market of La Batte, that ran along the riverfront, would have presented quite a challenge. They headed down the riverfront for less than a minute before turning right just after the Walloon Musee de L'Art. At the end of the Rue Velbruck they turned left and then, fifty yards later, right.

Ryan groaned and came to a juddering halt as he saw the mountain of steps rising steeply ahead of them. 'We're not going up there, are we!' he protested, pointing up the Montagne de Bueren.

'Scared of a few steps?' Craig's tone was mocking.

'A few steps! There must be at least five hundred!'

'Three hundred and seventy-four, if you must know,' said Craig; who had done his homework well. 'Hopefully it will teach you to stay off the pastries! We can have a rest at the top, but only if you run all the way!'

Having said his piece, Craig was off, bounding easily up the first flight of steps. Ryan knew he had little choice but to follow. He shook his head in despair and began the climb at a more sedate pace. Alone, Ryan would probably have walked much of the way, but he was determined to show Craig that he was up to the challenge. By the time they reached the top his heart was pounding and his legs had turned to jelly. Only an optimist could have described his slow progress as running.

Craig reached the top a good thirty seconds ahead of Ryan and, by the time Ryan approached the final few steps, was fully recovered. Craig had been a national standard athlete, and a graduate of the Australian Sports Institute, before becoming a fitness trainer, and he found the runs with Ryan far too comfortable for his liking.

'Good on yer mate,' he said putting his hands together in a silent, appreciative clap. 'Really didn't think you'd make it. Reckon you must be getting fit at last.'

'As you said, it was only a few steps!' Ryan gasped for air as his lungs and legs recovered from the tough ascent. His heart was pounding and a sheen of sweat lined his face, which was swiftly turning red. Despite the pain, Ryan was very pleased with his attempt on the steps.

He was about to say more to McDonald when the red headed trainer set off again.

'Aussie bastard; I thought we were supposed to rest at the top,' he muttered to himself as he broke into a jog after the fast-disappearing Australian.

The ascent of the Montagne de Bueren had brought them up to the old citadel above Liege. Not much remained of the citadel itself but the grounds provided excellent views over the old town and gave them a chance to run on grass. After circumnavigating the walls of the fort, they headed further east to run round the sports complex at Xhovemont. By now, Ryan had managed to shake off the worst of the previous night's excesses and was beginning to move more freely. Until he had hooked up with Craig, he had never really enjoyed the fitness aspects of the sport. McDonald had the knack of being able to put the technical aspects of training into layman's terms and, for once, Ryan was able to understand why he was being made to suffer. He had always realised that you needed to be very fit to drive a Formula One car; but it was one thing understanding the need for fitness, and quite another actually doing something about it. This was his second season working with McDonald and he had to admit the hard work was doing him good. Apart from anything else, he enjoyed the Australian's irreverent company and Craig helped keep his feet planted firmly on the ground.

McDonald slowed the pace down after they had completed a circuit of the sports complex. He reckoned he had made Ryan suffer sufficiently for his pleasures the previous night. The pair headed back the same way they had come, but this time they were able to chat.

'Is there any more news on Panetta?' asked Craig, his concern evident in his voice. Ryan found this human side of Craig's nature very appealing after the falsity displayed by much of the F1 community.

'I haven't heard anything more since yesterday, but it's pretty certain he's going to be out for the rest of the season.'

'I guess Warren's going to get his chance at last then.'

'Well, that's what you and I might have thought, but I'm afraid F1 doesn't deal in fairness. It looks like Somerset is going to bring someone else in.'

'Christ! It's a tough sport you guys play – what on earth does it take to get a break?'

'Plenty of luck, the right connections, and preferably money, plenty of money – ability is a pretty small part of the package.' Ryan spoke with feeling. He had enjoyed good luck and connections on his own way into the sport; but there was a large part of him that wished it was different and that ability was the key factor. Ryan enjoyed educating Craig in the subtleties of his sport. Craig now knew far more than he did when he had started with Ryan, but still had difficulty comprehending the political and economic dimensions of the sport.

Craig shook his head in disbelief. 'And I thought they wanted the best drivers in the best cars! Anyway, do you know who Somerset has in mind?' asked Craig, wondering if there was a chance to pick up another client.

'I don't know how official it is - but it could be Jason Kramer. Apparently he's an American Champ Car hot-shot but I know very little about him. I've seen his name in race results, but that's about all. Hopefully we'll know for sure in a few days. In the meantime; I think you'd better keep it quiet, a lot can change in this business!'

With that, Ryan suddenly accelerated to a sprint and moved away from Craig. He had a feeling that he'd already said too much, and wanted to stop the conversation before it went any further. It made a change to force Craig to play catch-up - although he knew he couldn't keep ahead of him for long. Craig caught him after just fifty metres and they then slowed to a more sustainable pace; and ran back to the Hotel together.

'What time are we leaving?' asked McDonald as they reached the hotel entrance.

Ryan wiped a bead of sweat away from his eyes before answering, 'I want to catch a train around two, so we had better get away from here by eleven. Is that okay by you?'

'Yeah, fine, are you having breakfast?'

'Just try and stop me!'

'Okay. Well, I'll see you in the breakfast room in half an hour then.' This time McDonald let Ryan take the lift while he went up the stairs.

After showering and dressing, Ryan escorted Victoria down to the breakfast room. There were not too many other people around as the mechanics and other team personnel had departed earlier. During the season, theirs was a hard life on the road - comparable to that of a large touring rock band. The cars had to be taken back to base for a thorough overhaul before any more testing could take place. Ryan was due at Brands Hatch, two days later, to test some ideas on suspension settings for the next race.

Ryan and Victoria were well into their breakfast before McDonald appeared. It frequently amused Ryan that McDonald could spend so long in a shower. Ryan was forever waiting around in changing rooms for McDonald to get dressed. It wasn't even that he needed to spend much time on his hair, for it was already cropped as short as can be. He just seemed to like being in the water.

It was just after eleven when the car pulled out of the hotel's small car park. Fortunately all three were prepared to travel light, for the boot of Ryan's Aston Martin was not designed for carting huge amounts of luggage. They had left most of their luggage with the team for transportation; so they needed little more than hand luggage for the trip. Although Liege was Belgium's third largest city it was, thankfully, only fairly small in size; so it was not too long before they were able to get away from the morning traffic and onto the E40 for Calais.

Once on the six-lane motorway, Ryan was able to put his foot down. The large Aston Martin V8 Volante was never happy being driven slowly in low gear. The speed limit in Belgium was 120 kph which, Ryan reckoned, meant he could get away with about 80 mph. He could not afford to collect too many speeding tickets, or his racing license could be put at risk.

The powerful convertible was Ryan's pride and joy. He knew there were better handling, and even better performance cars out there, but he had always wanted to own an Aston – and, for him, British Racing Green was the only possible colour. He had bought the car second-hand, as the V8 Vantage Volante model he wanted was no longer produced. Fortunately the Aston Martin service workshop at Newport Pagnell was able to restore the car to near mint condition; they had also fitted improved suspension and braking systems at his request. Due to its size the car could still be a real handful to drive, but Ryan enjoyed having to use his driving skills. Sadly, it was only at the nearer European races that he was able to give the car the long run it demanded.

Ryan checked the mirror before moving out to overtake a slower moving Peugeot in the middle lane. As he moved back into the middle lane he looked in his mirror again. As expected, he could just see the Lotus Elise overtaking the saloon. Ryan had first become aware of the red sports car half an hour into the journey. He rather enjoyed the Elise being on his tail as it helped him concentrate on his driving. His pride would not let him be easily overtaken by the lower powered sports car.

The Lotus was still with them as they pulled into the Eurotunnel terminus at Coquelles, on the outskirts of Calais. Ryan was a member of the Eurotunnel Club, which gave him access to a priority check-in lane. As a result, they were soon parked up waiting for instructions to board the train. While they waited, he looked around to see if could spot the Elise. The car had disappeared from view, and Ryan was disappointed not to get a look at the driver.

Victoria had reserved them a place on the 14:00 train, and it wasn't long before they drove the car into the brightly-lit but cramped interior of the train. Although it was possible to walk about on the train, the three of them were happy to stay in the comfort of the car during the thirty-five minute journey. Ryan switched on the powerful Linn hi-fi system he had extravagantly installed earlier in the summer, and selected an Eric Clapton album from the CD-changer mounted in the boot. The 950 watt Chakra system effortlessly filled the confined space with high quality music. Ryan had always had a fascination with sound equipment and, after driving, music was his second passion. The noise of the train, roaring through the long tunnel, was unnoticeable in the cocoon of music surrounding them.

There were no formalities on the other side of the channel, and within minutes they were on the M20 and heading for London.

They had barely gone five miles when Ryan thought he spotted the Elise. He only caught the briefest glimpse of a small red sports car in the heavy traffic. He eased back on the throttle and let a few cars pass in order to see if he could get a clearer view. He was right - there were three cars between the Aston and the Elise, but Ryan was sure that they had picked the sports car up again. He wasn't certain they were being followed, but his curiosity was certainly aroused.

'I think we're being followed,' he said out loud. Instinctively, the other two turned their heads.

'Which car, mate?' asked McDonald.

'Red Elise about four cars back.'

'I can't see anything,' complained Victoria.
McDonald moved his head from side in an attempt to get a better view.

'Yeah, got it, what makes you think they're following?' asked McDonald.

'They've been just behind us ever since we left Liege.'

'That doesn't mean a thing; lots of people come back home on that route!' said Victoria.

'Maybe,' said Ryan. 'But I think we'll do a bit of checking!'

With that he put his foot down - the sudden acceleration thrust Victoria and Craig firmly back into their seats. Ryan quickly overtook a couple of cars ,and then pulled over into the slow lane.

The female driver of the Elise had seen Ryan pull out to overtake the first car and had bided her time before starting to overtake herself. It was only after passing two more cars that she realised that she could no longer see the dark-green Aston Martin. She assumed the Aston had speeded up and so she accelerated. She didn't spot the Aston, tucked in between two large articulated lorries, as she sailed by in the outside lane.

'Now let's see whether or not we're being followed,' said Ryan. He pulled out into the fast lane and speeded up. Cruising up behind the Elise he flashed his lights. The driver of the Elise was too surprised to do anything other than let the Aston through. Ryan took a good long look at the driver as they slid alongside. He was more than a little surprised to find it was a woman. As they pulled ahead, he was sure that he would be able to recognise the girl - if he ever saw her again. The shock of blonde curls hanging down over her shoulders was fixed in his mind. Ryan kept station in the outside lane for a couple of miles after they got back in front of the Lotus. He could only occasionally see the Elise behind him. The red sports car had once again sought anonymity by drifting back to sit behind intervening cars. At junction seven, Ryan peeled off the motorway. The Lotus followed. At the top of the exit road, Ryan carried straight on round the roundabout and back down onto the M20.

The driver of the Elise cursed softly; she guessed that she had been rumbled, and rather than follow Ryan back onto the motorway chose to turn left at the roundabout. Just after the junction, she stopped the car and waited a few minutes, before making a U-turn and heading back onto the motorway. She would now have a rather more leisurely drive into London. As she didn't know where Ryan lived, she would have to find another way to get close to him.

For a few miles, Ryan kept an eye on his mirror, until he was certain that they were no longer being followed. He couldn't begin to guess why she had pursued them. He mentally shrugged-off the episode, and focused on the rest of the journey.

It was nearly half-past-four when they turned into the entrance to the underground car park of the luxury flat complex. Ryan opened the security gates with the remote control, and slowly drove the Aston down the ramp to the parking area. The three of them grabbed their bags and made for the lift. Ryan's penthouse suite occupied the entire 16th floor of a towering steel and glass structure in Chelsea harbour. As he unlocked the door an automated control system switched on the lighting and turned on Ryan's hi-fi. He enjoyed walking into a properly lighted room and it was a bonus to hear one of his favourite tunes. Home automation was one of his hobbies; and he had taken pleasure in setting up the complex system so that the level of lighting depended on the outside light level. As well as controlling his lighting, the system also looked after his security system, and provided touch-pad control over his home entertainment system.

As Ryan looked through his enormous CD collection for an album to play; Victoria opened the large glass doors that led to a terrace overlooking both the Thames and the Chelsea marina. She and Craig stepped outside into the dwindling evening sun. High above the river, the late summer breeze was chilling. Whilst the view was commonplace to Ryan, it was a treat for his friends. They stood in quiet companionship, looking down at the constantly moving river scene below them.

'What do you make of us being followed?' asked McDonald, walking backing into the huge living area with Victoria.

'I've got really no idea,' replied Ryan. 'But I think I'd better keep my eyes open for a few days.'

'Is this any help?' Victoria passed Ryan a slip of paper. He looked at the registration number on the note.

'It's not a number I recognise, but who knows - we may see it again somewhere.' He folded the piece of paper and tucked it into his wallet.

McDonald stayed for a coffee and a chat, but at seven-o-clock he regretfully got to his feet.

'I've got to head off,' he said. 'What's happening the rest of the week?'

'Tomorrow's a quiet day; but I guess that means we'll need to have a good workout doesn't it?' McDonald nodded in agreement.

'On Wednesday I'm due at Brands for testing - maybe you could come down there and we'll get a run in round the track?'

'That's cool. I'll see you tomorrow morning at eight then.'

'If you really must!' complained Ryan.

McDonald smiled at the pair of them and left - banging the door on the way out.

CHAPTER 4

Wednesday 22nd August, Brands Hatch - England

Ryan pulled left off the A20, and stopped a few yards in front of the tall green-metal gates that marked the main entrance to Brands Hatch. As he stopped, a uniformed guard wandered over. Ryan pressed the window switch and the window beside him quietly hissed down.

'Mornin' Mr Clarke, testing today, then, are we?' The blubbery face of the guard thrust into the open window. His piggy eyes roamed the inside of the car; enjoying a luxury he could only dream about. He had been on security at the track for nearly eleven years, and recognised Ryan by his car.

'That's right, a whole day of driving round in circles!' Ryan injected as much enthusiasm as he could muster into his voice - it wouldn't do to let people think he didn't enjoy his work. Although testing could be boring at times; Ryan was never happier than when sat behind the wheel of an F1 car. For him it was the ultimate power thrill and, even in a routine test session, nothing could ever be taken for granted; just as many accidents happened in testing as in races. When testing stopped being a thrill then it was probably time to give up motor racing.

In the background, a small group looked on excitedly. Some of them were wearing Vantec polo shirts and caps. A hardcore of dedicated fans was present at all the testing sessions. Slowly, they began to inch nervously towards the car.

'Great race Sunday – loved the way you stuffed that German bastard!' The guard was determined to make the most of his time with Ryan. The rest of his day promised little more than a lonely vigil by the gate.

'Yeah - quite enjoyed it myself,' responded Ryan, who couldn't be bothered to point out that Wittman was actually Austrian. 'Can you open the gates, while I deal with that lot behind you,' Ryan pointed at the fans, who were standing right behind the guard, waving pens and notebooks at him.

'Right you are then.' The guard eased his bulk off the window-sill and started to trudge over to the gates.

Ryan opened his car door and got out to greet the fans. Even after all his years in motor sport, he was still not sure what he thought about this aspect of the life. It was great to feel wanted, but it was often a chore he could do without. However, he understood the need to maintain good relationships with fans - apart from any other considerations, there could always be a journalist amongst them; so he put on his best face, and prepared to deal with the inevitable set of questions he was always asked.

Smiling, Ryan began to sign the requested autographs and answer the questions - from those fans brave enough to speak to their hero. A car horn interrupted the signing session, and Ryan looked round to see John Thornhill, the team manager, drive straight past the group and into the circuit. Thornhill smiled, and waved at Ryan as he slowly passed. Thornhill knew how little Ryan enjoyed the celebrity. Ryan raised his eyebrows in mock exasperation, and turned back to the milling fans.

Ryan spent five minutes with the fans, before climbing back into his car and driving into the track. He pulled up behind the conference centre, located along the sweeping Clark curve, just before eight a.m. There was a smattering of other cars in the car park. As much as he disliked the early start, at least it meant he had avoided the rush-hour traffic around Chelsea. From time to time he had checked his rear view mirror - but there was no sign that the red Lotus, or anyone else, was following him, and the journey proved very uneventful. Although there were large patches of blue sky, strong winds were pushing clouds across from the west. He made a mental note to check on the forecast.

Mechanics were bent over a jacked-up chassis as Ryan entered the pit garage, located half way along the main straight. Bits of green, logo-emblazoned carbon-fibre bodywork lay all over the enclosed space; even so, the pit had more in common with a hospital operating theatre than a car workshop. There was a high state of cleanliness, and all the tools were well organised. Apart from the risk of accidents, tools were costly - and the mechanics were not keen on losing their favourite implements.

He tapped Derek Archer on the shoulder. The scruffy mechanic stood up, and turned to welcome Ryan.

'Wotcha, how's tricks?'

'Not bad, how's the car shaping?'

Archer glanced at his oil smeared watch, 'Should be ready in about half an hour. Chris asked if you could see him, in his office, as soon as you arrive.' Archer pointed vaguely back in the direction of the corporate centre.

'Oh well, no rest for the wicked - better not keep the boss waiting,' said Ryan cheerfully. 'I'll see you later.' Ryan called out a greeting to the other mechanics on his way out. In the background he spotted the unknown mechanic who had taken part in the wheelbarrow race. The mechanic held Ryan's gaze for a second before lowering his eyes to concentrate on what he was doing. Ryan decided he'd better introduce himself to the guy later. He liked to know the people who worked on his car; after all they had his life in their hands. He hoped they would feel that responsibility more keenly if they personally knew the man behind the wheel.

Vantec had made Brands Hatch their home in 1987, when Chris Somerset had founded the team to race in Formula 3. The company's main office and factory were sited less than a mile down the road in Farningham, but, on practice days, the team also had use of several rooms in the green-glassed corporate hospitality centre. It was in one of those rooms that Ryan found Chris Somerset, seated on a comfortable black sofa, nursing a cup of coffee. Somerset was chatting to a young man that Ryan didn't recognise. As Ryan entered the room Somerset stopped talking; both men got to their feet.

'Ryan,' Somerset shook Ryan's hand, 'I'd like you to meet Jason Kramer; he's going to be your number two for the rest of the season.'

As Ryan shook an eagerly thrust out hand, he looked the American up and down. Kramer was tall for a racing driver, Ryan estimated his height at a little over six feet. He had a mop of dark curly hair, a wide mouth and large nose. A smart, cream-coloured, button-down, short-sleeved shirt exposed powerful arms that were thickly covered in dark hair. Confidence and controlled power radiated from him. Ryan sensed that he could be either a powerful ally or a determined foe. For now his dark-brown eyes smiled, and his greeting was warm enough. All in all, Ryan liked what he saw. He retrieved his crushed hand from the American's powerful grip before replying.

'Good to have you on board. I hope you can do more than just drive round in circles,' said Ryan alluding to the oval circuits the Americans seemed to prefer.

'I'm afraid you've got the wrong idea there, Mack. I was in Champ Cars, and we drove on road circuits - just like the one out there! In fact, a few years ago we raced on this very circuit,' responded the American, pointing a finger out of the window. 'Mind you I wasn't in Champ Cars then; so it's new to me!'

'Fair enough,' Ryan laughed his mistake off, but didn't miss the irritation that flickered across Kramer's face. It wasn't the good impression he had hoped to make with his new partner.

Somerset broke into the conversation.

'Ryan, can you show Jason the circuit; I want to get him into the car as soon as possible. When you've done that can we meet for a briefing at. . .,' he looked at his watch, 'half nine?'

'No problem,' replied Ryan. 'Come on then, Top Gun, let's go check out a proper motor racing circuit.'

Kramer got to his feet. He picked his crash-helmet up from the seat beside him, and shaking his head, followed Ryan out of the lounge.

Ryan thought it best if they got changed before heading out on a tour of the track. It also gave him a chance to point out some of the circuit's facilities. Although the team rented a few offices in the corporate hospitality centre - mainly in which to hold large meetings in comfort - they also brought one of their two motorhomes along to the track. The green motorhome was parked up alongside a pair of similarly coloured transporters. The well-appointed and luxurious motorhome not only provided changing and rest areas, but also meeting space and cooking facilities. A large covered area alongside the motorhome was filled with plastic tables and chairs - allowing Vantec's caterers to provide meals for the whole team. The entire operation was geared-up to ensure that maximum use could be made of the limited number of days allowed for testing.

Ryan walked Kramer through the currently empty eating space and up the aluminium steps into the motorhome. The drivers had each been allocated a small room in the van. Ryan showed Kramer to his room, and then returned to his own to get changed. His protective clothing was already neatly laid out on a cream coloured sofa that half filled the very small room. He quickly stripped off his own clothes and began to dress. As usual, Ryan struggled to get into the full length Nomex underwear. Once he had donned the green Vantec-badged Nomex overalls and fastened his thin-soled racing shoes his transformation into a racing driver was complete. He left the top of his overalls unzipped to the waist to keep cool.

Kramer was already waiting outside the motorhome for Ryan. The American was dressed in well worn deep red overalls. His racing suit was festooned with sponsors' badges; Ryan was amused to see logos from Sparco and Cosworth demonstrating common links with F1. A Team Radtke badge ran prominently across his chest. Ryan had used the internet to learn a bit more about his new colleague and knew that Radtke was the team that Kramer had last driven for. Ryan raised his eyebrows quizzically.

'They said it was too short notice to find me a Vantec suit. It seems you limeys are all much smaller than me! The boss said I could wear my old gear this morning. They're going to get a set out to me later today as we're supposed to meet the press this afternoon – I don't think they'll want me wearing this old tat!' Kramer pulled at the material to make his point.

It was the first Ryan had heard of a press meeting - but it made perfect sense, he just wished he had been told. He didn't like it when things happened around him without his knowledge.

'Well, I guess we'd better hide you in a car as soon as possible, but first we ought to take a tour of the track. I trust you can ride a moped.'

'You kidding me?'

'British humour old chap,' responded Ryan. 'Better get used to it. If you think I'm bad, wait until you meet the mechanics; taking the piss is an art form with those guys!'

Ryan escorted Kramer to the back of the Vantec garage. Parked up outside the pit were a row of Malaguti 49cc mopeds. The tiny "Phantom 200" scooters were ideal for buzzing around the spread out circuit. The bikes were smartly painted in Vantec livery and sponsors' logos covered the bodywork; no opportunity was missed in the ongoing struggle for funds. The Malaguti deal, including maintenance, was worth some £50,000 per season. It was one of the many indirect forms of sponsorship enjoyed by Vantec. If the bike manufacturer had not donated the bikes, Vantec would have had to use their own cash. As it was, Malaguti got a chance to be associated with the pinnacle of motorsport - and Vantec got free local transportation. However, it was only a small drop in the ocean, when balanced against the £50 million pounds it cost to run the team for a year.

The two drivers mounted the tiny bikes and rode down the back of the garage complex, joining the pit lane just before it emerged onto the Brabham straight. After quickly checking the road, Ryan drove out onto the empty main straight. Due to the inherent dangers in running powerful F1 cars, the track was exclusively booked for the testing session. Vantec was the only team testing at Brands Hatch, and as a result there was no other traffic on the circuit. Down the years, the merits of testing with or apart from the other British based F1 teams had been hotly debated; but Somerset had won the argument by saying that if it was good enough for Ferrari to test by themselves, then it was quite good enough for him. Apart from anything else it saved them having to drive up to Silverstone, taking everything they might just conceivably need. There were many advantages to being close to their factory. Repairs and adjustments were also that much easier to make. However, just like Ferrari, they did join the other teams for a couple of test sessions in Barcelona when the better Spanish weather was more practical than operating in the damp and cold of a British winter.

Almost as soon as they had joined the track, Ryan signalled Kramer to halt - just before the right-hand bend at Paddock hill. Ryan got off the scooter and pulled it onto his stand. Kramer did the same and was then surprised to see Ryan lie prone on the track.

'Taking a rest?' he asked.

'No, I wanted you to see the camber on the bend. It's pretty unique and can be just a bit scary.'

Kramer gave Ryan a quizzical look, surprised at what seemed timidity, before lying down on the tarmac alongside Ryan. He peered down the road - he could see that the road sloped upwards to the inside curve. On most corners the road sloped down to the inside kerb. From where he lay, Kramer could see very little - the road dived away from view down the hill. He nodded, appreciating that Ryan was right to sound a note of caution. Kramer got back to his feet followed quickly by Ryan.

'This is Paddock hill bend. It's pretty much a double-apex bend, with an adverse camber,' said Ryan. 'Get it wrong and you'll be playing sand castles over there!' Ryan pointed at the large sand trap that ran down the length of the steep hill.

'Better have a bucket and spade handy then,' quipped the American. Ryan was beginning to like his number two, and very relieved that the driver could take a joke.

'Well, to avoid needing a bucket and spade - the trick is to aim at that marshal's post over there,' Ryan pointed at a hut on the outside of the bend. 'Once over the top and turning right, you need to clip that kerb on the outside.' His arm swung to point at the sawtoothed red and white kerb on the inside of the track.

'Come on then, plenty more to see,' said Ryan, patting Kramer on the back. They remounted their bikes and headed down the steep right-hander.

Kramer was just as surprised by the tightness of the next bend at Druids, and halted at the top to look at the possible lines through the one hundred and eighty-degree bend. If that corner wasn't bad enough, the run down to the left-handed Graham Hill bend looked even worse. As they reached Surtees bend, Jason Kramer suddenly twisted the hand throttle to its full extent. He took a tiny lead before Ryan realised what he was up to and responded. The American raised a clenched fist in triumph and turned to grin at Ryan, who nodded his head in acknowledgement. Kramer eased back on the throttle to let Ryan come alongside. Together they completed the final bend and made their way back to the pits. By the time they stopped the bikes Jason Kramer had quite a lot to think about. Saying yes to the Formula One seat seemed a much bigger deal now that he had seen one of the circuits up-close.

As they dismounted, Ryan continued to brief Kramer. 'We just ran on what's called the 'Indy' circuit. The Grand Prix circuit is much longer, but is only used on major race days now. The Indy circuit is used most of the time because it's great for spectators and, more to the point, cheaper for the organisers!' It was a sore point with Ryan, who wished that they were able to run on the full circuit. He had been disappointed when attempts to return the British Grand Prix to Brands Hatch had failed. Silverstone was certainly more centrally located, but he found the circuit much blander than Brands Hatch, and far easier to drive.

There was a bit of time to spare before the briefing, so Ryan used the opportunity to introduce Kramer to the mechanics. At the rear of the garage, Warren Barton, the team's able young test driver, sat on a toolbox, and kept quiet as Kramer was introduced to the mechanics. Before Ryan had a chance to introduce him to Kramer, Barton got up and slunk out through a door at the back of the garage. Somerset had told him the bad news just half an hour previously, and he was still getting over the disappointment of not getting the drive. He was not ready to talk to the man who had taken away his chance of an F1 drive.

The mechanics had been sad to lose Panetta and they took a little while to warm to the charms of his American replacement. However, by the time the two drivers left the garage the mechanics were coming round. At least he cracked jokes, and they could understand what he said - most of the time anyway.

Kramer was keen to see the car. The nature of F1 circuits meant that the car was designed to handle differently to the Champ cars he was used to. Champ cars were designed for all-out straight-line speed - while Formula One cars were built to quickly navigate ever-changing combinations of bends and straights. Whilst he could see a number of differences in the bodywork, he knew that he would have to drive the car to really appreciate the differences. With the next race, at Monza, only eleven days away, he didn't have very long to get used to the Vantec.

As nine-thirty approached, the drivers made their way slowly back to the conference centre. Chris Somerset was waiting for them in one of the meeting rooms equipped with presentation facilities. A large table filled the room; eight chairs were already taken. Ryan and Jason, still wearing their racing overalls, found two unoccupied seats and sat down.

'Right, I think everybody's here,' said Somerset, looking round the table to check. 'I think it would be a good idea if we go round the table and you introduce yourselves to Jason

Kramer.' Heads turned as Somerset motioned towards the American. 'I'm sure you're all aware of Jason's Champ Car credentials!' There was a nodding of heads, and warm-hearted murmurs of appreciation from the assembly. The briefing was well attended; Somerset had wanted the key team members to meet Kramer as soon as possible.

'Scott Harding – Technical Director,' said the fifty-three year old man on Somerset's right.

The introductions continued round the table.

'Barry O'Donnell – Chief Designer.'

'John Thornhill – Team Manager.'

Kramer gave Thornhill an inquisitive stare, 'Am I missing something? I thought Somerset was the boss?'

Smiles broke out all around the table.

'John, you'd better explain that one,' said Somerset.

Thornhill coughed to clear his throat, 'I guess more accurately I am the Race Team Manager. I look after the organisation at races. I control the race strategy and tactics – in liaison with Chris and you guys. It's me you will be speaking to on the radio during races. You could say, that whereas Scott looks after the cars, I look after the people. Chris is however the team owner, and has the final say in all areas.' Thornhill looked to see if his explanation had been clear enough for Kramer.

'Okay, that makes sense to me. Thanks!' said Kramer.

Ken Eyre looked at Somerset for approval to continue. Somerset nodded.

'I'm Ken Eyre – Ryan's Race engineer.'

'Pat Norman – I'm your Race Engineer,' volunteered the person immediately to Kramer's right.

'Hi there, Derek Archer – I'm Ryan's number one,' said Archer proudly.

'Gary Perrault – I'll be your number one mechanic.'

'Okay, that's all the introductions completed; you'll get to meet them all properly later, but now we'd better press on - there's a lot to be done today,' said Somerset. 'Firstly Spa, and in particular Panetta. Alberto is fine; he's out of hospital - but his legs will take some time to heal properly. Apologies to Jason, but I hope we get him back into the team as soon as possible.' Somerset just stopped himself in time from mentioning that the team were only paid by Panetta's backers when he raced; instead he looked down the table to see Kramer's reaction. The American merely nodded in acknowledgement. Because Kramer had a place in the Demaison team lined up for the next season Somerset hadn't expected a negative reaction to his comment, but over the years he had learnt that drivers could be very touchy about such things. His conversation with Warren Barton earlier that morning had unsettled him. He had been sympathetic to Barton's plight but, at the end of the day, he had to do what was best for the team.

Somerset glanced at his notes before continuing, 'You may have seen it suggested in the TV coverage that Panetta locked a rear wheel and caused the accident himself. I have talked to Alberto - we've also had a good look at the telemetry, and I can confirm that it doesn't look like driver error. For some reason, as yet unknown, it looks like the rear offside brake locked up. We haven't had brake problems before, so let's hope it was an isolated incident. I don't think we need panic unduly, but I would like you all to be aware of brake responses as we go through the testing.' Somerset took a sip of water from the glass in front of him. 'I'll let the technical director go through the tests we want to cover in detail, but just to get you started: Ryan, I want you to set a benchmark on the track with the car set-up just as we had it for Spa. Once you've got a good representative time, we'll do some work on the suspension and see what happens.' He turned his attention to Kramer. 'Jason, I want you to familiarise yourself with the car. Follow Ryan through the first few laps to see his lines, and then just spend time getting up to speed. At the moment, the car is set up as it was for Alberto, but obviously we will have to change it to suit your needs. Talk to the guys here, and sort out what you want - but try the car first.' Somerset looked at Kramer who nodded in approval. 'Okay, well I've got to make a few phone calls, so I'll see you later – track-side. I'll hand you over to Scott now.' With that, Somerset gathered up his papers and left the room. Scott Harding made his way to the front of the room and began the more detailed briefing.

Ryan stood by his car, and watched as Kramer was helped into the second car. The mechanics had been given Kramer's height before he had joined the team, and had been able to make tentative alterations to the seating layout. Kramer was three inches taller than Alberto.

'The pedals are too close and the wheel's too far away,' observed Kramer. The mechanics now learnt that most of the extra inches were in the legs.

'Okay, let's have you out,' ordered Gary Perrault, 'I'll see what we can do.'

Kramer was due for a proper seat fitting later in the day, but for now they would concentrate on adjusting the pedals and steering wheel. The car had been set up for right-foot braking at Kramer's request, as that was what he was used to in the States. Ryan preferred to brake with his left foot, as it was found to be more efficient on a number of circuits. As it would take Kramer some time to adjust to left-foot braking, they weren't going to make the change now: not when there was so much else about the car for Kramer to get accustomed to. The last thing they needed was for him to have trouble finding the brake pedal!

Both drivers watched patiently as the mechanics made the necessary changes. When they had finished, Kramer lowered himself back into the cramped cockpit.

'The pedals are much better, but can you angle the wheel a bit?' Kramer indicated what he wanted with both hands.

'Fine, can you live with the pedals for the moment then?' asked Gary Perrault.

'Let's get a few laps in, and see, huh,' said Kramer, raising himself out of the seat again to allow them to alter the steering.

Ten minutes later, Kramer was reasonably comfortable in the cockpit. A mechanic handed him his helmet; he pulled it on over his head and tightened the straps. He now waited while Ryan got into his car. A mechanic attached an airgun to Ryan's car; the noise in the garage, as he started the engine, was deafening. The noise level was doubled as Kramer's car was also fired up. Ryan didn't waste any more time in the garage; he eased the Vantec out onto the apron in front of the pit. Slowly, he edged down the pit lane as he waited for Jason to appear. The second green car emerged a few seconds later, and pulled up behind Ryan.

Scott Harding and Ken Eyre, Ryan's race engineer, perched themselves on stools in the timing station alongside the pit wall, and studied the bank of monitors as the drivers picked up speed in the pit lane. When Harding was happy that all the necessary telemetry signals were functioning, he flipped a switch on the radio transmitter and spoke to Ryan.

'Ryan, can you hear me okay?'

'No problem.'

Harding then changed channel and checked that Kramer was also in contact. Satisfied, he concentrated on the screens again.

Ryan obeyed the speed limit in the pit lane, but once past the white line that marked the end of restrictions, he began to pick up speed. He would take the first lap easy, so that Kramer could follow his lines and get used to the circuit, but he assumed Kramer must be a good driver - or he wouldn't be sitting in the sister car.

As he entered the Brabham Straight, Ryan looked for Kramer in his mirror. Kramer had left a sensible gap between the two cars. Ryan took it easy down the short length of straight, giving Kramer a chance to watch his line into Paddock Hill. At the end of the straight, Ryan pulled over to the left, braking and changing down, before swooping to the right and down the hill. It was easy with no other cars around, but could be downright hairy in a pack.

Kramer followed Ryan's line into Paddock Hill as accurately as he could, knowing that on the next lap he would have to negotiate the tricky turn on his own. Once the car was back on a straight line he shifted up gear and the car began to pick up speed. Abruptly, the hill switched from being steeply downhill to steeply uphill. Kramer gasped as the compression hit him in the stomach. Well, at least he'd be ready for the shock next time round. He was still recovering as his car powered up the climb to Druids. Ahead of him, Ryan had opened up a slight gap.

Ryan slid his car expertly round Druids, and then shifted up a gear as he headed downhill towards the tricky Graham Hill bend. Brands Hatch was a drivers' circuit; still much admired among the racing fraternity. Realising that Kramer had been a bit slower through Druids, Ryan eased off a little to give Kramer a chance to see how he tackled the 90 degree left hander. Even so, Ryan rode the outside kerbing, before bringing the car back onto the tarmac and accelerating up the Cooper straight.

After the complexity of the first four corners, the rest of the short circuit was relatively straightforward - although the left-right jink through Surtees and Mclaren was still a trap waiting to snare the unwary. The final section of the circuit was a magnificent high-speed sweep through Clearways and Clark curve and up the inclined Brabham straight. Only on the main straight were the cars finally able to reach top gear.

In the other Vantec, Kramer was reasonably happy with the way things were going. He didn't like being so far back from Ryan, but accepted that there would be a learning curve. The car felt very nervous on the grooved tyres, and he wasn't certain how long they took to warm up, so he had been a bit too tentative through Graham Hill. He had then messed up Mclaren: he had correctly ridden the kerbs through Surtees, but had been caught out by the extent to which the car had been unsettled. By the end of the lap, he had lost at least a second to Ryan, but was looking forward to his next lap and another chance to master the roller-coaster circuit.

The timing and telemetry information weren't going to be important for a few laps, so Harding and Eyre were kicking their heels, waiting for the cars to come into view. At the finish line there was a 1.5 second gap between the cars.

'Not too bad,' said Eyre, 'Ryan's running about 2 seconds down on normal - so we need to see some more laps, but that was pretty fair from Jason.'

Inwardly, Harding heaved a sigh of relief. He needed to see Kramer run more laps, but the first lap could have been a complete disaster. Anyway, it looked like they had a real driver. He felt a bit guilty at not being able to use Warren, even though the decision had been Somerset's.

The radio crackled in Ryan's ear as the lap-time was read out: 41.872, over 2 seconds away from his best. Ryan put his foot down; he reckoned Kramer knew enough now to look after himself. His fastest lap over the 1.2 mile circuit was 39.32. He used the next lap to find the best lines and to drive as smoothly as possible. He would hustle when the tyres were at their peak. He was pleased with the lap as he again passed in front of the pits. His reward was a time of 40.239 - getting there!

After twenty laps, Harding was happy with the times set by Ryan - who had steadily reduced his lap-times until he was running consistently in the high 39s. Kramer meanwhile had also made good progress, and was only just over a second off the pace. They would need to personalise the car before Jason could get closer to Ryan. Pleased with the morning's work, he radioed the drivers.

'I think we'll take a break now, boys, come in at the end of the lap.'

While Kramer got together with his engineer and mechanic to discuss changes to his car, Ryan joined Eyre and Harding to look over the telemetry results. Provided that Ryan had driven well enough, the figures would act as a base for making comparisons with the suspension changes planned for the afternoon's session. The car had been set-up the same way as for Spa. The settings used there were not necessarily the best for Brands, but would still provide a good basis for the tests.

'Ideally, I'd like more downforce,' said Ryan.

'Sorry, you can't have it today as we need to check low downforce settings for Monza,' apologised Harding. 'You're just going to have change your braking habits a bit!'

'It's not going to look too pretty in places then.'

'We're more interested in how the suspension holds up; you're going to be riding the kerbs in Italy, and we don't want a suspension failure like last year.'

'Fair point,' agreed Ryan. Both Vantec drivers had failed to finish the previous year in Italy. Underwood's car had suffered a suspension failure, whilst Ryan had been taken out on the first bend. Monza was not a lucky track for the team.

'Why don't you take Jason off for an early lunch. I'd like you back here for one o'clock.'

Ryan collected Kramer, and took him out to the catering area beside the motorhome. The caterers were under instructions to feed the drivers healthily, so Ryan had to settle for a pasta dish with tuna, rather than the fry-up he would have liked.

The 'Penne al Tonno' was tasty enough, and Ryan tucked in willingly.

'What did you make of the car?' asked Ryan, spooning a portion of pasta into his mouth. He was glad it was Penne - he always had trouble eating Spaghetti.

'Skittish, I had to keep watching my rear-end.'

'Wait until it rains!'

'And you?'

'I'm checking the car out for Monza, so the settings aren't quite right for here,' explained Ryan. 'I think you should ask for a bit more downforce though.'

Ryan could see Kramer thinking about the tip.

'Yeah, I think you're right. I'll go and have a word after lunch.'

Ryan looked up as a large black shadow swept over the table.

'Seen this?' Derek Archer threw the magazine he was carrying onto the table. 'Someone's been making headlines.' Archer clumsily placed a heavily laden tray on the table and sat down; his body a tight fit in the narrow plastic chair. He watched with interest, as Ryan picked up the copy of Autosport and thumbed threw the already oil stained pages.

Ryan found the write up on the Belgian Grand Prix towards the middle of the weekly journal.

"WITTMAN WANTED CLARKE TO WAIT AT THE BUS STOP," screamed the headline, accompanied by a picture. The article didn't think much of the Austrian's claim that Ryan should have let him finish a place higher. The report of the race was sympathetic to Ryan, but the picture of the two drivers being restrained in Parc Ferme wouldn't do either driver any favours.

'I don't think Mr Somerset's going to be too happy,' said Archer cheerfully - tucking messily into the fry-up that Ryan wasn't allowed.

'I don't suppose Mr Wittman's too chuffed either,' agreed Ryan.

The two drivers didn't waste much time on the light meal; conversation was sparse, as both drivers were preoccupied with the driving. Kramer wanted to get back to the garage to see about adding more wing, so Ryan took the opportunity to go for a walk.

Despite the fair weather, clouds were racing across the sky on a chill wind that was blowing paper and sand about the track in little eddies. The track could be a dismal grey place when shorn of the brightly dressed crowds that filled it on a race day. Away from the empty grandstands, long grassy banks lined the road. Ryan walked along the Brabham straight. As he neared Paddock Hill bend he spotted Warren Barton, sitting despondently in the grandstand, his Vantec race uniform fully done up to counter the cold. Ryan climbed the concrete steps, and sat down on the wooden bench beside the test driver.

'Oh, hi Ryan.' Warren's greeting was less than enthusiastic.
'What's up?'

'I'm not feeling very wanted; first I lost out on Alberto's seat, and then I find they don't need me until later today. I guess you could say I'm pissed off.' The thin, ferret faced South-African ran a bony hand through the mop of blond hair that framed his face like a pair of curtains.

'I don't think the team could afford to take too many chances,' said Ryan. 'And you haven't raced at this level have you?' Ryan had a lot of sympathy for the unlucky South African.

'Maybe not, but at least I've driven the bloody car before!' said Barton bitterly. 'I was timing that session, and I've driven much faster than the Yank.' Barton waved a stopwatch in front of Ryan to make his point.

'Give the guy a break, he'd never seen the track or driven the car before this morning, I bet you weren't too clever first time out!' Ryan was becoming a little exasperated by Warren's negative attitude.

Warren changed the subject, unwilling to pursue the discussion over Kramer's pace in the car. 'I may only get one chance to show that I can make it as a driver - and that chance may have just gone!'

Ryan knew in his heart that Warren could be right. With the eleven F1 teams only needing twenty-two drivers it was very much a buyers' market. He had been exceptionally lucky to find an enthusiastic backer, in the shape of Chris Somerset, who had helped him up through the ranks of motor-sport - right from his early days in Formula 3.

'Your day will come; look what happened to Damon Hill. He was only the Williams test driver until Mansell pissed off to IndyCars. Four years later he was World Champion! So there's no point in sulking. Come and give Jason a hand. Make yourself useful.'

'No way, I may have to put-up with Kramer taking my place, but I'm not going to make it easier for him.'

'Suit yourself,' Ryan was disappointed in Warren's attitude, and thought it would only harm his cause. It was his life though. Ryan stood up; he'd had enough of the conversation. He'd done his best, but it was clearly not good enough to turn Warren around.

'Well, see you later, maybe.'

Barton merely grunted in response.

Ryan jogged down the steps and back to the garage for the afternoon session.

The second session was a mixture of stop and go, as the mechanics and engineers struggled with the new suspension parts to achieve the same performance as in the morning session. Eventually, they managed to get a series of lap-times that were just away from the best set earlier. It didn't look like they were going to make any more improvements, so they gave Ryan a break whilst they prepared for the final session of the day.

Kramer's session had also been frustrating; he had improved on the morning session, but was still over a second behind Ryan. In the end, Harding called a halt to the session and sent Kramer off for a seat fitting. Maybe a better fitting seat and another session the next day would help. The trouble was, they were running out of time. There was a feeling in the garage that the season was slipping away and that they badly needed more points. The cars would have to be packed off to Italy early next week, and they were only going to have the next day for testing, as Brands was booked for a race meeting on Saturday and Sunday.

Exiting Druids on the first lap of the final session, Ryan put in the usual squirt of acceleration and moved the car over to the left-hand side of the track. As the braking zone approached, he moved the car back over to the right and started braking. As he began to press down firmly on the brake pedal he felt something move down by his feet. To his horror, his left foot came to an unexpected stop. Ryan desperately lifted off the pedal and then reapplied the pressure. Whatever had caused the obstruction had moved again. This time the brakes began to bite; in the fraction of a second it had taken to reapply the brakes the car had travelled ten metres further down the track. Ryan scrubbed as much speed off as he could, but he knew the car was carrying too much speed to take the corner. Trying to turn could only lead to an uncontrollable spin, and if he were unlucky the car would roll. Coolly, he turned the wheel slightly so that he didn't plough straight into the tyre wall ahead. The car skated off the track and viciously bounced up over the serrated kerbing. The damp grass did little to slow the car as it bounded and skidded up the thirty metre slope. Ryan was no more than a passenger as the car made its short journey off the track. He tried to relax, knowing that to tense up would only result in him being hurt even more badly. Instinctively, he closed his eyes as the rear end of the car slammed into the tyre barrier - the violent impact crumpling the suspension and ripping off the rear-wing. Tightly strapped into his seat, Ryan was shaken in all directions; his right hand was wrenched off the steering wheel and the loose arm smacked painfully into the side of the chassis as the car came to a halt - a cloud of dust rising into the sky.

'Sod it!' Exclaimed Scott Harding, as the stream of telemetry data came to an abrupt halt. Something had obviously happened, but from where he was sitting he couldn't see that section of the track. His radio crackled into life.

'Ryan has had a bad off down at Graham Hill Bend,' reported the track-side spotter nearest the incident. He was one of a team of people watching the track. 'Ryan's okay. He's out of the car - but the car looks a right mess. A recovery vehicle is on its way.'

'Any idea what happened?' asked Harding, relieved that Ryan was all right.

'Ryan just went straight on at the bend. He was certainly going too fast to take the corner. I'm just on my way over there. I'll get him to speak to you as soon as I can. Out.'

'Roger and out.' Harding ended the conversation. He wanted to talk to the driver, but it would take some time for Ryan to get back to them.

Two marshals had rushed to the scene as soon as the car had come to a halt. One of the marshals looked on, his fire extinguisher at the ready, as the other helped Ryan out of the car. Quickly, they ushered Ryan away from the wrecked vehicle. After a minute, when there was no sign of a fire risk, Ryan brushed the marshals aside and went back to the car. He leant into the cockpit; from the floor of the pedal-well he fished out a spanner. He looked ruefully at the cheap metal tool and then at the expensively damaged racing car. He wondered which idiot had left the spanner in there. He had been very lucky with his team of mechanics, and this was the first time he had experienced any "finger trouble". He couldn't really see any of his regular mechanics making that kind of mistake, but there was a new mechanic. It really was time they were introduced!

The spotter, who had radioed-in, reached Ryan just as the recovery vehicle arrived at the scene. Whilst the recovery crew worked on rescuing the stricken vehicle, Ryan borrowed the spotter's radio.

'Scott, it's Ryan. Can you send a scooter round? I think I need to see the Doc - my arm's a bit buggered and I want to get some ice on it.'

'It's on its way - hold on a sec.' Harding switched channels and spoke to the garage. Derek Archer took the call and made it his duty to fetch Ryan. Harding switched back to Ryan.

'Was it you or the car?'

'Neither,' said Ryan, a little peeved that Harding even wondered that it could have been his fault. 'Some berk left a spanner in the car, and it got under the brake pedal going into Graham Hill. I couldn't brake. Can someone go and kick the mechanics for me!'

'No problem, they won't be able to sit down for weeks,' he assured Ryan. 'How bad's the car?'

'Can it run on two wheels and no rear wing?'

'Ouch! Okay, just get back here as soon as you can. I think testing's over for today.'

Ryan kicked his heels for five minutes, while he waited for the scooter to arrive. It was easy to recognise the scooter rider, as he wasn't wearing a helmet. Ryan hadn't expected Archer, but was pleased to see his chief mechanic; he would be able to tell him something about the newest mechanic.

'You okay boss?' asked Archer. He stayed on the scooter.

'Shaken, not stirred,' replied Ryan. 'Have you heard what happened?'

'No, I just got straight on the bike.'

'Well, you're not going to like it. Some prat left a spanner in the car.'

'You're fucking joking aren't you?'

Ryan handed over the spanner.

'Do you know whose it is?'

Archer looked it over. It was reasonably new, but there were no special marks on it and it wasn't tagged in any way.

'Sorry mate, could be anyone's.' He passed the spanner back.

'What's the new guy like,' asked Ryan.

'You mean Nick Phillips?'

'I guess so, we haven't been introduced. He was in Spa.'

'Yeah, that was Nick. He's a good bloke. Came to us from one of the Formula 3000 teams. He's done his time in the sport, got quite a few years under his belt, and he's fitted in really well. He works hard and seems careful enough. Accidents can happen you know.'

'Well, can you keep your eyes open. We don't really know what happened to Panetta. Two accidents - and both after Nick joined. I don't know about you, but it makes me bloody wonder!'

Archer nodded as he absorbed Ryan's observation; he wanted to defend his mechanics but that was hard to do when one of them had clearly put Ryan's life at risk. 'Okay, I'll watch him like a hawk. Now let's go find the Doc.'

Once Somerset had debriefed Ryan, he summoned all of the mechanics to the boardroom. The mechanics, in their oil-spattered overalls, felt out of place as they took their seats round the polished table. Word had already got round about the spanner, and the mechanics looked suspiciously at each other. A mechanic guilty of such an act could expect a very short career in motor racing.

'I guess you know why you're all here,' said Somerset. 'Someone left this in Ryan's car.' He threw the offending spanner down onto the table, not caring if it marked the polished surface. 'That mistake could have cost him his life; luckily, it's only cost us an expensive and time wasting rebuild.' He paused to look round the table; the mechanics all seemed to be studying their feet. He could feel their collective shame.

'Any idea whose spanner it is?'

There was no answer, just a shaking of heads.

'If one of you wants to own up later, you know where to find me. In the meantime, I want the spare car set up for Ryan - and I want the wrecked car rebuilt as soon as possible. No one's going home until I have three working cars again. Is that clear?'

The audience eagerly murmured their assent. Now was not the time to object to such a request. Social lives would have to be put on hold, and even sleep lost, as they collectively atoned for the accident.

'Okay, now go and get on with it,' Somerset curtly dismissed them. It had not been a good day. Preparations for Monza would not be as complete as he would have liked. The mechanics filed silently out of the room and headed for the garage.

Antoine, Demaison's latest manservant, sighed heavily as he saw the car's lights sweeping towards him up the drive. He looked at his watch – it was nearly midnight. Slowly, he got up from the uncomfortable wooden chair in the hallway and made his way over to the heavy front door; his master would expect it to be opened the moment he mounted the stone steps. The chauffeur had phoned five minutes earlier to warn Antoine of their imminent arrival. By using a code word, the chauffeur had also discreetly alerted Antoine to Demaison's mood. It seemed that yet again his master had lost heavily in the casino. Consequently, he would be in a foul mood. All of the servants had learnt to watch their step at such times. It was no surprise that the turnover of staff was so high, and Antoine was not sure how long he could stand his boss's mood swings. On nights like this, he knew it was best to become as invisible as possible. He opened the door and stood to the side.

Demaison ripped his coat off and threw it at Antoine. Even from a distance, Antoine could smell the alcohol and stale smoke on the old man. Without saying a word, Demaison stomped into the nearby study, slamming the door shut behind him. Antoine grimaced as he heard a loud "Merde" escape through the walls. He folded the coat over his arm, then quietly closed the front door, before ambling down the long hallway to hang the coat up. It was going to be a long night.

Once inside the sombrely lit room, Demaison went straight over to the sideboard. Carelessly, he poured himself a large brandy from an expensive crystal decanter; slops of amber liquid escaped from the glass and puddled on the antique surface. Demaison took a large swig from the glass, and then refilled it. Looking up, his eyes met Giselle's - his late wife's eyes seemed to be staring down at him in disapproval from the silver framed photo perched on top of the cabinet. He reached up and tenderly touched the photograph.

'My God! How I wish you were here,' he muttered apologetically; acutely aware of his failings. He knew he had never fully appreciated his wife while she had been alive. She had acted as a gentle brake on his wayward tendencies; now he was careering down a very slippery slope. He slid a finger across her fine pointed chin, and then removed his hand before turning away from the picture. Crossing the room, he slumped into a well worn armchair to wallow in his misery.

It had been a pig of a day. Bloody accountant he thought. The company accountant had summoned him to a meeting. The pen-pusher then had the nerve to criticise his boss's gambling. He said it was causing, ... how did he put it? Oh yes, 'financial difficulties'. He smiled with satisfaction as he remembered his pleasure at firing the man - no underling talked to him like that. The accountant wouldn't talk either. The photos he held of the accountant embracing another man would see to that! If you had courage and a little ingenuity he reasoned you could solve most difficulties! But what if the company truly was in trouble? Their engine supplier wasn't helping. Surely it was only an idle threat to take their blasted engines elsewhere - his was the only class team in the top six. They only made engines - what could they possibly know about running a racing team. The Japanese had never run a successful Formula One team; and their drivers! Pah! His chauffeur was better. However, he reluctantly admitted to himself that the team needed to do well that season. He smiled conspiratorially - at least he had taken steps to neutralise the opposition.

Kramer's fingers confidently tapped the long international phone number into his mobile phone. Settling back on the bed, he took a sip of iced scotch as he waited for a reply. After a dozen or so rings a male voice came back down the line.

'Demaison,' There was no warmth in the greeting. The ringing phone had surprised Demaison, and he had lifted the receiver out of habit rather than desire.

'It's Jason, I thought you'd like an update,' apologised Kramer, wondering if he had made a mistake in phoning so late.

A grunt came back down the line and then nothing. Eventually there was a response.

'Very well, but keep it short – I assume you can tell the time,' said Demaison sarcastically.

'It all seems so easy,' said Kramer launching straight in, ignoring the taunt.

'It's not meant to be easy - it's got to be effective,' the tone was sharp but the words slurred.

'Okay, okay,' reassured Kramer. 'It's effective enough - I managed to cause an accident today; it's cost testing time, and expensive repairs as a bonus!' He was feeling very pleased with himself.

'And they don't suspect you?'

'No way! They're all looking suspiciously at each other - I don't think they've really got a clue. After all, they're racing people not detectives!'

'Well just be careful, save it for race days. That's when I really need your help. I will remind you that we must finish in the top six at the end of the season.'

'Yeah, yeah, you've made your point. Just trust me huh!'

'All right. I'll see you in Monza then, as agreed,' replied Demaison, before abruptly replacing the receiver.

Kramer slammed his phone down on the small table beside the chair, and downed his Scotch in one. He hadn't got the appreciation he'd hoped for, but maybe that was his fault for calling so late. Disappointed, he opened the suitcase that was sitting on the bed beside him. He found the comprehensive report on Monza buried deep inside the unpacked case. He refilled his drink before settling back to plan his next move.

CHAPTER 5

5:15 a.m. Thursday 30th August, Chelsea - England

Ryan groaned as he became aware of the radio burbling away on his hi-fi. Already the bedroom lights were on. He had purposely designed the morning alarm system to be unstoppable. He was not a morning person and detested early starts, but it had been his decision to stay in London an extra day and not fly out with the rest of the team the previous afternoon. Beside him in the bed, Victoria had also been wakened. Sleepily, she rolled over and burrowed against Ryan's warm body. Ryan affectionately wrapped an arm around her bare shoulders and returned the hug; but knew he would have to get out of bed very shortly if he were to be ready for the taxi that was collecting him at six o'clock. Reluctantly, he removed his arm from Victoria and eased himself out from under her soft breasts. Once out of the bed he leant back over and gave Victoria a full kiss on the lips. Teasingly, her tongue sought his; he responded briefly, before disengaging and planting a friendly peck on her nose.

'You go back to sleep and I'll see you on Sunday.'

'Okay, see you Sunday then.' Victoria rolled back on to her side of the bed and closed her eyes. Once again Ryan marvelled at the ease with which she was able to fall asleep. He frequently struggled to get to sleep, and often spent many hours in bed awake with his thoughts.

After a quick shower and shave, he dressed casually in jeans and short-sleeved shirt for the journey. He would change into his team uniform at the circuit. He didn't fancy deliberately drawing attention to himself getting there. It was a small rebellion against the controlling influence of the team; he knew that Somerset would have preferred him to travel in full team outfit. Finally, he settled down on a sofa in his lounge with a cup of strong black coffee and waited for the taxi. He hated a last minute panic and had packed his bag the previous evening.

The cab-driver was on time, and by five past six Ryan was sitting beside the driver, as they headed up through Earls Court, in the silver coloured Lexus saloon. The team used the cab company on a regular basis, and the middle-aged driver, although aware of Ryan's profession, drove quickly but steadily. For this, Ryan was grateful - he could think of nothing worse than a young cab-driver trying to show off in an attempt to impress him; and he had suffered a number of hairy journeys down the years. Going against the early morning traffic, they made good time out to Heathrow.

British Airways flight BA0564, bound for Linate airport in Milan, lifted off runway 1 at 7:40 - a bare five minutes later than scheduled. The twin engines, generating twenty-seven thousand pounds of thrust, swiftly powered the plane steeply up through the low grey clouds blanketing southern England. Once up into clear blue sky the plane turned onto a heading for France. The journey, at a cruising speed of five hundred miles an hour, was scheduled for two hours.

'Would you like a drink?' asked the uniformed stewardess. She hadn't known who the passenger was until one of her colleagues had whispered in her ear. It still didn't really mean anything to her; but she had to admit he was rather dishy. Deliberately, she leant provocatively over Ryan - her blouse gaping.

'I'll have an orange juice - with plenty of ice if you have it,' replied Ryan, his eyes taking full advantage of the view offered. Shame about the boat race, he thought, as he looked up and smiled at the plain looking stewardess. He displayed a full set of even white teeth, the result of expensive and regular dentistry. He would have enjoyed a proper drink, but whilst he was happy to live it up away from race weekends, as far as he was concerned the race started now, and he would behave himself until the race was over.

Back in economy class, Nick Phillips, wearing a green Vantec polo shirt, was sitting on his own. There had been a shortage of space on the previous day's flight, and as the newest - and therefore deemed to be the least useful - team member, he had been left to make his own way. Nick wasn't too bothered; he had travelled round Europe with his previous team and was enjoying the chance to grab some time on his own. He hadn't noticed Ryan board the plane.

As the plane approached the French Alps, Nick pulled a wallet out from the rear pocket of his slacks and extracted a slip of paper. He read the note carefully - although he'd already checked it a number of times. The house wasn't too far from the circuit, but he'd have to be careful about how he got away from the team - and he wouldn't be able to stay very long. With luck, he would be able to get away after the race. He folded the piece of paper and slid it back into his wallet.

Even though Ryan was happy to travel in a racing car at over two hundred miles an hour on a tight circuit with his rear end only two inches off the ground, he disliked air travel. He hated not being in control of the experience, and he detested being pushed around the airports. Maybe one day he would get a helicopter - but he didn't yet earn enough money to make that an imminent reality. Once the obligatory meal tray had been removed, he closed his eyes and tried to ignore the stares of those passengers who had recognised him. Even in Club Class he was not isolated from his celebrity. It would be so much easier if they just talked to him the same way they talked to anyone else. Even when strangers did speak to him, the short conversations were generally only embarrassed requests for autographs. He smiled as he remembered the time a girl had handed him a pair of white knickers to sign; he had obliged, but hadn't felt it wise to ask if they were clean!

After ninety minutes of level flying the Airbus began the long descent into Linate airport. The airport was the smaller and lesser used of the two main Milanese airports. Consequently, there were fewer flights in and out of London, but that was more than balanced by its relative proximity to the race-track.

'So, you are a racing driver - yes?' asked the Immigration Officer, as he flicked through Ryan's dog-eared passport.

'That's right.' As Ryan answered, he spied Nick Phillips exiting the next booth. He was surprised that he hadn't spotted him on the plane - after all it was hard to miss the green shirt! He could only think that Nick had boarded the plane before him. Club Class was separated from Economy Class by a curtain, and once seated, he wouldn't have seen him. Club Class passengers were also let off the plane first. He wondered how the mechanic was getting to the track.

'I am very sorry, but your trip has been wasted, Ferrari will win this time,' asserted the Officer proudly - not noticing that Ryan's attention had wandered.

'I expect you're right,' murmured Ryan, retrieving his passport; he didn't want to get into a long debate, for his car was unlikely to trouble the home team.

Ryan was only carrying hand luggage and he passed through customs without any problems. Outside the air-conditioned terminal building, the summer heat hit him like a shock wave. After the relative cold of Belgium and Britain it was a pleasure to be back in hot sunshine. Looking round, he easily spotted Karen Goodbody who had been despatched to collect him. To his surprise Nick Phillips was standing next to her. At long, last it looked like Ryan would get to know his newest mechanic.

As Ryan walked over, he admired the thrust of Karen's large breasts inside the dark-green uniform blouse.

'Hi Karen - so they've got you on driving duty again, then!' He kissed the leggy blonde on the cheek and then turned to face his mechanic.

'Nick, good to see you - I think we need to talk!'

He thrust out his hand. The gesture took Nick by surprise; but he grasped the proffered hand and shook it firmly.

'Sure thing Ryan, I've been wanting to meet you.'

'Come on you two, you can talk on the way.' Karen impatiently hustled the drivers towards the large executive BMW that the team had hired for driving around sponsors and other important guests. She had spotted a traffic warden patrolling along the front of the building, and she was keenly aware that, along with several other drivers, she was parked in a no-parking zone.

Aptly named Karen Goodbody was the team's race secretary. The twenty-five year old had travelled down in one of the motorhomes on Tuesday. As well as sorting out a lot of the paperwork, she had played a full part in planning and executing the logistics for the trip. She had joined the team after graduating from Essex University with a degree in French. She could also speak Italian, and in quiet moments was teaching herself German from her laptop. Inevitably, people cracked jokes about her name, but she took no notice as she'd heard it all before. But she couldn't wait to get married so that she could at last change her surname. She wasn't going to let herself fall for a mechanic - but a racing driver, that would be an entirely different story.

'Would you like to drive?' she asked, waving the keys in front of Ryan's face.

'No thanks, I'm going to be doing quite enough of that later, thank you very much! Besides, I want to talk to Nick; we haven't had a proper chance to get to know each other yet.'

Karen hooted and swore along with the other Italian drivers as she fought her way through the airport traffic and out on to the Tangenziale. The year she had spent living and driving in Rome had not been wasted. She had volunteered to collect Ryan from the airport. He was just the sort of man she was looking for. Sadly, she felt unable to do anything about it. Firstly, she didn't like dating people she worked with, and secondly, she really liked Victoria. Still, she could enjoy his company - and he might be able to introduce her to some of the other drivers.

Maybe one of those dark-jawed Italians - or possibly a smooth talking Frenchman. She slammed the brakes on as a small yellow Fiat cut in front of her. 'Bastardo!' she yelled. In the back, Ryan grinned.

'So Nick, how are you settling in?' enquired Ryan, keen to get the measure of his mechanic.

'It's been great - so far. The other guys have made me feel very welcome. It's quite a step up from F3000. I mean the work's just the same – well, more or less; but somehow it seems more professional.'

Ryan was a little surprised by the intelligence and enthusiasm in the younger man's voice. Before he could think of a suitable response the mechanic was off again.

'Mind you, I was shocked by that accident you had. That's the sort of thing you only hear about - I never expected something like that to happen in F1, I mean, the guys are so careful'. There was a genuine sense of puzzlement in his voice.

'Oh well, no real damage done – except to the car and Chris's budget! But it could have been nasty!' replied Ryan, warming to the mechanic despite his earlier reservations.

The two men continued to chat animatedly as Karen drove them into the outskirts of Monza. By the time they left the main road, Ryan was far less certain that Nick was responsible for the two accidents that had befallen the team. However, to be on the safe side, he would keep a watchful eye on the mechanic.

The Monza circuit was set in the grounds of a royal park on the northern fringes of Monza. As they worked their way through the heavy traffic, they weren't allowed to forget that this was the spiritual home of Italian motor racing; wherever they looked, there were Ferrari flags and emblems, and there were enough Prancing Ponies on display to form a cavalry division.

The traffic was particularly bad that morning, and it was a slow grind out to the park; fortunately the car was well air-conditioned. Even though it was only Thursday, and there would be no official activity until the next morning, there were still plenty of Ferrari fans in evidence. The team and its drivers were revered and honoured throughout the country. Ferrari was not just a team from Italy - but Italy incarnate. The mood of the entire country swung with the fortunes and misfortunes of the historic marque. Its fans, the Tifosi, were the most fanatical in the world; and all of the other teams would be keenly aware that they were on away ground that week.

'I've organised a press conference for four o'clock this afternoon - in case you haven't yet changed your watches; that's in about three hours time.' Chris Somerset addressed Ryan and Kramer in the team motorhome, neatly parked in its assigned place in the paddock. 'Two purposes: firstly to introduce Kramer, and secondly to get that nonsense with Wittman out of the way!' He had not been amused by the reports in the motor sport press. He wanted to get the press off their back before the serious business started. He didn't want his drivers disturbed anymore than could be helped.

'Ryan, can you play it down - and try and say something nice about the car for once!' He looked up from his notes to check that Ryan was listening. Satisfied, he turned his attention to Jason. 'Jason, can you just say what a good opportunity it is for you to drive in Formula One and that people had better not expect too much from you. It would be nice if you could thank the team for giving you the chance - I will thank Pierre for lending you to us. It goes without saying that I want you both in Team shirts and caps.'

Kramer listened intently to what Somerset had to say. This was his first Grand Prix and he didn't want to make any embarrassing mistakes. He had flown down with Somerset from Heathrow. Unlike Ryan, he had wanted as much time as possible to explore the circuit. The nearest he had got, before arriving, was playing a motor-racing game on his Sony Playstation. He had found the game very useful, but there was no real substitute for seeing the track first hand. And the fans! He had heard about the Tifosi - but he was taken aback by the number of Ferrari fans already around the circuit. He had seen nothing like it back home. For sure, there were car nuts who would follow them around - but not in the numbers and style he was seeing here. Faces painted red, prancing ponies painted into the hair, Ferrari tattoos on arms - he didn't like to think where else! Amazing. It felt very alien to be a member of another team.

Ryan, though, had heard it all before and was happy when Somerset finally dismissed them. He stood up from the comfy leather sofa. 'You coming for a bite to eat?' he asked Kramer.

'Nah, I ought to have another look at the track. I'll catch you later.'

Ryan left Kramer with Somerset, and stepped out of the luxury van into the hot bright sunshine. It was a very short walk, for the team's café was located alongside the next motorhome.

Inside the tiny kitchen, Maggie Cousins was expertly chopping a pile of carrots with a very sharp knife and didn't notice Ryan enter the motorhome. The cuddly, dark-haired, 48 year old Scottish cook had arrived with the motorhome on Tuesday; and as usual it had been a struggle getting all of the power connections established. Wednesday had been busy - once the two large Scania transporters carrying the cars and the accompanying support truck had arrived. Her breakfasts were legendary; and the tired truckers had made short work of mounds of bacon and sausages. Now that the race team had arrived she was also having to cook rather healthier meals. She really cared that people went away thinking hers was the best kitchen in the paddock. Sometimes the races seemed almost incidental.

Maggie squealed as an arm unexpectedly wrapped itself round her waist.

'Get off!' she yelled, although there was warmth in her voice as she recognised Ryan. She liked most of the drivers - but he had always been her favourite.

Ryan hugged her for a few seconds, before reluctantly letting go and stepping back a pace.

'Hi Maggs, any chance of a fry-up?' asked Ryan, knowing full well what the answer would be.

'No way. You'll have to have something healthy - you know what Somerset's like.' Her voice had a soft Edinburgh burr; and anyway, the boss only allowed her to fry before nine in the morning.

'Oh well, I'll just have a cup of tea then.' Ryan wasn't really hungry, he just enjoyed teasing the friendly cook.

'Have you met Kramer yet?' asked Ryan, as Maggie poured his cup of tea.

'Chris brought him in yesterday; and he's been in a couple of times since. Seems all right - bit full-on for my liking though.' There was little warmth in her voice.

'You just don't like Yanks,' teased Ryan.

'Maybe not - way too loud and brash for me, ugh, but there's something else about Kramer. Can't put my finger on it – yet! Given time, I'll suss him. Anyway, how's Panetta?' This time, her concern was palpable.

'He's on the mend, but I don't think he'll be back this season.' Even as he answered, Ryan was conscious of the difference in the way Maggie felt about the two drivers. This gave Ryan food for thought - Maggie was a canny judge of character.

'Well, that's good news – of sorts,' she replied. 'Look, I've still got a mound of vegetables to chop,' Maggie waved a knife in the direction of the half-finished carrots; 'some of us have to work for a living, perhaps we can have a proper chat later.' She turned her back on Ryan and resumed chopping.

'No rest for the wicked!' Ryan playfully slapped her meaty rear-end, the flesh quivering under his touch.

'Out!' she yelled in mock anger, turning round and pointing her knife at Ryan.

He smiled broadly at Maggie, whilst raising both hands in a gesture of surrender, then grabbed his cup of tea and retreated to a table outside the motorhome.

'Wittman says you were driving dangerously, - were you?' asked the Italian reporter. The press conference was being held in the enclosure between the team's two motorhomes. The team didn't have enough seats for all of the reporters, and many at the back had to stand.

'Not at all,' replied Ryan. 'It was a straightforward overtaking move. His tyres were going off. There was no real problem.'

'Then why was he so angry?'

'You'll have to ask him that. For once, I was just lucky; the Vantec was working well - and Karl was maybe a bit unlucky.'

'Does this mean that the Vantec has improved a lot?' The question came from the Autosport reporter.

'We are very pleased with the progress we have made this year - but I am not sure that we will be up with the Ferraris and McLarens very often.'

'Will you have trouble with Wittman this weekend?'

'I don't expect to have any trouble; as far as I am concerned, the incident is closed. I would happily sit down for a beer with Karl!' lied Ryan. There was a smattering of laughter.

'Are you expecting to get in the points this weekend?'

'We always hope to get in the points. We have made a few changes, and hopefully we will have better luck than last year.' Ryan quite enjoyed fielding such simple questions at this stage. It was fairly easy to say positive things without being very specific; it would be much harder after the race - if things didn't go well. But if they didn't go well, then not many people would be wanting to talk to him! He was glad, though, that they had stopped asking him about Wittman.

'Who will be the number one this weekend?'

'I have been asked to take the number one role; but the team will support both of us equally.'

'What if Kramer beats you on Sunday?'

'If that happens - then the situation may have to be looked at.'

'I believe your contract expires at the end of the season. Have you signed a new contract yet?' It was the Autosport reporter again, keen to get any information about British drivers.

Ryan took a sip of water while he considered his reply.

'Negotiations are in progress - and I am happy with the way things are going.'

'If Kramer is as successful here as in the States, and Panetta returns, the team could have three drivers chasing two seats.'

Ryan hadn't considered it from that angle before. There was certainly not much to choose between himself and Panetta. Kramer was a bit of a wild card. It dawned on him that his position was even less secure than he realised.

'The team must pick the drivers it needs to progress. I will be doing all I can to show that one of those drivers should be me!'

Chris Somerset sat between the two drivers; and now intervened.

'If there are any more team questions perhaps they could be addressed to me,' he said. He wanted to steer the conversation away from the subject of driver contracts. 'Has anyone got any questions for Jason? I don't think he's had much to say so far. You can ask him some of the questions I haven't had a chance to!' joked Somerset.

Ryan had no further questions to answer as the reporters shifted their attention to Kramer, and his move into Formula One. Ryan listened with interest to the American's answers.

'How are you adapting to the car?'

'Very well - It's got four wheels and an engine so I figure it's pretty much like a Champ car!'

'Other drivers have attempted to make the change and failed - does that worry you?'

'Not really. Others have succeeded, look at Villeneuve; but I can't expect to repeat my American success without first learning the ropes. Besides, in America I was driving one of the very best cars - the Vantec's great - but it ain't no Ferrari!' That went down well with the Italian reporters.

'How are you braking?' The clued up reporter was aware that Kramer used the less orthodox right-foot braking method.

'By putting my foot hard to the floor and praying - how do you do it?'

There was laughter; the reporters sensed that here was a charismatic driver who would provide good copy. They were fed up with the corporate mouthpieces parading as drivers in some teams. It was refreshing to interview a driver who spoke his mind and had a sense of humour. They already found Ryan very amenable; it was a bonus to have two drivers worth talking to.

The press conference lasted a further ten minutes before Somerset brought it to a close. After the reporters had filed out, he congratulated the drivers on their performance. He was happy that the team had got some very good press. He just hoped that the post-race conference would be as positive.

After several years of experimenting with the qualifying process, F1 had sensibly returned to the tried and trusted three day format - with a 12 lap qualifying hour on Saturday. This was despite the grumbles from the smaller teams, who had enjoyed increased TV coverage in the era of single lap qualifying. As a result, Friday was the first really important day in the race weekend. Two timed practice sessions would enable teams to tune their cars - and judge their performances against each other. The hour-long sessions would be used to choose the best tyre compound and the right combination of suspension and wing settings. Monza is synonymous with speed. The pistol-shaped circuit demands low downforce but also tremendous stability in the chicanes. Resolving these contradictory requirements was the key to a good performance. Run too much wing, and the car would certainly stick to the road - but at the expense of straight-line speed. Too little wing, and the car would rocket down the straights - but struggle in the bends. If that wasn't enough to sort out; the wear on brakes was high at Monza and the right choice of brake discs also needed to be made. Friday was mechanics' day.

The first timed session began at eleven in the morning. Ryan joined the circuit at the back of a queue of cars. Teams were keen to get early laps in - allowing the mechanics time to make necessary adjustments. Kramer was held back for a couple of minutes but then also joined the circuit. Ryan and Jason completed a lap each, to shake the cars down, and then returned to the pit for a routine check. Both cars were passed as okay - the real work began as they rejoined the track.

After a steady out-lap to settle the car, Ryan began his first flying lap. He braked hard for the 'S-bend' at the start of the lap - dropping the car from 6th to 2nd gear. When he judged that the speed had dropped enough, he took his foot off the brake and let the car roll over the large red and white striped kerbs as smoothly as he could. Then he was quickly back on the throttle. He swung through the Curva Grande in 5th gear, still accelerating. As he ran under the canopy of trees lining the route the quality of light suddenly diminished, increasing the sense of speed as the car topped 200 mph. Ryan concentrated hard in the gloom as he approached the second chicane. Going through the zigzag bend he found himself wrestling with the steering wheel, and was unhappy with the amount of effort required to bring the nose round. He would give it another lap to be sure, but he suspected that the car was understeering. The tricky part was to decide whether it was the suspension or the wing settings that needed fixing. He would see what happened in the next few turns.

Another tight chicane followed on from the Curva Grande; and again Ryan let the car run over the kerbing - his body feeling every jolt as the car bounced over the serrated concrete. As his body absorbed the ripple of shocks, he concluded that the suspension was on the stiff side. Softening the suspension might also cure the understeer. The rest of the lap only served to confirm Ryan's diagnosis. He would have liked to pit straight away, but they would need a decent lap-time to act as a comparison for any changes they made. He completed the lap and then began another flying lap. Each successive lap had increased his knowledge of the circuit, and his driving was becoming more fluent and automatic. Despite the understeer and the lack of power, Ryan was fairly pleased with his effort as he eased up at the start of the in-lap. He would be interested to see how his lap stacked up against the opposition. Ryan let a flying McLaren through, and then waited until he had cleared the first chicane before he pressed the radio button.

'I'm coming in - I've got too much understeer and I want the front suspension softened,' he warned.

'Roger that,' responded Scott Harding. The slim fifty-three year old Technical Director pushed his heavy framed spectacles back up his beak of a nose.

'What do you think?' said Harding, turning to face Ken Eyre, Ryan's race-engineer.

The young engineer thought carefully before replying, aware of the many years of extra experience held by the older man. Formula One was increasingly becoming the domain of the young - but it was hard to ignore the knowledge and wisdom of a generation that had seen so many technical changes in the sport. He was even more conscious that Harding's expertise was in aerodynamics. One of Harding's strengths, though, was a willingness to listen to many points of view before reaching a decision.

'We can try, but it's already quite soft - I'm worried about hitting the kerbs if we soften it any more.'

'What about adjusting the wings then?' asked Harding.

'Not really an option as the car's slow enough here as it is. I'd better go wait for Ryan.'

Eyre eased himself off the stool and climbed down from the timing station. He carefully checked the pit lane before dashing across the tarmac to the garage, to prepare the mechanics for the task ahead.

Ryan had barely brought the car to a halt, before the mechanics grabbed the car and started to push it back into the garage. The four laps just completed had gobbled up seven minutes out of the sixty allowed for the session. Any adjustments would need to be made quickly. The mechanics jacked the car up as soon as Ryan got out.

'What's the problem?' asked Eyre, shouting to make himself heard above the racket as a car pulled out of a neighbouring garage.

'The car's understeering on entry to the corners,' said Ryan.

'Are you sure you want to soften the suspension, though?'

'Well, we don't want to slow the car with greater wing do we?'

'True, but we can't soften the suspension very much - those kerbs are lethal!'

'Okay. Well can we just soften it a bit and see what happens.? What did the lap-time look like anyway?'

They both looked up at the tiny monitor; the screen was filled with ever changing lap-times. Ryan's fastest lap of 1:25.992 put him in 18th place out of the 22 cars running. They couldn't afford to remain in that position. Kramer had found the circuit even more of a struggle and was down in 21st place.

'Ouch!' said Ryan.

Ten minutes later, Derek Archer, standing out on the wide garage apron, commandingly held up a hand to stop Ryan exiting as Wittman's Ferrari slipped past the Vantec garage. As the Ferrari gathered speed, and disappeared down the pit lane, he looked up and down the garages checking for any other dangers. Satisfied that no other cars were going to get in the way, he released Ryan onto the pit lane. Ryan accelerated up to the pit lane speed limit, and then waited patiently until the car crossed the white line that marked the end of the speed restriction, before flooring the throttle. The track was clear as Ryan shot out onto the circuit. He trusted his crew to check the traffic on the circuit before sending him out - even so things could change very quickly at 200 miles an hour!

The out-lap proved disappointing. The understeer was slightly less pronounced - but it was definitely still present. Sadly, softening the suspension had only served to introduce more roll in the corners - and the overall effect didn't seem very promising. Ryan decided he had better complete a timed lap to see if the figures told a different story. At the end of the quick lap he knew they were on the wrong tack. They obviously hadn't been able to improve the suspension for Monza. It looked like it was going to be another frustrating Italian Grand Prix. He pulled into the pits again.

As expected, the lap-time was slower at 1:26.201. Ryan asked for the suspension to be returned to its previous setting - and an increase in the angle of attack on the front wing. As he waited for the mechanics to complete the adjustments, Ken Eyre had even more bad news for Ryan. It appeared that the weather was changing. Already the track temperature had stopped increasing, and it looked like a storm was brewing. The forecast for the weekend was very unsettled. The suspension problems would give them little time to try out tyre combinations. If the weather became variable then tyre choice would be another lottery.

Ryan took the car out again with only 12 minutes left of the session. There was no chance of making any more major adjustments in the session. He would have to concentrate on gathering telemetry data that might help them make changes over the lunch break. The wing adjustment had indeed sorted the understeer problem - but he didn't need a clock to know that the lap-time had suffered. It looked like he was going to have to settle for a poorly balanced car if he wanted a reasonable time. He hoped that the tyre would stand up to the mistreatment that understeering would bring.

Ryan used the remainder of the session to see if changing his normal race line would help; but as he suspected, the circuit offered few chances to change cornering habits. Ryan could willingly have kicked the car in frustration at the end of the session. It was as if they had stood still from last year – a lack of power and handling problems. He shook his head in despair as he clambered out of the baking-hot car.

'Okay, so that was a waste of time,' said Scott Harding. There was nodded agreement from the other five men who sat round the table in the tiny office at the back of the team's main motorhome. Not for the first time, he was glad of the efficient air-conditioning in the cramped space. From that perspective, it was useful that Chris Somerset was elsewhere. He was busy talking to a group of potential sponsors, and had left Scott to run the debriefing.

'What do we do now?' asked Harding.

'I think we've got to risk the new suspension,' said Ken Eyre. Ryan's mouth opened in amazement. He thought they already were using the new system.

'Why on earth didn't we start with it?' asked Ryan incredulously.

'Because of the lack of testing at Brands,' said Eyre; diplomatically not reminding Ryan that it was his accident that lost them the time.

'You know, as well as I do, that the accident was nothing to do with the suspension!' said Ryan.

'Agreed,' said Scott Harding, breaking into the debate, 'But I didn't want to risk a new part, if there was a chance that other changes we've made since last year might have helped. As it happens, it doesn't look like they have done.'

'Well, you could have told us,' said Jason, who had sat quietly until now. He was equally peeved at the time they had wasted.

'Look,' said Harding. 'I wanted you both to drive as if this was the real car - I didn't want you both going out there thinking it didn't matter because there was a new suspension system waiting. But I think I was wrong. We can't afford to leave here in 18th place - or worse, so we'll risk it. Peter, can you go and get the mechanics started.'

'They were just waiting for the nod!' Peter Baldacci, the Chief Mechanic, got up and left the office. He had guessed they would have to try the new suspension ,and the mechanics should already have been preparing for suspension changes. He hadn't liked keeping the drivers in the dark, but sometimes it was better they didn't know what happened in the garage. As far as he was concerned they were paid to drive the cars - not to worry about how they were put together!

'Right, let's have a look at the figures!' Harding passed out copies of the telemetry data.

The hour-long lunch-break was as much for the benefit of the Track Marshals, and other officials, as anything else. There was no chance of any of the teams getting a break. The scene in the Vantec motorhome was being repeated, in varying form, in every team throughout the paddock. From all of the garages there came the clang of metal on metal, and the buzz of power tools, as mechanics toiled to make the changes needed to bring about fractions of a second of improvement. Overhead, the sky grew darker. In the distance, the sky was a shimmering curtain of grey from which rain was already falling.

Ryan sat patiently in the car as he waited for the green light to signal that the session was starting. He could see Harding and Eyre standing at the timing station. They were both studying the sky intently. The green light came on and almost immediately one of the Kodama cars headed out onto the circuit. A mechanic prepared to fire up Ryan's car but suddenly pulled the starter away at a signal from Derek Archer. Ryan's mechanic finished listening to the instructions that came over the radio, then bent over the car.

'It looks like it's going to rain in a few minutes, so we're going to put the "wets" on and wait!' he said.

Ryan nodded to show he'd got the message.

The car was jacked up and the tyres quickly changed. Now they just had to wait patiently for the rain. They couldn't take the car out if the track stayed dry as the "wet" tyres would quickly overheat and degrade. It was a huge gamble, as precious time was being lost waiting in the garage. Other teams, that had elected to go out on slicks, would have to come in quickly when the rains came –if they came. After two minutes, both Vantec cars were still sat in the garage. It had just started raining on the far side of the circuit. Going out now would be pointless. They would have to sit it out.

Ryan joined the circuit in a queue of cars. In the end, most of the teams had waited for fully wet conditions; and with the clock ticking, they all wanted to get their cars out as soon as possible. In front of Ryan, an American Thunderbird car was kicking up a great rooster tail of water. At least lack of power wasn't going to be an issue in this session, mused Ryan. Despite the added risks, Ryan enjoyed driving in the wet. The need to be more vigilant helped him concentrate, and the greater skill required to get it right, almost made it fun. But for the moment, the amount of water being thrown up into the air ahead of him made it very hard to see. However, by the time he reached the second Lesmos bend he knew the suspension change had worked. No longer was he fighting to bring the nose of the car round on the entry to the turns. The worsening weather conditions weren't going to help them assess the true worth of the changes, but he was much happier with the balance of the car. He slowed the car as yet again, the Thunderbird ahead of him twitched nervously. That was one team that wasn't going to threaten him. Ryan eased back from the Thunderbird to clear some space for the flying lap that was to follow. He didn't want the slower car to get in his way as he set a time. But with so many cars at different points on the track, they would be lucky to get a good clear run.

Ryan had just crossed the start line as ahead of him Ernie Patterson in the Thunderbird exited the first chicane. The American team had entered Formula One after the demise of Jaguar and were still relatively inexperienced - a fact that was frequently demonstrated by the calibre of drivers they employed. The team was still waiting to notch up their first points in the championship. The rookie American driving the car still had a rear wheel on the kerbing as he went back on the throttle. The slippery wet surface instantly pitched the red and black Thunderbird into a vicious tail-spin. Ryan was forced to slow violently as the Thunderbird pirouetted down the tarmac in front of him. There was space for Ryan to pass, but the incident had spoilt that lap. On the positive side he had managed to get past Patterson; who was clearly not at ease in the conditions. By the time he had got round to the start line again the rain was easing. The track was still very wet, but in the distance the sky was turning blue - just as if someone was pulling open a giant pair of curtains. Once the hot Italian sun came out, the track would dry quickly.

Two laps later the rain stopped. The track was still damp; but dry patches were appearing as the cars sprayed standing water away from the racing line. Times were improving, but soon there would not be enough water on the track to keep the tyres cool. As the tyres heated up they would become less effective - but until the track was properly dry it would be even riskier to put on slicks. Ryan watched and waited for the first brave driver to make the change. Another three laps passed before the radio crackled in his ear and he was ordered in.

All of the teams were forced to change tyres, and the next time Ryan ventured out there were even more cars on the track. It took a few laps, before Ryan was again able to find space to put his foot down and go for a time. On the dry track, with slick tyres, he was at last able to see the full benefit of the suspension changes. He was able to confidently throw the car into the corners and ride the kerbs. Sadly, the car was still under-powered, but they had definitely taken a step in the right direction. With fifteen minutes of the session remaining, Ryan pulled into the pit to see if a small change in the rear wing would help even more. The brief halt gave him a chance to look at the times being set. He had pulled up to tenth fastest - which was probably the best they could hope for. Kramer, who had struggled in the wet, had also improved once the track dried, but was down in 15th place. The places remained unchanged through the remainder of the session.

The atmosphere in the briefing after the practice session was muted. Clearly, progress had been made - but they were still too far off the leaders for comfort. Ryan had just started to look at the pages of telemetry data when Chris Somerset stuck his head round the door of the tiny office.

'Good afternoon all.' Somerset was beaming.

'I've brought someone along to see you - I think you'll be pleased with what he has to say. This is Andre Seiler - he works for Powerblok.' Somerset gestured at the tiny Swiss engineer standing behind him. Some of the team already knew Andre, who worked for their engine supplier.

The two men squeezed onto the bench seat, taking up what remained of the small space. After greetings had been exchanged, Somerset asked Seiler to give his news.

'We have found a small modification that will let the engine develop another 10 bhp. With help from your engine mapping we think this could be achieved by tomorrow.' Seiler's English was near perfect, with just the hint of a mid-European accent.

He glanced round the table, enjoying the pleasure and surprise shown on all the faces - it wasn't often that he was able to pass on such good news. He didn't think it wise to point out that the other two teams using Powerblok engines would also get the same benefit. He knew they would already be well aware of that.

Sitting quietly to the right of Seiler, Somerset was feeling guilty. Seiler would be far less happy if he knew that Somerset was looking to replace the Powerblok engine for the next season. Despite limited funds, the Powerblok company had put a lot of work into developing their engine, and had enjoyed the growing success they were getting with Vantec. The harsh reality, though, was that Powerblok were unlikely ever to rival the Katayama company, who had the backing of a multinational motor company behind them. The Katayama engine already offered more power, and the company was prepared to supply the team for free, in a deal worth $20m. As things stood, Vantec were paying Powerblok nearly £10 million pounds a season for their engines. In business terms it was no contest - but it didn't make Chris feel any better.

The briefing broke up as Scott Harding left with Chris Somerset and Andre Seiler to find Paul Morrison, who looked after the engine mapping. Ryan stayed behind to chat with Kramer. He wanted to see if he could help the American. The team needed both drivers to be challenging for the points; Kramer would also be under pressure because of his Champ Car success. Both drivers were in good humour by the time they headed for the hotel.

CHAPTER 6

Midday. Saturday 1st September, Monza Circuit - Italy

As the qualifying hour approached, the mood in the Vantec camp was very upbeat. The final practice session, earlier in the morning, had seen both Ryan and Jason move up the ranks. The engine modification had proved effective and Ryan was 9th fastest. Kramer was just half a second slower in 12th. The cars were still too slow to make the points - unless some of the other teams had trouble, but this was motor racing and anything could happen. At least they were in with a chance if a few cars fell off the track or broke-down. The skies were a clear bright blue, and there was an expectant buzz around the garage.

By midday, the temperature had already passed 85F. Qualifying had just begun and the team waited for one of the minor teams to go out and set a marker.

Finally, five minutes after the start of qualifying, one of the Thunderbirds ventured out onto the track, and Ryan got into the car. With each car only allowed to complete twelve laps in the session, Ryan, like most of the drivers, was planning to make four qualifying runs of three laps each. The first lap of each set would simply take the car round to the start of the timed lap. The third, or in-lap, would be a drive round to bring the car back to the pits. In each group of three laps, there would therefore be just one timed or 'flying' lap. During the whole session there would only be four chances to set a decent qualifying time.

Ryan sat in the cockpit and studied the tiny monitor that had been lowered from the gantry to rest at a comfortable viewing distance in front of him. As he studied the ever-changing figures, the Ferrari of Wittman's team-mate Frederick Barbosa screamed down the straight at the start of a flying lap. Even from inside the garage, Ryan could see the Tifosi going wild in the stand opposite. Any sign of Ferrari activity was greeted with an exuberant outbreak of flag waving and horn blowing.

At a signal from John Thornhill, the monitor was raised from in front of Ryan and the engine started. Mechanics covered their already protected ears as the powerful engine barked into life in the confined space of the garage. Ryan revved the engine gently, then rolled out onto the pit lane, picking up speed as he went. The first set of laps would be used to get in a qualifying time in case the weather changed, or the session was halted. The laps also gave them a chance to shake the car down and bring the tyres up to speed. If all went well, he would set his best times in the third and fourth runs.

After the first two runs, Ryan was sitting in 9th place behind one of the Team Demaison cars. Despite the good practice session in the morning, Kramer had not got up to speed, and had slipped back the ranks to 20th place. As the tyres warmed up, Ryan's car handled better, and his third run saw him sneak past the time set by Vigneron of Team Demaison and move up into 8th place. It still looked possible for Ryan to beat Stuart Underwood and move into 7th. Kramer had also got his act together - and was in 12th place with one more run to make.

Ryan relied on the Team Manager to decide when he should go out for his runs. Thornhill waited for Wittman to pass before he allowed Ryan to exit the pit. Wittman was on a flying lap. Ryan watched the Ferrari move further away as he took his own car round the out-lap at a more sedate pace.

The Italian circuit was nowhere more atmospheric than at the Parabolica; Ryan could almost sense the ghosts of long-dead drivers, as he passed the overgrown and weathered grey-concrete of the original banked circuit, on the outside of the present track. As soon as he hit the main straight he floored the throttle. The Vantec flashed across the start line at over 200mph.

Ryan drove the first sector of his final flying lap as well as he could ever remember driving at Monza ,and he confidently attacked the second sector. As he accelerated out of the second Lesmos, Ryan was surprised to see Wittman's Ferrari. Wittman, on an in-lap, should have been out of sight. There was still time for Wittman to move aside before Ryan reached the Ascari chicane, so, although surprised to see the car ahead of him, Ryan took no action. 'Shit,' swore Ryan, as he was forced to lift off the throttle. Wittman was clearly not going to let him through. Ryan was forced to follow Wittman through both bends of the chicane before the Austrian finally moved aside. Ryan shook his left fist in anger as he passed the scarlet Ferrari. He would like to see the TV replay; but it didn't seem possible that the block could have been anything other than deliberate. Clearly Spa still rankled with the Austrian. Ryan decided he wasn't going to descend to Wittman's level - but he wasn't going to do him any favours either. There was no chance to pick up time in the final sector, and, with no further laps left, Ryan qualified in 8th place. Kramer qualified in 13^{th,} having slipped a place to one of the Saubers just before the end of the session.

Somerset's mobile phone rang just before 10:30 the next morning. It was not a good time to take a call. He was in the canvas-roofed Vantec hospitality area located between their two motorhomes. A reception for sponsors and other invited guests was underway; he was surrounded by a group of six businessmen who were boring the pants off him. Awkwardly, he fished the phone out from the inside pocket of his jacket and checked the display to see who was calling. It was Toshihiko Shintaku, the managing director of Katayama motors. This was one call he had to take.

'Give me a second, I'm just with some people,' said Somerset, quickly putting the phone on hold. He was embarrassed at being unable to greet Shintaku properly, but he couldn't afford to let the people around him know who he was talking to. 'If you'll excuse me gentlemen; I need to take this call.' He held his phone up for the group to see, and then swiftly walked through the hospitality area before racing up the steps into the motorhome.

'Sorry about that Tosh,' said Somerset; putting the phone back into talk mode. It was a sign of progress that both men addressed each other by first name. Toshihiko was one of the least formal Japanese businessmen that Somerset knew; talking with some of his countrymen was often a diplomatic nightmare. Toshihiko was refreshingly different.

'I understand - I hope I haven't dragged you away from anything important,' said Toshihiko, anxious that he might have called at a bad time.

'No, to be honest, you've rescued me from a group of boring executives on a corporate jolly – I'm sure you have to suffer the same glad-handing!' Somerset fully understood the importance of his hospitality role; but he was a racing man and preferred to be where the action was. He didn't mind passing small talk with the sponsors, but he rather resented the need to speak to the sponsors' guests that he was supposed to entertain. They brought no money to the company, and few of them were genuinely interested in the racing. It was just another corporate outing for them - and a chance to name drop back at the office.

'Glad to be of service,' replied Toshihiko, offering no clue as to whether or not he felt the same way about corporate entertaining. 'How is Panetta?'

'He's fine; but he won't be driving for us again this season' Somerset appreciated the genuine concern in Toshihiko's question.

'That's a pity, I hope it doesn't spoil your season - but I understand that Kramer is a useful replacement.'

It came as no surprise to Somerset that Toshihiko was well informed. He had come to appreciate the consummate professionalism of the dapper forty-eight year old. It was easy to understand why he headed up the powerful multinational Katayama company.

'Well, we should find out today,' said Somerset ruefully, not yet convinced by Kramer.

'I wish you luck. Actually, it's drivers we need to talk about.' A more serious tone had come into Toshihiko's voice. He was aware that his next words would cause Somerset some concern.

Somerset listened patiently as Toshihiko continued.

'I have finally managed to convince my board of the merit in supporting Vantec instead of Demaison, but they have insisted on three conditions: firstly Vantec must finish in the top six.'

This Somerset already knew.

'Secondly, Vantec must finish ahead of Demaison. We need it to be clear that we are leaving for a more successful team,' explained Toshihiko. 'And finally the board is insisting that you run a Japanese driver.' Toshihiko stopped talking to let Somerset take in the new condition.

Somerset didn't reply for a few seconds as he brought his emotions under control. As a businessman he fully understood the necessity for the conditions. No company was going to provide $20m dollars worth of motor-engines without some payback. On the human level, though, he was upset at the need to release one of his drivers. A difficult decision lay ahead of him: Ryan was currently the team's best driver - and a personal friend, but Panetta was improving and also brought in £750,000 a year in sponsorship. The choice, whenever it had to be made, was going to be painful.

'That's great news Tosh,' he eventually replied - his voice flat. 'I think we can do business on that basis. Is there a driver you have in mind?' Somerset was worried; there were two Japanese drivers in the series already. Takano was having a good season with Kadama, and he couldn't see the Japanese team releasing him. The other driver, Yamushita, was not impressing with BAR.

'Of course, are you aware of Tomita? He is from our academy and is currently racing in Formula Nippon. We believe he is ready to move into Formula One.'

Somerset knew all about Katayama's driving academy. Takano, driving for Kodama, had certainly done well after graduating from the heavily sponsored driving stable. If Toshihiko said their driver was ready, then he was certainly a prospect worth looking at.

'So, what's the next step?' asked Somerset.

'Obviously, with those conditions, we cannot sign a formal agreement until the end of the season, but what we need now is an agreement in principle. Our lawyers are drawing-up an agreement, and will send it to you by the end of the week. We must have that agreement signed by Indianapolis.' There was a firmness in Toshihiko's voice. He had worked hard to get the deal past his board, and wanted to make it stick before either side had second thoughts.

'I can't see a problem with that, but I will need to study the agreement in detail. If there are any difficulties I will get back to you.'

Toshihiko smiled; he knew that there was very little room for manoeuvre and understood the need for a little face-saving for Somerset. The deal itself was just too good for Vantec to walk away from - even given the interference in their driver selection.

'I would expect nothing else! replied Toshihiko. Now I think I had better let you get back to the fun! It's been good talking to you, and I hope we can look forward to a future in partnership.'

'I hope so too. In any event, I'll contact you before Indianapolis to let you know what's happening. Thanks for calling'. With that Somerset pressed the end button. He wanted time on his own to think about the Katayama deal; but sadly he knew he would have to return to his corporate guests.

The track was bathed in hot sunshine as the race got underway the next day. Friday's rain was a distant memory. A wet race at Monza would have been a rare experience, and all of the teams were glad that the expected conditions prevailed. Good weather made the selection of tyres and race strategy a much more certain affair.

Somerset was balanced on a stool in the middle of the Vantec pit wall monitoring station. He was wearing a pair of Kenwood headphones; an attached microphone allowed him to communicate freely with the men alongside him on the pit wall, the garage, and the data analysts sat in the motorhome. The headphones also served to protect his hearing from the deafening scream of car engines operating at 18,000 rpm. The high pitched scream of a Formula One car in full flight was a thrill to be experienced - but too much exposure was definitely something to be avoided. The covered facility on the pit-wall was unkindly referred to by the mechanics as the "prat perch"; but despite its prime position right next to the track, it was impossible for Somerset to see the track itself without standing up. Instead, Somerset was keeping an eye on the overall situation by watching the continual TV coverage of the race. On a second monitor a list of driver sector times was continually being updated. From time to time, parts of the screen would change to green as a driver recorded a fastest sector or lap-time. Sitting on his left, John Thornhill, the team manager, was performing the same task, but with the added responsibility of keeping an eye open for any unwelcome announcements from the race stewards.

Scott Harding, on Somerset's immediate right, was more interested in what was happening in the Vantec cars themselves. By watching the in-car footage he was able to assess the drivers' performance, and even gain a useful insight into the conditions of the tyres. Sat on his right was Ken Eyre, Ryan's Race engineer; his eyes were constantly scanning lap-time information from race control and also detailed telemetry data passed to his Pelladyne laptop computer. Pelladyne Computing was another of the team's key sponsors; they provided the hardware for the sophisticated computer support - without which modern motor racing could not function. Eyre was able to keep an eye on over one hundred different data elements in Ryan's car - from oil pressure to water temperature. On the far left of the station, Pat Norman, Kramer's Race engineer, was doing the same for Kramer. The data was simultaneously being analysed by a team of engineers based in a cramped office in the back of the motorhome. Powerblok engineers were also receiving a feed, and providing their own analysis. It was no wonder some engineers had a jaundiced view of drivers - who in their eyes, had little more to do than, steer, change gears, brake and accelerate! Far more activity was happening every second off the race track.

It was a good job that Somerset trusted his team manager to handle the race; for he was finding it hard to concentrate as he pondered the potential Katayama engine deal. For Vantec to progress there was no doubt they needed a better engine. If he was to stay married, the team would have to progress. His wife Rosemary was fed up with the sacrifices that they had been forced to make over the past fifteen years. She had willingly supported Chris as he built the team up until they were successful in Formula 3. The money had just started to come in - when Chris sold their house to fund the move into Formula One. They were straight back to square one. Rosemary had made it abundantly clear to Chris that if they failed to reach the top 5 inside six years, then he would have to sell the team. This was the sixth year. He had managed to get another year out of his wife; but she was less than happy about it, and had promised to divorce him if he tried it again. As much as he loved his motor racing he loved his wife even more; although it was still a bitter disappointment that she didn't share his love of the sport. These days it was rare to even see her at a race. Still, he didn't need the distraction on race days, so maybe there was also a positive side to her absence.

Even though his mind was wandering, Somerset was still aware of the race; and he interrupted his thoughts to watch Ryan scream down the straight to be followed just a few seconds later by Kramer. As the cars howled off into the distance he once more considered the question of drivers.

Fortunately, Kramer was not an issue; he was due to join Demaison for the next season - but that still left three drivers for two seats; and Katayama had already decided how one of those seats was to be filled. He just hoped that the agreement being drawn up didn't give them a say in the other seat! Although he would try and fight any excessive conditions Katayama might try and impose, it was very much a seller's market. He pulled a rueful smile as he admitted to himself that he was prepared to sell his soul for a better engine.

It looked like a straight choice between Ryan and Panetta. In terms of their driving the gap between the two was shrinking; but while Panetta was clearly improving, Ryan only showed occasional flashes of brilliance - such as that glorious move at Spa. His heart said Ryan, but his brain said Panetta! But then there were also other drivers out there to consider– perhaps it was time for a complete change of line-up. He shook his head; it was enough to give him the ulcer that had been threatening for several years! It all came back to money, thought Somerset, as another lap was completed on the track. He comforted himself with the thought that there were still three more races left after Monza; maybe things would sort themselves out.

Ryan sat anxiously in his seat, desperately waiting for the pole-man to raise the lollipop and let him on his way again. Inside the static car, the heat was building rapidly, and he could feel an irritating trickle of sweat run down the side of his nose. To his right, he could see that the front wheel-man had his hand out - indicating that he had finished his job of replacing the wheel. A quick glance to the left told a similar story. What was the hold up? Unwelcome memories of horrific pit lane refuelling fires flashed through his mind. He stole a quick glance in his left mirror. The tiny mirror gave a poor view, but even so, he could see that the fuelling rig was off the car - and he thought he could see the rear wheel-man indicating that all was clear. He switched his vision to the other mirror. The wheel should have been replaced by now; but he could see a small group frantically working away. He thumped the wheel in frustration then re-focused his concentration. Whatever the problem behind him was, he needed to ensure that he was ready to go as soon as he was allowed. A poor pit stop was all he needed; he had come into the pit in a useful 8th place. Even through his helmet, and with all the noise around him, he heard yet another car scream past on the far side of the pit wall. He didn't know if it was a back-marker, or one of his close rivals, but he knew for sure that the over-long stop was costing valuable places. He didn't have any time to consider the situation further as the pole-man suddenly turned the lollipop over- indicating that he should put the car into first gear. Fractionally later, the pole was lifted clear and he was off again - on the final 16 lap stint.

Wearily, Ryan crossed the finishing line in 13th place. The track ahead of him was empty, and for the last ten laps his sole task had been to keep Steve Rider's Sauber at bay. The engine mods had helped, but, at the end of the day, the car was still not good enough on circuits like Monza. He had expected to hold onto a top ten finish but the poor pit stop had put paid to that. He had also seen Kramer's car parked off the track. Monza had been yet another big disappointment. To the left and right of the track he was aware of the wildly celebrating Ferrari fans. He didn't need to be told that Wittman had won. The Austrian had overtaken him eighteen laps from the end. He felt rather like a film extra in the presence of a star at a film premiere. In Ferrari country, after a Ferrari win, the other teams were an irrelevance. He would be pleased to get back to the hotel.

Ryan lay naked on the bed, with his eyes closed, and let the emotion drain out. Victoria sat curled up on the sofa in the hotel bedroom and quietly read a book. She had seen Ryan in this state enough times to recognise that it was best to let him be. In a couple of hours he would be back to his normal self.

Ryan felt absolutely frustrated. He could have done nothing more - but he knew the car was better than the result showed. After what Somerset had said at Spa he knew results were important. Monza had done nothing to help. To cap it all, it was Nick Phillips that had ballsed up that pit-stop. All his reservations over the new mechanic returned; well he'd have to see about getting him replaced. Maybe that was unfair. A wheel nut had cross-threaded, it could have happened to anyone but….. five places were lost whilst he sat in the pit. Beaten by his own mechanics - not even by another driver. As for Kramer - Ryan knew it was the American's first race in Formula One, but they could have done without him parking the car in a gravel trap. Well, at least Kramer was racing - even if his passing attempt at the first chicane was a bit rash. If he hadn't stalled the engine he could still have got away with it. Nil points.

The phone by the bed rang. Ryan let Victoria pick it up. He had left instructions with reception for calls not to be put through. She would sort it.

'Alberto! Hi, how are you?' Victoria squealed in delight. 'Mm, hmm, I'll ask him.' She turned to look at Ryan. 'Alberto's downstairs in the lobby. He asked if you'd like a drink.'

Ryan opened his eyes and sat up. 'Tell him I'll be straight down.'

As Victoria chatted happily to Alberto; Ryan headed for the bathroom.

Alberto was sitting on a sofa in the lobby - a pair of crutches by his side. Alberto suddenly surprised Ryan by getting to his feet unaided. He grabbed Ryan and kissed him on both cheeks. Ryan looked again at the crutches.

'What the fuck are those for, then?'

'I'm supposed to use them if I'm walking anywhere - but I don't need them very much. Mind you, they're pretty good for getting sympathy.' His eyes wistfully tracked a couple of young girls as they crossed the lobby behind Ryan.

'How long before you can drive again, then?' asked Ryan.

'The doctors say maybe another six weeks. I say maybe four. Too late for this season though. But I think perhaps you don't need me now. Despite his crash, Kramer looked pretty good.' There was a sadness in Panetta's voice.

'But not as good as you though. Italians have more style you know!' Ryan tried to cheer Alberto up.

'Style doesn't win races my friend! You didn't watch the race like I did. He was very, very quick. Even you might have trouble staying number one'.

As Ryan considered the implications of that statement he saw a familiar figure exit through the automatic door of the hotel. He turned his head to watch as the mechanic disappeared from sight. Where on earth was Nick Phillips going - all dressed up? If he had spotted him a fraction earlier he would have stopped the mechanic and taken him to task over the pit-stop. Oh well, another time. He returned his attention to Panetta.

'Let me worry about Kramer - you just get back into a car. Now, what about that drink?' Ryan picked up Alberto's crutches and passed them over. The two drivers chatted animatedly about the race as they headed for the hotel bar.

CHAPTER 7

9:40 p.m. Sunday 2nd September, near Milan - Italy

Pierre Demaison had arrived at the restaurant first. He had driven out to the small commune of Agrate Brianza, just a few miles outside Monza, on the pretext of visiting an old racing friend. Impatiently, he nursed a glass of red Chianti. The cheap restaurant was not what he was used to; and he had seen straight through the artificial presence of an old flour-mill. However, the anonymity of the location was ideal for the meeting he was about to have. Although there was nothing wrong with him meeting with Kramer, there were things they needed to discuss that were best kept private; and it was best that their association was kept to a minimum.

Whilst he slowly sipped his wine, he mused over the day's events. The day had certainly been one of mixed results. Thierry Vigneron had driven a fantastic race to place third; but the excellent result was marred by the retirement of Miguel Gonzales with a broken gearbox. It was only the second race of the season in which the team had scored any points. Their last points had been scored in Canada, where Vigneron had come fourth and Gonzales had just sneaked into sixth place. Despite his pleasure over Vigneron's podium in Italy, it still rankled with Demaison that the team had failed to score even a single point in their home Grand Prix at Magny-Cours. On the positive side, the team had vitally moved ahead of Vantec and into the top six.

Demaison looked up as the door opened. A young couple entered hand-in-hand, their eyes sparkling in anticipation of a good evening in each other's company He checked his watch and shook his head in irritation. Twenty minutes late. He wondered whether he should order another bottle. The door opened yet again and Demaison got to his feet.

The two men embraced; then Demaison held Jason Kramer at arm's length to get a good look at him.

'It's been a long time,' he said in English. Emotion choked his voice.

'It sure has - about five years by my reckoning. But the years have treated you well though.'

'A kind lie, my son. I am getting old and feel it.' They sat down and Demaison poured Kramer a glass of wine.

'Did you hurt yourself today?' Demaison had seen Kramer crash out.

'No, it was just a gentle spin into the tyre wall. I've hit walls far harder than that back in the States!' There was almost pride in his voice. In his book, a crash without injury was hardly worth calling a crash.

'And how is your mother?' asked Demaison.

'She's fine - but she's still tucked up with that asshole from Denver. I really don't know why she didn't hitch up with you.'

'She didn't want to live in France; and at the time my wife was still alive. It might have been a little inconvenient.' Demaison smiled at what his wife might have thought of such an arrangement. Instead, he had watched Jason grow up from a distance. He had been delighted when the young boy had taken up motor racing, and had assisted him financially when necessary. By contrast, Jean, his own marital son had greatly disappointed him. The boy certainly had brains. He worked as a manager in the company; but didn't have the balls for actual racing. Jason was the son he wished he had back home.

There was plenty for the two men to talk about; and they hardly noticed being served - or even eating the food that eventually arrived. Father and son chatted happily about both family and motor racing before, finally over cups of frothy cappuccino, Demaison turned the conversation round to the rest of the season.

'You understand that we must finish in the top six of the constructor's championship and that Vantec must be behind us?'

'Yeah, there's no need to remind me. I reckon we got off to a good start today - but I don't think I can crash out of every race! I'll have to work out another way. Have you thought anymore about what happens to me next year?'

Demaison was astute enough to sense the anxiety behind Jason's question.

'Assuming our plan works, I will take you on as our driver after the end of the season. Unfortunately, both Vigneron and Gonzales are under contract for next year; but I have a feeling that Gonzales may wish to resign from his contract before too long.' Demaison pulled out two photographs from his top pocket. The pictures of Gonzales and a young man were very explicit.

'You sure play dirty,' said Kramer, surprised at his father's ruthlessness - a germ of an idea beginning to form in his own mind.

Demaison poked his son in the chest. 'Winning is everything and don't you forget it! Now, I think we had best go our separate ways. I am not sure when we'll meet again. Good luck in Indianapolis!'

Nick Phillips was happier than he had been in a long time. His right hand tenderly stroked Alessandra's olive skinned wrist as he gazed in admiration at the twenty-year-old Italian girl. The half-eaten food on his plate had long since grown cold. His eyes made hundreds, if not thousands, of minute adjustments as they sought to appreciate every inch of her wonderful face; but always they would return to stare deep into her large brown eyes - as if drawn by a magnet. They had last been together the previous Christmas; and although he phoned Alessandra most days, he missed her physically - and time had dragged badly since then. Nick was desperate to make the evening as special as possible, for they were only going to have the one night together. Lost in their love for each other, the couple hadn't noticed Demaison and Kramer sitting just twenty feet away.

Just before 11:00 p.m, the scrape of chairs on the tiled floor briefly broke the spell. Instinctively, Nick looked towards the disturbance. Nick had been a motor racing fan from childhood, and easily recognised Demaison as the two men noisily got up from their table – but, from where he sat, Nick could only see the back of Demaison's tall dark-haired companion. As the two men slowly made their way to the exit, Nick puzzled over the presence of Demaison in the out of the way restaurant. The younger man reached the doorway first, and politely stood to one side to open the door. To his utter astonishment, Nick was rewarded with a brief but clear view of Kramer. He shrugged his shoulders; after all, it was none of his business. Then he returned his attention to his beautiful girl-friend.

CHAPTER 8

11:55 a.m. Sunday 16th September, Indianapolis Speedway – Unites States

Ryan closed his eyes, and tried to block out the hubbub around him. The half hour before the start was his least favourite part of the race. At least the photographers and celebrities had now left the grid; but the cars were still surrounded by mechanics and officials. Just yards in front of him, a young girl, dressed in a short white skirt and blue top, held a pole; the board on top of the pole indicated his name and grid position. In other circumstances, he would have admired the long shapely legs that emerged from her leather boots. He had briefly checked her out - but now she was just another unwelcome distraction.

Beside the car, Karen Goodbody held a large green umbrella over his head to help keep him cool. Wisely, she kept quiet, not wishing to spoil Ryan's concentration. She gritted her teeth as her arms began to ache from the weight of the umbrella; and tried not to think about the menial task she was having to perform. Dotted around Ryan's car, his mechanics feverishly checked and rechecked the tyres and a myriad of nuts and settings. They would only, grudgingly, leave the car when the signal to clear the grid was given. He sometimes thought his mechanics would only be happy if they drove round with him in the car!

He had given up trying to visualise the race and sat patiently trying to keep his nerves in check. He would be all right once the engine was running, but at present he felt quite alone - despite the throng of mechanics. He thought he could just make out the strains of a marching band over the sound system. The Americans had, as usual, put on a marvellous display to keep the huge audience amused in the run up to the race. He had kept away from most of the razzmatazz as it only seemed to make the adrenaline flow that little bit quicker; but he had been obliged to take part in the drivers' parade. All of the drivers had been slowly driven round the Oval Indy 500 circuit in six large pick-ups. It had been interesting to experience the oval circuit - but he was glad that they would be driving on the road circuit. The circuit had been created specifically for Formula One, and mainly lay inside the existing oval.

With just under two minutes to go the tyre covers were removed. They had done their job of retaining as much heat as possible - a factor so critical in the performance of the rubber. Despite all the performance gains made throughout the rest of the car, the tyres were still the single most important factor in determining race performance. Finally, on the one-minute-hooter, the engines were all started. Puffs of oily smoke rose from the back of the cars as twenty-two 850 bhp engines barked loudly into life.

Once the engines were noisily idling, the colourful human tide receded from the grid - leaving the cars resembling a school of beached sharks. Ryan looked back across from his 7th place on the grid to Kramer - who had impressed the team by qualifying just behind Ryan in 8th place. Kramer was on home soil, and at a track he knew well; even so, it was clear that the American was improving with every drive in a Formula One car. Ryan gave Kramer a thumbs-up sign that was immediately reciprocated. There was no time for further exchanges as the gantry lights turned green. The cars in front began to move off on the single formation lap that would help ensure that the cars were working properly. The slow lap would also help put some much needed heat and grip into the tyres prior to the start itself. Ryan let the car ahead move a healthy distance before revving the engine high and dropping the paddle-operated clutch with his left hand. The excessive engine revs spun the wheels - leaving a trail of black rubber that he would use for extra fractions of grip on the start. Then, he was away - quickly making up the gap to Underwood's red and white Kodama.

At the end of the formation lap, Ryan carefully stopped his car in a position to take advantage of the rubber he had laid down earlier. Now began the terrible wait while the remaining cars came to a halt on the grid. The last car to stop was the safety car. It came to a halt a respectful distance behind the powerful racing cars - its yellow, flashing, roof-top light barely visible in the bright sun. Up in race-control, the starter looked down over the cars, strung out at 16m intervals over 330m of the main straight. Satisfied that all was well, he pushed the button to begin the automatic start sequence. At one-second intervals a new red light glowed bright above the track. Once all five lights were lit, the start program would determine when the lights were extinguished and the race could begin.

As the lights began to glow, Ryan revved the engine and gently released the clutch paddle. When he felt the clutch beginning to bite he engaged the locking lever on the opposite side of the steering-wheel. As the fifth red light lit up Ryan breathed deeply to control his nerves and moved his finger on to the locking lever. Spectators covered their ears as the sound of twenty-two 850 horsepower engines filled the air. In the stands, along the pit straight closest to the action, fans covered their ears as the noise reached unbearable limits. There was the briefest of pause before all five lights were instantaneously extinguished and the race began.

Ryan released the clutch locking-lever and tried not to light up the rear tyres as he pulled away from the line. The massive acceleration thrust Ryan back into his seat - but as his car began to pick up speed a blue-sleeved arm was raised from the Renault of Cruz in front. With only 27 metres separating the front of his car and the rear of the Renault there was no time to consider the situation. Instinctively, Ryan lifted the throttle and jinked his car to the left; then he floored the throttle to ensure he wasn't rammed from behind by another car taking similar evasive action. Then he was past Cruz and back on the racing line - the car still gaining speed along the long main straight. Inside four seconds he was travelling at over 100 mph. All of the cars ahead of him had got away cleanly; and for once, there was no change in the order as they approached the first corner. As they reached the braking point for the sharp right-hander, his car was travelling at over 205 miles an hour.

With so many cars still around, Ryan took the normal racing line into the turn - braking early, and dropping down from 6th to 2nd gear. He had cut his speed to 65 miles per hour - the rapid deceleration forcing the nose of the car closer to the ground, and throwing Ryan forward sharply into his seat belt. As the nose of his car turned towards the apex, he was horrified to see another, faster moving, green car on his right. Already committed, there was nothing he could do as Kramer's car slid up on the inside. For a brief moment it looked like they might avoid each other - but luck was not running with them. Ryan's right rear-wheel touched Kramer's front offside wheel - it didn't feel a huge contact, but the touch spun Ryan's car through 180 degrees. Even as Ryan spun, the two cars carried on round the bend. At one point, the cars were nose on to each other, and Ryan could see Kramer wrestling with his car. Desperately, Ryan put his own car into reverse. To get out of the way he was forced to back off the track and onto the grass on the outside of the turn. Impatiently, he watched the rest of the field stream past. As the last car disappeared into the distance, he drove back onto the track and began to gain speed. The next turn, just yards up the road, was all he needed, to know that his race was over. The seemingly slight contact had clearly damaged his rear suspension. It was not something they would be able to repair - even if he was able to nurse the car round the remainder of the lap. In despair, he thumped the steering wheel with both hands, then toggled his radio switch on.

'Sorry, guys - that's it. The rear suspension is broken - I'm going to have to park her!' He switched the radio back off, this wasn't the right time for a long conversation. The team would have seen the accident on the TV - there was nothing he could add.

He drove the car off the circuit and parked it on the grass before turn three. As the marshals raced towards him, he climbed out of the stricken racing car.

Ryan watched the recovery team remove the car, before he began the walk back to the pits. He wasn't looking forward to meeting Somerset. He ran over the incident in his mind; but couldn't see that he had made a mistake. Hopefully, he could find a TV replay that would show what happened. At least the incident had only taken one of them out of the race - he just hoped that Kramer would make the most of his opportunity.

The walk back to the pits took almost ten minutes as he punctuated the journey with short halts to watch the cars go past. He was pleased to see that Kramer had retained 7th place,. He had even taken a few yards off the Williams just ahead. As he made his way back behind the Armco, Ryan could hear the crowd shouting at him. Mixed in with the odd cry of sympathy were a large number of insults about his driving. Some of the taunts hurt, but he was rather glad he didn't drive for Ferrari; the verbal punishment meted out by the Tifosi would have far exceeded the abuse now thrown at him. The walk, though, did nothing for his self respect and even less to cheer him up. He was pretty fed up by the time he reached the pit lane.

The familiar figure of Kirsten Reynolds blocked the entrance to the pits. The young ITV reporter, artificially clad in racing gear, was determined to get her interview. There was going to be no escape from the routine trial by television. Ryan thought it was a shame he only ever got to speak to her when things were going badly.

'Ryan, can we have a quick word?' asked the attractive brunette. Ryan nodded his assent; and prepared himself for the question that was bound to come.

'Whose fault was the clash? It looked, to us, like you chopped across Kramer.'

'Sometimes, things look different on the telly,' he replied, talking into the large microphone thrust inches from his face.

'Are you saying, then, that Kramer ...' Her words were drowned out by the passing cars as they began yet another lap.

'Sorry, could you repeat the question?' asked Ryan politely.

'Was the accident Kramer's fault?' The reporter reworked her question.

'Until I see a replay I can't really comment - but I believe I was following the racing line. I'd like to think it was a simple racing accident.'

'Do you think your team will see it that way?'

'I think we'll all have to sit down and see what happened. Obviously, we could have done without this - but I hope that Kramer can carry on, and perhaps finish in the points.'

'Thank you, Ryan - better luck in your next race'.

Inside the garage, Ryan could see that his own crew were dejected. Standing with arms tightly folded, their body language said it all. As the mechanics did their best to ignore him, Victoria strolled over and gave him a sympathetic hug - raising an eyebrow inquiringly. Ryan's mouth turned down in answer. The unspoken communication told Victoria all she needed to know about what Ryan thought of the incident. Ryan gave Victoria a quick squeeze to assure her he was okay; and then sought out Derek Archer.

'Sorry, Derek, I'd have liked to see more of the circuit.'

'It's not me you should say sorry to! I think Chris is pretty pissed off - maybe you should keep out of his way for a bit. I gather you said the suspension broke - is that right?'

'Well, you know how fragile it can be!'

'Not half as fragile as you bloody drivers!'

Ryan knew that Derek was only half joking - he cared more about the cars than the drivers.

'Was it your fault - didn't look like it to me?'

'I really don't know - I'm going to have to watch the tape first.' In the background, Kramer's crew kept a low profile. They were embarrassed that only their car was still running. Some of them suspected that their man had caused the accident. They kept their eyes fixedly on the TV monitor watching the race unfold. Now the team really did need Kramer to do something special.

Ryan thought it best to find Somerset straightaway and get the grief over with. At least Somerset's bad moods didn't last very long. Ryan carefully checked the pit lane before dashing across to the timing station. Somerset turned to face him.

'Well, what have you got to say for yourself?'

Ryan shrugged. 'I was on the racing line and turned in quite normally - and then suddenly, Kramer was there beside me,' said Ryan, defensively.

'Why do you think we put mirrors on the cars? They're not there for you to check your hair you know!'

'I looked - he wasn't there; so he must have come in faster and braked later. I had the line.'

'Luckily for you, that's exactly what they're saying on telly,' said Somerset, in a more conciliatory tone. He knew he would have a much tougher conversation with Kramer. Knowing drivers as he did, it was unlikely Kramer would concede that the accident was his fault; even after seeing slow motion replays, they were still inclined to blame anyone but themselves.

'Don't leave the circuit - I'll want to speak to both you and Kramer later.' With that, Somerset turned his back on Ryan and resumed watching the monitors. Ryan waited to cross the pit lane as a blue Demaison scorched away from a routine pit stop - laying down an unnecessary trail of black rubber.

'Can we go upstairs and watch from the suite?' Ryan asked Victoria. He'd watched ten laps of the race from inside the garage; but still felt like an unwelcome guest amongst the mechanics. The two of them made their way out through the rear of the garage and up to the purpose built suite. The TV was already on; but, surprisingly, there was no one else using the small lounge. Ryan peeled down the top of his overalls and slumped on the sofa. He'd worry about a shower after the race had finished; not that he really needed one - he hadn't actually done very much.

A slim silver coloured PVR, mounted underneath the TV, was being used to record the race onto its massive 120gb hard disk. As there was no one else in the room trying to watch the race, Ryan grabbed the remote control, and, using the "chase play" function, quickly located the race start. He watched the replay once at normal speed, and then again - stepping through one frame at a time. On television the accident looked much scarier than it had at the time. He had only been vaguely aware of the other cars taking avoiding action as he spun off the track. On the replay, cars were scattering in all directions and carefully picking their way through the accident zone. The replay told him all he needed to know. Relieved in the knowledge that he wasn't to blame, he fast-forwarded through the action until once again they were watching the race in real time.

Ryan was impressed with Kramer's driving. Knowing the track well, his lines on the oval section were slightly different from the less experienced F1 drivers. Despite the car still being down on power compared with the big teams, he had managed to inch closer to the Williams of Eddison on each successive lap. A good, first pit stop on lap 27 had brought him out just ahead of Eddison and into 6th place. As they approached the second series of pit-stops he was gaining on Stuart Underwood in the Kodama.

Kramer was unable to take Underwood in the pit stop; but by lap 63 he was pushing the British driver hard. On the next lap, Kramer wound the Vantec up down the main straight towards turn one. The car just topped 200 mph, before Kramer began a late braking manoeuvre up the inside of Underwood. Ryan held his breath as Kramer's car slid up the inside of Underwood - in what looked likely to be an exact repeat of their own clash. Underwood, perhaps aware of what had happened to Ryan earlier, had seen the move - and, rather than risk a coming-together, kept to the outside of the turn. Kramer only just held the Vantec together as the car exited turn one ahead of Underwood. He corrected the rear end of the car as it jinked in front of Underwood - and then with the car back under control, accelerated away. The move had been audacious but effective. The rest of the race was incident free - but Kramer had to work hard to keep Underwood behind him. His fifth place, and two valuable championship points, was a reasonable reward for the afternoon. Ryan had to agree that he would have been unlikely to have overtaken both Eddison and Underwood. He would still have words with Kramer - but judged his move less harshly now that he had seen the American drive so competitively. Even Somerset was likely to be pleased with the outcome.

Kramer was experiencing mixed feelings as he drove slowly back to Parc Ferme. Apart from his accident with Ryan, he knew he had driven well; and he had enjoyed the race. He had made his mark in Formula One; and would now be a force to reckon with. On the downside, he knew he had two tough conversations to brave. Somerset was going to be very unhappy about him taking-out Ryan, and his father was going to be less than pleased with him scoring Championship points - especially as Team Demaison had yet again failed to score any points. He would have to see Somerset as soon as possible - but he would wait before contacting his father.

Ryan listened to the post race analysis, before heading back to the pit to greet Kramer. It would be churlish to spoil his pleasure at a points finish; so Ryan decided to give him a chance to celebrate before tackling him about the accident. In the event, Kramer beat him to it - going straight over to Ryan on his return to the garage.

'Really sorry, pal.' Kramer held out his hand. 'I guess I just misjudged that one - but I thought you'd left the door open, so I went for it.'

'Apology accepted. But please don't do it again!' Ryan was surprised that Kramer had apologised so readily. Under the circumstances, there didn't seem much he could do about it - so he accepted the apology as gracefully as he could. He still wanted to talk it over properly with Kramer, but now didn't seem to be the right time.

'Look, I think I'd better go and shove some books down my shorts. I don't reckon the boss is too keen on me at the moment!' Kramer took his leave and headed off to find Somerset.

Kramer needn't have worried, for Chris Somerset had calmed down. The two points Kramer had gained left the team just one point behind Demaison - who had a total of eight points. Kramer had clearly demonstrated that he was a genuine racer. It looked like the team now had two competitive drivers; and an improving car capable of challenging for the top six. At the sharp end, McLaren had stolen the top points with a magnificent one-two performance. Sadly for Vantec, Kodama scored points with both drivers - and the fifth placed team was now seven points clear of Demaison in sixth place. But, with just a single point separating Vantec from the sixth place they needed, it was all still to play for. However, as Somerset faced the two contrite drivers in the suite above the garage, an hour after the race, he knew he still had to read the riot act.

'I understand that accidents happen,' said Somerset, circling unnervingly around the two men standing in front of him like naughty schoolboys, 'but it is totally unacceptable for two team-mates to drive into each other! We could be in the top six today - but instead, I have a damaged car and we're back in 7th place. And I don't suppose the sponsors were very happy to only see one car driving round carrying their expensive adverts - do you!' He needn't have worried on the last count - the accident had actually brought the sponsors increased TV coverage; and they were relishing the unexpected attention. He paused to check that they had got the message. Both drivers seemed to be studying the floor; but their eager nods showed that they'd heard.

'Well, I've heard both your stories - and Kramer has apologised; so we had better leave it at that; but if there are any repeats then I may have to start looking at contracts! Now get out!' He'd said his piece - and he felt better for it, but, at the end of the day, the trip to America had been worthwhile.

'You're staying around tomorrow aren't you?' The two drivers were on the way out of the motorhome, when Kramer grabbed Ryan by the arm. 'Say I take you out and show you the sights - we could have a real boys' night out. What do you say?' said Kramer, grinning infectiously.

'Okay, great!' Ryan had already planned on stopping over; he wanted to shop for some more home automation gear - sadly the States was still far ahead of the U.K in that respect. Victoria had to return home for work, so she wouldn't be a problem, and to be honest he rather liked Kramer - despite the earlier incident. At least they could talk about it over a few beers.

'All righty. I'll meet you in your hotel at eight-thirty, and we'll show Indianapolis how Formula One race heroes relax!

CHAPTER 9

5:55 p.m. Monday 17th September, Indianapolis – United States

Wearily, Ryan trudged back through the park in front of the large modern Hyatt Regency Hotel. At other times he might have appreciated the water fountains and stone sculptures that decorated the open space, but he had been on his feet all day and was looking forward to a reviving shower.

Inside the sand-coloured hotel, the magnificent twenty-one storey atrium containing the lobby gave the building an incredibly airy feeling. Exposed glass-fronted lifts ran up through the atrium to reach the guest floors. Ryan's attention, though, was immediately drawn to the surprising sight of a green Vantec jacket. As Ryan neared the reception desk he could see that it was the team's test driver. Barton was leaning casually on the reception desk; from the dark-haired receptionist's smile, it looked like he was getting on very well. The uniformed receptionist turned her attention away from Barton to greet Ryan with a bright warm smile. The unwelcome movement caused Barton to look round.

'Oh, hi Ryan.' There was no warmth in his greeting, and Ryan suspected that Warren was disappointed at being interrupted.

'I see you're keeping a low-profile,' teased Ryan, looking pointedly at Warren's conspicuous jacket.

Barton blushed, 'Thought I'd make the most of it,' he replied lamely. 'I don't often get to enjoy the benefits of the job like you guys.'

'Looks like it's working,' said Ryan, indicating the pretty receptionist with a glance. He was rewarded with yet another blush from the South African. It was proving far too easy to tease him - but he couldn't blame Barton for trying to utilise his motor-racing status.

'Anyway, I thought you'd left with the rest of the team.' Ryan knew that most of the team had flown out earlier that day.

'I haven't been to the States before - so I thought I'd stay over for a few days. Somerset doesn't need me until the end of the week.' There was a trace of bitterness in his voice. Barton changed the subject, 'Looks like you've been busy.' He nodded at the plastic carrier-bags that Ryan was clutching in his right hand.

'I think I've walked every inch of the city today,' exaggerated Ryan. He had started early in the morning, climbing 230 feet up to the observation platform on the Soldiers and Sailors monument. From the glass-encased balcony he had obtained a tremendous panorama of the city. Having got his bearings, he had then quickly visited the other key sights; making the most of a rare opportunity to do some sight-seeing. Of all the sights, he had been most impressed by the 19-storey RCA dome that was home to the Indianapolis Colts. He had never seen a roof supported by air-pressure before. It was a veritable sporting temple compared to the tatty concrete monstrosities that passed as stadiums back home. He had ended the day in the huge city-centre shopping mall - which accounted for the variety of bags he now carried. Unfortunately, he had been disappointed in his quest for yet more home-automation equipment.

'What are you doing later? Perhaps we could meet up for a drink?' asked Barton, hopefully. He would love to get Ryan on his own for an evening, and besides, the receptionist had wandered off to take care of some other guests and looked a lost cause.

'I'm afraid I've already got plans for this evening - some other time maybe,' Ryan didn't think it would improve Barton's morale to say he was going out with Kramer.

'That's a shame, but some other time would be good.' Barton suspected that another opportunity would be a long time coming.

'I'd love to stay and chat, but I need to get some stuff done before going out.' Ryan used the little white lie to bring their uncomfortable conversation to an end.

Up in his room, Ryan sat back in the dark brown leather chair and rested his feet on the matching leather footstool. Yet again he pressed the button on the remote control to change the TV channel. Having showered and dressed, he was idly flicking through the myriad of channels whilst he waited for Kramer. Sadly, much of the advertising was of a higher quality than the programmes. Game and Talk shows filled the channels. British television was going the same way, and for some time he had realised that the ability to access lots of channels really only meant the ability to watch even more rubbish than before.

Bored with the TV, he got up and walked over to the full-length window. Rooms in the city were at a premium over race weekends, and he had been lucky to get a room with a king-sized bed overlooking the State Capitol. The large floodlit dome couldn't have been more than four hundred yards from his hotel room, and the classically designed stone building was a welcome contrast to the steel and glass of much of the city. In the soft yellow light the building exuded power and elegance.

Ryan was still looking out at the night skyline when the phone in his room rang. The female receptionist politely informed him that Kramer was waiting in reception. He switched off the TV, slipped into a pair of comfortable shoes and grabbed his brown leather jacket. Despite his antipathy to Kramer's antics on the track he was rather looking forward to a boys' night out.

When Ryan emerged from the lift, Kramer was leaning conspiratorially over the counter talking to the receptionist. The girl was laughing, and it was evident that Kramer had an easy charm. Kramer had one last word with the receptionist, then touched her briefly on the arm and turned to greet Ryan. He shook Ryan's hand firmly and warmly.

'Forgiven me yet old boy?' he asked, in a mock British accident.

'Not yet,' answered Ryan tetchily. 'You can explain it to me again over dinner - I hope you haven't eaten yet, because I'm starving!'

'Fine, I know just the place. A few beers, some good blues music and the finest chilli. How's that grab you?'

'Sounds good to me - so long as we don't have to walk too far. I've already walked this town once today. Lead on - it's your town!'

Kramer propelled Ryan to the exit, his hand placed firmly in the middle of Ryan's back. Neither of them noticed the young man reading a newspaper in the lobby. Waiting until they had left the building, Warren Barton quickly folded the paper and placed it on the coffee table in front of him. He then got up from the sofa and walked purposefully after the two drivers. His angry disappointment had previously been directed solely at Kramer, but seeing Ryan in his company was another blow. It hurt that Ryan had not mentioned that he was seeing Kramer that evening. Once again, it seemed that he was being excluded.

Kramer led Ryan out onto the street. In mid-September the temperature in Indianapolis was very similar to that back in London. Ryan was pleased to be away from the sweltering heat of Monza, but the constantly blowing wind made him glad that he was wearing a leather jacket.

'You support the Indians, then?' asked Ryan, side-stepping a slow-moving old lady as he referred to the red baseball-jacket that Kramer was sporting.

'Yeah, when I can. But their season's just about the same as ours. Mainly I get to see them on TV.'

'So, are you from round here then?'

'Not originally. I was brought up in San Diego but I came out this way to learn to drive. Indianapolis was the place to be. I've also raced in the Indy 500 a couple of times - that's why I know the track well. I know the road circuit is different - but they haven't touched the main straight. I knew what the grip was like and could probably brake later than most of you guys.'

They turned left into Meridian Street and headed south - unaware that they were being followed.

'Well, I still can't see how you thought that move would work - not on the first lap with the whole field ploughing into the turn!' Ryan hadn't planned to discuss the clash in the street, but at least it got it out of the way.

'Give us a break. You know as well as I do, that the first lap is generally the best chance you get to make a few places. And you might recall it was only my second F1 race. I'm still finding my feet. I'm sorry - that's all I can say. It won't happen again,' apologised Kramer.

The explanation was plausible to Ryan, and there didn't seem to be anything to be gained by harping on about it. What was done was done. He'd keep a close eye on Kramer in the next race, though.

'Okay. I'll drop it - if you buy dinner, deal?'

'Deal.' Kramer exchanged an enthusiastic high-five that stung Ryan's hands.

The bar Kramer had in mind was just ten minutes walk from the hotel. It was a good job they had talked on the way; the music inside was incredibly loud, and conversation would have been difficult. On a stage at one end of the room, a band of ageing musicians was competently playing Sweet Little Angel. Ryan recognised the classic BB King track and nodded his approval. He didn't get to see live bands anywhere near as much as he'd like.

They found a relatively quiet table well away from the stage. Talking was not easy above the band - but at least they didn't need to shout to hear each other.

'You know your blues, then,' said Kramer.

'Not as much as I'd like. When I was a kid I wanted to be a guitarist.'

'So, what happened?'

'I saved up the cash from my Saturday job and paper round; got all the gear - but I just couldn't hack it. I thought I'd sound like Eric Clapton straight away. When it didn't happen I lost heart. Still, it really made me appreciate guys like him.' Ryan pointed at the guitarist.

'I know what you mean. When I was a kid I wanted to play Pro-football.'

'And?'

'Couldn't catch, couldn't run and was way too small!' They laughed at their collective failures.

'Can I get you guys a drink or something?' They hadn't noticed the denim-clad waitress sidle over. She now stood behind Ryan - bovinely chewing on a stick of gum, a pad and pencil at the ready.

'Budweiser okay with you?' asked Kramer.

'Yeah, whatever.'

'Bring us two Buds while we look at the menu, angel.' Kramer rubbed the back of her blue denimed leg. She felt she ought to be angry - but then again, they were both pretty cute.

'Don't play with what you can't afford,' she said, smiling, having settled on a mild rebuke.

Kramer laughed out loud. 'I think I can afford - just get us the beers and I promise to behave.'

The girl quickly came back with the beers, and then provocatively wiggled away to serve another table.

'Don't you have trouble with being recognised?' asked Ryan.

'Not here. Some places can be bad, but it's not like I've ever won the Indy 500 or anything. The people in here are more into music than motor racing. But, if anyone does ask - please don't say we're drivers!'

A low profile suited Ryan very well. He raised his bottle of beer to Kramer.

'We'll have a couple of beers and a bite to eat here; and then I know a little club down the road where we can find some more adult entertainment. You do like girls, I hope.' Briefly, a worried look flitted across Kramer's face.

'Almost as much as I like cars.'

'Well, some of these babes are pretty hot.'

'Hot's good. - just don't tell Victoria!'

'No way, man! This is boys' night. My lips are sealed - except when drinking of course!' With that, Kramer emptied his bottle of beer in one long draught and immediately signalled to the waitress.

Ryan followed Kramer's advice and had the chilli beef. He needn't have worried about going hungry - every time he visited America he was convinced the portions got bigger and bigger. The Mexican beef stew was hotly spiced, and Ryan was glad to wash it down with the cold beer.

Time passed quickly as the two drivers traded racing stories. Ryan found it refreshing to hear about new circuits and different drivers. Although there were differences between Formula 1 and Champ Car racing, there were far more similarities. The two drivers were linked by their enjoyment of controlling high-powered engines on the limit. As more beers went down, Ryan found himself exaggerating some of his stories. He was utterly convinced Kramer was doing the same. By the time they had finished the meal; they were driving cars faster than the cars actually went, on corners far tighter than in real life. Just after ten, Kramer called for the bill and slid across his gold Amex card in payment. The waitress smiled as she picked up the plastic, remembering what she had said earlier. This dude certainly could afford it!

The pair staggered out of the blues bar arm-in-arm. Behind them, Warren Barton followed cautiously. He didn't want to be spotted at this stage. Feeling awkward, he hung back in the shadows of an adjoining doorway as the two drivers stood on the kerbside. He waited to see where they went next. It wasn't long before a Metro cab drove into sight and was flagged down by Kramer.

'Shit!' Barton swore loudly as Jason and Ryan climbed into the back of the ageing, battered yellow cab. He wasn't sure how he was going to follow them. As the taxi disappeared into the distance, Barton took their place on the kerbside and looked anxiously up and down the road.

Ryan missed hearing what Kramer said to the driver, and was only vaguely aware that they were heading downtown. Eventually, the cab pulled up outside a nondescript brick building - in an area that had clearly seen better days. A closed steel door was jealously guarded by two large bouncers dressed in tuxedos. The buildings on either side were boarded up.

'It's okay, pal. It looks much better on the inside,' said Kramer, as Ryan looked at him quizzically.

A short corridor led from the solid outside door to an inner arched entrance. Even in the dingy light, Ryan could see the paint peeling from the walls. He was feeling decidedly uncomfortable in the squalid surroundings. Passing through the archway, he was taken aback by the size of the club. The street frontage had indeed been a poor advert for the interior. The club clearly extended across the buildings on either side. Chrome-railed stairs on each side of the large room led up to a second floor. A long well-stocked bar ran half the length of the left-hand side of the room. From overhead spotlights, a constantly changing pattern of coloured light was dancing on the shiny black counter. Despite the large mirrors that adorned the walls, clever use of soft lighting prevented the room from being overly bright.

Clusters of round tables sat on a platform surrounding the central dance floor. The tables were only sparsely occupied. A chrome rail ran round the edge of the platform, interrupted at regular intervals to provide access to the dance floor. On a separate raised-stage at one end of the dance floor, a near-naked dancer was gyrating provocatively round a shiny vertical pole in time to the slow rhythmic blues tune that was pumping loudly throughout the club. The pile of discarded clothes on the floor suggested that she was most of the way through her performance.

'Are you sure we want to be here?'

'Stay cool man, we've only just arrived.' Kramer sensed Ryan's discomfort. 'We'll have a drink - and if you really don't like it we'll move on.'

Ryan nodded his agreement and followed Kramer to one of the tables on the right-hand side of the room. Almost as soon as they had sat down a topless girl was hovering at their table. Ryan didn't hear Kramer order the drinks over the noise of the music. Despite his unease at the nature of the club, it was difficult to ignore the dancer's erotic performance. The girl had deserted the pole, and now lay on the floor writhing in mock ecstasy as her fingers moved inside her tiny, sparkling, silver g-string. Ryan was neither a prude nor naïve; but back home he avoided such displays because he was much more in the public eye.

The topless waitress soon returned with a loaded tray. Ryan tried not to stare at her large drooping, breasts as she placed a bottle of beer and a spirit tumbler in front of each man

'I reckoned that as we were only staying for one drink we'd better make it a good one - so I got us a bourbon chaser,' explained Kramer. 'Cheers.'

'Cheers,' responded Ryan, matching Kramer as he raised the bottle of Bud to his lips.

By now the drinks had begun to work their way through his system, and the pressure on his bladder signalled the need for release.

'Where are the toilets?'

Kramer pointed to a door in the far corner. Ryan got up a little unsteadily and made his way out to the toilet.

Ryan let the door bang noisily behind him and exited the filthy toilets as quickly as he could. His trip to the toilet, whilst very necessary, was an experience he didn't wish to repeat.

'Jason's been busy,' thought Ryan, spying the two blonde women sat either side of him. Kramer's right arm was draped over the shoulder of one of the girls, his hand teasingly stroking her exposed back.

Kramer stood up as Ryan neared the table.

'I guess it's our lucky day. These two charming girls wanted to buy us a drink - and I really don't like disappointing pretty women!' The women giggled. 'The stunning one on the right is Jo-Anne, and the gorgeous creature on the left is….,' Kramer struggled to remember.

'…Caroline,' said the blonde, helping Kramer out.

'The ugly brute who's just returned is Ryan.'

Ryan shook their proffered hands and sat down. Discreetly, he looked the girls over. Jo-Anne was a little shorter than Caroline; and he could see from the dark roots that - unlike her friend, she was not a natural blonde. He put her age at about twenty-six. A slightly-buckled nose spoilt an otherwise slim and attractive face. A red and black embroidered camisole hung down over black trousers. She seemed to have been adopted by Kramer; his arm was once again slung round her slim shoulders.

Ryan was surprised that Jason had chosen Jo-Anne over Caroline, for the taller girl was even more attractive. Well, perhaps Jo-Anne had chosen Jason; after all, the girls seemed to have found them. He was getting used to girls being more predatory than he had been brought up to expect. Caroline was dressed in a purple satin halter-top, the silky material clinging provocatively to her ample chest. Definitely more than a standard British handful there, he thought. She was slightly round-faced; that, and a suspicion of excess fat on her upper arms, prevented Ryan from classing her as a babe. He guessed that she was probably a year or two older than Jo-Anne.

Maybe they weren't mamma's idea of the girl next door - but they didn't look like tarts either. He relaxed. In for a penny, he thought.

'They thought we needed lightening up - so they brought some slammers over with them. Down in one ole buddy!'

Kramer slammed his glass on the table, and then downed the strong drink in one swallow. He was quickly followed by both girls. Ryan was left with little choice but to follow suit. The drink tasted unexpectedly bitter, but then it was a long time since he had last had tequila. A warm fiery glow quickly spread through his belly.

As midnight approached, the club began to fill out. The stage show was replaced by a DJ. Although not to Ryan's taste, the monotonous dance music was drawing people onto the large dance floor. By now, Ryan was laughing at even the slightest joke. He was having a great time and put that down to the drinks he had had. Internally, the date-rape drug Rohypnol was beginning to do its job. Exaggerating the effects of alcohol, it was steadily loosening his inhibitions.

'I wanna dance,' yelled Caroline, over the loud pounding bass.

'Go on Ryan, show the girl how it's done,' said Kramer. 'This I just gotta see!'.

Caroline grabbed Ryan's arm and hauled him, unprotesting, out onto the dance floor. Ryan enthusiastically attempted to copy the dancers around him. Amused smiles greeted his flailing arm and leg movements. Still sat at the table, Kramer and Jo-Anne were laughing uncontrollably at his efforts.

Ryan was in a world of his own; unaware that he was becoming less and less co-ordinated. As Caroline apologised yet again for Ryan's clumsiness she looked at her watch, and decided it was time to end the madness.

'I think it's time we got outta here,' she screamed, into his ear. 'I'm ready for something better than dancing!'

Ryan just nodded. He didn't know what was going on - but he was keen to get his hands on Caroline. Focused entirely on Caroline, he had forgotten all about Jason and Jo-Anne.

Caroline took Ryan by the hand and led him out of the club. Out on the street, cabs were already lined up, waiting in the hope of picking up a fare. Caroline spoke to a large coloured driver and then bundled Ryan into the back of his cab. As the cab set off down the dark street, she wrapped herself round Ryan and gave him a long slow smoochy kiss - her tongue eagerly exploring his mouth. The driver had seen it all before; but still kept one eye on the road and another on the couple in the back as he drove them out of town.

By the time the cab pulled up at the motel, Ryan was a mass of anticipation. As Caroline paid the driver he playfully fondled her white-trousered bottom. He was sure he could feel the elasticated edge of her knickers through the soft material.

Ryan thought nothing of it as Caroline led him straight to one of the motel rooms. Reaching inside her handbag, she found a set of keys and opened the door.

Once inside the room, Caroline wrapped her left-arm round Ryan's strongly muscled neck. Her free right-hand slid down his body to stroke his growing erection.

'I just have to use the bathroom, honey,' she said, disentangling herself.

As she disappeared into the bathroom, locking the cheap brown wooden door, Ryan began to undress. He was all fingers and thumbs, and by the time Caroline re-emerged, had just managed to get his shirt off. Caroline, on the other hand, had stripped down to bright-red bra and briefs.

'Let me help you, tiger,' she said, running a hand through the fine silky hair covering his chest. She deftly undid his shoes and pulled off his trousers.

'I think you should go to the bathroom now, don't you?'

Ryan needed no persuading. Caroline waited until she could hear Ryan peeing into the bowl before she grabbed her coat and quietly let herself out. Outside the door, she exchanged a quick grin with the shivering young blonde girl who had been waiting to take her place. The new girl, Jaqui, was also dressed in bright-red underwear and could have been Caroline's twin - if she hadn't been only fifteen years old. Keen to get out of the cold, Jaqui wasted no time in entering the motel room.

In the next room, the cameraman, hidden behind one-way glass, had watched the coming and going with amusement; but now his job began in earnest. As Jaqui made herself comfortable on the bed, he made sure the digital camcorder was switched on and focused.

Ryan came out of the bathroom, proud and naked.

'Come to bed, big boy,' beckoned Jaqui.

In his befuddled state, Ryan didn't notice that it wasn't Caroline on the bed. The bright-red lingerie held all his attention. The hidden camera continued to fill its voracious memory, as Jaqui stripped off and then mounted an unprotesting Ryan. As the couple rocked and bucked on the bed, the bedroom door opened yet again to let in another naked girl. The teenaged brunette joined Jaqui and Ryan on the bed. In his drugged state, this all seemed perfectly normal to Ryan - if a trifle lucky. He couldn't understand where the new girl had come from, but he wasn't about to complain.

Ryan's mind might have been willing; but the combined effects of the booze and drug had rendered him a less than wonderful stud. The girls made sure that the cameraman got sufficient pictures, before Jaqui decided it was time to move on to the next stage of the plan.

'It's Jacuzzi time,' she whispered, giving Ryan's ear lobe a little nibble.

The two girls helped an enfeebled Ryan off the bed. As fast as they could, they ushered him out of the room and along the outside of the motel to the pool. It really didn't matter that there was no Jacuzzi.

Ryan sensed that something wasn't right. The large expanse of water didn't look like a Jacuzzi to him. But even though his body stiffened in protest, the two young girls had more than enough strength to tip him into the pool. The girls checked that Ryan was floating before they dashed back to the room to grab their things. Behind the glass, the cameraman interrupted his clearing up to phone the police.

Officer Joe Peccorino slammed the squad-car door shut. While he waited for his partner to get out of the car he switched on his torch. Together, they cautiously approached the pool. The torch was not going to be needed for the area around the pool was brightly lit. The two policemen stood on the edge of the pool, and looked down at the inert figure sitting in the shallow end. Ryan's arms were resting on the poolside - as if he had tried to get out and failed.

'This goon's right out of it,' said Peccorino.

'Yeah. More sleeping beauty than bathing beauty,' replied Officer Mike Docherty.

'Okay, we'd better get him outta there – boy, do I hate getting wet!' Peccorino was peed at the thought of riding around in a wet uniform; all for the sake of a drunk. It's not as if the guy was doing anyone any harm; but they had been called, so they had to do something.

Peccorino poked Ryan with his nightstick. Ryan opened his eyes.

'Okay pal, bath time's over. Let's have you outta there!'

Despite the command, Ryan didn't move. His eyes closed as he blacked out again.

Peccorino looked at Docherty and shrugged his shoulders. 'You take his right arm.'

The two officers took an arm each and hauled Ryan out of the water; not caring that his limp body banged and scraped along the rough edges of the pool. Hidden in bushes, the cameraman busily snapped away. The pictures of Ryan, naked, in the company of the police, would join the pictures of him with the two under-age girls. The police may not do much about Ryan - but the papers would have a field-day.

Peccorino fetched a blanket from the car while Docherty checked Ryan over. Although Ryan had opened his eyes briefly when they grabbed him, he had blacked out again on the poolside. Docherty turned his head away in disgust as he caught a whiff of the alcohol on Ryan's breath. Why did people never learn their limits. He had no sympathy for the pathetic figure that lay dripping on the tiling at his feet. They should be catching real bad guys, not messing around with drunks in motel pools. More than likely the guy wouldn't even get booked. A wet uniform and a mass of paperwork for nothing. The 45 year-old policeman shook his head in frustration.

The Desk sergeant looked the naked figure up and down through tired eyes. It was three o'clock in the morning - the graveyard shift. Ryan was being propped up by the two policemen who had brought him in. He kept drifting in and out of consciousness.

'Another drunk?' It had already been a busy night, and the cells in the downtown precinct were filling up.

'Yes Sarge,' answered Officer Peccorino.

'What was he doing, then?' The Sergeant optimistically hoped for an interesting report of a naked drunk causing mayhem in a public place.

'When we got to him, he was just sitting, naked, in the swimming pool at the 'Sleep Eazy' motel', answered Peccorino.

'In the shallow end,' added Docherty, helpfully.

'I take it you checked him out with the Motel owner?'

The two policemen exchanged a pained look.

'First thing we did Sarge.' Peccorino answered for the pair of them. 'The owner says he's not a guest. He'd never seen him before – clothed or otherwise!'

'I don't suppose there was any ID?' asked the Desk sergeant,, addressing Docherty, whom he considered to be the senior of the cops.

'No such luck. We had a look round the pool and couldn't find any clothes - zilch.'

'So, we got this unknown naked guy in a swimming pool on private property?' The Sergeant played with his pencil as he looked Ryan up and down again.

'Any reports of any trouble?'

'No, we just got this call saying there was a naked man in the grounds.' Peccorino let Docherty do the talking.

'So, no felonies and no misdemeanours?'

'No Sarge.'

The Desk sergeant rubbed the palm of his hand back and forth across his chin as he considered what to do.

'Okay, get him some clothes, then throw him in with the other drunks to sleep it off. We'll speak to Sleeping Beauty in the morning.'

CHAPTER 10

3:45 a.m. Tuesday 18th September, Indianapolis – United States

It was still dark, and in the early hours of the morning, the wind felt even chillier as Kramer stepped out of the cab in front of the police precinct. Even though he had stopped drinking two hours earlier, the evening session had left him feeling very fragile. He'd far rather have been in bed than walking into a police station. He trudged up the stone steps into the unwelcoming precinct building. Kramer's previous experience of police stations had not left him with any love for the places.

'I'd like to report a missing person.' Jason Kramer stood in front of the battered reception desk. The police station was about as quiet as it ever got, but even so, several police officers were noisily exchanging friendly banter whilst tapping away at keyboards, writing up reports of the night's mayhem.

'When did you last see this person?' asked the Desk Sergeant. The tall dark-haired man standing in front of him looked very familiar. He racked his brains for a name.

'Only a coupla hours ago, but he's a stranger in town. He'd had a bit to drink, and we kinda got separated.'

'What's the guy's name?'

'Ryan Clarke.'

'The racing-driver?' The Desk Sergeant had watched the Grand Prix, and hearing Ryan's name it suddenly clicked, and he could now place the face of the man standing in front of him.

'That's right.' Jason was only slightly surprised that the policeman recognised the name. After all, millions of people would have seen the TV coverage of the race.

'Thought I recognised you. I saw the race – you're Jason Kramer aren't you?'

Jason nodded.

'Please describe Mr Clarke for me.'

'About 5 foot ten. 140 pounds. Fair curly hair. British. I think he's got some scars on his body. He told me he once had a bad accident and had to be cut out of his seat belt, he got badly nicked in the process.'

The Desk Sergeant made some notes on a pad with a well-chewed yellow pencil he removed from behind his ear.

'Where did you last see him?'

'In the Paradiso club. But I've been right round the area looking for him.'

'Wait there a second.' The Desk Sergeant asked a colleague to cover the desk, then he went down to the cells to take a look at the drunk Peccorino and Docherty had rounded-up. The disinfectant was fighting a losing battle against the noxious odours emanating from the half-filled cell block, and the Desk Sergeant blenched as he entered the drunk's cell. Ryan, clothed in a set of rough blue prison overalls, was snoring noisily on a bare bed. The cop unbuttoned the top of the prison outfit. At waist level there was a white scar. The Desk Sergeant fastened the buttons, and then quickly left the cell for the sanctuary of the front desk.

'Yeah, it sure looks like we've got your buddy downstairs.'

'Where d'ya find him?'

'He was picked up at the 'Sleep Easy' motel.

'Picked up - not found?'

'That's right – you're friend was found naked in the swimming pool. Someone called it in. Have you any idea what he was doing there?' The Desk Sergeant looked Kramer straight in the eye.

'Well, he was with a girl called Caroline; they both disappeared at the same time. I thought he'd just struck lucky!'

'Some luck! I guess this girl must have rolled him. We couldn't find any clothes or anything; no sign of a wallet.' The policeman was reluctantly coming round to the idea that Ryan was a victim rather than a villain.

'What's Ryan have to say about it?' asked Kramer, eagerly.

'Nothing, he's been out cold since he was brought in.'

Kramer nodded understandingly; it looked like he would have to wait for Ryan's view of events.

'Have you booked him?'

'No. It seems he hasn't done anything wrong.'

'So, can I take him away?'

'I wanted to have a word with him later.'

'Is that strictly necessary? I believe he's flying home later this morning. It was my fault he got lost - do you really want him to leave with a bad impression of Indianapolis?'

'No, but I think we need to find out more about this girl. What do you know about her?'

'Only that she was called Caroline. We met her in the club that night. I can give you a description.'

The cop tapped his pencil on the wooden desk while he thought it over. If Ryan was happy to let it go, then they would have one less crime to solve. It was very tempting to sweep the incident under the carpet. He reached a decision.

'Come back with some clothes, and we'll see.'

As Kramer had requested, the cab was still waiting outside the police station. On the quiet roads, it took no more than ten minutes to drive Kramer back to his apartment on the outskirts of town. Quickly, he gathered a few clothes together. Given the height difference between the two drivers, the clothes weren't going to fit - but Kramer figured Ryan was in no state to mind. Fifteen minutes later, he was back at the police station, once again leaving the cab-driver happily sitting outside - the clock running.

Entering the police station for a second time, Kramer had to wait while the Desk Sergeant processed a young kid that had been picked up for fighting. The kid was not co-operating, and Kramer watched in amusement as three cops wrestled with the fat and heavily-tattooed youngster. Eventually, the police bundled the kid off to the cells, and Kramer was able to talk to the Desk Sergeant.

'So, are you a race fan then?' asked Kramer, keen to get the policeman on his side.

'I catch a few on TV. That was the first F1 race I've seen though. I prefer the 500. There's more action.'

'That depends on where you're sitting!' Jason laughed.

'Clarke's the guy that turned in on you - isn't he?'

'Something like that. He's my team-mate, and I'd rather he didn't get mad at me again this weekend. Can't you do us a favour? Maybe one or two of you guys could use some tickets for the 500 next year?'

'Forget the tickets - but there's always the Police Charity.' They both knew an agreement had been struck.

Ten minutes later, Ryan was sleeping on the back seat of the cab - in an ill-fitting assortment of clothes. It had been like dressing a large rag doll as they forced his loose limbs into the easy fitting clothes.

It took the combined strength of Kramer and the cab-driver to haul Ryan's dead weight into the hotel, and it took all of Jason's charm to persuade the disapproving receptionist to give them the key-card for Ryan's room. Together, the cab-driver and Kramer awkwardly manoeuvred Ryan up to his room. Both men were relieved to dump Ryan on his bed. Kramer pulled out a wad of notes and paid off the cab-driver - who was more than happy with the relative fortune he had received, for what had been an easy night's work. He would also have a good story to tell; after all, how many cabbies got to ferry two F1 race drivers?

Once the cab-driver had gone, Kramer undressed Ryan, and then reckoning that there was no point in going home for just a few hours, settled down on the couch. It would also be wise to keep a close eye on Ryan in case he took a turn for the worse.

Ryan groggily came to. It was still dark in the hotel room. A few seconds later, he retched and realised why he had woken up. Uneasily, he struggled out of the bed, and only just managed to reach the bathroom before he threw-up. He hugged the toilet bowl for a few minutes, while his body did its best to rid itself of the accumulated toxins. Eventually, he was satisfied that there was nothing more to bring up. He rinsed his mouth with cold water and staggered sleepily back towards his bed; not noticing that he had stepped in the trail of vomit on the bathroom floor.

Kramer had dozed off, but the sound of Ryan vomiting had woken him up. It took him a few seconds to remember where he was, but then he smelt the sour vomit. He wrinkled his nose, then moved across to the window. He flung open the curtains, and noisily opened the window to let in some fresh air, just as Ryan emerged from the bathroom.

'Morning, pal.'

Ryan groaned. 'Is it?' His head was throbbing, and there was a nasty bitter taste in his mouth.

'You gave me quite a scare, old buddy?'

Ryan shook his head. 'Yeah how?' He tried to think what had happened. He had a vague memory of two girls - and some strippers, but nothing after that. He couldn't even remember returning to the hotel. He must have had a hell of a lot to drink.

'Hang on, I need the bathroom again.' Ryan made his way uneasily back to the bathroom; embarrassed at parading his nakedness in front of Kramer. Now that he was more awake, he grimaced as he spotted the trail of vomit on the carpet. He only just held on to the contents of his stomach as he saw the mess in the bathroom. He flushed the toilet, before raising the vomit-splashed toilet seat to pee. Outside, Jason settled into an easy chair, and picked up the previous week's copy of Autosport to read whilst he waited.

Ryan was embarrassed at the state of the bathroom. He could have just left it to the maid, but he had been raised to clear up his own mess. Using a face flannel and plenty of toilet-roll he was able to clean the place up; although it still stank. He quickly took a shower to clean himself up. Dressed in a large towelling-gown he rejoined Jason in the bedroom.

'What happened, then?' he asked.

'You mean you can't remember?' asked Kramer, rather incredulously.

'I remember a table dancing club, two girls and Tequila slammers.'

'Yeah - but what happened after that. One minute you were dancing with Caroline then...,' Kramer snapped his fingers, 'You were gone!'

Ryan shook his head.

'I don't know what happened next - I can't remember a thing.'

'Not even the cops?'

'What cops?'

'I found you in the police precinct. You'd been taken into custody - you mean you can't remember the swimming pool, and being naked either?'

This was just getting worse for Ryan. He could just about cope with the idea of misbehaving - he was no angel, but he couldn't understand why he couldn't remember any of the events that Jason was describing.

'Anything else?' Ryan hoped that was all.

'I guess you must have been rolled. Apparently there was no sign of your clothes - or your wallet!'

'Fuck it!' exclaimed Ryan 'They must have got my phone as well.'

'Guess so. Thing is, do you want to report this to the cops? They don't exactly bust a gut on muggings.'

Ryan held his head in his hands as he thought it over. It wasn't easy given the fugg that pervaded his brain. He suspected that Kramer was right, and he would become just another unsolved crime statistic. And, from what Kramer had said, he didn't fancy returning to the police station as an object of amusement. He sighed.

'I think I'm going to have to report it, or the Credit Card companies won't be very happy!' It was clear he was going to have to spend some time on the phone sorting the mess out. Fortunately, he'd not taken his PDA with him. The electronic diary held details of his Credit cards and all of his phone numbers. He'd also need to replace his missing phone. It was going to be a busy morning - his flight was at one o'clock, and he needed to check in by eleven.

'Look, do you want any breakfast?'

'Just get us a coffee, and some aspirin, will you? I'd better get dressed, and start sorting this shit out. As I haven't got any money or plastic - can you lend us some cash, and pay the hotel for me?'

'No problem.' Kramer fished out his wallet and handed Ryan a couple of hundred dollars – all of his remaining cash. He could always get some more from the hotel cash-machine downstairs. 'That do you for the moment?'

Ryan gratefully took the money from Kramer's outstretched hand.

'You're a pal! I guess I spoilt our lads' night out!' apologised Ryan.

'That's all right - made it kinda interesting, don't you think!'

Ryan snorted, 'That kind of interesting I can do without!'

CHAPTER 11

6:00 a.m. Wednesday 19th September, Gatwick Airport - England

'Good morning, sir - it's time to wake up.' The stewardess spoke with a soft mid-west American accent as she gently shook Ryan's shoulder.

Ryan rubbed his eyes, then glanced at his watch as he struggled to wake up. His Rolex Oyster showed the time in both the U.K and Indianapolis. It was six in the morning London time, and the U.S Airways flight from Pittsburgh was on the approach run to Gatwick. Ryan watched the stewardess as she moved on through the First Class cabin of the Boeing 767, rousing passengers that were still asleep.

Ryan had spent most of the journey asleep. Despite feeling lousy, he had had a busy final hour in Indianapolis. After a light breakfast, which refused to stay down, he phoned the police to report his stolen wallet and phone. He then cancelled his credit cards - fortunately he belonged to a card security scheme and only had to make a single call. He had still felt in a daze, as Jason drove him out to the airport and guided him through the formalities of check-in. He had dozed fitfully on the first leg of the journey to Pittsburgh. During the four-hour stopover in Pittsburgh, he had forced himself to eat a substantial meal. The nausea had passed, but he still felt uncommonly tired. He had never felt like this after other heavy drinking bouts, and he didn't think that he and Jason had hit it too hard. What puzzled him most was that he couldn't remember a thing after the stripper in the lap-dancing club. Neither could he understand how he got separated from Jason. In his befuddled state in the hotel, he had not really taken in all that Jason had told him. Never mind, he would just have to phone Jason and ask him. He was very glad he had slept his way through his short incarceration in the police cells. From what he'd seen of American police stations, he didn't much fancy being awake in an American prison cell!

Because of his extended stopover in America, Ryan had been unable to get away with a single item of hand luggage. Even though it had been a long walk from the plane to the luggage hall, he still had to kick his heels for the best part of twenty minutes, before his much battered green Delsey suitcase appeared on the crowded luggage carousel. Ryan quickly hauled the bag off the belt, accidentally banging into a large American who was bad-temperedly waiting. Ryan muttered a hasty apology and headed for customs. He planned on taking the Gatwick Express, and would have to take the connecting mono-rail service to the North Terminal for the train station.

Flashlights exploded feet from his face as he emerged into the busy arrivals hall. Ryan momentarily froze - like a rabbit caught in car headlights, before realising he had no option but to run the gauntlet of waiting pressmen.

The moment he was through the barriers, the waiting reporters rushed forward, thrusting microphones towards his face.

'Mr Clarke, what were you doing naked in the pool?'

Ryan heard the question clearly enough through the barrage of questions being fired at him. Before he could even say: "no comment", he caught the tail-end of another question.

'…enjoy two girls at once?'

Pale faced, he carried on walking whilst he decided what to do. He didn't know what the reporters were talking about, but this was obviously more serious than just being found naked in a motel swimming pool whilst drunk. And how did they know he was on that flight?

'Did you know they were both under age?'

The questions were getting worse, and he had no idea what was still to emerge. Ryan paused, and, as lights flashed, chose his words carefully.

'I have nothing to say at this moment. I will speak to you all later today, when I have had a chance to consult with my advisors.'

His lame statement was not enough to satisfy the journalists, and they continued to bray questions as he walked on. Ryan was convinced they would follow him if he took the train; he could not face a journey in their company, so he changed his plans and made his way to one of the VIP lounges, where he hoped to find a little peace and quiet. Above all, he needed time to think.

There were about a dozen people in the small lounge, and he could see one or two turn to each other and mutter as he walked by. He didn't know if they were talking about him, but he was beginning to feel like a leper as he took a seat.

'Have you got today's papers?' he asked, of a passing attendant.

'Certainly, sir,' the uniformed girl replied. 'Would you like the Times or the Telegraph?'

'Have you got the Sun and the Mirror?' he asked. He was embarrassed at having to ask for the tabloids - especially as he suspected he might be front-page news.

'I'll go and find them for you.' She smiled pleasantly, as she moved off on the errand.

When she returned, the smile was missing. Frostily, she handed the two newspapers to Ryan and promptly marched away.

"Grand Prix driver gets the ride of his life!" screamed the headline in the Sun. The sanitised picture that accompanied the story, clearly showed Ryan in bed with two girls; one of whom certainly looked quite young. Ryan wanted the floor to swallow him up. He felt his cheeks burning as he continued to read the story. Despite his embarrassment, he forced himself to read on; he had to know what he was being accused of. The pictures certainly gave him no chance of saying it wasn't true. He sighed deeply, as he finished the papers; then buried his head in his hands as he worked out his next move. If only he wasn't so tired.

After several minutes of deep thinking, he reached into the pocket of his jacket and fished out his new mobile phone. For once he had been grateful for airport shops; it had proved easier than he expected to buy a replacement phone. For once, having a new phone with a new number was a bonus - he could just imagine the many messages that would be waiting on the one he had lost. While he had waited for the connecting flight in Pittsburgh, he had charged up the phone and downloaded the phone book from his PDA to the snazzy small blue Nokia. Now, he rapidly searched through the address book for his business manager's number. He wouldn't appreciate being called at this time of day, but Ryan desperately needed help. He could really have used Victoria's PR skills, but under the circumstances, he didn't think she would be very willing to help. She was going to be yet another problem for him to deal with. The phone rang for a long time, before, at last, a sleepy voice answered.

'Tony Zervas. It's just gone six o'clock in the morning - so this had better be bloody good!' Tony had never been very easy first thing in the morning. By ten, he would be sweetness and light, but right now he sounded very disgruntled.

'Tony, it's Ryan, and it's nearer seven. We've got real big trouble. I'm at Gatwick - can you come and pick me up? Read the tabloids on the way, but please don't believe everything you see or read. Speak to you later. Bye.' Ryan rang off before Tony could reply. He didn't think it was a good idea to talk to Tony before he had properly woken up. Besides, he needed Tony to read the papers and get up to speed. He would phone him back in half an hour to let him know where to collect him. He turned the phone off again; he didn't want to be pestered while he worked out what to do. Above all, he didn't fancy having a public conversation about three-in-a-bed romps!

Ryan thought through his options. Clearly, the team would be pestered by reporters - so he would have to speak to Somerset sooner rather than later. Victoria was going to be another headache - he couldn't see how he was going to be able to square things with her. He was still very puzzled as to how any of this could have happened without his knowledge. He had been drunk before, even paralytic, but he had never been in a state where he couldn't recall his actions. He ordered a large Espresso from the girl who had fetched the papers. She was polite, but very reserved towards him. She clearly wasn't going to be joining his fan club! By the time he had finished the strong black coffee, he was beginning to feel more in control. It was going to be a really bad day, but he had finally come up with a plan of action.

He called the attendant over again. He could see that she was beginning to get annoyed.

'I know you don't like what you've seen in the papers, but I really do need your help. Is there another way out of here? I don't want to face the press again – not just yet!' He gave what he hoped was a winning smile.

'There is, but I'll have to check with the manager.' Her voice had thawed a little as she recognised Ryan's acute embarrassment. As she walked off, she thought about Ryan's request. She still didn't much like what he'd been up to - but she had no love for the press either. She had hated the way the media had hounded Princess Diana, and had no sympathy with the tabloids.

Presently, she returned with the young duty manager. He hadn't seen the papers, but, after some discussion, agreed to let Ryan out through the staff entrance. Ryan took his phone out again and called Tony.

'Tony, it's Ryan. Where are you now?'

'Just past Croydon - on the A23. I should be with you in half and hour or so. You really are a stupid bugger, aren't you? I don't know how we're going to get you out of this one!'

'I'm glad it's still: "we"! I thought you might just throw me to the wolves.'

'I still might - if you haven't got a good explanation, but, seeing as you are my bread and butter, I'm stuck with you for now.'

'Thanks, Tony - I really appreciate that. Listen, can you meet me just past the main South Terminal entrance - on the way out. They're going to let me use a staff exit. I don't want to leave my phone on, so I'll make sure I'm there before you. We can talk in the car. Okay?'

'Yeah, that's cool. Take care, you randy sod - and don't chat up any girls while you're waiting!' There was a hint of amusement in Tony's voice.

Tony had been Ryan's business manager for four years, and they complemented each other really well. Tony was part Greek - although no one quite knew which part! Most people suspected that there were even more nationalities present in his make up. He found most things amusing, but even while he smiled, he was likely to be considering where to put the knife in. The man was a born wheeler-dealer. If Tony couldn't help, then Ryan really would be in trouble.

Ryan waited in the lounge for twenty-five minutes, before getting up and seeking out the duty manager, who then led him out though the back of the VIP lounge and into the kitchens. It was a fair walk, before at last Ryan emerged into bright sunlight at the far end of the main entrance. He shivered in the cold early morning air, as he cautiously looked round the corner of the building and along the front of the main entrance. As he suspected, there were several cameramen and reporters standing in a huddle - no doubt reasoning that Ryan would have to leave the building eventually. He smiled at the thought of outwitting them, and moved back out of sight. Tony was late. Ryan had expected he might be, but he was still mightily relieved to see the familiar silver Porsche 911 cruise to a halt at the end of the terminal building - right in front of where he was standing.

Ryan threw his bag into the back of the car, and quickly got in. Tony pulled away before Ryan could even close the door.

Ryan felt himself being thrust back into the seat as Tony accelerated.

'Slow down, Tony, we don't want to get nicked for speeding as well!'

Tony took the hint and slowed slightly. He enjoyed showing off in the car, even though Ryan was a far better driver.

'Okay, what's the story then?'

'I really don't know,' said Ryan. 'It's obviously me in the pictures, but I don't remember anything about it at all. You've seen me drunk before - have you ever known me to lose complete recall of what I've done?'

Tony pulled the car out from behind a slow moving lime-green Renault, and put his foot down to overtake before answering.

'No. But I have known you to leap into bed with near strangers. Some people would say you just got lucky!'

'With a couple of underage girls? Do me a favour!' Ryan was not in the mood for any mickey-taking.

'Okay, okay I believe you. It's not your style. So how could it happen?'

'Drugs. I think I was drugged.'

'Yeah, with what and how?'

'I don't know, I really don't know - but I'd like to see a doctor before we do anything else.'

Ryan winced, as Tony slid down the inside of a car that was hogging the middle lane of the motorway. He wished he were driving; Tony might be an excellent businessman - but he was definitely not a very good driver.

'I buy that. If you're right, then that's got to be our best and only defence. If you weren't drugged - then you might find yourself working as a cabby next week!!' Tony laughed.

'If I give Doctor Foster a ring, can you drive me down to see him?'

'No worries. Whereabouts?'

'Sevenoaks.'

The private practice at Sevenoaks was convenient for Brands Hatch. Ryan had had to see Doctor Foster after a small accident a few years back, and had signed up with the Doctor as a result. Since then, their paths had crossed several times, and he was almost a friend. Foster was professional and very thorough, and fortunately very open to suggestions. Ryan hoped he would have no difficulty persuading the doctor to perform some tests.

As they sped north up the M23, Ryan fished his mobile from out of his shirt-pocket and phoned Doctor Foster. The phone rang for what seemed an age, and Ryan was just beginning to despair, when the doctor answered.

'Good morning, Doctor Foster, it's Ryan Clarke. I hope I didn't wake you?'

'No such luck, - I've just come in the door from my morning run.' The Doctor sounded a trifle out of breath. 'What can I do for you? Surely you haven't had an accident at this time of day?'

'No, no, nothing like that, but I do need to see you urgently. Could you see me first thing this morning?'

'Hold on, I'll just have a look at my list. Where are you at the moment?'

'On the M23, just approaching the M25,. I can be with you in fifteen to twenty minutes, if that's any help.' Ryan hoped he didn't sound too desperate.

'No problem, I can squeeze you in before my first patient at nine. The sooner you get here, the more time we'll have, but please don't bend the car - there's a good chap!'

Ryan exchanged a few pleasantries before hanging up. He sighed, and stretched to let out some of the tension. That was one potential problem resolved. He just hoped the doctor would be able to find something. If he couldn't – then, well, it didn't bear thinking about. One step at a time, he told himself.

'Listen, Tony, when we reach the M25, can you let me drive? I need you to phone Chris and set up a meeting for later this morning. I really don't want to speak to him until I've seen the quack. He's going to blow a whole shop full of fuses, so I want as much protection as possible. Is that okay?'

'So, Tony does all the dirty work huh!'

'That's right. For once, you can actually earn some of that fat commission I pay you! If you don't help me out of this one - then neither of us will be very marketable!'

'Are you sure you want to drive?' Tony took his eyes off the road to look at Ryan, who blanched as the car veered perilously close to a lorry on the inside.

'It's what I'm paid for! You do your job, and I'll do mine, and we'll both be happy.'

'Sure thing, boss.' Tony was in his element. He enjoyed a challenge, and this situation was certainly a new one on him. He smiled, as he thought about the prospect of raising his management fee - if he extracted Ryan from the mess. There was silver in every cloud, he thought. To Ryan's irritation, he began to hum: "Hi ho silver lining". Ryan shook his head; Tony was irrepressible.

It was only a short run up the M23 to the junction with the M25. Tony drove a further mile along the busy motorway before pulling over onto the hard shoulder. Even that early in the morning, the traffic was heavy, and Ryan felt badly exposed as he swapped places with Tony. Ryan quickly adjusted the seat, for Tony was several inches shorter. Choosing his moment, he carefully pulled out into the fast moving traffic. It was a relief to be back behind a wheel. He smoothly eased up through the gears, and worked his way into the fast lane.

After several miles of driving, he began to feel back in control. The familiar activity relaxed him, and enabled him to think calmly about the troubles to come. The meeting he was least looking forward to was the one with Victoria. Calm and serene, most of the time, he knew that when she did blow, she blew big time. He rather thought this would be one of those occasions. He wasn't sure she would be in the mood to listen to his explanation - no matter how convincing.

Ryan listened in as Tony phoned Somerset. Tony was very careful not to tell Chris that he was in the car with Ryan. The call was not very pleasant, but, grudgingly, Somerset accepted the suggestion of a meeting, and they settled on 11:00 at Brands Hatch. Tony grimaced as he put the phone down.

'I wouldn't say you were his favourite person at the moment. I hope you're right about the drugs.'

'So do I!'

After the steady motorway driving, Ryan was pleased when they turned off onto the local roads near Sevenoaks. Throwing the car round corners and playing with the gearbox was far more enjoyable, and far less likely to attract the attention of the police. He knew he really shouldn't, but he couldn't resist slamming the Porsche past a fast moving Mazda MX5 as they approached a series of tight bends. He threw the anchors on, and, in a screech of rubber, braked sufficiently to take the corner. He grinned, as he saw Tony nervously gripping the dashboard.

'Sorry, Tony - I needed that. Won't do it again.' Tony merely grunted; disappointed that he would never be able to handle the car like that - at least not without coming to grief!

The car crunched onto the gravel drive in front of the clinic just after 8:15 a.m. The sprawling, red-bricked Victorian building had been a cottage hospital until closed by the NHS. Dr Tim Foster had taken it over, and turned it into a private clinic. The clinic was well equipped, and was run like a very good hotel, right down to the large and immaculately groomed gardens. To salve his conscience, Dr Foster provided treatment for children free of charge, and frequently lent the facilities of the clinic to local doctors. As a result, the clinic had a very good local reputation, and Dr Foster was welcome everywhere.

Ryan shook Dr Foster's large hand. The handshake was warm and radiated confidence. The doctor may have had a run that morning, but his fitness regime was struggling to keep his large frame in check. He had played rugby, right up to his fortieth birthday, but had then declared it a sport not suited to the middle-aged. His face still bore the telltale scars of time spent in the scrum. Now, in his early fifties, he exercised to work off the corporate lunches he was forced to attend. He enjoyed treating sportsmen, and as well as a couple of racing drivers he had a number of golfers on his books. Ever since he had first treated him, he had followed Ryan's career with interest.

'I think it might be best if we talked alone.' Dr Foster nodded in the direction of Tony.

'Yes, of course. Tony, can you go and find something to do. We need to put together a press statement some time today, perhaps you could make a start on it.'

'Will do.' Ryan could tell that Tony was disappointed at being excluded from the consultation.

Dr Foster walked Ryan into a plush consulting room, and invited him to sit down.

'Okay, what's the story?'

Ryan handed over the newspapers. The doctor put the papers down on his desk, while he took out a pair of reading glasses from a red spectacle-case. From time to time, the doctor peered over the top of his glasses at Ryan, as he read the lurid descriptions of his activities. Eventually, Dr Foster carefully folded the papers, and handed them back to Ryan.

'So, what can I do for you? This doesn't look like a medical problem – unless you think you've caught something?'

'Ouch - I really hadn't thought of that!' Ryan was horrified at the thought of yet another unforeseen problem. 'I came to see you, because I believe I was drugged. I can't remember a thing about the incidents described, and that is just so out of character, it's untrue. Is it possible I could have been drugged?'

'Well, there are certainly one or two drugs that could have that effect. How long ago was this?'

The two men did their best to work out how many hours had passed since Ryan might have been drugged. Taking into account the fact that Indianapolis was five hours behind GMT, it could have been as long as thirty hours ago.

'We might be lucky,' concluded Dr Foster. 'Traces of drugs can stay in the blood for up to three days. Take your jacket off, and roll up your sleeve.' The doctor fetched a syringe, and a set of phials. Ryan turned his head away as the doctor slid the needle home as painlessly as he could.

'Well, we'll just take these away for testing. I'm afraid, that could take an hour or so. Maybe you'd like to wait in one of the lounges?'

'Not if they have newspapers. I'd rather have a walk in the garden.'

'As you wish. I'll send someone out to find you when I have the results back.'

Ryan got to his feet, and shook the doctor's hand.

'I hope you find something doctor.'

'We'll just have to cross our fingers, I'm afraid.'

After seeing Ryan out, Dr Foster took the blood samples down to the laboratory, and handed half of the samples to an assistant for testing. He didn't tell the assistant what to look for, as he had a feeling they had better go by the book on this one. The other samples he labelled and put into safe storage, in case any other interested parties needed to test the blood.

It was forty-five minutes before a middle-aged white-coated nurse found Ryan sitting on a bench in the garden. He had enjoyed the opportunity to sit quietly in the fresh country air. Peace and quiet were going to be rare commodities in the days ahead.

'Mr Clarke, the doctor will see you now.' She smiled sweetly at Ryan - she hadn't seen the papers that day.

Ryan sat nervously in the consulting room, as the doctor carefully studied the results of the blood tests. Eventually, he put the sheet of paper down and took off his glasses.

'I think we may be in luck!' The doctor sounded pretty cheerful, and Ryan appreciated the Doctor making it sound like a shared problem.

'There is a trace of a sedative, and no sign of any nasty little bugs'.

'That's a relief – Victoria's going to be very upset as it is!'

'I don't envy you that one.' The doctor shook his head; he had a fair idea of the reaction Ryan would face from his girlfriend.

'Have you been taking any medication recently, sleeping tablets or such like?'

'No, doctor. They're not exactly compatible with driving a high performance car at over 200 mph, and I was in Indianapolis to race, you know!'

The doctor grunted. 'You have a point. Do you remember anything at all of that evening?'

'I remember being in a lap dancing club, and seeing a girl strip on stage. I remember that quite clearly, but after that - nothing.'

'Well, that and the traces of sedative we've found, tie in with a drug called Rohypnol. Have you heard of it?'

'No, should I?'

'It's also been called the date-rape drug. I'm not saying you've been raped, but it makes people open to suggestion. It removes their inhibitions, and, even more importantly, causes a form of amnesia. All of this fits with what you have told me.'

Ryan sighed with relief.

'Thank you. That's just what I needed to hear. Now I've got to persuade an awful lot of other people. I don't suppose you could prepare a short statement of what you have found? I know you can't prepare a full report at such notice, but I need something to show the press.'

The doctor toyed with an expensive silver fountain pen as he thought it over.

'I think I can do something. I'm afraid it will have to be fairly vague, and full of reservations.'

The doctor turned to his right, and began to type on a notebook computer. Ten minutes later, he pressed the print key, and a page of headed notepaper spewed out of the printer that sat beside his desk. He passed the sheet over to Ryan.

'..I examined Mr Clarke at 8:45 today. Blood tests indicate the presence of a sedative. Preliminary findings suggest that this may be Rohypnol, although further tests will be needed to confirm the findings. Further samples of blood have been retained, and will be made available to appropriate parties on request.'

'Thank you very much, doctor. This may be the most important sheet of paper I've ever been given.' He folded the statement, and slid it into the inside pocket of his jacket.

Five minutes later, Ryan and Tony were on the way to Brands Hatch; with Tony driving. Ryan needed more time to think, so very reluctantly, he let Tony get back behind the wheel for the short journey to Vantec's factory.

Ryan waited for Tony to turn the engine off, then he touched him on the arm.

'I think it would be better if you went in first.' Tony could hear the worry in Ryan's voice; he nodded.

'Just let Chris read this, then phone my mobile and I'll come up.' Ryan handed over the statement from Dr Foster.

Inside the plush office, Chris Somerset was pacing up and down, fretting. The incident was an unwelcome distraction from the things that really mattered. How could Ryan let him down now? It was bad enough to lose one driver a season; he'd hate to lose Ryan, but could he continue to use a driver with the morals of an alley cat? It would be difficult for the team to be taken seriously. The press would be interested in the driver for all of the wrong reasons. The car and the team would be playing second fiddle. It would be like the tail wagging the dog. He looked at his watch. Ryan was late. He sighed deeply. He still didn't know what to do for the best. The intercom interrupted his thinking to announce Tony's arrival.

Tony knocked on the frosted glass door and entered.

Somerset was standing, but showed no inclination to shake Tony's extended hand.

'Where's Ryan?' There was a hard edge to his voice, and his face reddened. As he spoke, Somerset looked over Tony's shoulder expecting to see Ryan.

Tony blushed; it was going to be tough. The tabloids were all spread out on the table in front of them - somehow it seemed much worse spread across such an expanse.

'He asked that you read this first.' Tony passed over the sheet of paper.

'He thinks a little bit of paper will make it all right, does he?' The sarcasm was bitter. Tony made no comment. For all his bluster, Somerset took the time to read the paper, then he sat down and invited Tony to do likewise.

'Is Ryan here?'

'Yes, he said to call him when you'd read the doctor's note.'

'Get him in here - right now!'

'I'll have to phone him - can I use your phone?'

Ryan climbed the stairs, slowly. He was in no hurry for the meeting. On reaching the door, he checked his hair and made sure he was presentable. This was no time to upset Somerset further. He gave what he hoped was a confident knock on the glass door, then took a deep breath and entered.

Somerset sat with folded arms, and looked Ryan up and down for a few moments, before ordering him to sit down.

'I don't know what to think,' he said. 'I would like to believe the doctor, but you well know, I have found you in bed with other women in the past.' Somerset wagged a disapproving finger at Ryan. He was alluding to an episode that had taken place three years before, when he had accidentally disturbed Ryan in his hotel room. Such a free and easy love life was alien to Somerset, who had been faithfully married for thirty years. He didn't approve of blatant bed hopping, although he knew the drivers were easy targets for the girls on the circuit.

'I was not in control - I have no memory of any of this.' Ryan waved a hand over the papers in front of him.

'Can this ...,' Somerset reread the note, 'Rohypnol really do this?'

'I bloody well hope so - for there is no other explanation that makes sense to me.' Ryan could feel Somerset thawing, and hoped that a show of confidence would bring him round.

'This is a real mess. Even if you are blameless, some of this is going to stick.'

'I know that, and it's me it's going to stick to!' Ryan knew he was going to suffer for some time.

'I need you to drive at the top of your form. Indianapolis was not too good for you. If I stick up for you, you're going to have to be whiter than white for the rest of the season. As for next year...' Somerset left the question open.

'I know. The best thing I can do is put it together on the track. But what do we do now?' Ryan tried to steer Somerset on to a positive track. He didn't need reminding that his contract chances had just nose-dived.

'This is going to generate a lot of publicity. Maybe we can use that.' Somerset paused whilst he thought. His face had lost its redness, and he was beginning to exude a degree of positive energy.

'Okay, well, first we must issue the doctor's statement. The press won't let it lie there - but it may buy us a little time. Secondly, while they're interested in you, we might as well make good use of the coverage. It's not often Vantec gets press inches! I will phone round the sponsors, and see if any of them are interested in using you this week. In any event, you had better do the rounds of the sponsors. You are going to get fed up of apologising, but you got yourself into this - so tough! And next week, you are going to have to drive better than you've driven so far this season. Right now, we'd better get something down on paper. The PR people will dress it up later.'

Somerset phoned down for some coffee, and then the three of them set about producing the first draft of a press release - explaining that Ryan had been doped with Rohypnol, and what Rohypnol could do. It took half an hour to produce something that looked sufficiently plausible and authoritative. Somerset then dismissed Ryan and Tony. At Ryan's request, he reluctantly agreed to keep in contact via Tony.

Ryan desperately wanted some sleep, but knew he would have to face Victoria sooner rather than later. He closed his eyes, and tried to rest, as Tony drove them back to Ryan's flat in Chelsea.

'It looks like the press are here.' Tony's voice woke Ryan from the shallow slumber he had fallen into.

'Just drive round to the car park. I haven't got the remote with me, but you can key the number into the key pad.'

Tony drove past the press, round to the back of the luxury apartments, and down the ramp of the underground car park. He pressed a button, and his window glided down with a whisper. As Ryan called out the numbers, he keyed them into the metal keypad at the side of the gates. The gates opened and they were inside - away from prying eyes.

'I think, that's the first time I've appreciated your tinted windows!' said Ryan.

'They have other uses too,' boasted Tony.

'Yeah, well the less said about them the better. Look, do you mind waiting in the car until I've seen Victoria?'

'Are you sure you don't want me to talk to her?'

'You must be kidding - I don't think this row is suitable for substitutes. There could be blood!' Ryan was only half joking.

'Rather you than me, then. Don't forget I'm out here, though - I don't want to spend the night locked in your bloody car park!'

Ryan took the lift up to his apartment. It was not the fastest lift in the world, but he was still no nearer working out what to say to Victoria, as the doors swished open. He wasn't even sure Victoria would be in the flat. He hadn't felt like phoning, as he knew he wouldn't have a chance of getting his explanation in first. This was one of the few times he wondered about the wisdom of having given her a key. He crept up to the front door of his flat and listened. There was no sound from inside, but that didn't mean anything. He straightened up, and steeled himself. He slid the key into the lock. There was no chance of surprising Victoria if she was in there.

As he opened the door a few inches, he just had time to see a raised arm. Even as he pulled the door closed, a heavy glass ornament crashed into the door and shattered. It was a small irony that the only ornaments he possessed had been bought for him by Victoria. He just prayed that she had left his hi-fi and CD collection alone. He reached into his pocket, and found the doctor's note. He hoped it would work some more magic. Ryan slid the note through the letterbox; then he stood back, and waited.

Victoria watched the folded sheet float to the floor. She made no move to pick it up. He couldn't write his way out of this one. She sat and waited. Outside the door, Ryan also waited. He sat down, and prepared to sit it out. At least she couldn't throw things at him while he was outside. He checked his watch; he would give her ten minutes, and then try again.

In the end, it only took a few minutes for Victoria's curiosity to get the better of her. She walked over to the door, and carefully picked the letter out of the glass that lay below and around the sheet. She unfolded the piece of paper, and began to read as she walked back to the sofa. She had expected a scruffy hand-written note from Ryan, and was very surprised to see a well-typed statement instead. She looked to see who the author was before continuing. She recognised the doctor's name, and settled down on the sofa to read.

Ryan got to his feet as he heard his front door click open.

'You can come in - it's quite safe.' Nevertheless, Victoria's voice carried an edge.

Ryan pushed the door open, and tried to look around without making it obvious. Inwardly, he sighed with relief, as far as he could see, there was no damage other than the glass on the floor. He picked his way through the glass, and stood waiting for Victoria to speak.

'I'm not sure I believe this.' Victoria waved the note in the air.

'You know Tim, he's a good doctor - he wouldn't lie.'

'I also know he's a friend of yours. Maybe you took this Rohypnol stuff after it all came out in the press!'

'I wouldn't have had time- I was ill in bed in Indianapolis, right up to when Jason drove me to the airport,' Ryan gilded the truth slightly. 'Tony drove me straight to the doctor's, once I had landed. You can check with Tim, if you like, but you really don't need to. I wouldn't seek to embarrass myself, or you, with a display like they claim.'

'You're no angel, either!'

'No, I'm not. But I am a professional driver, and it wouldn't be worth ruining my career for a quick romp in a seedy motel. My contract was on the line before all this. I'm not that stupid!'

'Well, you can get out of this mess without my help. I'm taking a short holiday. Don't expect a postcard!'

Victoria abruptly stood up, grabbed a suitcase that had been sitting on the floor beside the sofa, and left the room, slamming the door on the way out.

Ryan heaved a sigh of relief, and sat down on the warm seat Victoria had just vacated. Her expensive perfume hung seductively in the air. He hadn't expected hugs and kisses, but at least she hadn't said she was leaving him. He could have used her skills, but he could understand why she didn't want to be involved in this one. At least, if she was out of the way for a while, he would only have himself to worry about. Things could have been far worse.

CHAPTER 12

1:45 p.m. Wednesday 19th September, Indianapolis – United States

After the dramatic events of the previous day, Jason Kramer had enjoyed an early night. Rising just before ten o'clock, he had made himself a leisurely breakfast, before setting out for a long slow jog. The physical activity was exactly what was needed to clear his body and relax his mind. By the time he returned to his apartment, he was ready to phone his father. He hadn't phoned since the race, and his father had already left several messages on his phone.

Jason hummed cheerfully to himself as he tapped the numbers into his phone. There was a short delay, whilst the signal made its way through the satellite network, until at last he heard it ring. The call was picked up moments later.

'Bon soir, Chateau Demaison.'

He didn't recognise the voice that politely greeted him in French; he supposed it must be one of his father's servants.

'Pierre Demaison. S'il vous plait.'

Jason's accent grated on the man at the other end. He switched to English for his response.

'May I enquire who is calling?'

Jason wasn't sure what the servants knew about him, so decided to play it formally.

'Yeah, it's Jason Kramer. The racing-driver.'

'Merci, monsieur. One moment, while I connect you.'

The servant knew exactly who Jason was - but it amused him to see the games his master played to keep the relationship secret.

He transferred the call upstairs to the master bedroom where Demaison was resting.

'Yes! Who is it?' demanded Demaison, tetchily.

'Jason Kramer, sir.'

'Well! Put him through, then.'

The servant regretfully put the receiver down. That was a conversation he would have enjoyed listening to. His master had been in a bad mood all week - and Jason was part of the reason.

'Hi dad, how are they hanging? Did you see the papers?'

The breezy greeting was too much for Demaison, who exploded angrily.

'Shut up and listen to me, you stupid boy!'

Jason stopped talking, but his mouth stayed wide open. He wasn't used to being talked to like that. He thought his father would be happy with what he had done.

'You have no reason to be pleased with yourself! I put you into Vantec to prevent the team scoring points, and what do you go and do - score two points!'

'Hey, hold it there!' Jason had recovered some of his composure. 'I did that to help make sure the team trusted me - I could have scored more points!' There was a note of boastfulness in his voice.

'I didn't want you to score any points! I spent the race with Toshihiko Shintaku - he's the Managing Director of Katayama Motors, in case you didn't know,' he added, sarcastically. 'He was very impressed with your drive – but he was supposed to be impressed with our drivers!' Demaison's voice rose until he was nearly shouting.

Both Demaison drivers had failed to finish; Thierry Vigneron had broken down with a transmission problem, whilst Gonzales had managed to spin off and stall the engine. It had not been a good display in front of their engine supplier. Not only had Sunday's race gone badly, but that very morning, he had taken a call from an angry supplier - threatening to stop supplying his team with suspension parts, unless some of what he was owed was paid. Demaison had to promise payment - but he would have to rob Peter to pay Paul. There was no spare money in the company. This would be the first of many such calls, unless he could persuade the bank to give him a bigger overdraft. What he really needed was results. If the results came there was always a chance of picking up another high-profile sponsor. Losing his engine supplier would tip the team into a downward spiral - and maybe extinction. No, it had not been a good week for Equipe Demaison.

'Okay, I'm sorry, but I still think the team trust me even more now. Even if I don't score again this season, they should still have faith in me! At least they should keep running me to the end of the season. You wouldn't want them to drop me - would you?'

Demaison had to admit that Jason's argument had some validity.

'Perhaps, but then you go and put it all at risk with your little photo shoot! I take it that was you?' Demaison belittled the newspaper stories.

'100%! I bet Ryan's sweating right now!' Jason was proud of his little scheme.

'And when he realises it was you who set it up? We could lose everything - and you wonder why I am angry!'

'Why should he think it was me? I fed him a good story - he thinks the girls set it up. Strange things happen in America. He was more than ready to believe some other scumbags were behind it all.'

'I hope for both our sakes that you are right. From now on you keep a low profile. You …are just a driver. If there are any stunts to be played - I will play them. Do you understand me?'

'Yeah, I get the message.' Jason looked down at the floor. What on earth did it take to please his father?

'Okay. No more tricks, and please don't drive too well at the Nurburgring!' With that, Demaison slammed the receiver down, abruptly terminating the call.

Jason expelled a sigh of frustration as he replaced his own receiver. He felt very crestfallen after his earlier cheerfulness. He had only been trying to help, and he thought he'd done a good job. Well he'd show his father.

CHAPTER 13

7:45 a.m. Friday 21st September, Chelsea - England

Ryan clasped his hands above his head and pushed them towards the ceiling until he felt the muscles in his back complain, then he unclasped his hands and reached out in a wide stretch. Finally, he lay back down in the comfortable king-size bed to enjoy the luxury of a long lie in. He had slept well, but only after he had suffered yet another repeat of the nightmare. The frightful dream had left him and his bed damp with sweat, and at just after three a.m., he had been forced to get up to change the sheet and find another duvet.

Knowing it would take a while for his mind to settle down again, he had donned a thick blue towelled dressing-gown and padded barefoot into the lounge. Although Ryan had wide musical tastes the majority of his music was rock based, and it had taken a few minutes to hunt through the alphabetically organised collection to find a suitable record to match his mood. Eventually, he had settled on a Seal album, and, after inserting the disc into his expensive Wadia CD player, had settled back on the sofa. The soothing music had slowly worked its subtle magic, and after half-an-hour he was struggling to keep his eyes open. Just before four o'clock, he had returned to his now cold bed. Once the bed had warmed up in his body heat, he had fallen into a deep and undisturbed sleep.

At 7:30, his home-automation system had begun its morning wake up routine. Lights on the hi-fi had blinked into life as the system switched on his radio. Too quiet to hear, the Capital Gold morning show began to flow from loudspeakers hidden in the ceiling of his bedroom. Steadily, the system increased the volume in tiny steps. Slowly, the music had penetrated Ryan's brain and eased him into wakefulness. Just before his eyes had opened, the bedroom ceiling light had begun to glow dimly. By the time his eyes were wide open, the lighting was fully on and the radio was operating at a sensible listening level.

Now Ryan glanced at the red digits on his bedside clock and cursed. In his tiredness the night before, he had failed to set the time correctly. There was not enough time to make it worth trying to go back to sleep, but at least he could relax in bed for a few more minutes.

Craig McDonald, dressed in a green and yellow Australian team tracksuit, a large black sports bag slung over his right shoulder, positively marched through the glass doors guarding the front entrance to Ryan's luxury tower block. The smartly suited concierge, who had been reading the Sun newspaper, rose from his desk to greet him.

'Morning sir, here for Mr Clarke again, are we?' The concierge knew Craig well; Ryan's trainer was a regular visitor, and sometimes stopped for a welcome chat - breaking up the tedium of his day.

'S'right. I'm beginning to think it'd make life a damn sight easier if I lived here!'

Given the high price of even the tiniest apartment, they both knew there was little chance of that.

'Your friend's been rather a naughty boy, hasn't he?' challenged the concierge, a broad smile displaying a crooked row of yellowing smoker's teeth. He had enjoyed reading the prurient stories in his newspaper - he'd enjoyed the pictures even more, but had mixed feelings over the whole episode. On one hand he felt sympathy for Ryan, as the driver had always treated him as an equal, unlike some of the stuck-up tenants of the tower. If pushed, though, he would admit to a little schadenfreude, and even a touch of envy. But, despite tempting cash offers, he had divulged nothing to the journalists who had besieged his desk in their attempts to build on the story. His was a cushy job, and carried with it a very small but desirable apartment in the luxury block. It was not something he was going to put at risk.

'Yeah, well, that's as maybe. I haven't had a chance to speak to Ryan yet - and I'd rather get his side of the story, before condemning him out of hand!' said Craig, gently chastising the concierge. He was beginning to realise the magnitude of Ryan's problems. As much as it was his job to keep Ryan physically fit, he had also taken it upon himself to look after his mental condition. Without the right mental attitude there was little to be gained from being superbly fit. The two sides complemented each other. Craig couldn't imagine the turmoil Ryan was going through, for he had never experienced anything remotely like this in his own life, but rightly guessed he faced an uphill battle.

'P'rhaps you're right. If you're going up, there's some post for Mr Clarke, and the papers.' The concierge turned to the pigeonhole behind him on the wall, and fished out a stack of envelopes and a small pile of newspapers.

'Thanks, can you give Ryan a call - I expect he's still in bed!' Craig took the envelopes and newspapers from the concierge, and headed towards the stairs, shunning the lifts as usual.

For once, Ryan was actually ready when the concierge announced that he had a visitor. While Ryan waited for Craig to make his way up to the penthouse apartment, he found his trainers and put them on. He was keen to fit some training in. Physically, he knew he needed to bolster his fitness levels, but more importantly, the training session would help re-establish the routine that had been missing for the past week. He hoped a good hard session would banish the mental demons, and help him focus on what was becoming a very important race for him.

Despite Ryan's apartment being on the sixteenth storey, Craig bounded up the thirty-two flights of steps and arrived breathless outside the front door. Ryan had already left the door open for him. He found Ryan sprawled on a sofa - his legs dangling over the end.

'Where are all the girls then? Thought there might be a bit of an orgy going on,' said Craig, looking round in an exaggerated manner.

'Ha, ha. Very funny!' Ryan knew Craig was only joking, but he was still in no mood to joke about it.

'Cheer up. Nobody's died. I can think of worse ways of making the papers. After all, it could have been young boys!'

Craig ducked, as a bright red sofa cushion sailed over his head.

'Anyway, this lot's for you.' Craig passed over the newspapers and letters.

Ryan put the newspapers to one side, and started to leaf through the envelopes. His curiosity always got the better of him. He had only handled five or six letters when he came across the expensive white envelope sporting the F.I.A Logo. The postmark was Swiss. He put the rest of the mail down.

'I don't like the look of this.' Ryan held the letter up for Craig to see.

'Maybe they want you to be the next President.' Craig tried to make light of it, but he knew that it was hardly likely to be good news. 'You could throw it in the bin.'

Ryan shook his head, 'I don't think that's going to work this time.'

'Well, unless you can read it through the envelope, you'd better open it.' Craig was just as curious as Ryan.

Ryan grimaced, then ripped open the envelope. He extracted the single sheet and read it quickly. Without a word he passed it over to Craig. It didn't take long for Craig to get the gist.

'...Complaints have been received concerning your behaviour after the Indianapolis Grand Prix. Accordingly, you are ordered to attend a meeting of the World Motor Sport Council, in Paris at 10:00 a.m. on Wednesday 26th September, to answer claims that you have brought the sport into disrepute.'

The letter went on to explain the consequences if he was found guilty. The penalties ranged from suspension, to exclusion and removal of his FIA Super Licence. He was allowed to be legally represented - if he so wished. The letter was copied to the team.

'Well, pal, you really are in the shit now.'

'Thanks for your support and encouragement!'

'Time we got some training in. You need to let off steam. We can talk as you train.' Craig motioned to the door.

Ryan reluctantly got to his feet. He knew that Craig was right, and that a hard dose of physical labour would help, but he really didn't feel like doing anything. Just when things seemed to be getting better, he had slid back down a snake. Well, that was true of most things in life, he reflected ruefully.

'I think we'd better start with a run,' said Craig.

'Whatever,' replied Ryan, despondently.

Ryan followed, as Craig led him down the stairs and out onto the street. Craig let Ryan stay silent as they jogged slowly down to the embankment; he realised Ryan would need some personal space to absorb the news. He would try and put Ryan's head back together later. For now, Craig was content to watch the river traffic, as he led Ryan along the Thames at an easy pace.

Ryan was in a world of his own. He had never envisaged being summoned before the Council. It seemed unreal that he risked being thrown out of the sport for something he didn't do. He felt that because he was drugged, it wasn't really something he had done. But he knew that argument wouldn't wash in Paris. He sighed deeply. He didn't see that there was anything he could do, other than make them try to accept the doctor's evidence that he had been doped. Perhaps the doctor could be persuaded to go to Paris with him? His hopes rose and then fell, as he convinced himself that the doctor would be too busy to spend a day travelling to Switzerland. Ryan didn't notice where they were going, but he was surprised when Craig came to a halt back outside the apartment complex. He had subconsciously followed

Craig, and had no idea of how far they ran, or how long they had been out.

'I don't think you were really with me there, were you?'

'No – sorry Craig. I needed to think.'

'Get anywhere?'

'Not really. I've never been in a situation like this before.'

'Well, let's go chuck some iron around. You've got a race next week, remember!'

'I wish!' Ryan was far from convinced he'd walk away from this one.

The sweat-stained pair walked into the apartment block and headed for the basement gym. As well as the splendid location, the presence of a gym on-site was a major factor in Ryan choosing the apartment.

Whoever had equipped the gym had done an excellent job. There were several multi-function workstations - alongside rowing and cycling machines. Large mirrors surrounded the room, an unwelcome reminder of the American club where Ryan's troubles began.

As Ryan powered away on one of the light-blue Concept 2 rowing machines, Craig dug into his sport bag for some suitable music to put on the music-centre that was provided for the users. Soon, loud rock music, courtesy of Rainbow, blasted out round the spacious room. Despite himself, the music lifted Ryan's spirits, and gradually he began to work with the machine rather than fighting it. By the end of the fifteen-minute rowing routine, he was moving backwards and forwards smoothly and powerfully, a healthy sheen of sweat visible on his toned muscles. Craig smiled as he recognised the good that the exercise was doing. Although he had earlier suggested that they talked in the gym, he now thought it best to keep Ryan focused on the training. They could chat properly after the session. That's when his job would really start.

Ryan had nearly completed a full session on the machines, when Craig called him to a halt.

'On your feet; I think you need to get rid of some more aggro.'

As Ryan stood up, Craig aimed a slow open-handed punch to the side of his head. Ryan instinctively blocked the blow, and smiled.

'You could've let me get up first!'

'Always expect the unexpected,' was Craig's response. He then backed away from the machines into an empty space in the middle of the gym.

The two men faced each other in ritual pose, and then bowed, before taking up defensive postures. Warily, they circled each other, before Craig launched the first kick. Ryan was too slow, and took a painful blow on his thigh. He smiled ruefully; he was going to have to buck his ideas up, or Craig was really going to hurt him.

Craig backed away, and waited for Ryan to get his composure back. He had introduced Ryan to Tae Kwondo during the winter break. Whilst Ryan was unlikely to ever match his own level as a black belt, he had been quick to pick up the basics, and his motor racing gave him the speed of reaction a true fighter would be proud of.

The chance to hit out at something was exactly what Ryan needed. Clumsily, he launched a simple combination of kicks and punches that Craig defended with ease. The two men separated again and began circling.

Craig nipped in and out with a quick punch that took Ryan by surprise. The rapid calculations, needed to mount a successful defence or attack, soon left no room for other thoughts, and focused Ryan's concentration.

Ryan purposely let Craig mount the next attack. Weathering a kick that he saw coming, he took Craig by surprise with an instant retaliatory kick of his own. The Australian yelped in pain as Ryan caught him in the stomach. Craig grinned. Job done.

The two men swapped kicks and punches for a further five minutes, before Craig called a halt. Together, they made for the pool. As they lay in the warm water, Ryan wanted to speak.

Craig stopped him. If they were going to talk seriously, he wanted to do it properly. Not shivering in a swimming pool. He ushered Ryan out of the pool and towards the shower.

Half an hour later, they were standing on the balcony outside Ryan's flat. The remnants of a hasty breakfast were spread across a round wrought-iron table behind them. For a few minutes, they stood at the railing and watched the river traffic moving gracefully far below. From where they stood, they could see right past the Houses of Parliament and round to Tower Bridge. The historic buildings were bathed in a glorious golden yellow. With clear blue skies overhead, it was a fantastic view. Eventually, Craig broke the silence.

'I only know what I've read in the papers. Maybe you'd better tell me what really happened.'

'There's not much more to tell. The papers got it pretty much right - as far as I know. After all, I don't remember a thing!' His voice was bitter.

'Well, tell me anyway. It's got to be better to talk about it, than to keep it all in. Besides, you're going to have to explain it all in Paris!'

'If you say so.' Ryan sounded less convinced. He'd rather ignore the whole episode, but he knew Craig was right.

'It all started so well.' Once Ryan started talking he warmed to the task, and soon the whole story, as Ryan knew it, came out: the Blues bar where they had eaten, the run-down entrance to the strip joint, the pole dancer and the arrival of the girls. He only had a half-memory of the police station and being rescued by Jason. He recounted how he had thrown up, and how awful he felt the next morning. He ended the tale with his arrival at Gatwick, and the unexpected press attention.

'So, who doped you then?' Craig had always been direct.

'I wish I knew.'

'Well, it was most likely to be someone who got close to you. They would have had to administer this Rohypnol. Did the doctor say what form it took?'

'He said it could be dissolved.'

'So, they doctored a drink you had. Did you ever leave your drink lying around?'

'Only to go to the toilet. But the others were still at the table.'

'Doesn't that make it likely that it was one of them?'

'I guess, but why?

'I can think of two reasons: firstly, they might have been looking to sell a story to the press. Any famous person would have done. You might just have been in the wrong place at the wrong time!'

'Sounds far-fetched,' said Ryan, 'what's your second reason?'

'That someone's after your seat. Get you into trouble and kicked out of the team. Who would benefit?'

'The only person I can think of is Warren Barton. He's been a pain in the arse since Kramer got Panetta's seat.' Ryan remembered his conversation with Warren, in the hotel, on the evening his troubles began. 'And Warren was still in Indy that night – that surprised me. He's got to be top of my list - but I still don't see how he could have arranged it all. He said he'd never been to the States before!'

'Tricky,' said Craig, 'what about Kramer?'

'He might have the opportunity, but I can't see what his motive would be. He's got a seat this year, and next year he'll be with Demaison - I can't think what he'd have to gain.' Ryan was stumped.

'But, didn't he introduce the girls to you?' asked Craig.

'Yeah, but he really didn't seem to know them. And, as I recall it, he couldn't even get their names right. He also took very good care of things the next day.' Ryan had been grateful for all that Kramer had done for him.

'Well, we'd better keep him on the list, for now.'

'In which case, you might as well add Wittman. I think he's still upset with me after that move in Spa. He bears grudges, and I wouldn't put a little mischief past him!' Ryan had already spent some time considering Wittman as a suspect. 'Then, I think we'd better add a fourth candidate - as I've also received a phone threat.'

'You serious?' Craig was stunned.

'Absolutely. Come on, I guess you'd better hear it.'

Craig followed Ryan back into the lounge. Ryan walked over to the phone, and quickly found the unwanted message. He turned the volume up so that Craig could hear.

'Did you enjoy the picture show? Well, my friends and I sure did. I wonder if next time things will be quite so painless? Do be careful - I'd hate to see you have an accident. I do hope you get my drift.' The female speaker spoke seductively, and there was a hint of the Mediterranean in her voice.

'Yep, that's certainly a threat. I take it you don't recognise the voice?'

Ryan looked sharply at Craig, who raised his hands into the air.

'Only joking. Maybe it's a female conspiracy.'

'In which case, we'd better include that woman who followed us back from Belgium in the red Lotus. I guess it's just possible that was her on the phone. If not, we've got a fifth candidate!'

'You sure you haven't been monkeying around with any powerful women? Revenge could be a motive.'

'Can't see it. I've been pretty faithful to Victoria over the last year.'

'Only pretty faithful?' Craig shook his head in despair.

'Only one girl, and she dumped me – I can't see her as a candidate.'

'So, that's the list then - for what good it does us! Three people we know, and two mystery suspects!'

'That just about sums it up,' said Ryan, despondently.

Craig sat down on the sofa beside Ryan. The two men sat in quiet contemplation for a few minutes, before Craig broke the silence.

'Okay, here's what we do!' Craig paused to ensure Ryan had his full attention.

'You, see if you can get anything out of Kramer. You're closer to him than me.'

Ryan nodded as Craig continued.

'Whilst you're doing that, I'll try and find out more about Warren Barton. Sadly, I don't think we can do much about the other suspects.'

'Guess so, at least we've got somewhere to start!' Ryan perked up at the thought of direct action, but then his mood sank again as he remembered the letter from the FIA. 'If they're trying to stop me racing, they might already have succeeded. If things go badly in Paris, I might not be driving again anyway!' Ryan sounded depressed.

'Come on. You know what I think about negative thoughts. If you think negative - you'll be negative. Turn it round, start looking at the positive. If you get through Wednesday - then you've got to race on Sunday. You can either give in to these threats, or face up to them!'

'Point taken. So, what do I do now?'

'First, I think you need to do some driving. At the end of the day, you're a racing driver not a detective. Get behind a wheel, and prove to yourself that you can still do it. Secondly, get as solid a defence as you can for Wednesday. You and the team can afford a good lawyer. Maybe Jason will help, and what about the doctor? Perhaps he could attend - he seems a good sort.'

'As usual, you're right. I like the idea of getting a drive in. I'll call Brands, and see if they've got anything I can take out tomorrow. I've got another sponsor to see this afternoon - more grovelling.'

'You know what they say - no publicity is bad publicity!'

Ryan picked up the phone, and dialled the driving school at Brands Hatch to see what could be arranged. He was in luck. The school retained an old Benetton Formula One car for scaring high paying corporate visitors. Despite the short notice, they had nothing booked for the car the next day, and as Ryan knew the chief instructor well, he was more than happy for Ryan to take the car out for a spin. It would be a pleasure to have the car handled by an expert for a change. They settled on a half-hour session, starting at 11:00 a.m.

Ryan came off the phone in a happier frame of mind. It seemed ages since he had last driven a racing car - especially as the race in Indianapolis had lasted less than one lap. He enjoyed driving at Brands Hatch, and he looked forward to renewing his acquaintance with the Benetton.

'Craig, do you mind tagging along for the next few weeks? I might need someone to watch my back.'

'Try keeping me away. If there's a whole gang of beautiful women out there, trying to get at you, I'd like a piece of the action!'

Ryan was delighted; he clapped Craig on the shoulder.

'Thanks, mate. Can you meet me at Brands tomorrow? Bring plenty of gear - I might need you around for some time!'

CHAPTER 14

11:15 a.m. Saturday 22nd September, Brands Hatch - England

  Ryan eased the ageing blue and white Benetton out of garage no 7 and onto the pit apron. At the end of the pit lane, he could see the traffic control light glowing green, beckoning him out onto the circuit. He paused briefly, imagining that he was making a crucial pit stop in the next race. He could see the pit crew frantically working round. As he visualised the lollipop man removing his pole, he engaged the clutch and the car began to accelerate. The rear end snaked a little under the sudden surge of power as he pulled onto the pit lane, and then he was away - picking up speed quickly. The entrance to Paddock Hill bend was no place to get carried away, so he watched his speed as he exited the pit lane onto the circuit.
  Although he had driven the ageing Benetton B196 several times before, it was still necessary for him to get used to the car's unique handling. The half hour he had spent with the car's engineers was not enough to set the car up as he would ideally like it, and so he waited to see how it behaved in the corners. Cautiously, he rounded Druids and then eased the car through Graham Hill bend. With the tricky bend behind, he floored the throttle and charged along the Cooper Straight towards McLaren. He eased off early for the left-right combination that caught so many people out. It would be far too embarrassing to park the car on the grass. Once on Clearways, he was able to build the speed up again - before he knew it, he was crossing the line at the end of his first lap. Sadly, they were only using the

short Indy circuit, but he was more concerned with driving than the geography of the circuit. At least on the short circuit he would get plenty of laps in over the thirty minutes he was allowed.

Three laps later, Ryan was confident he knew how the car would behave, and began to wind her up. He swooped down Paddock hill - his stomach lurching from the savage compression at the bottom of the hill as the steep drop switched into the climb up to Druids. He locked the right rear briefly as he swung slowly through the 180 degree bend of Druids, then bravely sought a very fast line through Graham Hill Bend. The wheels bumped up onto the kerbs, and it was a nervous moment before Ryan was certain he had kept the car on the track.

The few spectators were now treated to an unexpected display of grand prix driving. There had been no announcements, and they could only guess at who was behind the wheel. One thing, though, was obvious to the car-nuts and amateur weekend-racers - he was not one of them! The car barked, growled, howled and screamed in tortured fury, as Ryan hustled it round the 1.2 mile merry-go-round of a circuit. Braking was precise and late, corners were taken inch perfectly, and every yard of the few straights was used to build maximum speed. Fingers clicked on stopwatches in the grandstands, as the Formula One car screamed past at the end of each lap.

There were two spectators who did know the driver. Craig McDonald was on the pit wall. He couldn't see much of the drive, but he did at least get to chat with the pit crew. He liked the down to earth nature of the hard working and low paid mechanics. While they were the unsung heroes who kept the complicated cars on the road, it amused Craig to see himself as the unsung hero who kept the driver on the road!

The other knowing spectator was Chris Somerset, who was sat high up in the open stand overlooking Paddock hill. From where he was, he could see most of the track. He had been tipped off about Ryan's drive by the driving school. The head of the school had thought it best to check that Chris was happy for

Ryan to take a car out. Despite the risks involved, Chris was pleased that Ryan was showing a desire to drive. The sooner the demons of the past week were banished the better. Although he didn't want to see Ryan hurt - at least his own cars weren't being put at risk. Better still, it wasn't costing him any money! He looked at his watch and recorded the lap-time on his clipboard, before watching Ryan crest Druids again. He nodded with satisfaction, as he noted that Ryan had shaved another two-tenths off his time.

Ryan was driving well, and he knew it. He felt at one with the car. He was seeing the braking points clearly, and the car was reacting predictably to his slightest touch. He knew it couldn't possibly be as fast as his more modern Vantec, but it was certainly a car he would enjoy racing. As the laps slipped by, he felt more and more like a driver, and less like a puppet on a string. If only he could just get on with the driving!

It was with regret that he backed off the throttle and turned into the pit lane at the end of the short session. It was some time since he had last had such fun in a Formula One car. Usually, when he was testing, qualifying or racing he had to continually monitor the car, looking for the slightest change that may improve performance. Driving under those conditions was a job - and a very professional one at that. Driving for the sheer fun of it was something else. He didn't have to rush in to change tyre pressures, or wing set up, and he didn't have to worry about every 100th of a second. He knew he hadn't broken any lap records; the car was not set up well enough for that, but it had suited his driving style. He was more than satisfied with his morning's effort.

As Ryan parked the car, Chris Somerset packed his clipboard away in his briefcase, and got up from the hard blue-plastic seat in the stand. The uncomfortable seat made him rather glad that Ryan's session had been so short. Ryan wasn't the only person pleased with the morning's work. Somerset had always enjoyed watching Ryan drive, and he had just seen his driver put in a superb display. He had seen flashes of the brilliance that had made him a supporter of Ryan from his early days in Formula 3. He was no nearer resolving his dilemma over drivers for the next year, but the display he had just witnessed put another tick in the box for Ryan – if only they could get through the FIA charge. Somerset walked away from the track, a thoughtful but much happier man.

Craig McDonald was waiting in the garage, as Ryan stepped out of the car and removed his helmet.

'Well sport, at least it looks like you can still drive. I guess you could always get work as a cab-driver!' Craig smiled to show it was a joke.

He needn't have worried, for there was a broad grin on Ryan's face. Ryan had enjoyed himself immensely on the track, and knew he still had what it took. He smoothed his tousled hair down as he replied to Craig, 'I don't think I'd keep a cab licence for long, either – have you seen the speed limits out on the streets?'

The two men laughed, both realising that the track session had laid some ghosts to rest. Craig put a hand on Ryan's shoulder, and guided him out of the garage and over to the pit-wall. The next conversation wasn't for sharing with the driving school mechanics.

'Have you had a chance to speak to Jason yet?' asked Craig.

'No, but we're meeting up tomorrow with Somerset. I should get a chance then. What about Warren – any plans?'

'Yeah, I'm going round to his flat later. He doesn't know I'm coming - so I hope to catch him by surprise. That way, he won't have time to think up a story.' Craig was determined to get the truth out of Barton - one way or another.

'Sounds good. I reckon you should do all the detective work!' Ryan smiled wistfully.

Craig snorted, 'No way matey! You got yourself into this mess, you're going to have to do some of the work to get out of it! I'm not doing it all for you.'

'Oh well, it was worth a try!' In his heart, Ryan knew that it was his problem, and that he would have to deal with it. He was very grateful, though, for the support Craig was giving him.

Craig glanced at his watch, 'Look, it's time I made a move. I'll catch up with you tomorrow. What time will you be finished with Somerset?'

Ryan thought for a moment before replying, 'We're meeting at ten, but I don't know how long the lawyer's going to need. It's best if I give you a call when we've finished. Probably be mid-afternoon.'

'Right, I'm off to get some answers from Warren,' Craig slapped Ryan on the shoulder and jogged off towards the car park.

CHAPTER 15

12:30 a.m. Saturday 22nd September, Swanley, near Brands Hatch - England

Warren Barton was slumped on the beaten up sofa in his rented flat watching motorcycling on the TV, when his doorbell rang. He had been enjoying the race - although he was very glad he had four wheels underneath himself when racing! Irritated, he reached for the remote control and muted the sound, before getting up to answer the door. No doubt it would be a pair of Jehovah's Witnesses, or some other unwelcome visitor. He had no real friends in the U.K, and rarely received guests. Motor racing was his whole life. To his immense surprise, he opened the door to find Craig McDonald standing in the dank corridor outside.

'Nice place you've got here, Warren!' said Craig, by way of greeting, dismayed by the seedy surroundings.

'My other flat's in Monaco!' joked Warren, 'come in - if you dare!' He waved Craig in, with an extravagant sweep of his right arm.

Craig followed Warren back into the tiny flat. An awful, green floral wallpaper was doing its best to escape from the walls, and a damp musty smell assaulted Craig's nose. He knew test drivers weren't well paid, but he thought Warren could have done better for himself.

'This is only temporary,' said Warren, embarrassed by the condition of his lodgings and Craig's unasked question. 'I've got another, better, place lined up from next month.'

'And I thought you must like it here!' Craig's suspicions hardened as he wondered if Warren had come into more money from somewhere.

'It's bloody awful, but it is handy for Brands.'

Craig nodded, 'I know, I've just driven from there.' The journey had only taken him ten minutes. Swanley was a grey misery after the verdant countryside surrounding the race circuit - an unloved and unattractive town.

'Sit down,' Warren indicated a dilapidated armchair in the corner of the small room. 'Coffee?'

'Please,' said Craig, sitting down gingerly.

While he waited for Warren to return from the kitchen, he watched the bike race Warren was missing. It was a cracker, with Valentino Rossi duelling with Sete Gibernau. The lead changed hands several times in the space of a few laps, and Craig found the spectacle more exciting than many of the F1 races he had watched. He reminded himself that he was there to help Ryan, and reluctantly forced himself to look away from the screen. He was still thinking about his tactics, when Warren sneaked quietly back into the room, carrying a mug in each hand.

'You all right?' asked Warren, puzzled by the trance-like look on Craig's face.

'Yeah, sorry – I was just thinking,' apologised Craig.

'You paid to do that?'

'Sometimes!'

Warren handed a chipped mug over to Craig, then sat down on the sofa. Finding the remote again, he reluctantly switched the TV off.

'What brings you around here then?'

'I wanted to ask you about Indianapolis. I take it you know all about Ryan's little problem?' Craig studied Warren's face as he asked the question. There was just the slightest flicker of reaction. He was even more convinced there was good purpose to his visit.

'Who doesn't know about it? It's been in all the papers, and in Autosport.'

There was a hint of pleasure in Warren's voice that annoyed Craig. He gave up any idea of approaching the subject obliquely. He wanted out of there as quickly as possible – with the truth of Warren's involvement.

'Ryan says you stayed over unexpectedly.'

Warren was surprised at the edge in Craig's tone. 'Yeah, as I told Ryan, I hadn't been to the States before and was making the most of the trip. There was nothing suspicious about it.'

The answer was just too long, and Craig noticed Warren's eyes slide away from his as he answered. Craig was convinced there was more to be said. He put his cup down on a pile of newspapers beside the chair and got up. Warren watched, puzzled, as Craig moved behind him and towards the window. Once he was behind Warren, Craig moved aggressively, snaking an arm viciously round the South African's neck. Craig held Warren's head tightly in a painful headlock.

'What the fuck's that for?' mumbled Warren, his hands clawing at the arm under his chin.

'That's for Ryan! You're hiding something, and I'm going to find out what it is - one way or another!' menaced Craig, increasing his grip as Warren struggled.

'Okay, okay I'll tell you the truth …, now let me go!'

'Not until I'm satisfied you've told me everything - you'd better get on with it, unless you want a stiff neck tomorrow!'

'I followed Ryan and Jason to the first club.'

'Go on,' encouraged Craig, releasing his grip slightly.

'That's it, I tried to follow them after that, but they lost me when they got in a taxi. I had nothing to do with any of what happened later that night.'

'Then why did you follow them?' Craig was puzzled. If Warren was telling the truth, then he was a dead-end as far as their investigations went.

'I was pissed off that they didn't invite me out with them. I wanted to see what they did - see what I was missing out on. It's no fun being a doormat you know!'

Craig heard the truth and bitterness in Warren's voice, and withdrew his arm from Warren's head.

'Was that fucking necessary?' Warren glared at Craig, as he massaged his neck.

Craig held his hands up in supplication 'Sorry, but I had to know the truth. Someone's got it in for Ryan, and the way you've been behaving since Kramer has been on the scene, put you high on the list!'

'Thanks a bunch! Well, now you can cross me off your sick little list, and get out of here!' Warren pointed to the door.

Craig walked from behind Warren, and sat back down in the chair.

'Look, I know I'm not your pal at the moment, but Ryan does need help. Why not join us, and help find out who's behind all this? We could do with some extra help.'

'Fuck off! After what you've just done, you must be joking. Ryan will have to sort himself out. I'm staying out of this. Now piss off!'

'Suit yourself.' Craig got up from the chair and quickly headed to the door. He had a nasty feeling he had just made matters worse. He didn't mind that Warren now hated him, for he had never liked the driver, but he was worried that he had just given Ryan another enemy!

CHAPTER 16

10:00 a.m. Monday 24th September, Vantec Factory near Brands Hatch - England

Chris Somerset sat in his usual seat, at the window end of the board room table. Idly, he tapped the tabletop with his fountain pen, and glanced from Ryan Clarke to Jason Kramer. He was pleased that both drivers had dressed smartly for the meeting; he wanted them to make a good impression on the lawyer. He had summoned the pair to the office to determine how they would approach the meeting in Paris, with the FIA, on Wednesday.

Not for the first time, he wondered if Jason could have had a hand in Ryan's misfortunes, but looking at the pair of them, so comfortable in each other's company, he dismissed the idea. It bothered him that there were no other obvious suspects, and for the life of him he couldn't see a motive. That still left the possibility that Ryan had been responsible for his actions, but that theory ran aground when he asked himself how the pictures were obtained. Someone would have had to put in considerable work to set that up. Well, no matter what the incident was about, the main problem now was to get through the hearing in one piece. He couldn't afford to lose Ryan at this stage in the season. They wouldn't be lucky enough to find another free driver with Kramer's ability, and he had already decided that Warren Barton was never going to rise above being a test driver. Time to get on with it, he decided.

'Ryan, Jason has said he is prepared to testify on your behalf in Paris, if they'll let him.' Chris was already suspicious of the council's procedures.

'Thanks, mate.' Ryan turned his head to face Jason, and gave a little nod.

'It'll be a pleasure ….not!' Jason pulled a grimace.

'Before we all get carried away, I'd like to make sure we're all singing from the same songbook. Our lawyer will be here in about half an hour, and I'd like to make sure he only hears a single story. I know you've both been through it before, but I'd like to hear the whole story again - from the top. Ryan you start, take us up to the point where you lose your memory.'

Ryan stared into space as he recounted the tale. From time to time, Chris looked across to Jason, who nodded his agreement of the facts.

'I know we had a few drinks with the girls, but then nothing,' the puzzlement could still be heard in Ryan's voice. He just could not believe things could happen to him that he couldn't remember.

'And, you don't recall leaving the club?' asked Chris.

'No, the last thing I remember is being in the club. The doctor says that means that I was probably doped there.'

'Okay, we know you can't remember. It's your only real defence - so please don't suddenly start remembering, or we really will be in trouble!' Chris was only half joking, a recovery of memory at this stage, or on Wednesday, could prove very embarrassing.

'Now, Jason, can you please take the story on from there.'

'Well, it's like Ryan said, we had a few drinks with the girls and things were going really well. I spotted an old friend, on another table, and went over for a quick chat - Ryan was dancing with Caroline. When I returned, both Ryan and the girls had disappeared. Anyway, I had a good look round, but he was nowhere to be found. I sort of assumed he'd struck lucky - but I'd have thought one of the girls would have told me they were going.'

'Your view of lucky and mine are clearly quite different!' said Somerset, puritanically. 'How well did you know the two girls?'

'Not at all, I only met them for the first time that night; I guess they just took a fancy to us – unless, of course, they were part of it all?' Jason liked that touch. It certainly seemed that Ryan and Chris had swallowed the bait. Two mystery girls who bedded Ryan, and two others who took a shine to them in the club. It suited him that the others thought the four girls were all in it together - just so long as his name was kept out of the frame.

'So, why did they pick on Ryan? It wasn't blackmail.'

Ryan decided not to mention the threat he had received; he still didn't know if it was for real, and it could only complicate things. He didn't fancy trying to explain that one in Paris.

'True, but I guess they would have got good money from the papers,' offered Jason.

'But, it seems they knew he was a racing driver.'

'So did the three hundred thousand people who watched the race on Sunday.' Jason didn't like the way Chris was thinking; maybe his father had a point, this was not as easy as he had first thought.

'They wouldn't have known he would be in the club, and a stunt like that would have needed setting up.'

'Hey, things are different in America. Maybe they were always ready and on the lookout for a suitable victim. I've seen similar cases in the press in recent months.' There had certainly been one like it, because that's how Jason got the idea. He was having to think on his feet, but he had always been a consummate liar. They wouldn't be able to read anything in his face - he just prayed they couldn't read his mind!

'But, why Ryan and not you?' asked Chris.

'Perhaps the girls got the drinks mixed up.'

'Maybe, well, in which case you must both be more careful in the future!' Somerset sighed, 'We'd better go through it one more time, because those could well be questions they'll ask.'

They ran through the events again. This time, Chris keyed salient points into his Dell laptop. When they had finished, he printed a summary of the events for each of them.

'Right, this is the story that we are going to tell. Any disagreement?'

Quickly, Ryan and Jason read through the bullet points, then signalled their agreement with what had been written down.

Satisfied, Chris dismissed the pair of them. 'Ryan, why don't you show Jason round the factory. I'll have you paged when the lawyer gets here.'

'Come on, then, let's go see them repair the cars we wreck!'

Jason eagerly followed Ryan. Not only was he pleased to get away from Chris, and his awkward questions, but he also had a genuine interest in the factory. Back home, he had never been given the chance to seen them build the cars. The cars were largely assembled away from the team. He just got to drive the finished article. It would be interesting to see them making one from the bottom up.

Ryan had previously given the same tour to groups of sponsors, and he enjoyed the opportunity to show off his knowledge of the car building process. Rationalising the process, he decided to start in the design shop; after all, that's where the car really began – on a computer. Already work was well underway on the design of next year's car. Rather than disturb the busy design team, Ryan halted Jason outside the glass office. One of the designers looked up and waved. Ryan waved back, then quickly explained to Jason what was happening.

'Can we go in and have a look?' asked Jason.

'I'd rather not. If they're too busy they'll only tell us to get lost, and if they're not too busy they'll bore us to death! I think we'll go see something a bit more lively!' He led Jason off towards the body shop.

The work that went into making the carbon fibre chassis always staggered him. The whole process was highly complicated, and work never seemed to stop in the area. If they weren't creating new panels for a new car, they were busy creating spares. New nose cones were a frequent requirement, and Ryan's accident at Indianapolis had already presented them with a need to fabricate yet another.

Ryan halted just inside the door of the pattern making room. A router was noisily cutting through a large white panel of material. The operator was wearing ear defenders to protect his hearing from the terrible screech of the drill, as it cut its way through the panel. Ryan had to shout to make himself heard.

'They start by making patterns from Ureol – that's that white material they're machining,' Ryan pointed at the router. 'The cutting is controlled by computer - straight from the CAD design work we saw earlier.' He nodded towards the door. It was far too noisy to stay in the pattern making room.

Kramer followed Ryan into another workshop.

'In here, they assemble the patterns together into an accurate model that can be used to create a mould on which the carbon-fibre is laid-up. They do quite a lot of sanding to ensure the surfaces are smooth!'

Kramer could see what looked like a cockpit section being prepared.

'The model is checked with a digitising scanner before the mould is created, to ensure that it is totally accurate.'

'It's some process!' said Kramer, impressed.

'To use a phrase - you ain't seen nuthin' yet!' said Ryan. 'I'll summarise the rest of the process, then we can quickly walk through the other sections. The full tour really takes longer than we have available.'

'Fine by me.'

'Okay, here goes; first, the pattern is used to make a mould out of carbon fibre. The mould is then coated in release agent and baked. Then tooling blocks are fitted into the mould - they are removable patterns, used to make apertures and recesses for the suspension parts, and such like. So, that's the mould complete. Got it so far?'

Kramer nodded.

'Next, comes the tricky part – the laying up of the carbon-composites. The chassis is double skinned, and each skin can have up to seven layers of carbon-fibre. Between the two skins, there's a layer of honeycombed aluminium. So really, there are three main layers. The final skin is usually cured for about two and a half hours in the autoclave. As they are working on each skin, though, they may lay up a few layers of fibre, and then put the skin in the autoclave to help consolidate the material. The autoclave is really a giant pressure cooker. So, you can see the whole process is incredibly skilled, and very time-consuming.'

'I can see why they get pissed off when we break something!'

'Well, it doesn't stop there. Once the chassis has been baked, they've then got to finish it off. Drill fixing holes and other mountings. Let's move on.'

Ryan led Kramer through the laminating shop, where a laminator was busy with a hair-dryer, easing some carbon-fibre into a mould.

'It's not all high tech then!' observed Kramer, dryly.

'Does the job though! Look, there's the autoclave.' Ryan pointed to a large cylindrical machine at the end of the room. 'Looks like it's in use – nothing to see, though.'

Jason was staggered by the whole process; he had never realised how complex it all was. They finished the tour of the body shop, by watching a new nose cone being prepared for painting. Even the painting of the finished parts was a more complex task than he had envisaged. He could hardly believe it, when Ryan explained that even the weight of the paint had to be taken into account in the search for a lightweight chassis.

Compared to the dust and noise of the body shop, the race-shop was a far more clinical environment. The large airy room was fitted out with three bays, one for each car. Waist-high tool cabinets, surmounted by sturdy worktops, ran round the edges of the bays. In each bay, a car was perched on a cradle. Mechanics and engineers were hard at work, preparing the cars for the journey to the Nurburgring. Without their wheels, the cars looked about as useful as aircraft without wings. It was surprising what a difference, just adding four wide tyres made to the beast.

'Hey, lover boy's in town!' One of the mechanics had spotted Ryan. Immediately, a barrage of catcalls and whistles erupted. Ryan blushed, and raised a hand in acknowledgement. He chose not to reply to the comments, and waited for the hubbub to subside. Eventually, the mechanics tired of the game, and returned to their work.

'Why's that computer hooked up to my car?' asked Jason, who recognised his vehicle in the third bay. Ryan had a quick look before replying.

'It looks like they might be doing the engine mapping.'

'Yeah, now that's something I've always wanted to see. Okay if I go check it out?'

'Don't see why not, but don't pester them too much - or you won't have a car worth driving on Sunday! I want a quick word with Derek Archer, so, I'll catch up with you in a bit.' With that, the two drivers went their separate ways. Ryan joined Derek Archer in the first bay, where he was supervising the work on Ryan's car. The head mechanic was sipping from a large mug of tea. Nobody was supposed to drink in the area, but Derek had been a law unto himself from day one. Derek had been the first mechanic that the team had hired, and as a result, the burly mechanic got away with murder.

'How's it going Derek?' Ryan got in quick, in case the conversation turned back to Indianapolis.

'Not bad. Fortunately, you didn't do any real damage in America. The car's looking pretty good - and I think it should suit the Nurburgring. We've had her up on the seven-poster-rig, and based on the figures, she looks well set-up.'

Ryan nodded in appreciation, as Derek went through the results of the tests they had carried out on the suspension-testing machine.

'Now, you'll just have to stay clear of our Yankee friend.' Derek waved his mug in Jason's direction; tea slopped out of the large chipped cup and onto the otherwise clean floor.

'It's hard enough getting these babies to beat the other teams, without you two fighting each other.' To Derek's way of thinking, being taken out by a team-mate was an unspeakable calamity. It would take a lot of good driving from Jason before Derek was prepared to trust him again. Derek either took to people or he didn't, and right now, he had gone right off Jason.

'I don't think he did it on purpose, besides, he did grab a couple of good points that we needed.'

'That saved his fucking bacon. Chris was getting ready to fry him. But, he'd better not make a habit of it. I've put a lot of work into this old girl.' Derek patted the rear wing of the car affectionately.

Ryan looked at his watch. It couldn't be long before Chris was ready to see them again.

'I'd better go rescue that poor engineer from Jason, or he'll never finish in time. I'll see you later - if you're still around. If not, I'll catch up with you in Germany.'

Ryan left bay one, and strolled over to stand beside Jason in bay three.

'...It still seems incredible to me that you can play about with our rev limits using a computer. It's hard enough getting to grips with the mechanical side of it all, without trying to get my head round computers. It must be some really special software you use; I can't imagine it's written in Visual Basic.' Jason addressed his comments to the software engineer standing by the computer.

'Far from it - it's all written in the 'C' programming language.'

'I've heard of it, but never seen any actual code. What's it look like?'

'Your worst nightmare, a knitting pattern from hell, but if you're interested...' The software engineer's fingers flew across the keyboard, as he swapped out of the mapping function and into the development area. He enjoyed the rare opportunity to show off. Suddenly, strings of gobbledegook appeared on the screen.

'I see what you mean. And, you can actually change the program yourself?'

Ryan was surprised at Jason's interest.

'Can do, but most of the time we're just using the system to download settings to disk, which we take with us. We've got disks for each track, so we can make changes quite easily. If we wanted to, we could even transmit some changes to the car by radio, but that's dead against the rules, so it doesn't happen.' The engineer sounded disappointed.

'Too bad. I take it, you could perk the cars up a bit on the day - if you were allowed?'

'Too right. But, that's life!'

'I think Jason and me had better be going,' said Ryan, 'thanks for the spiel. We'll let you know if you got it right!'

'I'll know from the telemetry, well before you get round to telling me!' snorted the software engineer.

Ryan dragged Kramer away from the cars, and steered him out of the race shop. They were just finishing very welcome cups of coffee in the factory canteen, when the intercom demanded their presence in the boardroom. Neither of them relished going through the whole saga again, but hopefully this would be one of the last times.

A portly middle-aged man and Chris Somerset were chatting amiably, when Ryan and Jason entered the boardroom. Empty cups of coffee, and a half-finished plate of chocolate biscuits, suggested that they had been there for some time. Somerset introduced Ryan to Nicholas Marwick, the lawyer who was going to represent him in Paris. Judging by the lines round his face, the expensively suited lawyer had clearly been round the block. Ryan was pleased that it wasn't some fresh-faced kid, just out of college. Marwick's blue eyes twinkled, as he gripped Ryan's hand in a large and very firm handshake. The lawyer positively radiated confidence. Ryan wondered where on earth Somerset had found him. He suspected it must be one of his Masonic 'friends'; there always seemed to be a friend well placed to help out if needed. That sort of networking had never been Ryan's way, but it obviously had advantages.

As expected, the lawyer made both drivers go through the story again. Every now and then, he stopped them to ask piercing questions. His pen was hardly ever still as he made copious notes. Ryan had thought that the hearing was going to be tough, but after the grilling by Markwick, he had a much better idea of how tough. The FIA didn't summon many teams or drivers to appear in front of the Council, so there weren't that many lawyers around with experience of the process. The lawyer, that Chris had found may not have had experience of the FIA but he had apparently represented a few erring footballers in similar hearings. He had also consulted a German lawyer, who had actually been through an FIA hearing. He had decided that it was best to be over prepared.

After Ryan and Jason had finished telling their tale, the lawyer continued making notes. Ryan bit his lip anxiously as he waited for him to finish. He looked at Jason who shrugged his shoulders. Neither man knew what to expect next. Finally, the lawyer replaced the cap on his pen, and slid the expensive pen into the inside pocket of his jacket.

'Looking at the evidence in the newspapers, something definitely occurred that could be deemed as bringing the sport into disrepute. After all, there is no doubt it was you in the pictures! And that's not something you have tried to deny.'

Ryan was pleased that the lawyer didn't attempt to make fun of the situation.

'It is my belief that the council will concentrate on seeking an explanation for your behaviour in order to establish what responsibility, if any, you had for the events. Before we go any further, I will remind you that the ultimate punishment would be for the FIA to strip you of your license, and exclude you from the championship,' Marwick stared hard at Ryan - convinced he had the driver's full attention, he continued. 'Looking at the doctor's evidence, I do however believe that expulsion will be unlikely - there do seem to be some very good mitigating circumstances,' Marwick smiled, benevolently.

'That's a relief,' said Ryan, grinning, pleased to hear the professional opinion on his case.

Marwick held up a hand to stop Ryan. 'Before you get carried away, it is still possible they will penalise you in some way, you are not likely to come out of this unscathed. You might face a fine, or even have points deducted.'

Somerset pulled a long face at the mention of points being deducted.

Ryan sunk back into depression; the loss of any points could halt their challenge for a top six placing. He couldn't see Somerset offering him a new contract if that happened.

'Anyway, we have some work ahead of us. Although the World Motor Sport Council is not a court, it would be wise for us to prepare as fully as possible. I am afraid this may take some time,' said Marwick, concluding his speech.

The meeting continued for another hour and a half, as the lawyer marshalled the relevant facts, and coached each of them in the roles they may have to play.

It was a very quiet and worried driver who left Brands Hatch at the end of the long meeting. Jason had suggested they find somewhere to eat, but Ryan simply shook his head, and climbed alone into his Aston Martin. He didn't even check to see if Jason needed a lift. The only good news had been learning that Doctor Foster was going to attend the hearing.

CHAPTER 17

6 p.m. Tuesday 25th September, Paris - France

Craig McDonald was already waiting on the pavement as Ryan exited the Hotel de Crillon. Ryan shook his head as Craig, dressed in just a T-shirt and shorts, lay on the ground stretching, oblivious to the amused stares from passing pedestrians. Ryan stood self-consciously, with hands on his hips as he waited for Craig to finish his routine. Just as Craig stood up, Kramer ambled out of the hotel wearing a ludicrous pair of yellow cycling shorts.

'You guys going to stretch?' asked Craig, though he already knew the answer.

'Stuff that,' said Ryan. 'Have you any idea where we're going to run?'

'Well, I guess we don't want to get lost, so I thought we'd run along the river towards that big church on the island.'

'You mean the Notre Dame,' snorted Ryan derisively.

'Whatever,' replied Craig, not at all put out.

Without waiting for further comment on his choice of route, Craig set off at a brisk pace. Ryan and Jason had no option but to follow the quick moving Australian. Ryan had little chance to study the Place de la Concorde as they headed south towards the Seine. In the distance though he could see the Eiffel tower soaring high into the sky, dwarfing the ancient Egyptian Luxor obelisk that dominated the square. Both monuments witness to man's determination to reach towards the heavens.

In the early evening the traffic was still heavy, and McDonald jogged impatiently on the spot as he waited for the traffic lights to change at the southern end of the Place. After an interminable wait the lights finally changed and they were able to cross the road. Ryan had a disappointing feeling that the run was going to be a series such of interruptions - but at least it helped slow Craig down.

As they crossed the Pont de la Concorde a long sleek white river-boat slid majestically below their feet; the passengers waiving energetically at the runners above.

The three men turned left along the Seine; oblivious to the architectural magnificence of the neo-classical National Assembly building. Running on the pavements was not easy; in places the stone paving was uneven and from time to time they had to dodge fast moving Parisians on tiny push scooters.

Sunset was not for another hour and a half, but the light was already beginning to fade as they rounded Notre Dame. Despite the early evening chill, Ryan was already sweating. The physical activity, and splendid views, stopped him thinking too much about the hearing that was looming Sadly, they would soon have to turn back, for Chris Somerset felt they should go out on the town to eat, and had booked a table for eight-thirty.

As they crossed back over the Seine and began the two-mile return journey, it became clear that Jason was struggling. The American had fallen fifty yards behind Craig and Ryan, who were still moving at what was an easy pace for both of them. Craig glanced behind to check that Jason was out of hearing distance, and then spoke to Ryan.

'Looks like lover boy's not as fit as he should be.' Craig was amused at the American's lack of fitness. It was a clear indication that his work with Ryan was worthwhile.

'True, but he still drives well enough.' Ryan was enjoying his new level of fitness, but he wasn't going to give Craig the satisfaction of letting him know how pleased he was!

'Listen, while we've got a chance to speak, have you spoken to Jason yet?'

'Not really,' apologised Ryan. 'The time just hasn't seemed right - and I didn't want to risk upsetting him before tomorrow. If we win, then it won't really matter what happened, if we lose, then it's probably too late!'

Craig suspected that Ryan had bottled it. Perhaps he should have agreed to quiz Jason. They ran on a bit further in silence. Craig was happy to let Ryan stew in his embarrassment. Eventually, Ryan looked back over his shoulder to check on Jason's progress. Kramer had fallen even further behind.

'Don't you think we ought to let him catch up?'

Craig took the hint, and eased off the pace a little. It would still take Kramer a while to rejoin them.

'What about Warren, you haven't told me how you got on there?' asked Ryan.

'Well... I don't think he had anything to do with what happened in Indianapolis. He owned up to following you and Jason to the first bar, but lost you after that - apparently he was just feeling left out!'

'How sure are you?' Ryan was surprised at Warren's apparent childishness.

'Very, I had to lean on him quite heavily.'

Ryan looked at Craig anxiously.

'Don't worry - he's fine, but I don't think either of us will be on his Christmas card list this year!' Craig decided to keep his own fears about Warren's reaction to himself. If he became a genuine problem to Ryan, they could worry about it then. Now, there was nothing that either of them could do that would improve the situation. He didn't regret his manhandling of Warren. The guy was a loser, and Craig had to be certain he got the truth out of him. As far as he was concerned, the end justified the means.

'Hey, guys, you coulda waited for me!' Jason was breathing hard as he moved alongside the other two.

'Thought you needed the workout!' retorted Craig, unimpressed by Jason's fitness, 'I think you need to come out with us more regularly!'

'Uh uh! No way, not if you're going to sprint around like that!' Jason was unconvinced that he needed to be any fitter than he was.

The three men ran together at a slower pace past the enormous Musee du Louvre and into the Jardin des Tuileries. As they neared the end of the formal park they slowed to a walk to cool down. Despite his worries, Ryan was looking forward to the evening. Dr Foster and Chris Somerset were both excellent dining companions, and he suspected that Nicholas Marwick would also make good company. The three older men made a nice balance to the relative youth of Ryan, Jason and Craig. Somerset had been slightly taken aback when Ryan had said that he wanted Craig to come along. He didn't explain that he needed him to watch his back, and simply said he wanted to get some training done, and that he needed some moral support. Ryan had offered to pay for Craig, but Somerset would have none of it. He wasn't going to have people think he was cheap. Jokingly, he got Ryan to agree that if the appeal went badly, then Ryan would have to pay for the whole group. Six first class air flights and six beds in the five star Hotel de Crillon made it a very expensive affair.

As they exited the park and onto the Place de la Concorde, Ryan finally had a proper chance to study the glorious building that housed not just the hotel but also the FIA headquarters. The prestigious hotel may not be cheap but it was certainly very convenient. The Palladian facade and Corinthian columns lining the 100m length of the 18th century building bore witness to the building's origin as a palace. Not usually so observant, Ryan was struck by the resemblance to Buckingham Palace. The magnificence of the Hotel de Crillon was matched by its sister palace across the Rue Royale that housed the Navy Ministry. The two buildings dominated the entire north end of the Place de la Concorde. In the distant background, between the two palaces, the Greco-Roman styled Madeleine temple completed an architectural tour de force.

The three runners felt distinctly out of place, as they padded through the diamond patterned marbled lobby in their running kit. Light from the elegant chandeliers leant a golden hue to marble walls and columns. It was no surprise that the top hotel was favoured by the rich and famous. Ryan even thought he had caught a glimpse of Madonna earlier that day. As they passed, a smartly dressed businessmen turned to his colleague and said something in French. Ryan was fairly certain the man had just said something derogatory about them. Jogging may be very popular, but was not indulged in by many residents of world-class hotels!

Just after eight p.m, the six men left the hotel, and set off on foot for the restaurant on the South bank. They crossed the same bridge that the three younger men had run over earlier that evening. Now that it was dark, a different, more seductive atmosphere replaced the earlier daytime views. Red, white and green lights reflected off the water - constantly shimmering in the fast flowing water. Floodlights cast a warm yellow glow on the historic buildings they passed.

The restaurant Laperouse was located in the St-Germain-des-pres quarter. The group chatted convivially all the way, and the fifteen-minute walk from the hotel seemed much shorter.

'According to the books this is a real classic French restaurant,' said Somerset enthusiastically as they approached the entrance to the 18th century restaurant. He couldn't resist doing the tourist bit when given the chance on his away trips.

'Snails and Frog-legs bathed in an awful cream and garlic sauce you mean,' said Ryan who enjoyed winding his boss up.

'No, this is a proper Michelin starred restaurant and they also...' he stopped himself as he realised Ryan was only teasing. 'You'll see what I mean when we get inside.'

Even Ryan was speechless as they stepped through the entrance. Mirrors and portraits covered nearly every inch of the walls above dark wood panelling. Even more light sparkled off the array of glasses hanging over the bar.

'In the 19th century this place was famed for the writers who came here; Zola, Dumas and Hugo to name a few. It was also famous for prostitutes... ' Somerset paused. 'Under the circumstances I think we'd better forget that particular association!'

Before Ryan could think of anything clever to say the Maitre'D appeared. Having established that they had a booking he led them up a flight of stairs to one of the small private dining salons on the first floor.

'I thought it best that we had somewhere to ourselves,' explained Somerset.

The small dining room was as ornate as the entrance. Engraved mirrors and dark wood panels lined the walls. Ryan thought it was rather like being in the cabin of an old wooden ship.

As they studied the menu, written entirely in French, Somerset gave them the benefit of his knowledge.

He pointed at one of the mirrors, 'See those scratches. Apparently they were caused by prostitutes testing the diamonds they were sometimes given in lieu of cash.'

'Where on earth did you get that bullshit?' asked Ryan.

'A friend of mine recommended this place, so I looked it up in a guidebook! Anyway, it's also famous for its food - if you're interested.'

The group resumed their study of the menu. After a long wait a waiter ambled over to take their order.

The evening lived up to all expectations. Despite their half-hearted objections, Chris plied the drivers with drink. He knew they preferred not to drink in the days before a race, but he felt that these were exceptional circumstances - and one day would not make that much difference. However, he wasn't going to let them out of his sight, he didn't want to see any more lurid stories in his morning paper.

Ryan did his best not to think about the next day, but as he finished his breast of chicken in a Port sauce, he asked Marwick the question that had been bugging him all day.

'Nick, what do you really think my chances are?'

Somerset glared at Ryan, he had been keen to keep Ryan's mind off the hearing. Marwick sighed. He then reached for his napkin, and carefully wiped his mouth as he considered his reply.

'They're not good. As I said the other day, there is no doubt you took part in the events pictured. I think it will boil down to how much responsibility they think you had, and I guess, as to whether they think you have upset the reputation of the sport. Fortunately, it wasn't a sporting or sport related incident. However, they are not going to be impressed with the drug taking aspect. I think you will be punished, but I hope we can persuade them to be lenient. Now I think we had better change the subject - this was supposed to be a fun evening!'

Somerset shook his head. He had already asked Marwick the same question, and the answer didn't make any better hearing the second time round.

'Come on Ryan, have another drink, and lighten up.' Somerset leant over and refilled Ryan's glass.

'Okay, I'll try!' said Ryan, dispiritedly. He hadn't meant to ask the question, it had just slipped out. He wasn't really surprised at the answer, but was very disappointed with his own foolishness. He had been enjoying the evening, and was worried that he had spoilt things for everyone else.

While Ryan tried to recover his composure, Craig quickly started telling a joke. The filthy tale, was hardly fit for the surroundings, but soon had the others in stitches. Despite himself, Ryan grinned. Craig had a way with stories, and even Ryan hadn't heard the joke before.

By the end of the evening, gales of laughter swept the restaurant, and the tales became more outrageous. It seemed that the legal and medical professions were just as rich a source of apocryphal stories as the motor-racing circuit. They could have talked well into the small hours, but at 11:30 Somerset looked at his watch, then addressed the group.

'Gentlemen and drivers!' he paused for the inevitable jeers from Ryan and Jason. 'Thank you, it's been a great evening, but we have a long day ahead of us, so I think we should call it a day and head back to the hotel.' He snapped a finger, and gestured for the bill.

The walk back to the hotel took far longer than the outward journey. None of the men were sober, and it soon turned into a relaxed amble. Jokes and stories were still being swapped, as they stopped at the southern end of the Place de la Concorde to admire their Hotel bathed in light. It was after midnight when they entered the hotel.

The next morning, Ryan stared gloomily out of a large glass window in the restaurant. Rain beat a constant drum roll against the glass. Overnight the weather had changed dramatically. The dark skies and cold hard rain perfectly matched Ryan's mood. Unlike the weather, there was a chance that sunshine would not return to his life. On the fine china plate in front of him, a half-eaten croissant bore witness to his lack of hunger. He had been the first of the party to make it in to breakfast, but he didn't really feel like eating.

'Morning Ryan, sleep well?' Dr Foster was habitually an early riser. In spite of the weather, he was feeling cheery, he rarely got to take a break, and he was rather enjoying the whole affair.

'I guess.' Ryan had hardly slept a wink, but he was not ready to tell the doctor that, in case he started fussing.

'Well, cheer up - no one's about to die!' The doctor tried, unsuccessfully, to raise a smile from Ryan.

Ryan returned to looking out of the window, as a waitress asked the doctor if he wanted tea or coffee. The doctor ordered a coffee, then walked over to the well-stocked breakfast buffet table.

No one might die, but Ryan didn't know what he'd do with his life if he weren't allowed to drive again. Might just as well be dead, he mused.

Before long, the others joined them. They had to be up fairly early, as the hearing was scheduled for ten o'clock. Ryan envied their ability to laugh and joke. He was wrapped up in his own thoughts, and he let the animated conversation just wash over him, as he sipped his third cup of coffee. Only that morning he had learnt that the Place de la Concorde had been the site of the guillotine during the French Revolution. Right now, it felt just like that - a place of execution.

Nervously, he hung back at the rear of the group as they entered the building.

After spending just a few minutes in a plush reception area, the clocks chimed ten, and Ryan and the lawyer were shown into the large Council meeting room. A series of tables surrounded the room. The council members were sat together on one table, along with their own lawyer and a stenographer. Marwick and Ryan were motioned to a table facing the council. Notepads and pencils were laid out ready for them. Microphones and headphones were provided to enable translators to interpret the proceedings. The rest of the group remained outside the doors.

The British chairman welcomed them warmly, then got straight down to business.

'Ryan Clarke, this is not a court of law, however, you have been summoned before us to answer an allegation that, through your conduct, you have breached article 151c of the International Sporting Code. A breach of article 151c can be said to have occurred if a team member participates in any fraudulent conduct, or any act prejudicial to the interests of any competition, or to the interests of motor sport generally. If you are deemed to have brought the sport into disrepute, then we will have no alternative but to penalise you under the International Sporting Code. I remind you, that such penalties range from fines and suspension, through to disqualification. I note that you have wisely chosen to have legal representation. We shall begin, by hearing the evidence concerning the allegation. You will then have an opportunity to put before us anything you have to say on your behalf. After that, you will be asked to retire, so that the council may consider whether a breach has occurred, and if so, to determine an appropriate penalty. In the event that the charge is upheld, you will have a right of appeal. Is what I have said clear?'

'Yes sir,' answered Ryan, as loudly and as positively as he could. He could already feel sweat trickling from his armpits. At least the dark-blue suit he was wearing would hide any obvious signs.

The chairman addressed everyone present, 'Gentlemen, you have in front of you a folder containing a collection of newspaper articles. I apologise if some of the pictures are a trifle explicit. Can you please take five minutes to familiarise yourselves with the contents.'

Ryan opened the folder, and leafed through the articles. After the chairman's remarks, he was concerned that pictures he hadn't seen before, had emerged in foreign newspapers. He was very relieved to see that the pictures and articles were all from the British press, and he had seen all of those. He quickly finished his study, then looked round the room. Judging by their expressions, one or two of the Council members seemed to be enjoying themselves a bit too much. The ageing Italian representative, in particular, took an inordinate amount of time considering a single photo. Ryan could only hope that he would get a fair hearing.

If he had known what the Italian had been thinking, he need not have been so concerned. The elderly man had been a racing driver, in an age when drivers were expected to enjoy themselves to the full. The picture he spent ages studying, reminded him of a particularly enjoyable night in Rome. He really couldn't see what the fuss was all about. In his day, such behaviour would almost have been considered mandatory! He hoped Ryan wouldn't have to suffer too much, but he supposed the Council would have to put him through it for appearance's sake. He inwardly sighed at the wickedness of the modern world.

Satisfied that they had all digested the contents of the folders, the chairman again addressed Ryan.

'Do you agree, that the person shown in the pictures, and referred to, is yourself?'

Marwick rose to his feet. His size and bearing dominating the room.

'I would like to answer that question on behalf of my client. Mr Clarke accepts that there is little or no doubt that he could be the person in the pictures and articles. Because he has no personal recollection of the events, he is not in a position to absolutely confirm it is him. However, it is not our intention to dispute the identity of the person referred to. For the purposes of this hearing, we will accept that the pictures and articles do indeed refer to Mr Clarke.'

'Thank you, Mr Marwick, at least we are spared a lengthy debate as to identity.' The chairman nodded at Marwick, and gestured for him to sit down.

There was a palpable sense of relief around the table. It would have been extremely awkward if it had been proved that the person in the pictures was not Ryan Clarke. Several of the members were puzzled at Marwick's approach. If it had been them, they would have lengthily disputed the identity. The chairman continued.

'It is for us to decide, in due course, as to whether the incident does, in fact, constitute a case of bringing the sport into disrepute. Before we reach that stage, we would like Mr Clarke to explain his actions to us, in order that we might better understand his role in events.'

Once again Marwick rose from his seat. 'Mr Chairman, with your permission, I would first like to call Doctor Timothy Foster - he was the doctor who examined Mr Clarke on his return to England. He discovered the presence of the drug Rohypnol, that you have all seen referred to in the newspaper reports. Doctor Foster has kindly agreed to attend as an expert witness.'

'The Council have no objections,' the chairman signalled to an usher who waited by the door. 'Please ask Doctor Foster to come in.'

Marwick had hoped there would be no trouble introducing Doctor Foster, for he had privately spoken to the chairman several days previously. Still, he wasn't sure that the rest of the Council would be so accommodating.

Doctor Foster entered the room behind the usher, and was shown to a spare seat next to Nicholas Marwick - on the other side from Ryan Clarke. Some niceties were still being observed.

'Dr Foster, the Council welcomes you to this hearing. You may give your evidence from your seat.' The chairman sought to put Dr Foster at ease. There was no need. Dr Tim Foster had spent most of his adult life among men such as this, and no small part of it in courtrooms. On several occasions, he had attended tribunals on behalf of clients.

'Dr Foster, could you please outline your qualifications for the benefit of the Council,' asked Nicholas Marwick. The doctor confidently reeled off the details of his professional qualifications.

Even Ryan was surprised to learn that the Doctor had spent some time working in a drug rehabilitation clinic. No wonder the doctor had sounded so knowledgeable, on the day he had visited him.

'Thank you Doctor. Can you please explain what happened, when Mr Clarke consulted you on the 19th of September.' Marwick checked his notes, to make sure he'd got the right date.

'Mr Clarke came to see me just after eight-fifteen that morning. He said, he thought it was possible that he had been drugged. I thought it best, given the length of time that had elapsed since the incidents described in the newspapers, that I take a blood sample as soon as possible. He, himself, had no memory of the events. Due to the nature of what Mr Clarke was asking, I took the precaution of taking two sets of samples. One set I analysed that morning. The other set, I sent to an independent laboratory; I have their written report right here.

I'm afraid that it is quite technical, but they have managed a summary that bears a resemblance to normal English,' the Doctor hoped to lighten the atmosphere. He opened a folder, and extracted copies of the laboratory's report - passing them to the usher for distribution.

'With respect, gentlemen, I suggest that you don't read the report just yet. It merely serves to confirm what I am going to tell you.'

The Council members were warming to the doctor; they had feared they might be in for a dry and highly technical explanation.

'I am sure that you will have seen the statement I wrote on behalf of Mr Clarke. The blood tests, conducted by myself, and the other laboratory, confirm the presence of Rohypnol. I would now like to take a little of your time, to explain, in layman's terms, how Rohypnol works.' Encouraged by the nods from the far end of the table, the doctor continued.

'Rohypnol has been popularly called the 'date rape drug', as it has been implicated in a number of date rape cases in the United States. It is a legitimate drug, used for the short-term treatment of sleep disorders, but when combined with alcohol, it can make its users shed their inhibitions. It can also render loss of memory. It is fairly fast acting, and amnesia can set in within ten minutes of the drug being ingested.'

The doctor paused to make sure that the important point sunk in round the table.

'The effects can last for up to 8 hours. In recent years, a blue dye has been added to the drug to make it easier to detect in drinks, but it is possible to get counterfeit versions that have not been treated. This is especially true of the United States!'

Nicholas Marwick gratefully left the doctor to his own devices. He was pleased he didn't have to conduct a long question and answer session. He listened, along with the other council members, as the doctor eloquently explained - in simple terms -the affect the drug had on the body, how it could be administered, and examples of cases from medical journals.

'Mr Chairman, I have copies of the journal reports if you would like to see them?'

'Thank you Dr Foster, if you would like to pass the copies to the usher we will keep them for reference. I hope I speak for the rest of the Council, when I congratulate you on presenting your evidence in such an informative and authoritative manner.' The chairman looked round the table at the other Council members. They all nodded in agreement.

'Does anyone have any questions for Dr Foster before we excuse him?'

There was a lengthy period of silence, as the council members racked their brains to find a question that had not been covered in the doctor's comprehensive evidence. Finally, the French Council member risked a question.

'Does Rohypnol always render memory as ineffective as suggested in this case?'

'No, it doesn't,' replied the doctor, firmly. 'It is always extremely difficult to judge whether a person has genuinely lost their memory, or is merely being selective about what they choose to remember. One has to know the person concerned in order to form a valid subjective opinion as to whether that person has indeed lost their memory. Fortunately, I have treated Mr Clarke for a number of years, and I have no difficulty in accepting his assertion that he has no memory of the incidents that took place. His memory of events appears to stop at a point in the evening, and does not recover until many hours later. This is entirely consistent with the effect of Rohypnol. Mr Clarke was also very stressed, and confused, when I saw him.'

'Any more questions?' asked the chairman. He waited a few seconds. 'In that case, Doctor Foster, you may retire from the room.'

The doctor collected his things, and followed the usher out of the room.

They all waited until the doctor had left, then the chairman spoke.

'I would now like to ask Mr Clarke to give us his version of events.'

Ryan cleared his throat, and then with a confidence he didn't feel, addressed the council.

'Mr Chairman, and Council members, I would like to start my account at the beginning of the evening.'

Ryan paused, to check that they agreed, and then he began to recount the events of that evening - as he remembered them. From time to time, he glanced at a sheet of typed paper in front of him on the table; he neither wanted to miss anything, or get anything in the wrong order. His account ended with his visit to the doctor. He spoke for just over five minutes, but it seemed much longer as the row of faces, at the other end of the table, stared, unnervingly, at him.

When Ryan had finished speaking, the chairman addressed him.

'Mr Clarke, we would now like to question you further about your role in this incident. If you do not understand a question, please ask either myself, or your own lawyer, for an explanation.' The chairman looked at his fellow Council members. 'Gentlemen, do you have any questions for Mr Clarke?'

'Mr Clarke, have you ever taken drugs?' asked the German council member.

'Definitely not! Drugs and motor racing do not go together, and I would rather drive cars.' Ryan felt it best to keep quiet about the odd joint he had tried as a youth; only very good friends of his were aware of his youthful misdemeanours, and he hoped they could be trusted to stay quiet. He had been asked the same question before, and it wasn't too hard to sound convincing, but it was a tricky moment.

'Have you ever been in trouble with the police?' asked the Italian member.

'Never.' At least he could answer that one truthfully.

The next few questions all seemed to be concerned with establishing his moral character. Much to his surprise, they left his sex life out of the proceedings. It seemed that the council had accepted his version of events. Ryan wondered if Kramer was going to get a chance to testify on his behalf.

Before he knew it, the questions were over.

The chairman addressed Ryan. 'Mr Clarke, we have no further questions for you. Is there anything else you would like to add?'

Ryan looked at Nicholas Marwick, who shook his head.

'No, Mr Chairman.'

'Mr Marwick, is there anything you would like to say before we ask you both to retire?'

Nicholas Marwick was pleased that the questions had been much lighter than he had expected - although it was still impossible to calculate the outcome. For all he knew, they may already have made their minds up! Like Ryan, he was surprised that the council had not asked to see Jason Kramer - for they were well aware of his presence. On balance, he judged that there was nothing Kramer could usefully add. It was not worth over egging the pudding.

'No, Mr Chairman.'

'In which case, I would ask you both to retire from the room, so that we can consider our judgement. I thank you both for attending. If you would like to wait outside, we will call for you in a short while.'

The two men gathered up their things and left the room. There was nothing Ryan could do now - but wait. His driving future was going to be decided by a dozen strangers, none of them less than double his age.

They rejoined the others in the reception area.

'How did it go?' asked Somerset, eagerly. He had practically worn a groove in the carpet with his constant pacing! He had been frustrated at not being allowed to sit in on the hearing itself.

'So, so,' said Ryan, but he didn't actually have a clue.

'It's in the balance,' said Marwick, keen not to raise hopes too high.

'How come I didn't get called?' asked Kramer, who was actually rather relieved.

'No need I'm afraid,' replied Marwick. 'The more the evidence we provide, the more likely they'd be to find a hole. I needed you here just in case they disputed what occurred. I think the doctor did a great job.' Marwick nodded at the doctor, who dismissed the congratulations with a wave of his hand.

'My pleasure,' he said.

'Now we must wait. I don't think they'll take too long.' He could have told them that he and the chairman of the council had gone to the same public school, and that they had privately discussed the matter a few days ago. Still, he couldn't be too sure of the other Council members. Sagely, he kept quiet.

While they waited, they sat down to cups of freshly brewed coffee. Ryan wasn't in the mood for chatting, and he put his cup down on the table half drunk.

'If you don't mind, I need some fresh air, I'll be just outside the front door.'

He got up and walked out, leaving the others to continue their conversation. Outside the building, he undid the collar of his shirt, and took in a few deep lungfuls of air. Dust and dirt loosened by the rain had combined with the traffic fumes to produce the distinctive smell of a wet city. The fusty smell hung cloyingly in the drizzle that had replaced the earlier rain. Even the damp penetrating drizzle was welcome after being shut in the Council room. He sighed deeply. At least it would soon be over - one way or another. But what if things went against him? He knew he should try and be positive, like Craig was always telling him, but theory and practice were two very different things.

'Bit hot in there.' Craig McDonald had given Ryan a few minutes on his own, before joining him. He wanted to stop Ryan thinking too deeply about things.

'Yeah,' affirmed Ryan. He wasn't ready to chat.

Craig stood quietly, letting Ryan get used to his presence before he spoke again.

'Good job the forecast's better for the weekend. I don't think you'd want to drive in this.'

'I'd drive in anything given the chance,' said Ryan, bitterly.

'It could be a bit like last year at Spa. You were lucky not to get caught up in that pile up at the start.'

'That wasn't luck!' snorted Ryan. 'I was one of the few looking where they were going.'

Craig's simple ploy had worked. It was never difficult to get Ryan to talk about motor racing.

They were still talking motor races, when Marwick came out. Ryan was sure his heart was beating faster than normal, as he followed his lawyer back into the Council room. The last time he felt like this, was on a rare occasion when he had been called in to see the headmaster, way back in his schooldays. He sat down, and tried to still his pounding heart as he waited for the Chairman to speak. He didn't have to wait long.

'Ryan Clarke, we called you here to face accusations that you have brought the sport of motor racing into disrepute by your behaviour. There is no disputing the facts of your behaviour, and that behaviour has been judged, by all of us on the council, to have indeed brought the sport into disrepute.'

Ryan bowed his head. There was no chance of getting away from this cleanly. 'God, please don't let them take my licence away,' he prayed, with eyes closed.

'We cannot possibly let such behaviour go unpunished. Normally, we would consider suspending a driver's licence for such gross misbehaviour.'

'They're going to throw me out!' thought Ryan, in a sudden panic.

'But, it would be wrong of us to ignore the role that the drug Rohypnol played. Under such circumstances, we cannot properly form an opinion as to whether or not you were truly to blame for your actions. Taking your previous good behaviour into account, we are prepared to take a lenient view. We have therefore decided to impose a fine of £10,000, and to make a note on your file. You may also consider yourself to be severely reprimanded.

If we have cause to call you before us again, we will be forced to take this matter into account - and I cannot envisage us being so lenient again!'

'Yes - thank you God,' muttered Ryan, under his breath. He opened his eyes, and looked at Marwick, who winked back.

'Let that be an end to it. Thank you both for attending. I believe you owe a debt of thanks to Doctor Foster - whose evidence was both eloquent and persuasive. I declare this hearing closed.' The chairman banged his gavel. Immediately, the room came alive with the buzz of conversation as groups of people began to chat.

Ryan reached across to Marwick, and offered his hand. Marwick patted the back of Ryan's hand as he warmly shook it. 'That was a bit close,' said the lawyer.

'Give me a one hundred and fifty mile-an-hour crash any day,' replied Ryan, 'let's get out of here before they change their minds!'

CHAPTER 18

2:25 p.m. Saturday 29th September, Nurburgring Circuit - Germany

'...Hopefully I can build on that good qualifying position, and finish the season in the papers for all the right reasons! Now, if you don't mind, I have things to discuss with the team.' Despite holding a press conference the previous day, reporters were still pestering Ryan for interviews. The reporter for F1 magazine had caught him on his way back from the pits; the short interview had been conducted just inside the paddock entrance, with people milling around them. His Indianapolis adventure and the FIA hearing were both newsworthy stories. The season was nearing its climax, and the news-hounds were beginning to run short on new stories. Whilst he tried to be as frank and as helpful as he could with each journalist, the constant interruptions were becoming a real nuisance. Media attention was a price you paid for being a racing driver, but this level of celebrity was something he had never experienced before.

'Okay. Well, thanks Ryan. Good luck in the race tomorrow. I thought that was a great job you did today!' The English reporter was genuinely pleased for Ryan, one of only three British drivers in the championship. It seemed a very long time since Damon Hill had been World Champion, and the reporter would rather write about a fellow countryman doing well than waste several hours trying to find something interesting to say about Wittman.

Satisfied with his interview, he cagily looked around for another target before moving off.

Ryan ran a hand through his damp hair, and continued his slow amble back to the motorhome. As he wandered through the busy paddock, he couldn't help but notice that people were unsure how to react to him. He was aware that some people turned away, or even looked down at the ground, but despite the odd negative reaction, he smiled with pleasure as he reflected on the result of the qualifying session. Tenth was his second highest grid placing of the season. He knew he had driven well, but much of the credit was down to hard work in the factory.

All season, the team had struggled with a measure of understeer on the Vantec, Finally, in late August, Barry O'Donnell the Chief Designer decided to experiment with a slightly longer wheelbase. Wind-tunnel results had only shown a very marginal improvement, but Somerset thought it worth pursuing the experiment on the track with one of the cars. As a result, the factory had worked long and hard to prepare a single chassis in time for the Nurburgring. Somerset had only informed the drivers of the change when they had arrived at the circuit.

The wind-tunnel results may not have been conclusive, but Ryan knew after just one lap in practice on Friday that the change was worthwhile. The car was far more stable in the corners, which allowed him to get on to the power faster on the exits. The final proof had been in qualifying. Once the tyres were on song, each successive timed run was faster. After all the nonsense of the past two weeks, Ryan was delighted to make his mark on the track.

As Ryan neared the team's motorhome complex, he saw Wittman coming out of Maggie's canteen. The Austrian mounted a red scooter and drove straight at Ryan. Wittman stopped his bike a yard in front of Ryan, but remained seated. Ryan decided to ignore the Ferrari driver, who rarely had anything friendly to say. Surprisingly, Wittman just stared as Ryan side-stepped the bike and walked on. Ryan had only gone another five yards when Wittman shouted,

'I hope the girls have kept the bed warm for you!'

Ryan bristled, and momentarily stopped in his tracks, before he shrugged and walked on. It had been such a pathetic taunt from the driver. He had heard far worse, and he wasn't going to let the obnoxious Austrian get to him, but it broke the spell and brought him back down to earth with a bump. Qualifying was just that, he would have to do even better in the race if he was really going to shut his critics up.

What Ryan couldn't understand was, what Wittman was doing in Maggie's canteen? It was unlike Wittman to stray very far from the Ferrari pitch. He had few friends, and seemed happiest surrounded with his own coterie of arse-lickers. Well, there was only one way to find out, so Ryan changed his mind about going straight back to his motorhome and made for the canteen. It would be interesting to see what Maggie made of the Austrian's visit. At least he could get a drink while he was there, he was feeling quite parched after the drive and the interminable interviews.

The awning-covered hospitality area was doing good business. There were only a dozen tables, and most of them were occupied. There were no women in sight. Groups of men were excitedly discussing the qualifying session that they had just witnessed. Paddock and security passes dangled from every neck like Olympic medals. The value of these medals, although difficult to obtain without money or fame, was rather more prosaic.

Conspicuous by their absence were the team mechanics – they were still busy working on the cars, readying them for the torture they would face the next day. Their work would continue late into the afternoon.

In his bright green racing overalls, Warren Barton stuck out like a solitary cucumber left on the supermarket shelves. The driver was sitting by himself, nursing a cup of coffee, as far away from the other occupied tables as he could get. Barton was staring at the table, and didn't look up as Ryan entered the area.

Ryan could understand Barton's dissatisfaction. Once again, he had travelled out to a Grand Prix, only to spend his time sitting around waiting for something unforeseen to happen to one of the drivers - to remain totally focused, ready to step into a car at very short notice, was a difficult ask for anyone. The spare driver needed to know the track as well as the main drivers, yet would have little opportunity to drive the circuit itself. With qualifying over, Barton's chance of driving in Germany had slipped even further away. Ryan decided to have his talk with Maggie before joining Warren.

He made his way through the collection of cloth covered plastic tables that constituted the dining area, and popped his head into the trailer, where Maggie was hard at work preparing yet more meals. Maggie had her back to Ryan.

'Ello darlin', any chance of a fry-up?' asked Ryan, in his best impression of a South London mechanic.

Ryan was grinning broadly as Maggie angrily turned round, ready to chastise whichever poor sod dared to call her darling.

'I might have known it was you,' she said, smiling, no trace of anger in her voice, 'Well done. I hear you've had a good one.'

'Yeah, pretty good - makes a change doesn't it!' Ryan changed the subject, he'd had enough of talking about the session, 'What did Wittman want? I was surprised to see him in here.'

'So was I,' said Maggie vehemently, wiping her hands on her apron, she detested the Ferrari driver. 'He didn't have anything to eat or drink, though. Said he was looking for someone, but didn't say who.'

'I don't suppose it was me, because he didn't stop when I saw him just now.'

'I guess we'll never know. Funnily enough, he was the second person in here: "Just looking for someone". Jason's been in as well - I think he was after you. Said he'd be back in the motorhome.'

Maggie reached into an apron pocket and fished out a small bottle of pills. 'I found these just now, when I was clearing up. I don't remember seeing them earlier. Maybe they're Jason's? Could you pop them back to me if they're not? Someone must need them.'

'Yeah, sure.' Ryan took the bottle from Maggie. He wanted to take a close look at the tablets. It would certainly be interesting if the tablets proved to have non-medical uses. Perhaps more important, though, was to know who had left them. He had a sudden thought. 'How long has Warren been out there?'

Maggie unconsciously wiped her clean hands again, 'He came in about ten minutes ago. You could ask him if he saw anyone leave the bottle. They could have been left at anytime in the last half-hour,' Maggie paused as she carefully picked her words, she wasn't one for malicious gossip. 'I don't think Warren's in a very good mood,' she said.

'That's an understatement, Maggie, I'd say he's severely fucked off!' Ryan grinned as Maggie blushed, he enjoyed teasing the matronly woman. Even though she frequently heard far worse from the mechanics, she still reacted endearingly to foul language. 'I think I'd better have a chat with him. Bring us a mug of coffee will you - when you're ready!' he added quickly. Then he turned and retreated from Maggie's territory. As much as he disliked the idea, he thought he'd better have his talk with Warren. It was crucial that the team all pulled together, and he was, after all, the team leader.

Warren looked up sourly as Ryan's shadow loomed over him. He looked away, and said nothing. Ryan sat down. 'Fuck you,' he thought.

'Hi Warren, how goes it?' he asked, as cheerfully as he could.

Warren looked directly at Ryan, his jaw set firm and his eyes narrowing.

'Like you care!' Warren looked away again, discouraging further conversation.

Well, that's taken care of the social chit-chat, thought Ryan. There didn't seem much point in trying to jolly the miserable driver along. He still wanted to know about the tablets, so he risked another question.

'You didn't see who left these did you?' Ryan shook the bottle in front of Warren's face.

'I told your sidekick, you can sort your own puzzles out,' Barton practically spat his reply out, then pushed his plastic seat back and stood up. Without a further word, he stormed out of the tent - leaving a half finished cup of coffee on the table. His rushed exit caused a few heads to turn, and conversation in the tent came to an abrupt halt. Ryan shrugged his shoulders. The excitement over, the other groups resumed their conversations.

Ryan sat in quiet contemplation. He hadn't expected such a negative reaction from Barton. He must have a word with McDonald. He guessed that Craig hadn't told him everything about his meeting with Barton. It didn't look like they were making any progress as detectives - but he could have done without creating another enemy. It didn't bode well for the team either – the last thing they needed was internal warfare! He was still puzzling over the whole business, when Maggie quietly placed a mug of steaming coffee in front of him and left. She had witnessed Warren's stormy departure, and reckoned Ryan needed some time on his own.

Ryan studied the pill bottle as he drank his coffee. Turning it over in his right hand, he could see no markings - or any other indication of the contents or user. He opened the bottle and closely examined one of the pills. The white oval pill was unmarked. The pill looked ordinary enough, but then he wouldn't know a dodgy pill if he saw one. He removed another couple of tablets and put them in his pocket. He would see if he could get someone back home to identify the tablets. With any luck, Dr Foster would check them out for him. It was a pity that the doctor hadn't come out to the race. It would have been good to have a quick answer.

Climbing up into the motorhome, Ryan could hear a rush of water from the shower. Kramer had obviously beaten him to it. Despite his more than reasonable 12th place on the grid, Jason had escaped the attention of the media. Ryan placed the pill bottle on a small table, then decided to check his e-mail while he waited for Jason to finish his shower. He fetched his notebook computer from where he had left it on his bunk, and settled down on a sofa in the tiny lounge to log on.

Ryan powered the computer up without trouble, but as soon as he tried to access the e-mail service he ran into problems. He thought he had seen most error messages over the years, but he couldn't make head or tail of the garbage that now appeared on the screen. He logged off and on again several times over the next few minutes as he tried everything he knew, but all to no avail. Before long, he was swearing and thumping the machine as successive attempts to read his waiting mail failed. He was still fiddling, as Jason emerged from the shower, his lower body wrapped in a large bath towel. He was drying his curly black hair on a smaller towel.

'Having trouble?' asked Jason, amused.

'Like you wouldn't believe!'

Kramer sat down on the sofa beside Ryan, and looked at the screen.

'Hmm, see what you mean. Hand it over - I'll see what I can do.'

Ryan passed the computer over without much hope. He wasn't prepared for what happened next. Kramer's fingers flew over the keyboard, he couldn't have been more at home in a racing car. As the American swapped in and out of accessories and programs on the computer, Ryan could only watch in amazement.

'There, that should do it. Try your mail again.' Kramer sounded triumphant as he handed the computer back. Ryan connected to his mail service, and typed in his password. This time the mail messages appeared in readable text.

'That was brilliant, Jason - where on earth did you learn to do that?'

'Oh, that was pretty simple stuff,' he replied proudly. I did a computing course at school. I've worked with computers for years. Even used to build my own. Any more problems, you know who to call. Look, I'd better get dressed, I don't want to sit around in a damp towel. You'll want to read your mail in peace anyway.' Jason stood up, and hastily grabbed his towel as it started to drop to the floor.

'Before you go - are those yours?' Ryan pointed at the pills on the table.

'Can't be mine, I haven't taken anything for years!' Kramer shook his head.

If he was lying, he was a good liar. Ryan let it go. He'd just have to wait until he could get the tablets checked out.

'Fair enough, I'll return them to Maggie then, she's the one who found them.'

Ryan shook his head as the young American exited the lounge and headed for his cabin. He would love to be able to get around a computer like that. Ryan quickly checked the waiting mail. To his surprise, there was a message from Victoria. He opened and read the short mail. Victoria apologised for not being present at qualifying, but she was hoping to be there for the race. It wasn't a chatty message, but at least she appeared willing to see him again. He left the remaining fifteen mails unread - after checking that there was nothing suspicious or urgent. By the time he made his way to the shower, he was humming cheerfully. Despite Barton, things were definitely looking up.

The weather was bright but windy the next afternoon. As he drove the racing car slowly up the hill towards the Veedol chicane, Ryan could see puffy white clouds moving briskly across the otherwise blue sky. For once the forecast was good, and it promised to be an interesting race. In the practice session that morning, his best lap placed him eighth fastest. He was confident that the car was set-up as well as it could be for the German circuit. Now it was down to him. If he failed to race well, he could wave goodbye to his F1 career.

Ahead of him, the cars began to weave left and right as they took their places on the grid. Ryan brought his own car to a gentle halt on the right of the track. This was definitely the worst part of racing. The wait until they were released by the lights seemed endless, and then there was the double risk of running into a stationary car ahead or being rammed by an over-enthusiastic starter from behind. The 16 metres between cars were not enough to make him feel comfortable.

As the first light turned to red, he clunked into first gear. One by one, the remaining lights on the overhead gantry ahead also turned red. Once the fourth light came on, he depressed the throttle pedal with his right foot until the engine was pulling eleven thousand revs. He could feel the revs vibrating through his left thumb as he held down the clutch locking lever on the steering wheel. The instant the lights went out, he released the lever. A puff of smoke escaped from the rear as the 800 brake horsepower engine thrust the car off the line. Ryan controlled the wheel-spin with the throttle, and short changed into second. Satisfied that the rear wheels were hooked up properly, he floored the throttle. Mercifully, it was a clean start, and soon the whole field of cars was streaming down to turn one. As they approached the turn, Ryan edged over to the left side of the track and slotted in behind the Demaison of Gonzales. He wanted to keep his main rival in close sight.

The silver and black McLaren of Weiss had faultlessly screeched away from pole position, and held the racing line as they approached the Castrol curves. Wittman, in the Ferrari, was tucked in right behind. Behind the two leaders, the other cars were still side by side in pairs.

It was just one of those things. Despite the millions of pounds poured into designing and building the cars, they were still very fragile creations. A powerful screaming F1 car, charging down the road at two hundred miles an hour, could turn into an expensive ornament in a fraction of a second. As Weiss turned into the left hander that was the second part of Castrol, the electric system on his car failed. Bereft of gears, his car now formed a mobile chicane that the rest of the field would have to scramble round.

Wittman had initially thought that Weiss was simply slowing for the turn. When he realised that the McLaren was going nowhere, he sought to pull out and round the car. He might have got away with it, if he hadn't clipped the offside rear wheel on the McLaren. The slight touch spun the Ferrari over to the right. Wittman cleverly caught the spin, but a fraction too late to prevent the second McLaren spearing into his side.

With the whole field now approaching the turn, things became very confused. It was every man for himself. Underwood, who had started third in the Kodama, only had one direction in which to go - he cut across the grass to the left of Weiss, and rejoined the track in first place without any real trouble. Eddison, in the Williams, who had been behind him on the grid, followed into second place. Those drivers who had stayed on the right hand side of the track weren't quite so lucky. As the second McLaren collided with Wittman's Ferrari, they were all forced to slow drastically, the cars concertinaing into a slow moving queue. Fortunately, the pace of the accident took both cars involved off the track to the right, but sharp carbon fibre fragments littered the track.

Ryan was right behind Gonzales, on the left of the track. They both followed Takano, who was in the second Kodama car, as he picked his way through the debris littering the tarmac. Once past the site of the accident, Ryan found himself unexpectedly promoted to fifth place. The cars picked up racing speed as they headed downhill to the Ford curve.

Ryan fully expected to see a red flag being shown, for he couldn't see how the race could possibly continue with three cars parked on the first bend. He was therefore surprised to see the safety car board being held out by a marshal. Still, that could work out better for him. As they wouldn't need a restart, he would be able to close up on the first two cars that had managed to pull away.

They joined up with the safety car at the end of the lap. As they approached the accident site, the stricken cars were already being moved out of the way. The track was cleared quickly, and they were only held behind the slow moving Mercedes for a couple of laps. In the middle of lap four, the safety car turned off its flashing lights. A short while later, the car pulled into the pit lane. The race was on again.

After the excitement of the first lap, the race settled down into an altogether less eventful affair. By the end of the forty-first lap, there was no change in the order at the front. Ryan chased Gonzales round the track for lap after lap, without finding a way to get past. Even the first pit stops, on lap twenty-five, failed to resolve the tight battle. Three times he made fake passing moves at the Veedol chicane to see if Gonzales would react. The Spaniard was too experienced to fall for a simple trick like that, and resolutely stuck to the racing line. The Vantec and Demaison cars were clearly very well matched: unless Ryan could think of something special, he'd have to rely on Gonzales making a mistake. To keep his options open, Ryan continued to hassle the car in front.

On lap forty-two, Ryan got on the radio. He wanted to know if it was possible for him to make time on Gonzales if the Spaniard pitted first.

'When do you want me in?' he asked. 'Can we run long, or do we take Gonzales in the pits?'

'I don't think you're fast enough to stay out. We'll try and take him when he comes in. Be ready.' John Thornhill the team manager had been thinking along similar lines, and had already decided on the tactic.

The Vantec team was not allowed to let their crew out of the garage, and into the pit lane, until the very lap the car was due in. They would have to wait until there was some movement from the Demaison crew - then they would have to move fast.

The forty-third and forty-fourth laps came and went without any sign. By the end of the next lap, Thornhill was beginning to worry. There was not much fuel left in Ryan's car. If the Demaison didn't come in soon, he would have to bring Ryan in regardless. Half way through the forty-sixth lap, Thornhill was forced to radio Ryan.

'Come in, Ryan. We can't stay out.' It looked like the gamble had failed.

But even as Thornhill ended the call, there was movement in the garage next door. The dark-blue liveried Demaison crew swarmed out of their garage and took up their positions on the concrete apron. Due to the team being ahead of Vantec at the end of last season, the team had been allocated the garage immediately before Vantec's.

Ryan was very relieved to be called in - he too was becoming increasingly concerned about the fuel situation. He made a good job of following Gonzales round the rest of the lap, trying to keep as close as possible whilst also conserving fuel.

The two cars peeled off into the pit-lane, line astern. Ryan quickly brought the Vantec down to the allowed speed; it would be stupid to earn a penalty for speeding in the pit lane at this stage. There were only yards separating the two cars as they reached the first of the garages. The Demaison peeled off to the right. As Ryan drove past, the Demaison mechanics were already rushing into action. It was going to be a very close run thing.

Ryan put Gonzales out of his mind, and concentrated on making an accurate stop. Any chance he had of beating the Demaison out of the pits lay with him and the crew being disciplined - and very quick.

Ryan stopped the car as his front rear wheel came under the hand of the nearside mechanic. The drivers, unable to see the line on the ground, relied on a mechanic to mark the correct stopping position. As the car came to a halt, it banged gently against the front lifting trolley. Clouds of black brake dust billowed out from each corner. The moment the car was lifted off the ground, the eighteen mechanics began their well rehearsed manoeuvre.

Even as the four wheel-nuts were being removed - by mechanics with compressed air wheel guns - fuel was being pumped into the near empty fuel tank behind Ryan. The length of the stop would be dictated by the amount of fuel loaded. At a consumption rate of just over 3 litres a lap, Ryan would need the best part of 48 litres to take him to the end of the race. Fuel was gushing into the tank at eleven litres a second. The whole stop would take under 7 seconds.

A mechanic had wiped Ryan's visor as soon as the car had been raised, and now Ryan had nothing to do but hold the engine at 4,000 revs in neutral. After just four seconds, a mechanic on the nearside front wheel raised his right arm to signal that his work was done. Fuel was still flowing as work on all four wheels was completed and the car was lowered to the ground with a bump. Ryan waited impatiently for the signal to select 1st gear. Any second, he expected the dark blue Demaison to drive past. He could see nothing in his mirrors. As always, the refuelling seemed to take an eternity, then suddenly the pole-man flipped his board over, and Ryan selected first gear.

The pole-man was now the key player in the action. Ryan would drive out of the pit on his say so alone, for he couldn't see what was happening behind him.

Rob Johnson had worked the pole for a number of years. Despite all his experience, his mouth was dry with fear as he tried to judge the situation. Not only did he have to make sure his own team had finished their work, but that it was also safe for Ryan to go. Anxious, he could see the Demaison team was nearing the same point.

At last he could see the two men on the fuel-rig starting to pull the heavy nozzle away from the car. Johnson again looked back down the pit lane. The Demaison pole-man was just removing his own pole. It was now or never. He whipped his own pole away from in front of Ryan, and prayed he hadn't made a terrible misjudgement.

There was a screech of brakes as the Demaison was forced to slow, but they had done it. Ryan's car fishtailed slightly as he hit the pit lane just yards ahead of the Demaison. Ryan was unaware of quite how close it had all been. All he knew, and all that mattered, was that he was ahead of Gonzales.

Once back on the circuit, the Vantec had a clear advantage over the Demaison. Ryan gradually pulled out an increasing lead over Gonzales. Nearly all the teams were now making routine pit stops, and it was several laps before Ryan had a good idea of what was going on. According to the pit boards, he was steadily gaining on the third placed car of Takano ahead of him.

Things were rather quiet over the next five laps. Behind him, Gonzales was posing little threat, and Ryan had to concentrate on driving carefully as he slowly closed the gap on Takano. To his amusement and delight, he started to come up to the backmarkers. It was a rare treat to see blue flags being waved on his behalf. The slower cars, however, posed no real problem to either Takano or Ryan.

Ryan finally caught up with Takano on lap fifty-one. Takano was being frustrated by the Williams of Eddison. Ever since the pit stops, he had been following the Williams closely. Several times, the Japanese driver had feigned to overtake on the entrance to the Veedol chicane, but Eddison had been expecting the move, and had defended his line perfectly. Takano had settled for taking a gamble later in the race, but now he also had Ryan to worry about.

The three cars sped round the 3.2 mile circuit one behind the other. For his part, Ryan couldn't see how he could possibly get past Takano - never mind Eddison. It looked like he would end up in the points, but just off the podium. He reminded himself that nothing was settled until the flag dropped, and continued to harry Takano round the hilly circuit.

On lap fifty-seven, as they rounded the Dunlop curve at the bottom of the circuit, Takano again tucked himself under the tail of Eddison. Takano pressured the Brazilian harder than he had done before. It didn't look like the tactic was working any better than before, but as the drivers braked for Veedol, there was a puff of blue smoke from the right rear wheel of the Williams. Eddison had locked a wheel. As the Williams bounced up over the kerbing and onto the grass, both Takano and Ryan took advantage on the road. After exiting the chicane and the turn into the home straight, Ryan found himself in third place. He knew that he had driven well, but the high placing was due to a high measure of racing luck. Still, on so many other occasions things had worked against him.

There were still five laps to go. Takano started to pull away, but Ryan was more concerned that the Williams would get back at him. By the end of the next lap, it looked like the fight had gone out of the Brazilian; either that, or his brakes really were shot.

The final lap couldn't come soon enough for Ryan. He desperately wanted to finish on the podium. But now noises from the car, that hadn't bothered him earlier in the race, were causing him concern. Unsettling noises weren't his only worry. The only way he had got out of the pits ahead of Gonzales had been by taking on less fuel; now he would have to hope they had put enough in. At the beginning of the final lap, Thornhill came over the radio.

'Go easy - fuel is tight. You have nearly two seconds in hand.'

Thanks chaps, thought Ryan, as he eased off the throttle, you sure know how to make a guy relax.

On the hilly circuit, the little petrol that remained was sloshing to and fro in the tank. Ryan nervously rounded the bottom bend, and started the climb up to the RTL curve. To his relief the engine pulled cleanly. Another mile to go. On the straight before turn ten, he took a good look in his mirrors. Eddison was closing again.

As they approached Veedol for the last time, the Williams was close enough to have a go. Ryan took a defensive line through the crucial chicane, and prepared to block Eddison into the last corner. But he needn't have worried. The brakes on the Williams were going off, and Eddison had reluctantly decided against a final attack.

There was only a short distance to go after the final corner. Ecstatic, Ryan drove across the line - past the waving chequered flag that had so often marked the end of a frustrating race. He took both hands off the wheel, and pumped them into the air - saluting his team, who had become a waving and gesticulating green mass lining the pit wall. Having passed his team, Ryan banged the steering wheel in delight, and let out a loud whoop.

Stuart Underwood was already out of his car as Ryan drove slowly into Parc Ferme. Ryan hurriedly got out of his car, and dashed over to congratulate Stuart, who was chatting excitedly to Takano. Both Kodama drivers had just recorded their best results of the season - although Underwood was no stranger to the podium. Underwood broke away from Takano, and embraced Ryan.

'Well done. I bet you didn't see that coming.' Underwood was grinning broadly, surprised at how the race had turned out.

'No way. But they all count. I really needed that one though!' Underwood could hear the relief in Ryan's voice. Unlike some of the other drivers, he had taken no pleasure from Ryan's misfortunes, and was genuinely pleased that his old racing partner had returned to the track in style.

Before they could talk anymore, they were ushered towards the weighing room. Before disappearing from sight, Ryan spotted his own crew, behind the wire at the far side of the enclosure, and gave them yet another wave.

The three drivers were quickly weighed, before being hustled towards the podium. Ryan handed his helmet over in exchange for a sponsor's cap, before climbing the stairs to the rostrum. He took his place on the platform and looked around him. He was determined to enjoy the moment. He had been on podiums in previous racing series, but never in F1, and never in front of crowds as large as this. Below him, he could pick out his team, and he smiled broadly as he saw a group of them attempting to lift John Thornhill onto their shoulders. To his surprise, he suddenly spotted Victoria's face amongst a group of his mechanics. He hadn't known for certain that she was even in Germany. He pointed towards her and waved vigorously; to his delight, she rewarded him with a blown kiss.

Ryan respectfully stood to attention as "God Save the Queen" thundered out over the tannoy to salute the winner. He closed his eyes, and let himself imagine that they were playing the anthem for him. He didn't even mind standing through the Japanese anthem that followed, being up there, after all that had happened since Indianapolis, seemed a miracle. He was happy for it to last as long as possible.

One moment, he was clapping as Underwood received the large winner's trophy, and the next, he was being announced to the crowd - a smaller 3rd place trophy was thrust into his hands. He then joined Takano, and climbed up onto the winner's platform to congratulate Underwood; flash bulbs exploded all around. How different these flash bulbs seemed.

The three tired drivers posed happily for a few photographs, before the obligatory bottles of champagne were handed over. Ryan took a quick slug of champagne from his own giant bottle, and watched Underwood and Takano drenching each other in spray - the suited officials hastily retreating from the podium. Satisfied with a mouthful of champagne, Ryan joined in the fun, pouring a copious amount down the back of Underwood's neck, as he in turn took a face-full from Takano. The drivers finished the ritual by spraying the remaining champagne over the cheering crowd below. Then, with no chance to clean up, they were led away to the media centre for the post race press conference.

While Ryan was enjoying himself on the podium, Kramer headed briskly towards the motorhome. He hadn't expected Ryan to do so well, but it looked as if the excellent result was going to make his own job a whole lot easier. He had been delighted to see, what appeared to be, the whole Vantec team swarming towards the victory stand.

'Enjoy your last podium, folks!' muttered Kramer, as he boarded the van. He quickly made for his cabin. Dumping his helmet unceremoniously on the bed, he reached for his briefcase. Unlocking the smart black leather case, he rummaged around until he found what he was looking for. He held the tiny USB memory stick up to his lips, and kissed it. 'Okay baby, time for you to do your stuff!'.

Leaving his room, Kramer walked to the back of the van where the data engineers worked. The tiny office was not as empty as he'd hoped. Most of the engineers had gone, but one man was busily tidying up. Kramer's eyes rapidly scanned the work bench. The laptops were still in place and switched on.

He addressed the engineer, who was in the process of coiling a power lead, 'Hi, any chance I can have a look at my race telemetry? I'm off back to the States tomorrow, and this is the only opportunity I'll have.' Kramer's tone was almost pleading.

'I don't see why not…do you need any help?' The engineer was in a good mood, and more than happy to help the American.

'Yeah, perhaps you could just log me on and get my results up. I'll be here all day otherwise!' Kramer thought that was a nice touch; he didn't want the engineer to know how useful he was around computers.

The engineer smiled; he was accustomed to drivers not knowing their way round the system. He placed the lead, now coiled, in a packing case, and moved over to one of the computers. Seconds later, he had Kramer's data up on the screen.

'Thanks pal, I should be okay from here.' Kramer mounted the stool in front of the laptop, and began to scan the results for the benefit of the engineer. After a minute, he turned round to the engineer.

'Say, you couldn't fetch us a coffee or something? I'm as dry as the Arizona desert.'

'No problem, how do you want it?' The engineer knew his place in the pecking order, and to be honest, he quite fancied a drink himself.

'Strong black and no sugar, oh and a sandwich - any sort will do!' Kramer wanted the engineer out of the way for as long as possible.

The data engineer walked out of the office, leaving Kramer alone.

Kramer wasted no time, and slotted the memory stick into one of the USB ports at the back of the laptop. Now he needed some luck. He switched out of the telemetry results, and into a directory view of all the folders on the computer. First, he checked that the system had recognised his memory stick. To his relief, it was clearly showing up as a new drive. He mouthed a silent thank you for the wonder of Windows - its handy plug'n'play features made it so much easier to use external devices. Next came the tricky part: finding the engine mapping application he had seen on his factory tour with Ryan. At the time, he had made a mental note of the application name shown on the screen. The program had been shown as "Engine Mapper", but, sadly, he knew that screen program names didn't always match the underlying file names. He accessed the file search function, and after narrowing the search to only look for application files, keyed in a variety of search terms: *engmap, eng, mapp*. He pressed the search key. It wasn't long before a short stream of results appeared on the right-hand side of the 17" TFT screen.

Kramer knew he didn't have time to explore all five results to identify the one application he was after. Instead, he mentally added up the file lengths, and checked that all five applications would fit in the 256mb memory of the memory stick. Satisfied, he selected all five applications and dragged them across to the assigned drive. The 127mb of data would take nearly four minutes to copy. While the process was underway, he swapped back into the telemetry screen. Even if the engineer returned before the process was complete, it was unlikely the guy would realise anything was happening in the background.

Jason needn't have worried. The engineer had to wait for Maggie to prepare a ham sandwich, and then spent a further few minutes chatting. Jason had time to remove the memory stick, and close down the applications he had opened, before the engineer re-appeared. He was genuinely studying his own telemetry results with interest, when at last a mug of coffee was placed in front of him. The engineer mounted the stool next to

Kramer, and for the next ten minutes the two men went over the telemetry.

While he nervously waited for the post-race Press conference to begin, Ryan poured himself a glass of orange squash from the large jug in front of him. He was careful not to knock the microphone that rose from the table like a strange breed of black tulip. Ryan sat on the left-hand side of the table. The very cheap table was hidden behind a grey F1 board for the benefit of the cameras. Another board, displaying the name of the race, ran along the front of the table in front of him. Behind him yet more boarding, geometrically decorated with snazzy F1 logos, provided a back-drop. It looked far more professional from the other side of the TV screen! Out front, reporters jostled for position. Ryan knew he would be third in line for questions. He also knew he may have to field questions in languages other than English – which wasn't a prospect he looked forward to!

'Congratulations on your win today.' The British television interviewer paused briefly, before continuing to address Underwood. 'But, I don't expect you thought you would reach the front as easily as you did.'

'It's never easy with cars flying off the track in front of you - but that's racing. Today it worked in my favour, the next race, I may be the one stranded in the gravel.'

Ryan listened with amusement to Underwood's confident explanation. He hoped he got just as easy a question. The interviewer asked Stuart Underwood a few more questions, before moving on to speak to his Japanese team-mate. Ryan liked Takano, who was a very genuine person, but sadly his English frequently let him down, and he had a tendency to clam up in interviews. Today was one of those days, and the interviewer was unable to get anything of interest out of the driver. Ryan adjusted his sponsor's cap, while he waited for the interviewer to reach him.

'Ryan, it's been quite an eventful fortnight for you. Last week it looked like you might not even be racing, and now a good third place. Can you explain it?'

'I just took my chances,' said Ryan, wryly. 'I came here to put Indianapolis behind me, and that's what I think I've done!' He hoped that was a final reference to Indianapolis.

'I know you benefited from the first lap accident - like the others, but your race seemed to hinge on the pit stop, where you came out ahead of Demaison. It looked very close to being a serious accident, wasn't it a bit risky?'

'The pit stop was in the hands of the team. I just drove away when told to do so. I can't imagine them letting me out if it was going to be dangerous. We were just better disciplined than Demaison.'

As Ryan faced the cameras in the media centre, Pierre Demaison was in his team's garage being interviewed by French Television.

'Are you a little disappointed with the two points your team scored today, given the good qualifying position?'

'For sure. We started in seventh place, and after the events of the first lap, I thought we could be looking forward to collecting several points - and with the car going so well, maybe even a podium place.' Demaison affectionately patted the blue nose-cone of the car beside him.

'It looked like the damage was done in the pit stop, when Gonzales was beaten out again by Clarke. It looked a very dangerous move by the Vantec team; will you be making a protest?'

Demaison breathed deeply, feeling the anger sweep through his body. He suppressed his emotions and put on a smile, then replied as urbanely as ever. 'No. I get on very well with the Vantec boys. It was just a normal racing incident. We came in first, and we should have made the better stop, but it wasn't to be. After that, it proved impossible for Gonzales to get past Clarke.'

'So, now, with just two races to go, your team lies in 7th place in the championship. Where do you expect to finish?'

'We have a car that is very competitive with the Vantec, and I would hope that we can beat them to end up in 6th place. It is a little unrealistic to expect us to catch any of the top five teams now, but anything can happen in motor racing, and the flag will only drop on the season at the end of the last lap in Japan. I look forward to some good racing in the last two Grand Prix!'

The Demaison PR man politely ushered the journalist away. He knew how much of an act his boss had just put on, and didn't want to be around when he finally exploded. He racked his brains to find something useful to do far away from the garage.

Demaison lovingly stroked the quiescent racing car, while he waited for the garage to clear.

'Merde, merde, merde!' he yelled, not caring how the noise echoed round the hollow garage, or that it could be heard outside in the pit lane where mechanics were hard at work clearing up. Someone was going to pay for that terrible pit stop. No mechanic was going to spoil his season and expect to keep his job. Besides, setting an example would keep the rest on their toes. But even worse, Vantec had moved ahead for the first time in the season. It was time for the gloves to come off and to take direct action. Demaison paced round the garage like a caged tiger as he considered the options.

CHAPTER 19

8:30 a.m. Friday 5th October, Chelsea - England

The low growl of the Aston's V8 engine reverberated noisily round the underground garage, as Ryan drove up the ramp and into the outside world. He halted at the edge of the main road, and glanced left and right, before turning right. Curious, he thought, as he saw the white Ford transit van parked opposite the flats. He had noticed it as he had returned the previous evening, and was surprised to still see it there in the morning. The dented and rusty van looked out of place in the exclusive residential area. He kept his eye on the rear mirror as he continued down the road. As he turned the first bend the van disappeared from view. He put it out of his mind, and concentrated on the drive down to Brands Hatch.

He was feeling positively cheerful. The third place in Germany had done wonders for his public image. His picture filled the inside back pages of several papers, and he had even been asked to write a column for one of them. He had been very flattered to be asked, and had co-operated fully with the reporter assigned to ghost write the article. Now he was due down at Brands Hatch for yet another photo shoot. Due to the unpleasant weather, he sincerely hoped they were going to be able to work indoors. There was a chill in the air, and frequent heavy showers were interspersed by long periods of grey cloud. Strong gusting winds were whipping up the early autumn leaves. Ryan hadn't seen the sun since they returned from the Nurburgring. At least they were off to the Far East tomorrow. If nothing else, it would be a lot warmer.

Despite going against the rush hour flow, the traffic was still heavy, and as he inched forward through the jam to get over Vauxhall bridge, he puzzled once again over the mystery of the pill bottle. Rather than drive down to see Dr Foster, he had chanced taking the tablets to a local pharmacist in Chelsea. The pharmacist had peered at one of the tablets through his glasses, and then taken it out to the back of the shop. It was some minutes before he returned to announce that the pills were German in origin, and were simply sleeping tablets.

Oh well, thought Ryan, at least that let Kramer off the hook. Perhaps after all, it was Wittman attempting a little mischief - he couldn't imagine the Austrian actually needing sleeping tablets. Surely he could just talk himself to sleep, thought Ryan, pulling an amused smile.

But the mysteries were certainly mounting. He still didn't know why the red Lotus had been following them on the way back from Spa. He hadn't caught another sight of the car. But from what he could recall, he wouldn't have minded meeting the female driver again! And then there was Jason's skill with the computer. He couldn't see how Jason had found the time to become so skilled; must just be a genius, he reflected. Well, at least Jason wasn't going to be one of his worries for a few days. Kramer had dragged the old version car round the Nurburgring to a decent 12th place. Disappointed, he had asked if he could return to the States before joining them in Malaysia for the next race. Somerset had willingly agreed; he didn't need a sour Kramer to spoil the good publicity that Ryan was generating.

The wet weather had attracted more traffic than usual onto the road, and it was one of the slowest trips down to the track that Ryan had experienced for some time. Behind him, a reasonable distance down the road, Ricky, the driver of the white van, was pleased with the way things were going. The Aston was proving very easy to follow in the slow moving traffic, and his van blended in with the other vans out and about on their legitimate business. He glanced in his wing mirror to check that the dark-blue Ford Mondeo was still accompanying them.

Once he had seen Ryan join the A20, the van driver didn't worry about following too closely. It was pretty obvious where Clarke was going, and Ford Transits weren't designed for chasing Aston Martins down fast roads! He slowed just a little as the Aston became a spot in the distance, and then he reached for his mobile phone.

'All right Steve, how's tricks?' Ricky listened impatiently as Steve listed his current ailments; he began to wish he hadn't asked.

'Okay, well never mind all that. He's on his way to Brands as expected. He's in the Aston, the lucky fucker! Give us a bell when he reaches you.' Ricky ended the call. He didn't care enough about Steve to want to spend any more time chatting. They had sent Steve down to Brands to do a spot of reconnaissance, and to act as a spotter. The plan could be considered risky, given that it depended on Clarke going to Brands - they would have to abandon their scheme if he didn't. But the boss man had assured them that Ryan would definitely be going to the track. Maybe it was going to be a lucky plan. Ricky hadn't known many jobs go exactly as planned; he just hoped, for once, that this would be an exception. It was a shame that the target was British, though; he rather liked what little he had seen of Clarke, but money was money, and the five thousand pounds for the job was going to be very handy.

Somerset was waiting in his office, in the Brands Hatch hospitality centre, for the photographic team to arrive, when the phone on his desk rang.

'Somerset,' he answered brusquely, expecting to hear that the photographers had at last arrived. He was therefore somewhat surprised to hear the caller announce himself in a Japanese accent.

'Chris, it's Tosh,' the caller paused to let his name sink in. 'Have I caught you at a good time?'

'No problem, what can I do for you?' Somerset was wary; he had been expecting a call at some stage from the Katayama boss. He was pleased that they had tied up their agreement in principle before Indianapolis, but knew that Ryan's escapade would not have gone unnoticed.

'I wanted to congratulate you on your excellent result in Germany,' replied Toshihiko, sincerely.

'Thank you, we…'

'…But,' Toshihiko cut Somerset off, 'some of the board are very concerned about the driver line-up for next year. I am sure you appreciate that Clarke has done himself no favours in recent weeks!' Toshihiko was being typically diplomatic. He was personally comfortable with Ryan's position in the team, but some of the older, more traditional, members of the board held stronger opinions.

'I think your concern is totally unwarranted. Ryan has been absolved of all blame, and redeemed himself brilliantly at the Nurburgring,' bridled Somerset, irritated at what looked like interference in his team.

'I agree with you,' soothed Toshihiko, 'but you must remember, we only have an agreement in principle. I urge you to ensure that nothing else untoward happens this season, or I may find it hard to keep my board on side! It may be for the best, if you considered replacing Mr Clarke next year.'

Toshihiko's advice sounded rather like a threat.

'We have already agreed to run your driver next year. I think the remainder of the team is for me to determine,' said Somerset, his voice pinched, struggling not to get angry.

'Absolutely. I am just asking that you take all of the aspects into consideration,' said Toshihiko, confident that the engine supplier had the whip-hand. Vantec could not afford to jeopardise the agreement – not if they wanted to move up the racing ladder. Opportunities to obtain new and better engines came round very rarely. 'Perhaps we can meet in Malaysia,' continued Toshihiko, in a conciliatory manner.

'That sounds like a good idea,' said Somerset, keen to maintain a good relationship - although he suspected Toshihiko would only browbeat him again over drivers.

After discussing a meeting point and time, Toshihiko ended the call.

Somerset replaced the handset, and walked over to the large window overlooking the circuit. The track had witnessed so many of his team's triumphs in the junior ranks of motor-racing. Toshihiko's call had upset him, and he was slowly beginning to appreciate what getting into bed with the large multi-national company would mean. Powerblok, their current engine supplier, had been a new company - glad to work with a rising team, and had consequently been easy to control. Katayama were an entirely different proposition. Just how much of a team boss would they allow him to be, he wondered?

Forty minutes later, the van driver reached for his bleeping phone. They were just passing Swanley, on the M20.

'Can you lot shut up for a second!' he yelled at the three occupants in the back of the van, who were noisily playing cards. The men quietened down, just enough for Ricky to hear the man on the other end of the phone.

'Steve here, Clarke's just driven in. What do you want me to do now?'

'Walk out to the main road and turn left. I'll pull up just past the entrance. We'll have a chat there. We should be there in about ten minutes.' Ricky checked his watch.

Ricky drew the Ford Transit up on to the side of the road, a hundred yards past the entrance and left his indicator blinking. Moments later the Mondeo also swung up on to the grass, just ahead of the van. However, there was no sign of Steve - no doubt he was still sitting snug in his car. No harm in making Steve walk a bit, thought Ricky. The idle sod wasn't going to have to do the dirty work that came later.

'Why the fuck did you park right up here!' moaned Steve, as he eventually reached the van. He hadn't enjoyed the walk up the slight hill, and was panting from the unaccustomed effort.

'Sorry Steve, didn't want to be too conspicuous. Wasn't that far was it?' asked Ricky sarcastically, enjoying Steve's obvious discomfort.

Steve shot him a black look, before climbing into the back of the van. A moment later, the driver of the Mondeo joined them. They had all been briefed the day before, in a private room behind the bar of a pub in Lewisham, but the leader wasn't going to take any chances. Ten minutes later, briefing over, Steve opened the door and climbed down to begin his walk back. It had started to rain again, and he was decidedly wet by the time he got back into his own car, parked in the Thistle Hotel car park, just outside the entrance to the circuit. It could be a long wait, and he wondered if he could afford to pop into the hotel for a coffee. He decided against it; you never knew. It wouldn't do for him to miss Clarke leaving. He settled down to watch the gates. When Clarke did reappear, he would have to act quickly.

Ryan parked his car in the car park by the hospitality centre, and stepped out. He looked about him. Despite the car park being nearly full, the rest of the track seemed deserted. From the unusual silence, he deduced that there were no cars of any sort on the track. He pulled a face, and headed for the offices.

'About bloody time! I've been here ages!' Craig McDonald closed the car magazine he'd been reading, and stood up to greet Ryan, the glossy publication still in his hand.

Ryan looked at his Rolex wristwatch. 'Actually, bang on time, old chap!'

'Just teasing. I'd only just sat down when you turned up. Didn't even have time to read this rubbish you're supposed to have written!' Craig waved the magazine in Ryan's direction - a collection of advertising inserts fell from the magazine and fluttered to the carpeted floor.

'I wouldn't bother if I were you; there's no great insight in there.'

'Pity! Look, sorry I couldn't be with you yesterday, I trust things have been quiet.' Craig wasn't sure how much Ryan had told anyone else.

'Yeah, no problems. But I'm glad you're here. Fancy a run later?' Despite the appalling weather, Ryan was feeling guilty about his lack of recent training.

'A run would be good. It seems pretty quiet out there today - we might even be able to use the circuit. A couple of laps of the track should do the trick.' Craig had always fancied running on the track itself. Given the rain, it would be a lot easier than slogging round the grass and mud.

'Fine. I'll catch up with you when the photo boys have finished. Got your mobile on you?'

Craig nodded.

'Okay, I'll give you a bell when I'm through.'

McDonald sat back down to read the glossy auto magazine, as Ryan headed for the stairs - smiling sweetly at the receptionist on his way up to Somerset's office.

It was a good two hours before Ryan was able to rejoin Craig. Originally, they had hoped to do the filming at the track, but the bad weather put paid to that. After a short discussion, Somerset agreed that they could film in the Vantec factory up the road instead. Time was wasted as all of the film equipment was packed back into the photographer's smart black Range Rover. Somerset, though, was glad to be able to return to the factory, as he had plenty to do before they decamped for Malaysia.

'Leave the Aston. I'll give you a lift up the road,' offered Somerset.

'Fine. Provided someone can drop me back later,' replied Ryan, who suspected that Somerset wanted a word with him.

'As much as I think the walk would do you good - I'm sure I can find someone to bring you back!' It was a common problem, as their factory was located a distance from the circuit.

As the two men reached the bottom of the stairs, there was no sign of McDonald. The trainer had clearly found something to amuse himself elsewhere.

A minute later, they were sat in the comfortable black leather seats in Somerset's silver Mercedes CL-class coupe. Somerset inserted his key into the ignition, then turned to face Ryan without switching the engine on.

'So, how are things at the moment?' asked Somerset.

It was an open-ended question that posed any number of traps for Ryan to fall into. He decided to bat the ball back into Somerset's court.

'Pretty good. I think we're getting some good publicity - Germany did me a lot of favours!'

Somerset nodded, 'Agreed, but that was only one race; you may not be so lucky in the next. If you want to get on the podium again, you're going to have to drive even better next time. The court's still out on you, you know!'

Somerset still felt unable to talk directly about the status of his discussions with Katayama Motors. He didn't want to unduly worry Ryan, but he wanted to get the message across that Ryan still had some work to do.

'That was the best result we've ever had! Surely I've done enough to impress you!,' said Ryan, peevishly.

'One swallow doesn't make a summer, you know. I'm not the only person you need to impress!' It was the closest Somerset was prepared to go to the truth. With nothing more he could say, he switched on the engine.

Ryan's emotions were back on the roller-coaster. He had always thought Somerset made all the decisions. This was the first time he had heard that his fate might lie in someone else's hands. It was a sobering realisation, and Ryan was happy to sit in silence as Somerset drove them the short distance to the factory.

Back in the sterile factory environment, the photographers had filmed Ryan in and out of the car, in and out of his full racing uniform. The magazine had even provided a pneumatic young blonde model for the pictures. Despite his reservations about appearing in more pictures with scantily clad women, it sure beat being filmed with just a car for company! He hoped the PR people had judged things correctly. Then, after all the photography, he spent a further half-hour with a reporter - who seemed to want to cover his whole life story. Ryan wasn't objecting. This was the first time one of the big monthly lifestyle magazines had wanted to cover him.

Steve was becoming ever more impatient as he sat in his car, just outside the main entrance to the circuit. He had failed to spot Somerset and Ryan leaving in the Mercedes, and he hadn't noticed Ryan's return two hours later. He hadn't expected to wait so long. What if Clarke had taken a different exit? Surely, they weren't expected to sit around all day. He looked at his watch again, it was nearly two. He shook his head, he'd give it another fifteen minutes then he'd phone Ricky.

The fifteen minutes were nearly up when he spotted the familiar green Aston approaching the gates. He quickly pressed the stored number to dial Ricky.

'Go!' Steve didn't need to say anymore. Out on the main road, about a mile from the entrance, Ricky relayed the signal by walkie-talkie to the rest of his team. Immediately, they swung into a series of pre-planned actions.

A mile down the hill from Brands Hatch, a man in a donkey jacket and hard hat manhandled a triangular sign-board out into the middle of the A20. The word 'Diversion' stood out in bold black lettering underneath a broad black arrow. The arrow pointed down a lane leading to Farningham - a plausible alternate route away from the area.

To ensure there were no undue surprises, a similarly dressed man waited until Ryan had passed, then placed a 'Wait' sign just before the entrance to Brands. For what they had in mind it wouldn't do for an innocent motorist to get in the way. The critical stretch of the A20 was now isolated.

Just a little way up the lane, Ricky pulled the white van off the road, and checked that it couldn't be seen. In the back of the van, the two remaining members of the gang donned black Balaclavas, and grabbed their weapons. Further up the road, the driver of the Mondeo got into position.

Ryan turned right onto the A20, which to his slight surprise was clear of traffic. He was quite used to having to sit and wait. Must be my lucky day, he thought. As Ryan picked up speed on the main road, Craig was just pulling out of the circuit gates in his ancient but highly tuned Mustang

'Shit,' swore Steve, as the powerful black and rust coloured car turned in the same direction as the Aston. There was nothing he could do, but watch and hope that Ricky had covered such an eventuality. His distress was compounded, as a 1000cc Ducati motorbike followed just seconds later. He shook his head. His job was done. He turned the ignition in his car, and cruised out of the Hotel car-park and up to the A20 - his right indicator blinking bright yellow in the deepening gloom.

Now what? Ryan slowed slightly as he spotted the diversion sign. Must be more roadworks - strange, he couldn't remember seeing anything as he drove up earlier. Never mind, he knew the road he was been directed down. It would be fun to throw the car round the twisty lane, and besides, he wasn't in any real hurry. He swung the car left into the lane, and waved at the man standing by the diversion sign. The fake workman motioned him down the road with a sweep of his arm.

As soon as the Aston disappeared from view, the man grabbed the road sign and re-sited it at the edge of the lane - this time pointing drivers away from the lane. He'd spotted the Mustang approaching, but he didn't really care what that driver thought. He'd been told to move the sign as soon as the Aston had turned off the main road.

McDonald was puzzled. He had just glimpsed the rear end of the Aston as it turned down the lane ahead. He couldn't read the road sign that the man had just moved, but never mind, he was going to follow Ryan anyway. He didn't bother to indicate, he just swept left into the lane - his wing mirror clipping the sign as he went.

The man in the donkey jacket was taken completely by surprise. He had been holding the road sign as McDonald knocked into it. The unexpected movement took the man with it. Board and man clattered to the ground. The man winced as he landed on top of the walkie-talkie in his pocket. He rolled over and sat up - then reached into his pocket for the radio. He just had time to spot that the aerial had been broken off, when a red Ducati blatted past him, heading down the lane after the Mustang. He tried to call Ricky, but it was no use. He grimaced, as he thought about what Ricky would have to say! He got to his feet, and gingerly began to jog down the lane. If he got there in time he might at least be able to help.

Ryan clipped the edge of the road as he swung the heavy car round the tight left-hander. He began to squeeze the throttle, then lifted, and stamped on the brake pedal instead. Ahead of him, a dark-blue Mondeo was camped at an awkward angle across the road, the front end of the Ford was up against a tree, and Ryan could see a figure slumped across the steering wheel.

Ricky grunted with satisfaction as the Aston passed his hiding place, then drove out onto the lane and followed at a leisurely pace.

Ryan peered through the windscreen at the body. There was no sign of movement. Anxiously, he grabbed the door handle, hoping the door wasn't locked. The door wouldn't move - but Ryan did. He spotted a raised arm reflected in the window. Instinctively, he ducked inside the swing of the baseball bat - lifting his right arm in protection. The bat crashed painfully into his shoulder as he turned toward his assailant. His attacker hadn't expected any retaliation, and off balance; Ryan was able to wrestle him towards the ground. As the two men crashed to the tarmac, Ryan glimpsed two other masked men rushing to join in. Three against one! The situation looked decidedly nasty.

Ryan rolled over so that his attacker was on top, and aimed a well-directed punch into the man's face. The man grunted as his head jerked back. Despite the awful pain in his nose, Ryan's attacker stuck to his task.

McDonald slammed on the anchors the moment he spotted the mayhem ahead on the road. He gave a loud blast on the car's horn, as he pushed open the car door.

Two men, who had been rushing towards Ryan, halted at the sound of the horn. Ricky, the larger of the two turned to face McDonald. He motioned his partner on towards Ryan. Ricky thumped the pick handle into his palm, and gestured towards McDonald.

'Come on then, my son, if you think you're hard enough,' he sneered.

Back at the Mondeo, Ryan was continuing to roll around with his attacker. The second man had just joined the action, and Ryan had already taken a bruising kick in the back. He would have to do something soon. He rolled again, smashing his opponent's head into the side of the car. The move looked promising, so he repeated it. This time his attacker rolled off in pain. One down, but he was stuck on the ground. He fended the next kick off with his hands. He desperately needed to get to his feet.

Nick Phillips took in the scene quickly. In the foreground, he could see McDonald facing a man brandishing a pick handle, behind them - on the ground; he could see Ryan about to take a beating. He revved his powerful bike and aimed at the man confronting McDonald.

McDonald heard the roar of the Ducati, and then felt a blast of air as the bike sped past, inches from his shoulder. The handle bars of the 500 pound bike hit Ricky on the left hand side, spinning him to the ground. Nick skidded the bike to a halt, yards away from where Ryan was still attempting to fend off new blows from his latest attacker. Regretfully, Nick laid the bike on the tarmac; there was no time to get it onto its stand.

Clad in bike leathers, and helmeted, he was better protected than the others. He steamed into the fight - leading with a foot. His wayward kick caught Ryan's attacker in the back of his left leg. As the thug turned his head to see where the new attack was coming from, Ryan grabbed his right leg and tugged. The man thudded to the ground - his pick handle skittering down the road.

Craig was actually disappointed that his brutish looking opponent had been dropped by the bike. He had been looking forward to teaching the guy a lesson. Worried, Craig ran towards Ryan - leaving Ricky lying on the ground.

By the time Craig reached the Aston, the two thugs had got to their feet. Nick was busy helping Ryan up - which gave the men a chance to make a break for it. Craig was in no position to stop two men, and, reluctantly, let them run past him - back towards their stricken leader.

The driver of the Mondeo had watched the whole thing, and, once he'd spotted the reinforcements, had decided against joining in. He started the car, and backed away from the tree against which the car had been resting. He'd only met the others the previous day. He didn't owe them anything, and the money wasn't going to make it worth taking a beating. He sped off down the lane, the rear end of his car fishtailing in his anxiety to get away.

Ricky sat on the ground, nursing what he suspected was a broken arm. He shook his head in disbelief as he saw the Mondeo make a getaway. The little shit - he'd deal with him later. The two men who had attacked Ryan were running back up the road towards him. The fight had gone out of them, and they looked apprehensively back at Ryan, Nick and Craig, as if they expected an attack at any moment.

They needn't have worried. Craig was more concerned about Ryan, and Nick was torn between helping Ryan and checking his bike over! Ryan wouldn't have minded finding out what it was all about, but couldn't afford any more injuries before the next race. Instead, they stood as a group and watched as the gang bundled into the white Transit and drove off. The man who had worked the signboard at last made it up the lane on foot. He flagged the van to a halt, and clambered into the back. Belching black and blue smoke, the van continued on its way.

'What the fuck was that all about?' asked Nick cheerfully - having checked his pride and joy, and found no damage.

'You tell me!' replied Ryan, who wasn't willing to talk about his problems with Nick. 'But great work! Boy, was I pleased to see you. How come you came this way?'

'Oh, I live just a couple of miles up the road. I often come this way. Look, do you want to come back to my place and get cleaned up?'

Ryan looked at Craig.

'Yeah, could be a good move. We need to get some ice on those bruises as soon as possible.'

'Thanks, Nick. You lead - but don't go too fast, I don't want to lose you!' Ryan had just changed his mind about the young mechanic. Mentally, he crossed Nick off his list of suspects. At least some good had come out of the incident.

The young mechanic grinned. He really would have something to talk about down the pub later. It wasn't every day he took a Formula One driver home.

CHAPTER 20

7:00 p.m. Wednesday 10th October, Kuala Lumpur International Airport -Malaysia

Ryan contracted the muscles in his right leg, waited until the tension became unbearable, and then relaxed; straight away, he felt the stress dissipate. He repeated the exercise on the other leg. He was glad there was only another half-hour to go before they were due to land. Naively, he'd thought that by stopping off in Australia for a few days with Craig, it would then just be a short flight to Malaysia. The reality was still a seven-hour flight. Thankfully, the need to change planes at Jakarta had given him a chance to stretch his legs. It wasn't just his legs that were complaining; he was still suffering from the beating he had taken. Shifting in his seat, he winced as his bruised side caught the edge of the armrest. He smiled at the reminder of how ridiculous he must have looked, lying fully dressed, on the sun-drenched beach outside Sydney amid all the thong-clad sun worshippers. Only Craig McDonald and Nick Philips knew about the attack, and he wanted to keep it that way.

Even as he mulled over the few restful days in Australia, he knew he wasn't just physically tired. It was nearly the end of the season, and he was growing mentally weary. The levels of concentration needed to drive a car at extreme speeds, and the pressures of the Formula One circus, all took their toll. Ryan felt like a puppet on a string - pulled every which way by the puppet masters that controlled his life. The end of the season would bring temporary relief, but all too soon he would be back on the treadmill - or at least he hoped he would! He tried to think of something else; it seemed ridiculous to be moaning about a job that most young men could only dream about. There were certainly rewards. Across the aisle of the 737, he could see an attractive stewardess leaning towards a fellow passenger. The girl's provocative curves lifted Ryan's spirits, and he let his eyes linger appreciatively over her long nylon clad legs.

'It sure looks a fantastic hotel,' enthused Craig, who sat in the window seat next to Ryan.

Ryan glanced at Craig, who held up a glossy magazine article for Ryan to see; he had managed to find an advertising feature for their hotel in the airline magazine.

'Bloody close to the airport, though ,' moaned Craig. 'It says here, it's close to the control tower. I hope we're going to get some sleep!'

'It'll be fine,' assured Ryan. He had stayed at the 5-star Pan Pacific hotel before. The hotel was as good as could be expected for a modern building, and at just over two miles from the Sepang circuit, was an ideal place to stay. At least they didn't have to face a long journey from the airport.

'Cabin crew to standby.' The pilot issued the routine command as the plane began the descent into Kuala Lumpur. Ryan fastened his seat belt and waited patiently for touch down.

It was certainly unusual not to need any transport to reach their hotel. They collected their luggage, and made their way over the bridge that linked the airport to the impressive ten-storey hotel building.

The spacious green tiled lobby was alive with activity as they checked in. A number of other teams were also staying at the hotel, and Ryan found himself nodding and waving to familiar faces. It was at times like these that he realised how insular the Grand Prix circuit could be. With engineers, mechanics, office and support staff, the teams alone accounted for a travelling band of over five hundred people. On top of that, there were the regular press and TV crews. Every two weeks during the season, the same horde descended upon yet another lonely and deserted race-track. The gathering of the teams signalled the beginning of something important, but the real buzz came when the thousands of fans began to pour through the circuit gates.

Ryan woke refreshed the next morning. The planes hadn't disturbed him, and a gentle hum from the air-conditioning had done its part in helping him drop off to sleep. Craig was already waiting for him in the breakfast room - tucking healthily into a rack of toast. The Australian had been out for a run, and glowed with energy. He waited for Ryan to sit down before speaking

'It's a bit hot and sweaty out there,' said Craig, his mouth full of toast.

'Well, if you must go for a run, you've only got yourself to blame. I'm going to let the car do all the work.'

They both knew that wasn't going to be the case. Due to the humidity, Ryan would be in extreme physical distress by the end of the race on Sunday.

'What's the plan for today?' asked Craig, still chewing, and waving a piece of toast in the air. A small sliver of marmalade slid off the toast and dropped onto the crumb spattered white tablecloth. It was never difficult to work out where Craig had been eating.

'I don't have to drive today, but I've got to be at the track for eleven to discuss the set-up for the weekend. After lunch, I want to take a good long look at the track. We should be back here quite early.'

Craig grunted. It didn't seem too hard a schedule. He knew Ryan was still sore from the beating, but the bruises were easing. More importantly, if they kept in the public eye, there didn't seem to be much risk of another attack. Craig was taking his minding duties seriously. The ambush had been a timely reminder that someone meant business. He was going to stick as close to Ryan as he could.

The teams were all at the track and, after the hubbub of check-in, the hotel was much quieter in the morning. The two men, comfortable in each other's company, chatted happily over a long but light breakfast. Any cares Ryan might have had were banished by the bright sun that flooded the airy restaurant.

To help him get about, the team had provided Ryan with a moped. The tiny vehicle struggled under their combined weight, but Ryan and Craig still managed to arrive at the circuit just before eleven.

Despite their team uniforms, the Asian security guard on the gate insisted on checking their passes thoroughly. Entry to the paddock was a carefully controlled right. No pass - no entry; it all helped build the cachet that went with access to the cars and stars. Even though it was only a practice day, a small number of fans had gathered at the paddock gate, hoping to catch a glimpse of their heroes. Impatiently, they sat on the moped waiting for the guard to let them through. Craig glared angrily at yet another fan who reached out to touch Ryan.

Eventually, the guard opened the gate. Ryan drove the scooter up to the Vantec garage, situated mid-way along the pit-lane. After the bright morning sunshine, it took his eyes a few moments to adjust, before he could see clearly what was happening inside the shady chamber.

'Shit! Shit! Shit!' A mechanic waved his hand painfully in the air, as a spanner clanged to the ground.

Ryan smiled partly in sympathy and partly in amusement. Some things never changed, mechanics would always end up covered in cuts and bruises. It was as if the cars were reluctant patients, and took every opportunity to get their own back.

'All right Nick?' said Ryan, recognising the unfortunate mechanic.

'Yeah, just a scrape.'

The other mechanics had already forgotten the incident, and were busy carrying on with the myriad of tasks that needed to be completed to get three race cars up and working.

'Is Chris around?' asked Ryan. He was due in a meeting with the boss, and it never did to keep Somerset waiting.

'I think he's over with Scott and the others in the motorhome.'

'Cheers, I'd better get over there then. Is everything going okay?'

Nick shrugged his shoulders. 'Seems to be, but - you know, we're never told what's going on!'

'Yours not to reason why, huh! Well, I'll see you later.'

Leaving Craig in the garage with the mechanics; Ryan walked over to the motorhome. By the time he had covered the short distance, he was dripping with sweat. After the coolness of the hotel, the heat and humidity of Malaysia took some getting used to. He could understand why Chris Somerset and Scott Harding had retreated to the air-conditioned motorhome.

It was not the team's normal motorhome - for flyaway trips they hired local vans. Ryan ascended the few steps into the motorhome. Ryan found them all in the lounge area. Seated with Chris and Scott, were John Thornhill – the team manager, Ken Eyre - the Chief Race engineer, and Derek Archer. Jason Kramer completed the group.

'Sorry if I'm late,' apologised Ryan.

'You're not late, we've all only just got here. I thought we ought to go through the initial set up plans,' explained Somerset.

'Okay, good. What's the weather forecast?' Ryan always liked to check the conditions first.

'Good, if you like weather like this,' said John Thornhill, wryly. 'No change forecast - so the heat's going to be the biggest problem.'

'No surprise there, then!' said Ryan.

'Well, at least it should make tyre choice easy,' offered Jason.

'Making them last will be a bigger problem, though!' replied Chris.

No matter what the conditions, there always seemed to be one snag or another.

'Leaving tyres aside for the moment – Jason, you'll be pleased to know we've also got a long wheelbase car for you this time,' said Chris proudly.

The team had been delighted with the performance of the new chassis in Germany, and everybody at the factory had worked hard to get a second car ready for Sepang.

'Brilliant! Thanks, guys!' Jason was keen to get to grips with the new car.

The group settled down to a long technical discussion over the many different aspects of car set-up. Computer simulations helped provide a default set-up, but this would be the first time the new car had run on the Sepang circuit. Engine mapping, gear ratios, suspension and wing settings were all gone over at great and detailed length. Even though the car had run well in Germany, there was still much to learn about the handling of the newer longer wheelbase. As the technical arguments bounced endlessly between the engineers, the two drivers sat restlessly, eager to get out and look at the track. To their chagrin, Ryan and Jason were only asked to contribute at infrequent intervals. Eventually, after an hour and a half, there was agreement over car settings and strategy for the weekend. Satisfied, the engineers went away to brief their respective areas - the mechanics would have to work all afternoon to ensure the cars conformed to the agreed set-ups. As it was lunch-time, Ryan and Jason went off in search of food.

After a simple meal, Ryan took one of the mopeds and slowly made his way round the circuit, re-familiarising himself with the braking and turning-in points. To his surprise, Kramer had elected to discuss the circuit with his race engineer before venturing out. Touring the circuit on his own suited Ryan, who wanted to take his time. More selfishly, he was happy not to pass on too many tips to his team-mate. He was number one in the team and wanted to keep it that way. The improvement in the American's performance was beginning to worry Ryan. He reasoned Kramer was old enough, and ugly enough, to look after himself.

Unlike some of the European circuits, on which they tested all too frequently, the Sepang track was an adventure each time they returned. At this stage in the season, it was good to have something to think about.

If only more circuits were like Sepang, mused Ryan, as he motored past the magnificent stands lining the main straight. The Malaysian circuit had been purpose built, and the designers had made an excellent job of it. Not only was the circuit good from a driver's point of view, but it provided excellent views and facilities for the spectators. The double-fronted main grandstand was an awesome creation; flanked on both sides by half-mile long straights, it accommodated 30,000 spectators. Ryan shook his head at the sheer scale of the building.

His inspection completed, Ryan collected Craig from the garage, and they returned by moped to the hotel. Having been out in the sun for nearly an hour, Ryan was desperate to get back and have a cold shower. Despite the climatic conditions, Ryan was feeling very positive. On the back of his success in Germany - with Indianapolis fading into history, he was looking forward to the weekend.

It was Saturday afternoon, when Ryan felt a hand on his shoulder. 'Can we please have you in the car now, Ryan?' asked John Thornhill. Ryan slowly got up from the pit wall seat, reluctant to leave the welcome shade.

'Cometh the hour, cometh the man!' muttered Ryan, as he picked up his green and white helmet and headed over to the garage. The start of the qualifying hour was just five minutes away, and the team liked to get an early run in before the track became too crowded.

Ryan was feeling quietly confident. Over the course of the previous days, they had managed to progressively dial the car in. With stable weather conditions forecast, Ryan expected to go well. The only real surprise had been the pace of Jason, who was just getting used to the long-wheelbased Vantec. Any lingering doubts Ryan may have had about Jason's ability, were dismissed in that morning's warm up session - the American had gone one tenth quicker than he had. Ryan was going to have to find something a bit extra in the next hour. It may be a team sport from the constructor's point of view, but for the drivers, the first person to beat was always their team mate. Direct comparisons of driver abilities could only be made when drivers were in the same car. It was a race within a race.

After studying qualifying sessions from past years, Ryan had come round to the idea that 4-lap stints might prove better than the traditional 3-lap practice. Four-lapping gave two quick laps a stint - while three-lapping wasted more laps getting in and out of the pits. Thornhill had taken a lot of persuading before he agreed to let Ryan try it his way.

Ryan's first run was intended as a warm-up to make sure the car hadn't changed since the morning session, and ensure a place on the grid. Rarely did drivers fail to qualify these days, but it was always wise to take the pressure off by guaranteeing a start place early on. Ryan needn't have worried; the car was working well, and after the two quick laps he was safely inside the 107% mark - and would definitely be starting the race.

While he waited to go out again, Ryan studied the monitor hung down in front of him, and tried to make sense of the ever changing figures. His fastest lap of 1:42.801 made him 12th at that early stage. Ten minutes later, the time didn't look so useful - and he had been relegated to 16th. Already his clothing was damp with sweat, and he took frequent sips from his water bottle in a vain attempt to keep cool. Beside him in the garage, there was a sudden explosion of noise as Kramer's car was fired up.

Ryan grimaced as Kramer's first section time lit up green on the screen. The second sector also proved quicker than Kramer had been before, and it was no surprise that by the end of the lap Kramer had run half a second faster than Ryan. Kramer's 1:42.377 put him in 8th place.

Ryan waited until Kramer had returned to the pits before exiting for his second run. Ryan had expected Jason to go quicker - but not by such a large margin. As he drove round his out lap, he began to focus on the coming quick-lap, mentally noting the corners he would attack harder than before. As he sped up the penultimate long straight, he looked hard in his mirror. Seeing no one charging up from behind, he eased off a fraction to let the car ahead of him pull away. He wanted a clear run for his fast lap.

Ryan carried as much speed through the final turn as the hairpin would allow, and then floored the throttle. The car flashed past the start-finish line and he was committed. The first complex of turns, at the end of the half-mile home straight, were crucial - and Ryan knew he had to be on the edge. He let himself feel the movement of the car beneath him, and put his faith in the braking point he had selected. As the speed dropped from 185 mph to 60 mph, it felt as if the car was pushing him into the steering wheel - the front of the car dipping in the massive deceleration. There was a puff of smoke as one of the wheels began to lock. Ryan just caught the rear end in time. He drove through the next bend on instinct, and then began to accelerate again. It had been a hairy moment for those watching, but Ryan was happily at one with his machine. He slung it round the remaining bends with less trouble, and knew he must have put up a good time. To be on the safe side, he kept the power on as he crossed the start-finish line at the end of the lap. He would carry on for another fast lap.

As he reached turn one again, he knew the moment had gone. He found himself braking slightly earlier than on the previous lap. The next corner proved he was no longer operating at the edge. It was no surprise when the intercom crackled into life.

'In this lap.' The message was short and unemotional.

Ryan eased off and tooled slowly back to the garage. There were smiles all round as he turned off the engine.

'Well done, Ryan,' said John Thornhill over the radio. '1:41.5, 4th place.'

The monitor was once again lowered in front of him, and he studied the figures with interest. He didn't think he was going to go any better, but it would be interesting to see how the others responded.

For several minutes his time remained unbeaten, but then, in quick succession, both of the Kodama drivers went faster. Their superior power plants gave them a big advantage down the two long straights. More cars screamed past the pit without challenging his time, but, with ten minutes of the session remaining, Eddison in the Williams sneaked past. Ryan was back on the fourth row of the grid in seventh place.

Five minutes from the end of the session, Ryan pulled out of the pits for his final run. He eased the car round the out-lap - carefully extending the gap between himself and one of the Williams ahead. Down the penultimate straight he picked up speed. As he swung round the final bend, he quickly straightened the car and got on the throttle. Sound waves bounced between the two storey pit complex and the main stand, as the engine screamed up to 17,000 revs.

At the end of the first timing sector, Ryan was just three hundredths off his best and looking good. On the timing wall, John Thornhill watched the live TV coverage, as, in a rare moment, the Vantec was tracked round the circuit. Ryan was driving well, and it looked like he could pick up another place or two. After negotiating the eight turns that made up the second sector, Ryan had made up a further two hundredths of a second, and was in touch with his best time.

'Sod it!' Thornhill banged his fist on the bench in front of him, in frustration. Even as the cameras continued to follow the Vantec, the spoken commentary was telling a different story. Up ahead, and out of Ryan's sight, a Williams had tangled with a slower car going into the final turn. It was not a major accident, but the yellow flags came out instantly. Ryan was going to have to lift off. The run was spoiled.

At the end of the lap, Ryan cruised into the pits. He was only slightly disappointed - as well as the run had been going, he was not convinced he was going to improve on his earlier mark. He was more than happy with his driving, and for once the car felt good beneath him. He was ready for the race.

Ryan stayed in the pits for some time after the end of the qualifying session. He wanted to see how that final run had compared with his best lap. Despite the overwhelming mass of data collected by the race engineers, the drivers were given fairly simple charts to study. Ryan knew his way around the computer system well enough to overlay a chart of his last run over that of his best run. The peaks and troughs of engine revs on both laps told a similar story. Ryan nodded in satisfaction. As far as he was concerned, he would be able to do pretty much the same thing lap after lap.

Craig McDonald had waited patiently for Ryan to finish. Together, the pair headed back through the paddock in the hot Malaysian sun.

'Isn't that Jason?' Craig grabbed Ryan's arm, and pointed over to the perimeter fence.

Fifty yards away, a tall man in green driving overalls appeared to be in conversation with a shorter bespectacled man on the far side of the wire fence.

'Sure looks like it. I wonder who he's talking to?' Ryan's curiosity was aroused, and he began to jog over towards the fence - followed moments later by Craig. They weren't quick enough. Before they had got halfway, Jason pulled away from the fence, and walked off, without spotting the pair bearing down on him. Ryan slowed to a walk; it was too hot to rush after Jason.

'I guess we'll never know now,' said Craig, catching up with Ryan. He was puzzled - it didn't seem very likely that Jason would have friends the other side of the fence.

'Maybe it was just a fan.' Ryan didn't sound very convinced.

Later that evening, Jason Kramer laid the heavy leather-bound menu back down on the table, and looked round the spacious expensive restaurant. This was his sort of town. He had been impressed with Kuala Lumpur from the moment he first glimpsed the giant Petronas Towers. To an American raised on images of space exploration, they looked just like huge rockets poised for blast off.

'Is it wise for us to be seen like this?' he asked the man sitting across from him at the table.

'You are my driver - you know' said Demaison, sipping from a glass of red wine. 'Sometimes it is best to be obvious; if we met in some dark corner, then people really would talk!'

'Well, it's certainly some place. You must be pretty flush to stay here!'

Irritated as he was by the comment, Demaison resisted the urge to reply truthfully.

'Money comes to money,' he replied, 'in your language, you would probably say I am a player!'

'Yeah, right, winning is everything huh!'

Demaison gave a tight-lipped smile in reply.

Further conversation was stilled while a waiter took their order.

'Our cars are running very well,' observed Jason some time later, as he moved his spoon playfully around the bowl of fish soup in front of him.

'Then, you will just have to drive badly won't you,' replied Demaison, meaningfully pointing a soup-spoon at Jason. The accompanying smile was frosty. He was still disappointed that Ryan was even driving. He wasn't sure if Jason knew about the botched ambush. In any event, he wasn't prepared to discuss his failure with his son.

Driving badly wasn't what Jason had in mind. He had other plans up his sleeve. He smiled as he imagined telling his father how he had scuppered Ryan. That was for the future; right now, he'd better not upset the apple cart.

'Do you have anything particular in mind?' asked Kramer, curious to know what plans his father had made.

Demaison leaned conspiratorially towards his son. It took just a minute to explain his ideas to Jason, who merely nodded his head in agreement.

Forty-two laps into the race the next afternoon, and Jason Kramer was enjoying himself. He had started in 11th position - just four places behind Ryan. The car had been working well, and he had easily cruised up behind 10th place man Barsotti - passing the Renault under braking into turn 15 at the end of lap 8. It had then taken him quite a bit longer to catch the next car - Barsotti had clearly been holding the pair of them up. Nevertheless, five laps later, he had pulled up behind the Williams of Collett.

The Williams and the Vantec circled the track in tandem. The cars were evenly matched, and although Kramer took a good look down the long final straight, he couldn't find enough power to pass. Collett pitted first on lap 18. Kramer pushed over the next lap in an attempt to buy time, but it wasn't enough to give him the advantage he needed. The Vantec pit stop was as good as it had been all season - but the William's team was also very well drilled. The two cars resumed their parade round the long 3.44 mile-long circuit.

Up ahead of Kramer's battle for 9th place, Ryan was also pursuing a Williams. In his case it was the car driven by Eddison. As much as he pushed, Ryan was unable to close. Eddison was as good a driver as Ryan, and also had a demonstrably faster car.

On lap 45, the situation was changed for them. The generally reliable McLaren engine of Weiss, who was leading the race, let go - accompanied by an impressive cloud of oily smoke. Weiss wisely got the car off the circuit as quickly as possibly. If he could have seen the flames licking the underneath of the chassis, he would have got out of the car even faster than he did! He only had one foot out of the cockpit as one of the marshals sprayed foam over the burning rear end of the car.

Weiss's misfortune was Ryan's gain. He was now in the points. With eleven laps to go, and no real challenge coming from behind, he was feeling confident.

As Kramer saw his own lap-board, at the end of the next lap, he realised that Ryan must now be in the points. He smiled to himself, and hoped that all his hard work had been worthwhile.

Seated on a grass bank, on the far side of the circuit, the young Asian man peered through his round spectacles at the screen of the small laptop nestling in his lap. He had been waiting for the moment when Ryan hit the top six. He was finding his first Grand Prix all a bit confusing, as the backmarkers were making it hard for him to follow the race. Still, the TV coverage clearly showed Ryan in 6th place. Satisfied that the time had come, the man swapped from the TV picture to a simple screen with just a few boxes on it. He moved his finger over the mouse pad until the cursor rested over the button marked 'Transmit', said a silent prayer, and then clicked the left mouse control. His work was done. He switched back to the TV coverage to watch the results.

The man had chosen his position well. He was seated close to one of the radio beacons used to communicate with the cars. A rapid stream of data left his lap-top and passed through a separate small transmitter on the ground next to him. Soon, a mixture of commands and data was winging through the air to Ryan's car.

In the Vantec pit, there was consternation. Ken Eyre, Ryan's race engineer, was sitting with the Powerblok engineer who had first spotted the anomaly. Ken flicked the radio button.

'John, look at Ryan's engine revs - I think we have a problem.'

From his seat on the prat-perch, John Thornhill looked at the screen. He couldn't see a problem, but then he was no expert. Two seats to his right, Scott Harding was also studying the screen.

'What am I supposed to be looking at?' he asked.

Ken Eyre looked at the screen again, and shook his head, the anomaly had gone.

'Doesn't matter. It seems to have cleared itself.' Ken was puzzled; he knew what he had seen. Still, problems that cleared themselves were fine by him.

On the next lap, the anomaly returned again. This time, the problem was still evident as both Thornhill and Harding looked at their screens.

Eyre came on the radio again, 'John, the engine guy's very concerned the engine's going to blow if the engine keeps over-revving like that. I think we're going to have to ask Ryan to back off a few hundred revs.'

'What do you think, Scott?' asked Thornhill.

'It's a no-brainer, I'm afraid. Best do what Ken suggests.'

'Okay, it looks like he's got enough in hand.' John pressed the radio switch to speak to Ryan.

'Ryan, your engine is over-revving, keep it below 16,500 revs.'

Ryan was bemused; he could tell no difference in the engine from earlier in the race. But he didn't have all the information that the engineers had. Reluctantly, he backed off. Frustratingly, the Williams ahead of him immediately began to pull out a gap. He looked in his mirrors. There was no one in sight - at the moment.

'Look at that!' the engineer pointed excitedly at an even larger blip on the screen. Whatever the problem was - it was definitely getting worse. 'Do we bring him in?' he asked, worried.

Ken Eyre shook his head, they would have to try and keep him out on the track. With just four laps left; they'd have to take a chance. 'No, but I think we'd better slow Ryan a bit more – say 16,000 revs?'

'It's your engine!' The man from Powerblok shrugged his shoulders. It was not the decision he would have taken. He hastily scribbled a note in a small notebook. If questions were asked later, he wanted to make sure it was clear that keeping Ryan out wasn't his decision.

'Ryan, hold below 16,000.'

Two laps later, Ryan thought he spotted a dot in the rapidly vibrating mirror. By the end of that lap, he knew he was in trouble. The long straights demanded maximum power, and he wasn't allowed to use it. Ryan shook his head in desperation as Vigneron's Demaison glided past. Seconds later, Collett and then Kramer followed suit.

The man on the bank clenched his fist in satisfaction. He would let Ryan complete another lap, and then he'd end the transmission. They would never know he had even been mucking about with their telemetry. He just hoped that Kramer kept his word over the cocaine. Not only was his own stash running out, but he knew people who were prepared to pay him good money for a regular supply.

The remaining laps were an agony for Somerset, who was watching the race from the pit wall. It hurt him to see Kramer and both Renaults pass Ryan's cruising car. Ryan eventually crossed the line in eleventh place. Ryan's misfortune was bad enough - but what really hurt, was seeing Vigneron cross the line in 6th place. He took no consolation from Kramer's creditable eighth place. The single point Vigneron had grabbed was enough to bring Demaison level with Vantec in the Championship. The fight for sixth place in the championship was going to have to be fought out in Japan.

CHAPTER 21

9:20 p.m. Wednesday 24th October, Flower Garden Hotel, Suzuka - Japan

Craig watched with concern as Ryan pushed the tiny piece of raw red tuna round his plate with a chopstick. He had already finished his own starter, and sat patiently for several minutes as Ryan played with the food on his plate. Ryan's mood had clearly changed since the flight down to Kochi. After the Malaysian grand prix, the two of them had spent a week on Lizard Island north of Cairns, off Australia's Queensland coast. Five days of sunbathing and diving in the exclusive resort had left the pair of them very relaxed, but now Ryan seemed depressed.

'What's up?' asked Craig, over the loud babble of voices from the diners all around. 'You were okay earlier today; nothing's happened has it?' There was concern in Craig's voice.

'No - nothing's happened, but all of this could come to an end on Sunday.' Ryan's hand described an arc round the room.

'Well, that sure wouldn't bother me - I hate Japanese food.' Craig felt uncomfortable in the smart hotel restaurant.

'I didn't just mean the restaurant, you Australian oaf!' Ryan laid his chopsticks to rest on the plate. He guessed Craig was trying to cheer him up.

'I thought things were looking up. Stuff Demaison on Sunday, and Somerset's surely got to give you a new contract.'

Despite the many hours Craig had spent with Ryan, both in and away from the races, he had never fully understood the political wrangling that went on in Formula One. It was supposed to be a sport, wasn't it?

'If only life were that easy!' said Ryan, sharply. 'You saw Autosport last week, Vantec's the only team that hasn't sorted its drivers out. That means, that if it all goes pear shaped, there'll be nowhere else for me to go - and that'll be the end of Ryan Clarke, Formula One driver. If you're not moving up in this game - you're moving down, and there's no further down than not having a drive! Not many drivers make it back in again; there are just too many good youngsters waiting to step in. A test drive somewhere is the best I could hope for – that's not for me, look at Warren! Vantec is my only hope now.'

'But, surely you're in the driving seat; Kramer hasn't got a contract either, and Panetta can't be a serious threat - he's only just started driving again.'

'If Kramer hasn't got a contract sorted, then he could also be up for one of the Vantec seats - and he's been pushing me hard.' There was respect in Ryan's voice. It had come as a shock to Ryan that Kramer had not been given a contract at Demaison.

'As for Panetta, he's young, improving and, more importantly, brings a lot of money into the team! And let's face it, I haven't exactly done my case much good this year, have I?'

'If you put it like that, then there's not too much to worry about is there!' teased Craig.

'And if I'm out of a job - then so are you!' said Ryan, pointing a finger at Craig.

'Now, you have got me worried!'

'So, you can see why I'm down?' Ryan lapsed back into a moody silence.

Craig nodded, then shut up as he desperately tried to think of something to say to lighten the atmosphere. Their worries would have been greatly magnified, if they had known of Somerset's agreement to run a Japanese driver. As it was, Somerset had kept details of the engine deal to himself. He had reasoned that letting anyone else know, at such a crucial stage in the season, could only unsettle the drivers. There was also the real prospect that the deal might not materialise.

They were still ruminating, when a familiar figure glided up to stand behind Ryan.

A pair of slender bare arms slid over Ryan's shoulders, and expensively ringed hands stroked his chest.

With his head imprisoned in an ample female bosom, Ryan was unable to turn round. He sniffed the air appreciatively - he'd recognise that scent any day.

'Hi, Roxy.' Ryan managed to inject some enthusiasm into the greeting.

'That's not much of a welcome, especially as I've bought a friend.' She released Ryan from her grasp, and let him turn round in his chair.

Standing just behind Roxanne Prendergast was Thierry Vigneron, Demaison's number one driver.

'Thierry! Good to see you.' It was no surprise to see another driver in the hotel restaurant. The small hotel was the only one close to the Suzuka circuit, and they would nearly all be staying there.

'I didn't know you knew Roxy,' said Ryan, addressing the diminutive Frenchman, who was dressed head to toe in black. Ryan recognised the expensive cut of an Armani jacket.

'She's rather taken me under her wing.' A broad smile spread across the Frenchman's face, displaying an uneven row of very white teeth.

'I can't think of a better set of wings! Will you join us?' Even though Thierry Vigneron drove for Demaison, Ryan always found him good company away from the track.

Thierry Vigneron looked enquiringly at Roxy.

'Love to - but you guys had better not talk cars all night!' she said.

'Thank God for that,' said Craig, 'Ryan's been boring me all evening!'

As Thierry and Roxy sat down at the table, Ryan beckoned to a white-jacketed waiter who had been hovering attentively in the background. The waiter adjusted the table settings, and took a drink order while the newcomers studied the menu.

Thierry was on top form, and was soon regaling them with hilarious tales of his failed sexual conquests down the years. According to him, jealous husbands and irate fathers were forever chasing him down garden-paths. Ryan didn't believe a word of it; Vigneron had an enviable reputation with the ladies. Under the round table, Ryan felt Roxy's nylon-clad foot slide up and down his calf. The girl was incorrigible. If he hadn't already been laughing at one of Thierry's story's, he would have had a hard job keeping a straight face.

By the time their main courses arrived, Ryan's appetite had returned. Not wanting to risk a stomach upset so close to the weekend, he had settled for a simple chicken Kamameshi. Eagerly, he tucked into the chicken and rice casserole, which, to his surprise, was rather like an Italian risotto.

While they waited for dessert to be served, Thierry excused himself from the table, and made his way confidently towards the toilet. As he made his way through the crowded room, heads, mainly female, turned to follow his progress. The driver was easily recognisable.

'When did you two hook up?' Ryan was curious.

'Oh, only yesterday. We came in on the same plane - and have just sort of stuck together since. He is rather good company, don't you think?'

'Absolutely, but he's not the sort to hang round with one girl for long - so just watch yourself.'

'I think I can look after myself - which is more than can be said for you!' There was no anger in her voice. She was surprised, though, to find herself pleased that Ryan still cared. She had followed Ryan's misadventures with dismay.

'You don't need to worry - he's got me to look after him!' interjected Craig, who was feeling a bit left out.

'Okay, tough guy, but you'd better stay close to Ryan - some people aren't quite what they seem.' There was bitterness in her voice.

'Anyone we know?' Craig glanced across the table at Ryan, as he asked the question.

'Oh yeah, someone you know real well! Mummy always told me stay away from Americans.'

'Kramer!' exclaimed Ryan and Craig, simultaneously.

'Uh huh. I think he got the wrong idea about me from somewhere, and he got a bit too fresh in Malaysia. Still, a knee in the balls soon put a stop to that.' Roxy smiled at the memory. 'Not at all like Thierry - I practically had to drag him into the bedroom!'

Ryan couldn't imagine Thierry putting up much of a struggle.

'And Thierry's not a bastard, unlike Jason. According to Thierry, Jason's illegitimate. Says he heard it from one of the mechanics. I think Thierry knows who the father is, but he wouldn't tell me. He just said it's someone quite famous. He also said that Jason treats his mum badly. Well, I can certainly believe that!'

Roxy made a habit of collecting paddock gossip, and kept her ear to the ground. Although Roxy's revelation surprised Ryan, he suddenly realised he actually knew very little about his team-mate's private life, even after the time they had spent together in America.

At that moment, Vigneron reappeared. He smiled and waved at people he knew as he weaved his way slowly through the restaurant.

'You wouldn't believe what just happened...,' Thierry left them hanging in suspense as he sat back down. 'There I was taking a leak, "pshhhhhh....," Ryan, Craig and Roxy burst out laughing at Thiery's over the top sound effects - all round the room, heads turned to see where the noise was coming from.

'...ah, the relief, you can't imagine! Anyway, as I finished, I looked over to the left, and standing beside me was a young Japanese girl, who immediately thrust a notebook and pen in my face. I was too surprised to do anything other than give her a bloody autograph. Still, when she studies it carefully she'll see I signed it "Big Willy"!' A broad white grin spread across Thierry's beaten-up face.

The group once again burst into laughter. The earlier conversation about Kramer was forgotten as the group swapped autograph-hunting stories.

Just after 11 p.m, Ryan glanced at his watch.

'It's getting a bit late - if you lot don't mind too much, I'd rather like to get an early night. Tomorrow's going to be a bit hectic. And I'd like to get a breath of air before turning in.' The heavy rice dish was sitting uncomfortably in his stomach, and he wanted to let the food settle properly before he went to bed.

'I'll come with you,' said Craig, taking his minding role seriously.

'We'll leave you to it; I'm ready for bed,' said Roxy, yawning theatrically, Thierry smiled broadly. He was also keen to get to bed - but he wasn't planning on sleeping.

Ryan and Craig said their goodnights to Thierry and Roxy in the lobby of the hotel, and watched as the pair got into the lift, Thierry giving Roxy's pert rear a huge pinch, much to Ryan's amusement.

Once outside the hotel, Ryan took a deep breath and filled his lungs with cool night air. He was pleased to be away from the hubbub of the busy restaurant. With so many teams and spectators in the area, the hotel was full. The two men strolled casually round the floodlit hotel grounds. Ryan was too wrapped up in his thoughts to appreciate all the care that had gone into the design of the garden, but he sniffed appreciatively at the air, savouring the mixed fragrances of pine, magnolia and cherry.

'What did you make of Roxy's story about Kramer?' asked Craig, as they crossed a wooden Japanese style bridge over a meandering stream, their way lit by warm yellow light from hanging stone lanterns.

'Not much. I certainly don't care that he's illegitimate - or who his father is!'

'But what about his bothering Roxy?'

'A bit surprising, but you heard her; she's a big girl, and very capable of taking care of herself. Besides, she does give out a lot of signals - I'm not sure Kramer was completely to blame!'

'Yeah, well, I don't think much of guys who treat girls badly!' Sometimes, Craig showed a very Victorian attitude to behaviour.

'Rather sounds like you're jealous!' The thought of Craig and Roxy as a pair amused Ryan - she would eat him alive.

'Well, I wouldn't say no, but I'm too busy baby-sitting you at the moment!'

After two laps of the grounds, the pair headed slowly back to the hotel. As they strolled down the carpeted corridor towards the elevators, they could see Karl Wittman waiting for a lift. Ryan didn't relish a conversation with the Austrian - but could see no way of avoiding him without looking foolish.

'Karl.' Ryan's greeting was perfunctory, and accompanied by the briefest of nods. The Austrian said nothing, but turned his head and stared at Ryan for an uncomfortable few seconds, before turning again to face the lift.

'Please yourself!' said Ryan, irritated by Wittman's attitude. He turned towards Craig, 'You know, I've always thought his car had more personality.'

It was fortunate for Ryan that the shiny brushed-metal lift doors reflected every movement. He leant sideways, as Wittman's clumsy haymaker whistled past his right ear, and then put all of his weight into a short powerful punch to Wittman's stomach. As Wittman doubled up in pain, the lift doors slid open with a whoosh. Ryan stepped inside - quickly followed by Craig. He had no desire to prolong the confrontation.

'Sorry Craig, I know that wasn't very sensible - but I've wanted to do that for some time.'

'Fair enough, but you were dead lucky; I don't think there were any witnesses.' Craig had scanned the corridor before getting into the lift.

'Thank God! But I think I've just given you someone else to protect me from.'

'I can cope, but if I were you, I'd give Karl a wide berth - both on and off the track!'

CHAPTER 22

Evening Saturday 27th October, Flower Garden Hotel, Suzuka - Japan

Pierre Demaison slid a grey-haired arm out of the sleeve of his elegant dark blue suit, and looked at his watch. The expensive gold Patek Philippe watch had been a gift from Prince Rainier of Monaco in 1955, the result of winning the Monaco Grand Prix. He grunted impatiently, it was still only 17:45 and Gonzales was not due to see him for another fifteen minutes. He moved forward to perch on the edge of the black leather sofa in his hotel suite. He picked up the sheet of paper lying on the coffee table in front of him, and for the umpteenth time that afternoon, stared at the championship standings:

1.	Ferrari	151 pts
2.	Mclaren	133 pts
3.	Williams	38 pts
4.	Kodama	34 pts
5.	Renault	33 pts
6.	Demaison	11 pts
7.	Vantec	11 pts

He shook his head and sighed deeply. Eleven points were a meagre return for all of the time, effort and money expended through the long season. By the same time the previous season, his team had amassed 35 points, and was in 5th place. This year, it had taken the team until the 6th race in Canada to score any points at all. Having managed to score points in Montreal with both cars, Demaison had hoped for an improvement in the team's fortunes - but they failed to score again until the 13th race in Italy. To Demaison's disgust, the team had failed miserably on French soil. The home race at Magny-Cours saw Gonzales drive home in 9th place, Vigneron failed to finish - his car breaking down on lap 47 with a gearbox seizure. After the Italian Grand Prix, the team had picked up a fifth place in Germany and a sixth in Malaysia. Just five scoring results, out of the thirty-two starts prior to the last race of the season. Without doubt, it was the team's worst performance in its long and distinguished history.

He no longer needed the company accountant to tell him they were in financial trouble; the shortfall in money was evident throughout the factory - if you looked carefully. The total number of staff had shrunk by five, leaving significant gaps. A number of other people had also left and been replaced, but they had been unable to pay enough to attract the very best people. Even more serious, though, was the reduction in the teams research and development programme. In Formula One, it is necessary to make continual improvement just to stand still in comparison with the other teams. The faltering development programme was sending the team to the back of the grid - just as effectively as having no development programme!

The only hope for the team, would be to have a better season next year - but if the team lost Katayama as their engine supplier, there would be little chance of them racing their way out of trouble. Hanging on to sixth place was the only way to guarantee a continued supply of Katayama engines. Good engines were hard to come by, and the Katayama motor was indisputably the best of the independent engines. There was no chance that Ferrari, Mercedes or any of the other car manufacturers would provide his team with an engine! He grimaced at the prospect of the team having to make do with under-performing Powerblok engines.

He picked up a pen from the table in front of him and violently drew several lines underneath the team lying 7th in the championship. Demaison were only ahead of Vantec by virtue of a 4th place in Canada. Keeping in front of Vantec was going to be the name of the game. He smiled ruefully as he drew a final line right through his rival's name, then slammed the pen down on the glass-topped table. At least he had a couple of aces up his sleeve - Kramer could be relied upon to play his part, and in a few minutes he was going to arrange some insurance against the threat from Ryan Clarke.

Even better for Demaison, the qualifying session earlier that afternoon had left the team in a good position relative to their British rivals. Gonzales had outshone Thierry Vigneron for only the 3rd time that season, but more importantly - having qualified sixth fastest, he was two places ahead of Ryan Clarke. Despite his disappointment at Thierry Vigneron qualifying in 9th place, the presence of Jason Kramer ahead of Clarke was almost as good as having two drivers ahead of Vantec. With luck, they would get the result they needed on the race track.

Finally, at ten minutes past six, there was a rap on his door.

'Entre!' shouted Demaison; his irritation at Gonzales' late arrival was ill-concealed.

The slim body of Cesar Gonzales slid cautiously into the room. The 35 year old driver was surprised at having been summoned to see Demaison in his hotel. Demaison had a chance to talk to him at the track earlier that afternoon. It was certainly unusual to see his boss away from a racing circuit.

'Pardon chef', Gonzales was apologetic, 'the traffic was very bad'. Even as he uttered the excuse, he was aware how lame it sounded for a racing driver.

Demaison grunted, and gestured for Gonzales to sit down. Gonzales took his place on a second leather sofa facing Demaison. The coffee table acted as a physical barrier between the two men. Even though Gonzales had driven for Demaison for six years, there had been little close contact between them. Demaison had always had his favourite drivers in the team - and currently his favourite was Thierry Vigneron. Gonzales suspected that this was largely because Vigneron was also

French. Gonzales owed his place in the team due to the sponsorship he brought from the Repsol oil company.

Gonzales draped an arm along the top of the sofa and crossed his legs, before staring at Demaison through his dark brown slits of eyes. Like all racing drivers, he had a very concentrated stare - born from years of focusing on distant targets on the track. He didn't wish to be insolent, but he was determined not to be intimidated by Demaison. He had never witnessed Demaison in a rage, but had heard muttered stories from disgruntled mechanics.

Demaison took his time, and studied his number two driver for what seemed an age, before speaking.

'In your own words - tell me what we need to achieve this weekend?' There were no wasteful pleasantries. Demaison got straight down to business; he was keen to understand how much Gonzales appreciated the situation. They had been through it all that afternoon after qualifying, but he knew that the drivers didn't always pay full attention to the political and business side of the sport. Frequently, the drivers had their own agendas. It was, after all, a very selfish sport. A driver had to look after himself.

'We need to finish in the top six and stay ahead of Vantec,' replied Gonzales carefully.

'And why must we do so?'

'Because we want to finish as high as we can in the Championship - and Vantec are our only rivals.' The puzzlement in Gonzales' voice was evident. It was obvious that they needed to perform as well as they could, and he couldn't understand why Demaison was taking this tack.

For his part, Demaison was pleased with the answer. It seemed clear that the team's financial problems had not filtered down to the drivers. How much could he afford to tell Gonzales?

'I am pleased that you were listening this afternoon', there was just the slightest hint of sarcasm in his voice. 'It is not just important that we finish ahead of Vantec - it is *imperative* that we do so'. Demaison placed heavy emphasis on the word imperative.

'As our leading driver tomorrow - the responsibility for doing so lies with you!' Demaison jabbed a pudgy finger at Gonzales. 'There is no guarantee that Thierry will be able to get past both Vantecs'. This time there was regret and disappointment in his voice.

Gonzales nodded his head in agreement; there didn't seem any need to speak. This was all obvious - he wondered if he was missing something. Well, he'd let Demaison do all the talking. The purpose of the conversation must eventually show itself.

Demaison leant forward, and picked up a blue-covered folder from the coffee table.

'This is your contract for next season.'

Again, Gonzales just nodded. He had signed the papers a month previously.

Demaison tossed the folder across the gap between them. Gonzales reacted instinctively to catch the folder before it landed in his lap.

'Turn to the last page,' commanded Demaison brusquely.

Gonzales did as he was told, and quickly found the final page. As expected, the page contained space for the signatures that would confirm acceptance of the contract. His own signature crawled untidily across the left hand side of the page. But his was the only signature on the legal document.

'I don't understand - where is your signature? We both signed this contract at the same time.' Gonzales was seriously worried.

'I think you must be mistaken' said Demaison smoothly, 'I have not yet signed your contract for next year.' He stared into Gonzales' eyes. He held the stare until, eventually, Gonzales looked away. No apology, no explanation; that was how he would approach this.

Gonzales was out of his depth. Demaison had taken him by surprise the previous month, when he had invited him to sign a new contract. His manager had not been present at the brief ceremony, but Gonzales had been happy to tidy up the paperwork. He had satisfied himself that the papers being signed were those agreed with his management team. Signing in the absence of his manager had not seemed a big deal at the time, especially as the team manager had also been present to witness the event. He shook his head in bafflement.

Before Gonzales could muster a response, Demaison went on the attack.

'I have no doubt you are aware that all of the other teams have filled their drives for next year.' Demaison knew from Kramer, that Vantec had not sorted out their team - but all of the other teams had gone public with their line-ups. He couldn't see a slot becoming available in Vantec for Gonzales - so he was content to let his inaccurate statement stand. He continued, 'I will sign you for next year if you finish ahead of both Vantec drivers tomorrow.' He paused to let Gonzales absorb the information.

Gonzales visibly brightened at the news, and once again looked directly into Demaison's eyes. Demaison's green eyes were twinkling, and his lips were curled in amusement. He was sure he had Gonzales - but he had to be certain.

'While it would be preferable for us to beat Vantec cleanly on the track, we cannot let them finish ahead of us. If there is the slightest chance of a Vantec getting past you, I expect you to do whatever is necessary to prevent it happening.'

He didn't need to spell it out any clearer - Gonzales knew exactly what Demaison was suggesting.

'What you are asking is both difficult and dangerous. I could even lose my licence!' Gonzales bridled, his voice raised. His eyes flashed angrily, and he could feel his cheeks burning.

'Let me remind you, that failing to do what I ask will also result in the end of your career,' said Demaison smoothly. He was rather enjoying the confrontation.

'No!' shouted Gonzales 'I will not do what you ask - you had better find another driver for tomorrow.' He stood up.

'Sit down!' hissed Demaison, 'it is foolish to act rashly when you don't know all the facts!' He glowered at Gonzales, who hesitantly sank back onto the sofa.

'I had hoped that you would be sensible about this - but clearly you need more persuading. Perhaps, this will help you make a rational decision.' Demaison hunted for, and found, a manila folder. He glanced inside, to make sure he had the correct file, and then slid the folder across the table.

Gonzales took a deep breath and picked up the folder. He knew that Demaison was capable of fighting dirty, and was aware of his vulnerability. He opened the folder – inside, there was a single large photo. The picture showed Gonzales gazing compassionately at another man - his right arm tenderly draped around the man's shoulders. In its way, the picture was innocent enough, but the damage lay in the fact that both men were naked.

'I wonder if your wife and son know of your interests?' said Demaison, studying Gonzales. He saw a slight flinch. He hadn't been sure on that point, but the confirmation in Gonzales' eyes was enough. He liked to keep tabs on all his drivers - and the private detective had not come cheap. Gonzales had made a very good job of keeping his sexual activities quiet, for there had been no paddock gossip suggesting that he was gay. Not much escaped the watchful eyes up and down the pit lane.

'I have more pictures,' said Demaison, ramming the point home. 'I do hope you won't make me use them! If you fail to do what I ask tomorrow - you will not just be finished as a racing driver - you will also be finished as a man!' Demaison paused briefly to look at Gonzales. Hatred was still flashing from his eyes, but his shoulders had sunk in capitulation - he had him.

'Now get out. I suggest you spend some time thinking about the race tomorrow. Do this right, and we can start next season with a clean slate.' Finished, Demaison pointed towards the door. He thought it was a nice touch to leave Gonzales with a little ray of hope - even if it wasn't true. He had no intention of keeping Gonzales on the team - he wasn't having a fairy drive one of his cars. He liked his men to be men.

Gonzales got slowly to his feet, and slunk towards the door. In a petty act of defiance, he slammed the door behind him.

CHAPTER 23

Midday Sunday 28th October, Suzuka Race Circuit - Japan

'Before I get on to today's race; I'd like to begin by thanking all of you for the hard work you have put in - not just on this weekend, but over the whole season...'

While Chris Somerset continued his welcoming speech, Ryan looked round the select group crammed into the lounge of the motorhome. As well as himself and Chris Somerset, there was Jason Kramer, Scott Harding, John Thornhill, and the race engineers and chief mechanics for each driver. Ryan wondered how many knew how important the race was going to be. Taken on one level, he thought Chris's speech sounded a lot like a farewell, but there didn't seem to be any concern on any of the faces.

'...and that brings us to the race. I don't need to tell you that we have had a good weekend - so far, but there is still a lot of work to be done if we are to reap the benefits.'

There were nods of agreement all round. The team had not only got both cars onto the fourth row of the grid, but the cars had gone even better in the final warm-up.

'We must finish ahead of Demaison. To achieve that, either Ryan or Jason will have to get past Gonzales - and we all know how difficult it is to overtake in Formula One!' Somerset looked directly at the two drivers as he spoke.

Ryan nodded to show he understood; Jason merely smiled. Somerset took the smile for a show of confidence. Kramer was driving well and had qualified in 7th place - one place ahead of

Ryan in 8th. To their disappointment, Gonzales had qualified the Demaison ahead of both of them in 6th place. Worryingly, Vigneron was camped immediately behind Ryan – ready to pick up the spoils if there were any problems. It was not the starting scenario Somerset would have preferred. Demaison would begin the race with the advantage. Vantec's fortunes rested on a tight scrap round the tricky Suzuka circuit.

Despite the confident words, Ryan could see Somerset's hands shaking. Ryan was nervous for the same reason - today could be his last race as well. Ryan's apprehension was centred in his stomach. Several trips to the toilet had not shaken off the tight knot that had formed. From past experience, he knew the feeling would probably disappear once he stepped into the car, but he hadn't suffered as badly as this since his first race for Vantec.

Ryan turned his head slightly to see how his team-mate was coping.

Kramer shot him a grin and held a thumb up.

Kramer was clearly in good spirits. Was he happy because it was his last race - or did he know something Ryan didn't? Kramer's grin was infectious, but after Roxy's revelations, Ryan still didn't know what to make of his colleague.

'The forecast for today is fine, no chance of rain - so that settles the tyre issue.'

Ryan turned his attention back to what Somerset was saying.

'There is no question of making anything other than two stops - so we'll make those fairly evenly spaced; Kramer on laps eighteen and thirty-six, Clarke on nineteen and thirty-seven.' Somerset looked at both drivers to check they had heard.

'Unless anyone has had any new thoughts, we will go with the set-ups from this morning.'

There was no disagreement. It was the end of a long season, and they knew just about all they were going to know about the car. The morning set-up had proved itself, and no one was keen to risk changing it.

'Okay, good! Now go to it - and good luck!' Somerset beamed at the group, then dismissed them with an airy wave of his hand. He hadn't slept at all the previous night and was running on nerves. It was going to be the longest day of his racing life.

With that, the briefing ended. There was still over an hour to go before they needed to get the cars onto the track, but the engineers and mechanics were keen to get back to the pits.

'Good luck Ryan; let's just hope the telemetry behaves itself this time!' said Ken Eyre, as they got up from the bench together. Ken sounded more confident than he actually felt. They had stripped the engine after Malaysia and had found nothing at all wrong with it. That pointed the figure squarely at the software system - but days of frantic and thorough testing had revealed nothing. He could only hope that the problem in Malaysia was a one-off.

'Yeah, too right,' replied Ryan, who was not concentrating on what Ken Eyre was saying. He really wanted to have a word with Kramer, but as his race engineer spoke to him, he could see Kramer already leaving the motorhome.

By the time Ryan exited the van, his team-mate was already a distant figure.

Ryan picked his pace up, and was gaining on Kramer, when he spotted an unwelcome figure clad in red racing overalls. Ryan hurriedly looked around for cover - the last thing he needed was a confrontation with Wittman. Luckily, the Kodama hospitality area was close by. Ryan stepped into the awning-covered area out of Wittman's sight.

'Hello, Ryan.'

The tone was friendly, so Ryan turned to face the speaker. A young blonde woman, smartly dressed in a black trouser-suit over a white top, sat at a round cloth covered table. Dark sunglasses hid her eyes.

'Do I know you?' he asked.

She slid her sunglasses upward, perching them high on her head, before replying.

'Actually, no. But I did spend several hours chasing you up a motorway earlier this year!' She sounded amused, and her green eyes twinkled.

Ryan leant across and grabbed her slender arm.

'Hey - steady on, you're hurting me!' she said angrily.

'Why were you following me?' he hissed. He wanted to shout, but the area was busy, and he didn't want to make a scene.

'If you just let go - I'll tell you.' She glared up at him.

Ryan released her arm, and sat down opposite her.

'Well?'

The girl rubbed her arm.

'You don't know your own strength,' she said.

'Sorry, but I'm a bit stressed. Please - tell me why you were following us.'

'My name is Samantha Beswick, I'm a freelance financial journalist and also a motor racing fan. I was putting together a story about the economics of Formula One. I recognised your car when you left Liege, and in a moment of madness, thought I could catch up with you and snatch an interview.' She was aware how weak her account would sound.

'Couldn't you have just phoned and arranged an interview like everyone else?' he asked.

'It seemed too good an opportunity to miss - but I didn't realise it was so hard to follow someone in a car! Besides, I had to go overseas the next day to cover a different assignment.'

'Suzuka's a long way to come for a story.' Ryan was still suspicious; after all it had been a woman who had threatened him over the phone.

'I was over in Japan anyway. I've been covering the Japanese financial recovery. Maybe you can answer a few questions for me, now?' she asked optimistically.

'Love to - but I've really got to go.'

'I think you owe me - unless you want me to report your earlier behaviour.' She smiled.

The gentle blackmail worked.

'Okay, but make it quick.'

'What do you know about Demaison?' she asked.

'The team or the man?' The question puzzled Ryan, who had expected to be asked about himself or his own team.

'Start with the man.'

'Pierre - he's well liked in the paddock. A racing legend - always has a good word for people. He's even helped our team out this year. Lent us Kramer after Panetta had his accident...'

'Now, why would he do that?'

'To give Kramer F1 experience. He'll then be fully trained up when he rejoins Demaison.'

'But aren't they in danger of losing their engine supplier to Vantec?'

'Is that right?' Ryan wondered where on earth she'd heard that.

'I see you're not going to help me on that one.'

Ryan shook his head, 'I'm just a driver.'

'If it was true - how far would Demaison go on behalf of his team?'

'As far as I can see, he's always played fair.'

'But what if he was in deep financial trouble, and desperately needed his team to do well or go under?'

'Is that possible? I haven't seen any rumours in the press.'

'Well, I have my sources outside motor racing, and if what they say is true, then Demaison is in real trouble.'

'Look, that's all very interesting, but I can't think about that right now - I've got to race. We'll just have to see what happens, won't we?' Ryan stood up.

'Okay, well thanks for your time - maybe I'll catch up with you after the race. Good luck!' She smiled at him. It was a shame they had got off to a bad start, for he was just her type.

Ryan left the hospitality area and headed back towards the motorhome - disturbed by the implications of what he had just been told. Just how far would a man like Demaison go?

It seemed unreasonable that Ryan should bump into Demaison so soon after his chat with the journalist. But Ryan hadn't even reached the Vantec motorhome before he spotted him. The Frenchman was hugging Kramer. Ryan knew that Pierre was given to extravagant gestures, but, even by French standards, the greeting seemed over familiar. As Ryan came closer, Demaison released Kramer and took Ryan into his arms.

'Bon chance, mon ami. May you have a good race - but maybe not too good, huh!'

There was no hint of trouble in Demaison's voice, but Ryan didn't think the greeting he had received was quite as warm as that meted out to Kramer. Still, Kramer was almost one of Demaison's own drivers.

'I'm going out there to win, and if not to win - to come second. At the very least, I intend to beat those dogs you call racing cars!'

'Well mon brave, first you have to catch Gonzales - only then, will we see if your rust bucket is good enough to get past,' fired back Demaison - giving as good as he got.

But Ryan was not disappointed. Anger had flickered in Demaison's eyes.

'Perhaps we'll both be up on the podium.' Ryan gestured towards the stands - he didn't want to start a war.

Kramer tugged on Ryan's arm. 'Come on, we'd better start getting ready - they won't hold the race for us.'

The two drivers took their leave of Demaison and climbed into the sanctuary of the motorhome.

'That was a bit strong with old Pierre!' there was amusement in Kramer's voice.

'Just enjoying a wind up.' Ryan said no more, and left Kramer looking bemused in the lounge, as he headed for the toilet.

Ryan took his place on the grid twenty-three minutes before the race. He could have joined the grid later, but he preferred to get into place and get settled - even though the general hubbub did little to soothe the nerves. Having parked the car on the markings, Ryan got out to let the engineers get to work. It was nearly 40 degrees C on the track, and he had hardly got out of the car, before engineers were feeding dry ice into the sidepods to cool the engine.

Thoughtfully, Karen Goodbody had bought a large golfing umbrella onto the track. Ryan ducked into the shade and gratefully took the cold drink she offered him. As he slowly sipped the cold glucose drink, he soaked up the theatrical atmosphere of the track. The large Ferris wheel, and noisy fair in the background, made the place seem like a mini Disneyland - but the track itself was no joke. Its Dutch designer had created one of the world's best circuits. The bumpy and undulating figure-of-eight track offered every kind of challenge - from blindingly-fast corners, to slow tight-chicanes. After Spa, it was Ryan's favourite circuit.

The grid was buzzing with frenetic energy, and was no place to relax. As well as all the mechanics, camera crews were struggling to keep up with their reporters - who buzzed to and fro between the big stars, hoping for an interesting sound-bite. It was both amusing and irritating to Ryan. Whenever he'd watched a pre race build up on TV, he'd never heard anything worthwhile come from the lips of the pent-up drivers. It all seemed a pretty pointless exercise. He smiled wryly, at least they rarely bothered him.

Eventually, Ryan had to get back into the car - and even in the shade of the large umbrella, he rapidly started to heat up. He sat quietly, staring ahead - trying to visualise the start. His concentration was broken several times, as mechanics reached into the car to fiddle with god knows what. He felt like a patient on an operating table - unable to influence what was being done, but knowing it was for his own good. All the time, his pulse was rising as the adrenaline kicked in. However safe motor racing had become, it was still a thrilling experience, and his heart would be pounding at over 180 beats per minute throughout the race.

With two minutes to go, the car was fired up. Ryan sighed with relief as the engine roared into life on the second attempt; a misfire and an ignominious start from the pit lane would have undone all the good work in the qualifying session. With the engine burbling away behind him, the mechanics drifted away from the track. Ryan and the other drivers were now on their own.

Ryan made the most of the momentary peace before the gantry lights turned green and the formation lap started. Kramer moved away faster than Ryan. Almost immediately, Rider in the Sauber, one row behind Ryan on the grid, came up alongside - before dropping back into position. Once the cars were away from the home straight, the formation lap settled down into its normal procession.

As they neared the chicane at the end of the lap, Ryan began to extravagantly haul the steering-wheel from side to side - jinking the car from left to right as he sought to build up some heat in the tyres. In front of him, cars began to pull left and right as they found their places on the grid. Ryan looked for his own mark and pulled up just short of the line. Ahead of him, a heat haze rose from the boiling hot engine of Gonzales' blue Demaison.

As the overhead gantry lights began to turn red, Ryan started to press down on the throttle - feeling the car strain against the clutch. Two, three, four, five - all of the lights were on. It was only a fraction over a second before the lights went off - but it seemed far longer. Then the wait was over, and he released the clutch.

Just ahead of Ryan, Kramer's clutch control was poor. The American spun his rear wheels, wastefully coating the circuit with rubber before the tyres found enough grip to handle the power of the engine and propel the car forward. The small mistake allowed Ryan to slide past on the inside.

As the two columns of cars hurtled downhill towards the first turn, Ryan noticed Kramer slot in behind him. The steep drop into the turn made it seem as if he was actually accelerating into the corner. Although there had been no dramas up front, Ryan had to push hard to stop a gap growing between himself and

Gonzales ahead. With the first bend out of the way, Ryan began to relax, his nerves dissipating in the physical act of driving.

The snaking uphill section through the Esses was as challenging as ever. The combination of short straights and left-right turns demanded constant gear changes. The concrete barriers leant the section an almost street circuit quality. Ryan had to concentrate hard to negotiate the twisting road. He had a momentary view of the sky as he crested the ridge, before he was slung terrifyingly round the 180 degree Dunlop curve. It felt like he was in a centrifuge. To make matters worse, the road was bumpy, and Ryan felt every jolt as the car bottomed out.

Ryan was still unable to make any impression on the cars in front, as he braked, banged down two gears, and swept imperiously through the first part of the Degner curve. The track narrowed into the second part of Degner. There was no room for complacency as he rounded the tight corner.

The horizon rushed towards him, as he approached the Spoon for the first time. At last Ryan felt he was making ground on the Demaison. His confidence was misplaced - he had gone in too fast, and the Vantec slid towards the outside of the track. He had to work hard to pull the car back in for the tighter second apex. His slight mistake had wasted valuable fractions of a second, and allowed Gonzales to regain the yards he had earlier lost. Ryan cursed, and set about chasing the Spaniard down again.

The race soon settled into to a finely tuned game of tag, with Ryan chasing, but never quite getting close enough to Gonzales. Frustratingly, Ryan would close right up on the Spaniard's tailpipe as they braked into Spoon, but the Demaison would pull away again as they rounded the bend. The two cars were well matched, and Ryan began to despair of getting past him for the vital championship point the team needed.

At least Ryan didn't have to worry about being overtaken. Kramer was playing shotgun behind him. Kramer was far enough behind Ryan not to get in the way, and driving well enough to prevent other cars from joining the battle for sixth place.

The pit stops began on the 18th lap, and Ryan briefly held 6th place as Gonzales peeled off first into the pit lane. In clean air, Ryan put his foot down; he would only need a small advantage to leapfrog Gonzales with a well-executed pit-stop. By the time he had rounded Degner, Ryan had put in his fastest 1st sector time of the race.

With Takano five seconds ahead of him in the Kodama, Ryan anticipated no problems as he rounded Spoon, and began the long climb up to 130R.

'Shit!' Ryan swore as he spotted the first of the waved double yellow flags. He lifted slightly as he rounded the left-hander and saw the reason for the flags. One of the Thunderbirds was parked half on the track and half on the grass. Marshals were frantically trying to clear the stranded car. Fortunately, the car was off the racing line as Ryan approached the chicane; but the damage had been done, and any chance of passing Gonzales in the pits had been lost.

Thierry Vigneron, in the second Demaison, had not given up the chase, but was having his own private battle with Steve Rider in the leading Sauber. Pitting on lap twenty, right behind Rider, he had the satisfaction of driving past the Sauber as the Sauber pit crew struggled to disengage their fuel hose. The Demaisons were still in 6th and 9th places - sandwiching the two Vantecs.

The frustrating game of tag continued, as Ryan did his best to pressure Gonzales into making a mistake. But the Spaniard was having one of his good days, and the two cars went round the track as if tied by elastic - the gap between them expanding and contracting as they navigated the circuit's 18 corners.

Ryan had to try something if he were to beat the Demaison in front, but his options were narrowing as the laps counted down. He pressed the radio button as they approached the thirty-fifth lap.

'How many laps of fuel have I got?' he asked.

'Three for sure, maybe four.' There was a hard, nervous edge to Thornhill's voice.

They had planned to pit on lap thirty-seven. From what Thornhill was saying, they could maybe pit as late as lap 38 - but it was a risk. Nothing ventured, nothing gained.

'I'm coming in on thirty-eight,' commanded Ryan, switching off the radio; he didn't want to debate the issue. If he got it wrong Somerset could rightly have his hide, but till then, he was going to try it his way.

He slowed slightly and Gonzales moved away from him. Ryan let the gap grow until he was satisfied that the Vantec was out of the dirty air caused by the Demaison. If he drove carefully, he might just save enough fuel to use to good effect once Gonzales pitted.

As Ryan bounced right and left over the chicane kerbs, he saw Gonzales peel off to the right and into the pit lane. He guessed Gonzales had made about four seconds on him in the last two laps. Now he would see if his calculations were right.

Over the next two laps, Ryan concentrated like never before - driving as smoothly and as quickly as he could. On near empty fuel tanks, the two laps he was now driving would be faster than Gonzales managed on a full tank and cold tyres.

Lap thirty-six was fast, but not as fast as Ryan would have liked - it seemed unexpectedly hard to pick the pace up without a visible target to chase. He had no way of knowing how much time he had recovered, or how much he still needed. He couldn't afford to radio in for information - and the pit board information, held out each lap, was inaccurate.

Ryan was more than pleased with his next lap, and it was not until he was nearly half way through lap thirty-eight, that he again became conscious of his need to conserve fuel. It would have to be a slower lap if he was going to make it back to the pit. From the Hairpin onwards, he accelerated cautiously out of each turn. After a long ninety-seconds, he braked for the chicane before the pit lane entrance.

The engine spluttered as he bounced over the first kerb of the chicane, and Ryan's heart skipped a beat. The remaining fuel was slopping about the fuel tank, and the engine misfired again as he bounced over the next kerb. Back on an even keel, the engine picked up, and with relief he pulled into the pit-lane.

For once, the pit-lane speed restriction was a pleasure. Ryan slid the car to a halt in front of the lollipop man and tore off a visor strip. To left and right in front of him, the wheel-men thrust out hands to signal that their job was over. He sat impatiently, waiting for the refuelling to finish. Ryan hoped that the crew had done their sums properly. If they had, then they would need to put in less fuel than Gonzales had needed - and even more time would be gained. At last, the lollipop man turned his sign over and Ryan selected 1st gear. There was a clunk as the fuel line was yanked away from the car - and then the lollipop began to lift. Ryan wasted no time, and dropped the clutch. The lollipop had barely cleared the height of the car, before Ryan was fishtailing out onto the pit-lane. He pressed the radio button.

'How's it looking?'

'Good...'

There was a pause, as Thornhill looked down the track to see Gonzales just entering the straight.

'...Bloody good, now go for it!'

Ryan could hear the ecstasy in Thornhill's voice.

As he came out onto the main straight, Ryan glanced in his mirrors. Gonzales was in sight and closing fast - but he was behind, and that was all that mattered.

As a Sauber screeched off the apron and onto the pit-lane, Chris Somerset turned to study the monitor. Now that all of the planned pit stops were over, it was a straight race to the finish. The race had settled down into a fairly steady progression - with Weiss in the lead; nearly three seconds ahead of Barbosa, who was surprisingly heading Wittman, his Ferrari colleague, by a couple of seconds. Faustino, in the second McLaren, was hanging on to the rear of Wittman - and had a growing cushion over Takano. Ryan occupied the last point scoring position - but was being attacked by Gonzales, with Kramer a little further back.

'Well, John, it's going to be tight - at least there are only thirteen laps to go. I don't think I could take much more.' The excitement in Somerset's voice betrayed his words.

John Thornhill didn't reply to Somerset; he was busy listening into a conversation between Scott Harding and their Powerblok technician.

Sat on the other side of Somerset, Harding and the Powerblok technician were studying the telemetry. Together, they peered at the stream of figures pouring across the tiny screen. Red warning signals were intermittently flashing on and off. Thirteen laps could be twelve laps too many! Scott looked across to the engineer - who simply shook his head and grimaced.

'Chris, John - we've got a situation brewing here.' Harding kept his voice flat and steady - he didn't want to over excite Somerset.

Somerset climbed off his stool, and moved over to stand behind Harding and the engineer at their station. He didn't need to be an engineer to see that the flashing red lights meant trouble.

'Malaysia?' he asked.

'Could be, but it's not quite the same set of symptoms. There are other things happening here that I don't understand.'

'What are the options?' Somerset felt a knot growing in his stomach.

'One; We bring Ryan in and take a look. Two; we ask him to slow as in Malaysia. Three - we do nothing.' Harding paused to think about the implications of each option, before continuing his assessment. 'If we bring Ryan in, or ask him to slow, we are throwing a point away - although Kramer's not far off. If we do nothing - the engine could seize and throw Ryan off the track!'

Somerset closed his eyes, and puffed his cheeks out as he came to a decision.

'We'll do nothing for another lap or two while we check it out.' Somerset turned to the engine technician. 'How quickly could you get a second opinion from your office?'

'A couple of minutes - we are feeding them a data stream already.'

'Okay, well do it!'

The next two laps were a nightmare for Somerset. On the track, Ryan was managing to pull away from Gonzales by fractions each lap - but how much damage was being done to the engine? Finally, Somerset felt a tap on the shoulder. It was the Powerblok engineer.

'Head Office say there is a real and imminent risk of the engine seizing. The bearing temperatures are climbing steadily - and even if we don't yet understand the other signs, we know that one is fatal, sorry.' The engineer bowed his head in shame - feeling a corporate responsibility for the disaster that was unfolding.

'Scott?' There was a note of despair in Somerset's enquiry.

'I don't think we have a choice; we can't risk Ryan's life - there could be a bad accident if the engine seizes and throws Ryan off at speed. We must ask him to slow and come in.' Harding shrugged, it was all part of racing - and he wasn't keen on risking a driver's life, championship points at stake or not.

'Bring him in then,' ordered Somerset.

'John – did you get that?' asked Harding.

'Yeah – I'm on it,' replied Thornhill.

Somerset tore his headset off in frustration, and with head bowed, stormed across to the garage. The puzzled mechanics, made way for the boss, as he marched straight through the garage and out to the paddock to seek refuge in the motorhome.

'Ryan, you have a growing engine problem - slow and come in.' Even over the crackle of the radio connection, Thornhill's tone was emphatic.

Ryan shook his helmeted head in disbelief. This just couldn't be happening to him again. The thought of his career ending in dismal retirement was too much to bear. He didn't reply

'Ryan, did you get that?' asked Thornhill anxiously.

Ryan ignored the question, and concentrated on maintaining the gap over Gonzales while he tried to listen to the engine. The car had been behaving well since the last stop. If anything, it was going even better than before. He listened to the rise and fall of the revs as he changed down into turn 7 and then accelerated towards Degner. He couldn't hear anything unusual. Still, he had nearly a lap to assess things.

'Ryan, you are in danger; I am ordering you to slow down – now!'

There was no ignoring the firmness in Thornhill's voice. Ryan pressed the radio button.

'Roger.'

Ryan lifted and moved off the racing line. As he approached the first Degner curve, Gonzales slid past on the inside.

Ryan sighed; Kramer would also pass him shortly. Ryan's career now rested on the American getting past Gonzales. To Ryan's surprise, Kramer didn't pass him until they had gone round the hairpin. Ryan couldn't think why it had taken Kramer so long to reach him. Kramer should have been up the road after Gonzales a whole lot sooner.

Thinking about Kramer raised the earlier image of him with Demaison in Ryan's mind. Instinctively, he knew that the hug he had witnessed was more than just a greeting between friends. In his mind's eye, Ryan suddenly saw a similarity in the faces of the two men. They could almost be brothers – no, not brothers: father and son. Ryan experienced a sharp intake of breath as the realisation hit home.

Ryan concentrated on his driving as he steered round the ultra slow Spoon curve. But the genie was out of the bottle, and more images of Kramer sped through his mind as he began the long drag up to 130R. He wasn't sure why he began to accelerate again, but he knew it was the right thing to do.

As his car began to close on Kramer, he reviewed events since Kramer had joined the team. All of Ryan's problems had occurred after the American had joined - but how many could be down to Kramer? Possibly the dropped spanner - if so, then Kramer hadn't wasted any time. And Indianapolis? Certainly Kramer had an explanation for all that happened - but if his account was not to be trusted, then anything was possible. But they got on very well, and Kramer had even helped fix his computer - hadn't he? Ryan's leg tensed, and he almost braked as he appreciated the possibilities of Kramer's skill with a computer. The clincher was the unexpected revelation that Demaison was in real financial trouble. If Kramer and Demaison were linked, then a motive was obvious! He was no longer in any doubt - the cause of all his troubles was up ahead, driving a similar green Vantec. Furthermore, he instinctively knew there was nothing wrong with his own car. Computers played far too big a role in motor-racing!

Ryan swung the car through the final chicane, and looked to see how far Kramer was ahead of him. It looked like just over three seconds. The Vantec crew stared, open-mouthed, as Ryan sped past the entrance to the pit-lane and into the home straight.

'Ryan, stop playing games - you must come in!' Thornhill was not only incensed, but sounded very concerned.

'The car is fine - I repeat, the car is fine.' Ryan ended the conversation with satisfaction, then ripped the radio lead out of its socket. He knew he wouldn't be able to persuade the team of his theory, and he didn't need Thornhill pestering him lap after lap.

Ryan was almost correct in his estimation of the gap to Kramer. As they began lap forty-four, Kramer was 4.2 seconds ahead. Gonzales was a further three seconds up the road from Kramer. Ryan swept through the snake of turns three, four, five and six. By the time he reached Degner, he could visibly see the gap closing. With a bit of luck, Kramer wouldn't be expecting him.

Once they reached the Hairpin, Ryan wouldn't be able to hide his progress. If Kramer was awake, he would see Ryan closing on entry - as he himself left the tight corner. Ryan was right. There was a perceptible increase in pace from the leading Vantec. The race was on.

Suzuka was new to Kramer - but Ryan had raced in Japanese Formula three for two years, and knew the circuit well - but would it be enough? At the end of the lap, the gap had dropped to 3.5 seconds - but Kramer was now alert to Ryan's charge. Kramer hadn't been gaining on Gonzales before, but now both Vantecs were moving quicker than the Demaison.

In the Vantec garage, the mechanics could only follow the progress of the cars from the sector times displayed on the overhead monitor. The TV coverage was only intermittently displaying pictures of the two Vantecs racing in midfield. The team knew there was supposed to be a problem with Ryan's car, but none of them had heard the radio interchanges. Despite their concerns, they witnessed a succession of quicker sector times from both drivers - but Ryan was showing best. By the end of lap 47, he was driving quicker than anyone on the track. Finally, on lap 48, a cheer went up as Ryan recorded the fastest lap of the race.

As Ryan crossed the line at the end of lap 49, he didn't need the pit board to tell him the gap to Kramer. Another good lap, and he would be up Kramer's tailpipe. Ryan knew he was driving well - but couldn't explain why. After all that had happened, he thought he would probably be trying too hard - but somehow it was as if all of the bad things that had happened were behind him. His subconscious mind had taken over the driving of the car, and was utilising all of his experience and knowledge. He had entered the zone. Some days it was a struggle to pick out and hit the braking and turning points, but now the car seemed to be on rails. The car was sweeping imperiously through the corners. Ahead of him, Kramer was becoming ever more ragged. Ryan hoped that the pressure was getting to him.

At the end of the lap, the two Vantecs flashed across the start-line together. Ryan slipstreamed as best he could, and then pulled over to the right of Kramer as they reached the pit-lane exit on the inside of the track. Ryan had gambled that Kramer would stay away from the pit exit. With the increase in speed from the tow up the straight, Ryan slid alongside Kramer and began to brake for turn one. It was hardly an ideal line for the right-hander, but Kramer would have no option but to go the long way round the outside.

Kramer quickly assessed the situation. His plan was clearly not working. He also knew his car was not performing as well as Ryan's - and if he was to gain his father's respect, there was only one realistic option. If he judged it just right, then it would look like a simple racing accident. Ryan was after all taking a chance by going up on the inside. Kramer turned his wheel in Ryan's direction.

Ryan felt a shudder from the rear, as Kramer's front wheel made contact with his own left rear wheel. Ryan felt the back of the car go light - but caught the movement on the throttle, and then he was round the turn. In his mirror he saw the other Vantec career off the track. Ryan smiled grimly. That was his enemy out of the way, but he still had a lot of hard work to do.

The knock had cost Ryan a little time, but he could at last see Gonzales. Ryan looked at the gap and saw it would take him a lap to close up. The race was going to have to go down to the final lap. Ryan relentlessly closed on his rival through the remainder of the penultimate lap. He was beginning to struggle with his own tyres, but ahead of him, Gonzales was clearly having bigger problems - and Ryan could see the Demaison struggling into some of the turns.

Somerset was sitting in despair in the motorhome, head in hands, when Thornhill reached him on his walkie-talkie.

The team manager sounded uncharacteristically excited, 'Chris, you'd better get back here right now. Ryan's still out on track - and he's actually challenging Gonzales!'

This was the last thing Somerset had expected. 'I'm on my way!'

Somerset levered himself off the bench seat, and dashed from the motorhome, puzzling over the turn around in their fortunes. Lifting himself up onto the stool, he listened intently as Thornhill rapidly brought him up to speed.

'Ryan hasn't obeyed the order to come in - but despite the telemetry, the car still seems to be running okay. I really don't know why,' he exclaimed, throwing his hands in the air. 'Anyway, he had a coming together with Kramer a lap ago. Not yet sure what happened there - but anyhow, Ryan is now chasing Gonzales down.' He stopped speaking as he heard the cars approaching the main straight. The two men watched as the cars flashed past, both listening carefully for any sign of engine trouble.

The gap, at the start of the last lap, was too great to permit a move at the end of the straight - and Ryan resigned himself to making a late challenge. Ryan closed dramatically on the Demaison at the Hairpin - but the closeness was a mirage, for Gonzales was able to get on the throttle earlier than Ryan, and again pulled out a gap after the turn.

The same happened at the Spoon, but then they were on the long run to 130R and Ryan closed to within striking distance. Ryan carried greater speed through the challenging 6th gear bend than Gonzales, and immediately pulled over to the right. The nose of his car soon came level with the Demaison's cockpit. The right hand side of the track was not the best line for the approaching Casio chicane – but, by drawing level with Gonzales, Ryan had stolen the inside. It was no longer a matter of speed. The race would be determined by the braking capabilities of both cars.

Gonzales was in a quandary - Demaison's instructions had been all too clear. The final chicane was an ideal place in which to take Ryan out. In 1988 the corner had witnessed a collision between Prost and Senna - and it was also where Berger rammed Irvine in 1996. Gonzales knew his off track behaviour was questionable, but on the circuit, he had always played fair. He also knew he was reaching the end of his career. He was certain he didn't want to drive for Demaison again - contract or no contract. In the short run up to the turn, he made his decision.

'Sorry, Dolores,' he muttered. They would both have to suffer the consequences. His predilection for young men would come as a big shock to his wife – but at the end of the day, he cared far more about what people thought of his driving.

Ryan pushed his foot hard to the floor - the rapid braking thrusting his body painfully into the seat belts. The brake cylinders glowed bright red as the carbon fibre brakes bit hard. There was a puff of blue smoke from the right hand rear as the wheel locked, and Ryan was forced to let the brake up a little. The Vantec shot ahead of the Demaison - now alongside and also braking hard. The speed continued to scrub off as Ryan hauled the steering wheel over to the right. The front of the car refused to turn in. Ryan forced the brake pedal down again. As the car lost even more speed, the front wheels began to bite and the nose began to follow the turn. Ryan held the advantage through the left and right turns that immediately followed.

Ryan yelled with relief as he emerged onto the Suzuka straight ahead of Gonzales. His right foot floored the throttle – and, as he flicked up through the gears, the screaming engine was the sweetest sound in the world. He wanted to swoop over to the pit wall to salute the team - but he wasn't going to take any chances. Once across the finish line, he began to brake. When the car was under control, he raised both hands and pounded the steering wheel in delight - whooping deliriously inside his helmet.

Pierre Demaison angrily ripped the headphones from his head and left them bouncing on their coiled lead as he got up from his stool in the prat-perch. Before any of his colleagues could react, he marched across the pit lane and out through the back of the team's garage. Two minutes later he was standing beside his private helicopter. The pilot had been asleep but a vicious kick in the shin had soon woken him up. Now on his best behaviour the pilot quickly started the engine and completed the safety checks. Then, like an angry wasp, the small helicopter rose nosily into the air.

Somerset was rushing towards Parc Ferme when the mobile phone on his hip rang. Pushing through the mass of people heading in the same direction, he brought the phone to his ear just as a helicopter clattered overhead.

'Hi Chris, it's Tosh. Congratulations. Great race!' The Japanese caller paused. 'When can we have a look at your chassis for next year?' he asked.

After all the drama, it took Somerset a few seconds to realise what Toshihiko was getting at. There was only one reason why Katayama would want to examine his chassis.

'You mean, we've got the engine deal?' asked Somerset, stopping in his tracks and placing a hand over his free ear so he could hear better.

'Subject to any post race nonsense,' said Toshihiko, hedging his bets in case the FIA had anything to say about the race. 'Please keep it to yourself until we are ready to publicly confirm the news. I just thought you would like to know at the earliest possibility!'

'That's fantastic news - of course I'll keep it under wraps. I'll call you back later - it's rather difficult to speak right now.'

The two men exchanged farewells, and Somerset continued his walk to Parc Ferme. This time he felt like he was walking on air.

By the time Ryan got back to Parc Ferme, Somerset was eagerly waiting for him. Ryan undid his belt, and lifted the steering wheel off before standing up in the cockpit. He smiled broadly at Somerset through his open visor. Before he had a chance to speak, a pair of arms encircled his waist, and he was lifted from the car. Once his feet were on solid ground, he found himself in a tight bear hug. Ryan had never seen Somerset so emotional - but after everything that had happened, nothing would ever surprise him again! He responded to the warm embrace - and it was several seconds before Somerset released his grasp.

'Bloody fantastic! We've done it - 6th place in the championship.' Despite Somerset shouting, Ryan could only just hear him over the hubbub in the enclosed paddock. Ryan patted Somerset on the back.

'No problem. I was in control all the way.'

'Very funny! But next year - you really will obey orders.' Somerset poked Ryan firmly in the chest.

'What do you mean – "next year"?'

'I mean you've just got yourself a new contract!' said Somerset. After the way he had just driven, Somerset knew that Ryan had to fill the second seat alongside the Katayama shoe-in. It was a pity for Panetta but the Italian was still young and would have other chances. As for Kramer – he had hardly distinguished himself.

'Now let's go find the others - I don't know where Kramer's got to? I guess he's too embarrassed to see me!'

'Somehow I don't think we'll see Kramer again,' said Ryan, smiling. It was clear that Somerset still didn't know the truth. 'Look, it's a long story - I'll tell you all about Kramer later, but right now there's someone I need to see.' Ryan pointed at Victoria, who was waving excitedly from the other side of the wire mesh surrounding Parc Ferme. With the season over it was time to mend a few bridges.

EPILOGUE

8:45 a.m. Tuesday 30th October, Spa - Belgium

Pierre Demaison switched off the engine, and sat quietly on the start line looking down the track to La Source. Despite the bright sun, the autumn air was chill. It was a fine morning. Demaison settled himself for the task ahead. It had only been two days since his rapid departure from the Japanese Grand Prix. He had excused himself from his colleagues as soon as he had seen Ryan Clarke round the last bend. His was one of the first helicopters to fly away from the circuit. Demaison smiled, recalling the surprise on the pilot's face as he had kicked him awake. It was typical of modern standards. If only other people had his standards, he wouldn't be in the position he was in now.

Too late. There was no way to turn the clock back now. Losing their engine supply was the final straw; there was no money for another engine, or much else - and he was fully to blame. Well, he didn't want to be around to see his team fold, or, even worse - sold on. He shook his head woefully at the thought of someone else taking charge - he could almost hear them criticising his stewardship. He smiled bitterly - even his own son had let him down. Well, that was all in the past. The future was now – himself, a car and a race track. Demaison undid the seat belt.

He reached across to the passenger seat and retrieved his old racing goggles. He studied them briefly, then wiped away a speck of dust before donning them. Ah, happy days. He could see himself as a young man sitting in the 1958 Demaison -

wrestling with the large heavy steering wheel. He looked ruefully at the small modern racing wheel in front of him. The navy blue Maserati Spyder was far too modern for his liking, but at least he could feel the cold air in his hair.

He turned the ignition and gunned the motor - listening to the harshly revving 4.2 litre V8 engine. Satisfied, he sat still for a second.

'Au revoir Giselle!' He floored the accelerator and released the clutch. Clouds of blue smoke billowed out from the rear tyres as the wheels fought to gain grip. Then the car was on the move - rapidly picking up speed. The car's manual boasted a 0-60 mph time in just five seconds. La Source was on him all too soon, and he was forced to slow the car to take the tight left-handed turn. Now he faced the long run down to Eau Rouge. He accelerated hard - his body pushed back into the comfortable bucket seat.

Only deserted stands bore witness to his defiant charge. The car topped 150 mph at the foot of Eau Rouge. Demaison experienced a wave of nausea as downhill turned to uphill. He won the struggle to keep his foot on the floor as the car flicked left into the first section. Even before the car had settled, Demaison hauled the wheel back over to the right for the right handed flick up the hill.

Demaison smiled - he had done it, he had gone flat into Eau Rouge. His smile was triumphant - but already the rear end was losing grip.